I'M STARTING TO WORRY ABOUT THIS

BLACK BOX OF DOOM

ALSO BY JASON PARGIN

Zoey Is Too Drunk for This Dystopia
If This Book Exists, You're in the Wrong Universe
Zoey Punches the Future in the Dick
Futuristic Violence and Fancy Suits
What the Hell Did I Just Read
This Book Is Full of Spiders
John Dies at the End

I'M STARTING
TO WORRY
ABOUT THIS

BLACK BOX
OF DOOM

JASON PARGIN

ST. MARTIN'S PRESS
NEW YORK

First published in the United States by St. Martin's Press, an imprint of
St. Martin's Publishing Group

I'M STARTING TO WORRY ABOUT THIS BLACK BOX OF DOOM. Copyright © 2024 by Jason Pargin. All rights reserved. Printed in the United States of America. For information, address St. Martin's Publishing Group, 120 Broadway, New York, NY 10271.

www.stmartins.com

Endpaper art: desert scene © Melok/Shutterstock; sky © Night Foxsong/Shutterstock; rabbit © AMStudio_yk/Shutterstock; cube © Radachynskyi Serhii/Shutterstock; bomb icon © Polina Tomtosova/Shutterstock; tire tracks © My Portfolio/Shutterstock

Designed by Steven Seighman

The Library of Congress Cataloging-in-Publication Data is available upon request.

ISBN 978-1-250-28595-9 (hardcover)
ISBN 978-1-250-28596-6 (ebook)

Our books may be purchased in bulk for promotional, educational, or business use. Please contact your local bookseller or the Macmillan Corporate and Premium Sales Department at 1-800-221-7945, extension 5442, or by email at MacmillanSpecialMarkets@macmillan.com.

First Edition: 2024

10 9 8 7 6 5 4 3 2

DAY 1

But I am very poorly today and very stupid and hate everybody and everything.

—CHARLES DARWIN,
in a letter to a friend, 1861

1

ABBOTT

Abbott Coburn had spent much of his twenty-six years dreading the wrong things, in the wrong amounts, for the wrong reasons. So it was appropriate that in his final hours before achieving international infamy, he was dreading a routine trip he'd accepted as a driver for the rideshare service Lyft. The passenger had ordered an early-morning ride from Victorville, California, to Los Angeles International Airport, a facility Abbott believed had been designed to make every traveler feel like they were doing it wrong.

He rolled up to the pickup spot—the parking lot of a Circle K convenience store—to find a woman sitting on a black box, one large enough that she probably could've mailed herself to her destination with the addition of some breathing holes and a piss drain. It had wheels, and she was rolling herself back and forth a few inches in each direction with her feet, working out nervous energy. The millions of strangers who would become obsessed with that box in the coming days would usually describe it incorrectly, calling it everything from a "footlocker" to an "armored munitions crate." What the woman was actually sitting on was a road case, the type musicians use to transport concert gear. This one was covered in band stickers, a detail that would have been inconsequential in a rational society but would turn out to be extremely consequential in ours.

Abbott rolled down the window and braced himself, doing his usual scan for reassuring signs that the passenger is Normal (he'd developed a sixth sense for the weirdos who, for example, wanted to sit in the front). The woman on the box wore green cargo pants and a dazzling orange hoodie that looked to Abbott like high-visibility work gear. Though, if she were on the job, the bosses weren't strict about the dress code: She wore a faded trucker cap that said, WELCOME TO THE SHITSHOW. Below that was a pair of oversize sunglasses with lime-green plastic frames and, below that, smeared lipstick that looked like it had been hurriedly applied in the dark. Her hair was short enough that it appeared to have been buzzed without a mirror while driving down a bumpy road. It did not occur to Abbott that all of this would be an excellent way to thwart security cameras and facial recognition software.

Abbott, his nervous system already hovering a finger over its big red Fight-or-Flight button, asked, "You got the Lyft to LAX?"

He was hopeful she'd say no, but there was no one else in the vicinity aside from a rail-thin man by the tire air machine having a tense argument via either Bluetooth or psychosis.

"Oh my god," said the woman on the box, "I have a huge favor to ask you. HUGE. I am in so much trouble with my employer."

She removed her green sunglasses as if the situation had become much too serious for such eyewear. Her eyes were bloodshot, and Abbott thought she'd either been recently smoking weed or recently crying, though he knew from personal experience that it was possible to do both simultaneously. He was now absolutely certain that the favor she was about to ask was going to be illegal, impossible, or just a string of nonsense words. He wasn't sure how to respond without accidentally agreeing, so he just stared.

"Okay," she said, after realizing it was still her turn to talk. "Yes, I ordered a trip to LAX, but in the time I've been waiting, I found out that's not going to work. This is a big problem. BIG problem."

Her voice was shaky, and Abbott decided that she had, in fact, been crying. He instantly sensed two opposing instincts in his brain quietly begin to go to war with each other.

"This box I'm sitting on?" she continued. "The guy who hired me has to have it by Monday, the Fourth of July. I can't ship it, because I can't let it out of my sight—I have to stay with it, wherever it goes. And I can't fly, for reasons that would take all day to explain. Now, I'm going to ask you a question. It's going to sound like a hypothetical or a joke, but it's an actual question. Okay? Okay. So, how much would you charge to drive me to Washington, DC?"

Abbott took a moment to make sure he'd heard her right before replying, "Oh, that's not something you can do in a Lyft; the maximum trip is only—"

"No, no. You'd clock out of your app or however you do it. I'm asking you, personally, as a citizen with a beautiful working car—what is this, an Escalade?"

"A, uh, Lincoln Navigator. It actually belongs to—"

"I'm asking what you would charge to take me all the way across the country. And your reflex is going to be to say no amount of money because I'm talking about totally putting your life on hold for more than a week, without notice. Restaurants, hotels, lost business, canceled Fourth of July plans, additional stress—it's a lot to ask. But I'm willing to pay a lot. Or rather, my employer is willing to pay a lot. Look."

She twisted around and dug into a tattered duffel bag that Abbott hadn't previously noticed. When she came back around, she was holding two thick folds of cash, each bound with rubber bands. He physically recoiled at the sight of it, mainly because not a single reasonable person has ever carried money that way.

"This is one hundred thousand dollars," she said, waving the cash around like a mind-control amulet. "The guy who hired me has this kind of money to throw around, and no, he's not a criminal, he's a legitimate rich guy, if such a thing exists. No, I can't tell you who he is. All I can tell you is that he needs this box by the Fourth at the latest, and it has to be kept quiet. Today is Thursday. We can make it easily; we don't even have to travel overnight. Four days of leisurely driving and we'll get there Sunday evening, no problem. One hundred K is my starting offer for you to make this drive. Make me a counteroffer."

At this stage, Abbott was considering this request in the exact same way he'd have considered a request to be transported to Venus in exchange for a baggie of rat turds: He just wanted out of the crazy conversation as quickly and safely as possible.

He said, "I'm sure there are plenty of people within a few miles of here, probably a million of them, who'd love to take you up on this. But I really can't. I'm sorry."

She shook her head. "No. No, you're perfect for this, I can tell already. And I can't keep asking people; I have to get on the road, and I have to do it now. The more drivers I have to ask, the more people know about this, and that's bad. Secrecy is part of what I'm paying for. And I'm not crazy, I know how I look. Though I will have to tell you about the worms at some point. But no, I'm dressed like this for a reason. How about one fifty?"

A third fold of cash was added, and Abbott had to force himself to look away from it. He prided himself on not being enslaved to mindless greed, but way back at the rear of his noisy brain was a tiny voice pointing out that this amount of money would let him move out on his own and tell his father to fuck off (though it would definitely have to be done in that order). It would be *freedom,* for literally the first time in his life. He imagined a factory farm pig escaping into a sunny green pasture and seeing the clear blue sky for the first time. Though he was having trouble imagining the pig looking up. Could pigs do that? He'd have to google it later. Wait, what did she say about worms?

The woman grinned and sat up straighter, the posture of an angler who's just seen the bobber plop under the surface. It kind of made Abbott want to refuse just to spite her.

"But there are rules," she said, a finger in the air. "You can't look in the box. You can't ask me what's in the box. And you can't tell anyone where we're going until it's over. After that, you can tell anyone anything you like. But no one can come looking for us."

"Well, there's certainly nothing weird or suspicious about that. So, why don't you just rent a car and drive yourself?"

"No driver's license. I used to have one, but the government took it away. They said, 'You're too good of a driver, it's making the other drivers look bad, you're hurting their self-esteem.'"

"I just . . . I really can't, sorry. You say I'm perfect for this, but I assure you I'm the absolute perfect person to not do it. That's, what, like, fifty hours of driving? I don't even like to drive for *one* hour."

"You drive for a living!"

"Oh, I just started doing this a couple months ago to—"

"I'm just teasing you. I know you probably didn't grow up dressing as a Lyft driver for Halloween. But no, you're my guy. You're not married, right? I don't see a ring. No kids, I can see it on your face. If you have another job, it's one you can walk away from; it's not a 401(k)-and-health-insurance situation. You probably live with a parent, so even if you have pets, there's somebody to feed them while you're away. You're old enough that nobody's going to assume you were abducted. You're, what, twenty-four? Around there?"

"Twenty-six. Did you just deduce all that on the fly?"

She smiled again and made a show of leaning forward, narrowing her eyes as if to examine him. "Ah, see, there's something you need to know about me: I can *read minds*. I can tell you're skeptical, so let me give it a shot. Ready?"

She narrowed her eyes farther, comically exaggerating her concentration. At this point, Abbott was 99 percent of the way to driving off and marking the ride as canceled.

"You have trouble getting to sleep at night," she began, "because you can't turn off your brain. Usually, it's replaying something stressful that happened in the past or rehearsing something stressful that could possibly happen in the future. You then have to down constant caffeine just to function through the day—I bet you've got one of those big energy drinks in the center console right now. You sometimes get really good ideas in the shower. You can't navigate even your own city without software that gives you turn-by-turn directions. You get an actual, physical sense of panic if you can't find your phone, even if you know it's still somewhere in your home."

She was rocking in her seat, rolling the trunk's tiny wheels back and forth, back and forth.

"You don't have a girlfriend or a boyfriend," she continued before Abbott could interrupt. "You've never had a long-term relationship, and at least once in your life, you thought you were dating someone while the whole time *they* thought you were just friends. You actually don't have any close friends. Maybe you did when you were in school, but you don't keep in touch. You've replaced them with a whole bunch of internet acquaintances—maybe you're all members of the same fandom or a guild in a video game—but you'd be traumatized if any of them suddenly showed up at your front door unannounced. Sometimes, out of the blue, you'll physically cringe at something you said or did when you were a teenager. When you use porn, you may have to sort through two hundred pics or videos before you find one that will get you off. You're sure that humanity is doomed and feel like you were cursed to be born when you were. Am I close?"

Abbott had to take a moment to gather himself. Forcing a dismissive tone with all his might, he said, "Congratulations, you've just described everyone I know."

"Exactly. It describes everyone *you know*."

"I really do have to get back to work, I don't—"

"Don't get offended, please, none of that was intended as an insult. I'm only saying that I know you're an outsider, just like me! I think the universe brought us together. But I'm not done, because this is the big one: The reason you're hesitating to make this trip, even for a life-changing amount of money, isn't because you're worried that I'm a scammer or that my employer is a drug lord and this box is full of heroin. No, what you fear above all is *humiliation at the hands of the unfamiliar.* What if you get a flat tire on a highway in Tennessee—do you even know how to change it? What if we wind up in the wrong lane at a toll road and the lady in the booth yells at you? What if you get a speeding ticket in Ohio—how do you even pay it? What if you get into a fender bender and the other driver is a big, scary guy who doesn't speak English? Then there's the absolutely *terrifying* prospect of spending dozens of hours in an enclosed space with some weird woman. What if you embarrass yourself? Or, worse, what if I say something that makes you embarrassed on my behalf? You'll have no mute or block button, just unfettered raw-dog, face-to-face contact, with no escape, for days on end. What if I'm so unhinged that we literally have nothing to talk about, no shared jokes, no way to break the tension? What if, what if, what if—all of these scenarios that humanity deals with a billion times a day but that you find so terrifying that you wouldn't even risk them for a hundred and fifty thousand dollars in cash. So the question is: Would you do it for two hundred?"

She fished out a fourth hunk of bills. The escalating amounts actually didn't make an impression on Abbott; at this point, the dollar figures all registered as equally impossible sums of money. But the hand that held the cash was trembling, and he sensed the thrum of desperation inside the woman, the vibe of one who has exhausted every reasonable option and is now trying the stupid ones.

"A hundred now," she said, "and a hundred after we arrive in DC. If you think it's a trick, that we'll get there and I'll steal back the money at knifepoint, we can swing by somewhere and you can drop off the first payment. You can even take it to your bank, let the teller do the counterfeit test on the bills. If we hurry."

"How do you know I wouldn't do that and then just refuse to drive you?"

"Because *I can see into your soul.* You would never do that. Not just because it's wrong but because you'd be torn apart by the awkwardness of that conversation, of having to see the look on my face when I found out you'd double-crossed me. Also, you'd soon realize that you wouldn't just be screwing me but my employer. And even if he's not a criminal, you can guess that's probably a pretty bad idea. He could send guys in suits to your house to demand the money back, and just think how awkward *that* would be."

Abbott heard himself say, "Can I have time to think about it?" and knew that his automated avoidance mechanism had kicked in. He'd been developing this apparatus since his first day in kindergarten when the Smelly Girl had asked him to play with her and, in a panic, he'd had to come up with a plausible excuse not to (he told her his family's religion forbade touching plastic dinosaurs). These days, it was pure reflex: If an acquaintance invited him to trivia night at the bar, a ready-made, ironclad excuse would fly from his lips before he'd even given it a thought. Sure, sometimes he'd find himself wondering if maybe he should be filtering these invitations before they were routed directly into the trash. Here, for example: On some level, he knew this offer deserved more consideration. But his request for time wasn't about that, it was just one of the stock phrases he deployed to get to a safe distance where plans could be easily canceled via text or, even better, by simply avoiding that person for the rest of his life. Sure, this woman was in some kind of distress, but that would be no burden to him once she was out of sight—

"No, you can't have time to think about it," said the woman on the box. "I meant it when I said we have to leave right now. *Maybe* we can swing by your place to pack up some clothes and whatever medications you're on—you're on a few, right?—and to tell the parent or grandparent you live with that you'll be back late next week. But it has to be real quick, in and out."

"I can't even tell my dad where I'm going?"

"You'll tell him that a friend needs you to help with a job that pays a bundle, that it's being done on behalf of a celebrity and has to be kept quiet so the press doesn't sniff it out. And that it's nothing illegal. That's, like, ninety percent true. Or eighty percent. It's mostly true."

"Is your employer a celebrity?"

"He's not a movie star or anything, if you're trying to guess who he is. But your dad shouldn't question it." She waved a hand in the vague direction of Los Angeles. "Out there, you've probably got a hundred professional fixer types doing jobs like this as we speak."

"Then go find one of them. If you think I'm such a loser, what makes you think I can even get us there?"

"All right, enough of that." She stood and put on her lime-green sunglasses. "You don't even have your heart in it anymore. Come on, help me load the box. It's really heavy. We've been sitting out here too long, and people are starting to stare."

In the coming days, many words would be spent speculating as to why Abbott had agreed to the trip. Was it the money? Or did he genuinely want to help this woman he'd never met? The truth was, not even Abbott himself knew. Maybe it was just that by the time she was lugging the box toward the rear of the Navigator, it'd have simply been too awkward to stop her.

MALORT

Considering he was 275 pounds, bald, covered in tattoos, and wearing mirrored sunglasses, Malort could have wound up with many nicknames. But a drunken bet in a Milwaukee dive bar decades earlier had resulted in a bicep tattoo of a Jeppson's Malört bottle, the Chicago-area liquor so infamously bitter that the label featured a lengthy paragraph apologizing for the taste. His friends had all agreed the tattoo and nickname fit him, but never dared to explain their rationale in his presence. He did have to drop the little dots above the *o* in recent years, as nobody knew how to add those in text messages.

The man they called Malort rolled up to find that the Apple Valley Fire Department had apparently arrived just in time to turn the shack in the desert from a smoldering ruin into a wet smoldering ruin. Only two and a half walls of the flimsy structure were still upright, exposing the charred interior like a diorama. It told a fairly simple story of a loner hiding from and/or rooting for the apocalypse. From where he sat, there was no sign of the black box, and he had a sinking feeling it was long gone.

He stepped out of his metallic red Buick Grand National and approached a young man whose build and face made him look like a kid who'd dressed up in his dad's helmet and turnout coat. He was hosing down the aftermath to cool the embers and looked like he would have a stroke if two thoughts appeared in his brain simultaneously. He noticed Malort, and a beam of curiosity pierced his haze.

"This your property?" asked the kid.

It was a dumb question, thought Malort. The type of guy who sets up in a wilderness survival shack probably doesn't get around in a sparkly Buick that surely lists at least one pimp in its CARFAX report. He took the dumbness of the question as a good sign. Instead of answering, Malort pulled out his phone and pointed the camera at the scene, acting like he had an important job to do. Generally, if you can project enough confidence and purpose, all the uncertain nerds of the world will just part like the Red Sea.

He stepped toward the smoldering structure with his phone and, without looking at the kid, grumbled, "Is there propane?"

"There was. It already popped; that's what blew out the sides here. The ruptured tank is on the floor. There's some kind of apparatus attached. Maybe a booby trap, or maybe they were trying to deep-fry a turkey? You ever seen one of those go wrong? Nightmare. So, uh, are you a friend? One of the neighbors?"

Malort peered into the half-standing structure from afar, trying to stay out of the hose splatter. The other firefighters hadn't seemed to register his presence, most of them distracted by the task of spraying down the landscape to keep stray sparks from triggering a brush fire.

"The strangest thing just happened," rumbled Malort. "You know the big house over the hill there, behind the fence with all the barbed wire? The crazy bastard who lived there owns all this, it's all his property. So, I was chasing an intruder through that house, then they went round a corner and vanished into thin air. I looked all around, saw neither hide nor hair of 'em. A few minutes later, I looked out the window and noticed the smoke over here."

"Oh, really?" said the kid, who didn't seem to understand what that had to do with this.

"Nobody dead in there, I take it?"

"No, sir. Looks to me like they either left the propane to blow on purpose or left it unattended on accident."

"So there's no corpse in *there,* but if you go over the hill and look in that house behind the barbed wire, you'll see the owner is dead on the floor of a workshop where he was making Lord-knows-what. Though I wouldn't advise poking your head in unless you've got a strong stomach. They'll have to identify him by his teeth and prints, considering the condition his face is in."

Malort studied the smoking remains of a bed, now just a blackened frame and springs. The morning sunlight and the spray of the hose was decorating the scene with a festive little rainbow.

"Is that true?" asked the kid, trying to piece together the implications. "Did you call it in?"

"I'm not much for callin' things in. Though you should tell your people to wear protective gear when they go over there. I don't know what the guy had in his shop, but there were homemade radiation warning signs on the door. You can decide for yourself whether a homemade radiation sign is scarier than an official one." Malort studied the shack's exposed ashy guts and asked, "Have you seen any sign of a road case? One of them black boxes with aluminum trim, about the size of a footlocker?"

"No, sir. I mean, we haven't dug around inside there, but I haven't seen anything like that. Hey, uh, Bomb and Arson are on their way. You should tell them about the dead body."

"Nobody has come to take anything from the scene?"

"Not since I been here. I didn't catch your name?"

"And nobody saw the occupant leave? Or what vehicle they were driving? Might have been a blue pickup."

"No, sir." The kid was glancing around now, presumably for someone senior to come to his rescue.

Malort zoomed in with his camera, focusing on the bit of intact wall at the foot of the bed. There was a schizoid scatter of pictures and drawings pinned to the wall, blackened and curled. The residue of a mind gone to batshit. He snapped a photo. He then studied the floor around the bed . . .

"Point your hose away," growled Malort. "I'm gonna check somethin'."

He stomped toward the shack, kicked over the burned-out bed frame, and yanked away a waterlogged rug underneath. There it was: a hatch that opened with a metal ring.

"Huh," said the kid as Malort yanked the hatch open. "They got a basement?"

"They've got a tunnel and a bomb shelter. Follow it back a hundred yards or so and you'll wind up under that house behind the fence. It turned out my intruder didn't vanish; they slipped into a bedroom closet, climbed down a ladder, ran over, popped out here."

Then, thought Malort, they'd rigged it so he'd get a face full of propane tank shrapnel if he tried to follow.

The kid looked amazed. "Damn. Is this like a cartel operation? I have a buddy who said they busted a place that had tunnels running all through the neighborhood—"

"Sir!" shouted a new voice from behind the kid. "What's your business here?"

It was the older guy, coming to assert his authority. Malort tensed up. The dude was in his fifties or sixties, but that only put him in the same range as himself. And you generally didn't want to tangle with a firefighter; they had muscles from hauling gear and bad attitudes from breathing toxic chemicals and remembering the screams of burning children.

"He's looking for a big box," said the kid. "He says the old guy who owns this land is dead over in that house behind the fence. And now he's found a secret tunnel under the Unabomber hut. And the house is radioactive, maybe."

"Who are you?" asked the older man, ignoring the kid completely.

Malort put his phone away. "I was just leaving."

"No, you're not. I'm gonna need to see ID. Hey!"

Malort ignored him and made his way back to the Buick. The senior fireman was talking into a radio now, hurrying to get himself between Malort and his car.

"You just wait right here."

He put a hand on Malort's chest. Malort stopped, looked slowly down at the gloved hand, then back up to meet the old dude's eyes. There he detected the same apprehension he'd seen on the faces of authority figures since his growth spurt in middle school. He decided that, if things continued to progress in this fashion, he would open with forearm blows to the head and then delegate the closing argument to his boots. No doubt the other firemen would try to jump in, but you can't waste your life worrying about stuff that's not gonna happen until thirty seconds from now.

"Everybody," announced Malort, "get out your phones and start recording, because if this old fuck doesn't get out of my way, what happens next should really be something to see."

He balled his fists, and his heart revved into another gear. As stimulants go, an early-morning ass-kicking was only a notch below speed. The old man gave him a perfunctory hard look and then backed down, allowing Malort to get behind the wheel of the Grand National unimpeded. The old man made a big show of photographing the license plate to save face.

As Malort backed up, he leaned out his window and said, "Never challenge a man in a Buick. He's got nothin' to lose."

As he headed back to the main road, he pulled up the pic of the shack's interior and zoomed in on the charred paranoia collage. Written on a handmade banner above the darkened scraps were three words:

THE FORBIDDEN NUMBERS

2

ABBOTT

The short trip to Abbott's home afforded him just enough time to engage in his favorite pastime, which was carefully tabulating all of the ways in which the universe was wronging him in that particular moment:

1. His new passenger did, in fact, insist on sitting in the front, undeterred by the pile of objects he kept in that seat specifically to prevent that. She had just climbed right in and pushed aside his carefully arranged barrier of lip balm, asthma inhaler, vape pen, throat lozenges, antacids, and bag of Flamin' Hot Cheetos, the woman blundering into his private world like a wet dog rolling onto a chessboard in mid-match.
2. She kind of smelled bad. She stank of smoke, but not cigarette smoke—it was the acrid stink of plastic and other materials that only burned when things went badly wrong. He didn't know what exactly could go wrong with a human metabolism to make a person smell like that and didn't want to know.
3. And this was the worst of all—she simply wasn't upset enough. As soon as they were in the vehicle and rolling, her teary panic evaporated, and out from behind that cloud beamed horrible, horrible sunlight. It's not that Abbott was opposed to others being happy (though he found the miserable were generally less exhausting to be around), but Abbott himself was definitely *not* happy, and in the aftermath of any transaction, this kind of mismatch in demeanor generally implied that one party had gotten screwed.

"I haven't been on a road trip in for*ever*," she cooed, gazing at the passing megachurch and Chevy dealership like she was taking in the Jungle

Cruise at Disney World. "I'm so excited! Do you realize that only seventy years ago, there wouldn't have even been a highway from here to DC? You'd literally have been getting off on little country roads, some of them gravel, to get from one end of the USA to the other. If you go back, like, three lifetimes, it's a trip you wouldn't expect everyone to survive; somebody in the party would be dead of tuberculosis or bear attack before you got halfway. There are so many parts of the world where they still don't have this, a wide, perfectly smooth road from basically anywhere to anywhere."

"Yeah," muttered Abbott as they stopped at a red light. He immediately took the opportunity to act like he was engrossed by something on his phone.

She glanced over and said, "Hey, have you ever noticed that when you're watching a movie or reading a book and a character mentions social media, it makes you cringe? Like if a character says, 'We're blowing up on Twitter!' or 'We've gone viral on TikTok!' it's just really off-putting. Corny."

"Oh, really?" mumbled Abbott, wondering if this woman was going to stop talking long enough to let him think.

"You know why I think that is? I think we hate being reminded that this is how we spend all our free time. We want our fictional characters to go out and do things in the real world. If they show the protagonist zoning out on the sofa with their phone, it's always portrayed as pathetic, like, 'Look at this poor sap.' That's weird, right, considering that's probably the exact position we're in when watching them do it?"

Abbott cleared his throat and said, "Hey, uh, when I get to the house, I'll have to talk to my dad. This is his car, and I'm just letting you know right now that he—"

"Let me stop you right there. Remember, I can read your mind. You're already planning how you're going to use 'My dad won't let me go' as a way to get out of the trip. Maybe you'll say he won't let you have the car, even though you've clearly already gotten permission to use it for work, and this is work. I bet you find yourself doing that a lot."

"Doing what?"

"Instead of just saying what you'd prefer, you off-load the choice to someone or something else. Instead of 'I don't want to hang out with you,' it's 'I have work that night' or 'I'm not feeling well.' Nothing is ever expressed as your own needs and wants, so you never have to defend your choices or own the consequences later. I used to do it all the time."

"Fine, *I don't want to take you on this trip.*"

"Yes, you do! Are you honestly telling me the version of you a month or a year or ten years from now won't be happy that you rescued a desperate person, went on an adventure, and got a couple hundred grand to jump-start your adult life? Sure, you don't want to do the work *right now,* during the hard part. Nobody does! But the real 'you' doesn't exist in the moment; you exist in the long term. *That* you, the whole you, will be glad you did this."

"I don't want to do it, because what you're asking me to do is objectively crazy and certain to end in tragedy."

"I bet you do that a lot, too. Catastrophize. Everything outside your comfort zone is a worst-case scenario waiting to happen. The reality is this: Somebody with lots of money needs a job done, and you were in the right place at the right time—nothing crazier than that. And in a week or so, it'll be completely behind you; all you'll have is the money, some cool memories, and a few thousand more miles on your old man's car. Even that will be good for it. City driving is torture for cars; they need to get out and run! By the way, you've never asked my name, and we've reached the point where it's going to be too awkward for you to ask and you'll have to play some roundabout game to get me to say it. Let me save you from that: It's Ether. E-T-H-E-R."

"Do you have a last name?"

"Nope. Just Ether."

"Okay, I'm starting to think this is a prank."

"And what's your name?"

"It, uh, would have shown on the app when you ordered the ride."

"Yeah, but for all I know, you have a cool nickname you prefer to be called, like 'Dutch' or 'Poncho' or 'Killer' or 'Professor BigNutz.'"

"Abbott is fine."

"Good to meet you, Abbott. Remember, when we get to your place, it's in and out, real quick. Right?" She shot a nervous glance into the rearview mirror and then tried to play it off by saying, "Ugh, I've gotta remove this lipstick. I look like the Joker, one of the versions that does a sloppy job with the makeup to let you know *their* movie is for grown-ups."

She took off the WELCOME TO THE SHITSHOW hat and ran a hand through her razed hair, like she'd never felt it before. Abbott decided then that she had, in fact, cut her hair that very morning, maybe minutes before they'd met. That, oddly enough, was what caused him to silently add one more item to his packing list.

He spent the twenty-minute drive home silently rehearsing every possible disaster that could occur in the course of this trip—which, it turned out, wasn't enough time to even scratch the surface of all his vividly dire scenarios.

"Nice house!" exclaimed Ether at the sight of Abbott's dad's McMansion, the exterior of which Abbott had always thought looked like stucco that the crew had drunkenly mixed with piss. "We're close to the lake, right? Do you ever go? Ride a Jet Ski around, all that?"

"No. Dad goes out there and fishes."

"Do you ever go with him?"

"If he ever offered that, I'd assume his plan was to drown me. I'll be right back."

He took the Navigator's key fob inside with him, along with the two bundles of cash. He figured it was possible Ether could still hot-wire the vehicle and take off with it, but so what? He'd have a free hundred grand, and the stolen Navigator would be his dad's problem.

The house was empty; Abbott had known his father wouldn't be home, as the man worked six and a half days a week. He went to his own bedroom and packed ten days' worth of T-shirts and cargo shorts, adhering to his habit of including far more pairs of underwear than he'd need as if he were going to just be continually soiling himself amid a nationwide shortage of pairs for purchase. He packed his eye drops, anti-dandruff shampoo, athlete's foot spray, fingernail clippers, sleep mask, two types of skin ointment, hemorrhoid cream, and three different kinds of antacids. He went to his medicine cabinet for both of his prescriptions and noticed that one of them—the most important—only had two pills rattling around in the bottle. He felt a little jolt of panic and made a mental note to refill it before leaving town. He almost packed the white noise machine he needed for sleep but was pretty sure there were phone apps that did the same thing. He'd have to remember to download one, lest he be left alone in the dark with his slithering thoughts. He considered grabbing a second pair of shoes and decided he was being ridiculous.

He went to pack up his laptop, which was still on the little folding table positioned in front of the section of wall he'd painted bright green. Then he reconsidered and took a seat in front of the laptop and logged on.

"Uh, hey, gang," he said into the laptop's camera while stuffing items into his bag. "It's Abaddon, something came up, so, uh, no streams this week and probably next. I have to hit the road. I'll be checking in with you when I get the chance. Thanks for all your support, I'll be back on by Monday the eleventh, I think. You guys enjoy your Fourth of July and your long weekend if, uh, you've got a job that even gives you days off. As I was packing, I remembered I have to get my brain pills refilled and realized how ironic it is that they're for my anxiety, but nothing gives me anxiety like the prospect of running out. Or maybe that's not ironic—does anybody know what that word even means? Anyway, I'm in the process of packing and imagining myself going into withdrawal while flying down the interstate at eighty miles an hour—"

He was interrupted by two brief beeps of the Navigator's horn outside.

"Ha, uh, I guess she's getting impatient. Alright, I have to go, if you don't ever hear from me again, it means I've been murdered and dumped in a ditch somewhere. Bye-bye."

He closed the laptop and wrapped the charging cable around it, having no idea that he'd just recorded what would become by far the most-viewed stream of his lifetime. The question now was what exactly to tell his dad. He could send a text, but that would simply yield a return call and, eventually, his father chasing him down to put a stop to the whole thing. No, he needed to be long gone before his dad even knew about the trip. After Abbott returned with enough money to spring himself from this prison, it wouldn't matter. Hell, he could drop the Navigator off while his father was out on a jobsite and simply never have to talk to the man again. The sheer thought of it sent a flash of warm, golden light through his system, the sensation that he believed other people called *hope*.

He found a pen and a full-size sheet of paper that wouldn't be easily overlooked and wrote,

Got offered a cash job
Last minute
Need to help a friend move some stuff
Taking the navigator
Back within 10 days probably
    —Abbott

He then pulled out one of the wads of cash and peeled off five hundred-dollar bills, placing them on top of the note and weighing both down with a brushed-steel saltshaker—an electric one that ground the salt for some fucking reason. He didn't even know why he was leaving the money. Maybe he just wanted to prove that the job was real. That's how it worked with his dad: Nothing was real until there was money to show for it.

Abbott then went up to his father's bedroom for the last item he'd added to his packing list. He opened the bottom drawer of the nightstand and grabbed the box that contained his father's handgun. Inside, the automatic was nestled in black foam, a spare magazine resting alongside it. Abbott only hesitated for a moment before taking the gun and returning the closed box to the drawer. There was no reason for his father to even notice it was gone. If an intruder happened to break in during Abbott's trip, well, tough luck. Dad would have to go for the golf clubs in the closet.

He stuffed the gun under the clothes in his duffel bag, having no way of knowing that the charred remains of the bag and its contents—including that gun—would be examined by a forensics team less than five days later. He gathered everything and headed downstairs. He paused at the front door to take a look around the living room, wondering if he would ever set foot in this house again. He decided that from here on out, that would be the goal that kept him going, making sure he'd never have to.

"You came back! And you packed!" Ether giggled and clapped like a little girl as he approached. "I was sure you were gonna ghost me. You know how I thought you'd do it? I thought you'd go inside and call a friend who needs the money. Then you'd just hide in there until they pulled up, like,

'Hey, Abbott told me you need a driver?' There'd have been no reason for me to not just go with them instead."

Abbott stopped and realized that would, in fact, have been a perfect way to get out of this. Was it too late to try? Ah, who was he kidding, he had nobody to hand the job off to.

Ether noticed what he was carrying, and her eyes narrowed. "Oh, your laptop. Uh, there's something else we need to talk about. You have to leave that behind. And your phone, too."

Ah, okay, thought Abbott. So this wasn't happening after all. He felt a weight roll off him, the exquisite relief of canceled plans that extroverts will never know.

"I know you think this is a deal-breaker," said Ether before Abbott could voice mostly those exact words. "But I've already ditched my phone. We can't have any device that can be tracked. I'll even disable the GPS in the car. We'll have to navigate the old-fashioned way, with a map. And we'll be cash-only, no credit cards."

"Because the cops are after you."

"No. The police don't know about this, and there's no reason for them to care even if they did. But there are people who want *that*." She pointed to the back, where the box sat ominously.

"Your trunk full of heroin, you mean."

"The box does not contain heroin or any other kind of drug. I promise. But even if it did, you're not a conspirator; you'd be no more responsible than a cabdriver whose fare had a bag of coke in their suitcase. But no phones—that was a requirement from my employer."

"It doesn't matter. I can't do this without my phone."

"Those things didn't even exist fifteen years ago! I bet you're having a physical reaction right now at the thought of being untethered from it. Look at how well they've trained us! Constant sharing, constant tracking, everything offered up for scrutiny. See, that's the one thing the system can't tolerate today: privacy. In private, dangerous ideas happen, unique individuals are formed, cool secret boxes are moved. They can't have that, can they?!?"

Ether was getting worked up, and Abbott got the distinct impression that, if allowed, she would continue on an uninterrupted rant on the subject for the next fifteen hours or so. Jesus, this woman's red flags could supply a Communist parade.

"Okay," she said, calming herself. "I can see you're reacting like what I just said is crazy, that I must be some kind of fringe anti-technology weirdo, so just forget I said all that. I'm not the Unabomber."

"The what?"

"The Unabomber? Real name Ted Kaczynski? The math genius who went to go live in a cabin in the woods in 1978, wrote an anti-technology manifesto, and then spent the next couple decades blowing up people with mail bombs? It doesn't matter. What I want you to do is turn off your catastrophe reflex and think it through. For any nontrivial task you use that phone for, we can find a work-around. Trust me, I've been doing it for the last two years. Now please, *please,* can you take your gadgets inside so we can get moving?"

"So the other people who want that box, who are definitely not the cops, they have the power to track our devices?"

"I don't know, but I can tell you from experience that it doesn't take a cop or a super-hacker to track somebody. Anyone can do it, using software they can get for free. Stalkers do it all the time. Now come on, we have to go."

He stared her down for just a moment but sensed her distress bubbling back to the surface and, for the second time, allowed it to sway him. He went back in and took the devices to his room, feeling naked without them as he reached the front door and again wondered if this would be the last time he'd see that living room or if he'd just see it again one minute from now after it turned out he needed to come back and do a third thing.

"Can't you feel it?" asked Ether as he buckled into the Navigator. "The call to adventure?"

"No."

"That's so sad! What has the world done to kill our sense of wonder? This, right here, what you're about to do, this is every downtrodden schlub's dream come true. Every fantasy blockbuster has the same premise: A reluctant nobody is finally put into a position where he or she *has* to go on an adventure. Luke's aunt and uncle are dead, Harry Potter's home-life is a shit sandwich, Neo's job sucks, Bruce Wayne's parents got eaten by bats. The dream isn't that the chance for adventure will come along—you can do an adventure any time you want—but that circumstances will line up just right so that *you simply have no more excuses.* Now here it is! That's your ring back there, and the realm needs you to drive it to Mordor!"

She gestured to the box behind her, not knowing that a blackened remnant of one of its metal corners would later be recovered from the rubble and sold at a true-crime-memorabilia auction for $625.

"There's a knot in my guts," replied Abbott, "but it isn't the thrill of adventure, it's my self-preservation instincts telling me to turn back."

"No, you've got it backward," she said as they pulled into traffic. "Are you honestly telling me you're not bored? Like, every day? Your phone can numb the feeling moment-to-moment, but it's still there in the long term, the boredom. Well, that sensation exists for a reason! It's your instincts telling you to go exploring. *That boredom is your call to adventure.*" She swept her hand across the windshield. "We have the whole country in front of us! The greatest and wealthiest and most dazzling empire that has ever existed!"

"Uh-huh," muttered Abbott. "Ah, I need to swing by Walgreens first."

Twitch chat logs from the stream posted at 8:04 A.M., Thursday, June 30, by user Abaddon6969:

> **SteveReborn:** My laptop fan is making a noise like it's haunted.
>
> **DeathNugget:** Good luck abs! Enjoy your trip!
>
> **Tremors3:** Now what am I supposed to do on my holiday weekend, talk to my family?
>
> **SteveReborn:** Is there a way to tell if your laptop is getting too hot?
>
> **SkipTutorial:** I'm doing a poll, if you were stranded on a desert island with a bunch of people with no food and you had to resort to cannibalism to survive, who should be eaten first: An old man, or a baby?
>
> **DeathNugget:** Crack an egg on it, see if it cooks.

Tremors3: Wouldn't you get way more calories off the old man?

SkipTutorial: But he might have knowledge that would help you, maybe he's an old seaman.

ZekeArt: Is it just me or did abs seem stressed?

DeathNugget: Got indigestion from all that chicken. Some of it even made it into his mouth.

SteveReborn: Maybe a family member got sick.

Covis: What sex is the baby?

SkipTutorial: I'm afraid to ask why that matters.

ZekeArt: I went back and watched the clip, the way he was acting. I don't know, guys. This feels ominous to me.

DeathNugget: Everything feels like that to me, all the time.

CathyCathyCathy: Why would you have to eat a whole person, why couldn't you go around and have people cut off bits of themselves to make stew?

DeathNugget: You'd have a whole island full of people limping around, sepsis spoiling their meat.

SteveReborn: Will an overheated laptop on your lap lower your sperm count?

Tremors3: God I hope so.

KEY

Retired FBI agent Joan Key wondered if she'd finally made enough small talk to get to her actual point. She'd been sipping diner coffee for the last fifteen minutes and could already feel it activating her reflux. The square-torsoed man in the suit across from her was droning on about his son's soccer team and steadfastly avoiding any bureau talk, either out of concern that she missed it too much or that she didn't miss it enough.

". . . So now we're in these last couple of months of high school, and

I'm wondering, did he have any kind of normal experience there? It's so different from when I was a kid. Did I tell you that he doesn't even drive? He never got a license, he has no interest in it. When I was his age, I was obsessed with cars. So now he's about to go off to college, and I think he's emotionally about thirteen years old."

The speaker was Patrick Diaz, a boxy LEGO figure of a man who had probably looked like an FBI agent in his mother's ultrasound. Joan, whom everybody just called "Key," had crashed his solitary breakfast at a Riverside diner, and Patrick had foolishly assumed she'd just wanted to catch up.

"That's crazy," said Key, which she hoped was sufficient to convince Patrick she'd been listening. "So, do you remember when that little bit of plutonium and cesium was stolen out of that DoE van at a San Antonio hotel in 2017 and never recovered?"

Patrick, who had been systematically working his way counterclockwise around a plate of eggs, sausages, and hash browns, dropped his fork and gave her a look he usually reserved for interrogations.

"You didn't make it six months? I told you to get a hobby. Go talk to Hershel; he took up photography. He takes pictures of barns, travels the country. He does exhibits. You two can travel the countryside, get into trouble, have sex. I've been in locker rooms with the guy; he packs serious heat."

"You do remember it, right? I mean the thing I was talking about, not whatever you just said."

"Do I remember a bunch of alarmist headlines generated by a trivial amount of nuclear material getting stolen, the capsules geologists use to calibrate their tools? Are you actually asking if I remember, or is this just a preamble to the conversation you really wanted to have? And here I thought you actually missed me."

"And do you remember," said Key, persevering through Patrick's tone, "how there's a theory that the theft was connected to a chain of similar incidents, including a quantity of iridium-192 that went missing from a Strasburg, Ohio, warehouse a couple of years back? Again, a trivial amount, but if it turned out the same party was dedicated to collecting all of these trivial amounts on the black market, then mathematically, they would end up with a nontrivial amount."

"Yes, in the sense that it's technically possible that every stereo stolen from a vehicle in the last ten years is secretly being assembled into a gigantic sonic weapon that, when activated, will cause everyone on earth to simultaneously shit themselves."

"So, there's this thing I've been chasing down in my spare time, and my gut is telling me that it's either a nothingburger or an all-hands-on-deck crisis and absolutely nothing in between. But if it's going to happen, it's going to happen soon."

"How is your health these days?" asked Patrick, who had resumed eating in a particularly infuriating manner. "If you're about to tell me I'm changing the subject, I seem to remember that the stress of the job ruined your ability to digest food. I remember sitting in a bar while you asked me how to identify dried blood in your stool. Then you got out your phone and showed me a picture of your bowel movement. I was eating a bowl of chili at the time, and you noted the similarity."

"The job was stressful because of stonewall conversations like this. What if I'm onto something? What if there's an incident and it comes out later that we failed to connect the dots? You won't even let me tell you what it is!"

"Joan, everyone who has ever pursued law enforcement as a career, at any level, has had but one dream: to one day conduct a rogue off-duty investigation, finally shooting the bad guy off a tall building, causing him to fall until he impacts the windshield of a parked car below. But that doesn't happen in real life, and frankly, this only tells me that you got out just in time."

"Then this is your chance to talk me out of it. But you can only do that if you let me tell you what I know."

"You think somebody is intending to do what, exactly? Make a dirty bomb and use it on the Fourth?"

A "dirty bomb" was a bomb that used nuclear material but not a nuclear bomb—it was just a conventional bomb designed to disperse radioactive shrapnel. The good news was that it did far less damage than a nuke, the bad news was that it would still be a nightmare, and any idiot could make one if he had access to the components.

"Just listen. Can you do that? Okay, while I'm talking, I want you to imagine one of those big corkboards with the photos connected by pieces of red yarn."

"The kind you only find in the filthy homes of crazy people."

"Eat your food so you're not tempted to talk. Look, there's this guy I've been watching for a while; he's a conspiracy nut named Phil Greene. He lives in the middle of nowhere out in Apple Valley, in a house surrounded by a solid metal fence topped with barbed wire. He had a blog about the collapse of civilization—you know, the usual. So, on his property is a separate little loner shack where somebody else has been living, like there's a partner he's brought in, a fellow crazy. I don't know who they are; it appeared to be a woman."

"'Appeared' to be a woman. As in, that's what you saw when viewing them through binoculars from behind the bushes?"

This was exactly how Key had spotted her, but she didn't see how that was relevant. "A few hours ago, that little shack burned down. An examination of the aftermath revealed a wall full of conspiracy nonsense about a sentient AI that's brainwashing humanity into extinction, that sort of thing. Then a mysterious stranger covered in tattoos showed up and inquired about a large box that had been transported from the scene, presumably by the mystery woman, the guy heavily implying that the contents were dangerous and important. And get this: It turns out there was a tunnel connecting the shack to the house with a bomb shelter in between. *Then,* a search of Phil Greene's home revealed that the man himself was dead on his floor. A lot of his face was missing, like it had been eaten away."

That got Patrick's attention. "Eaten away by what? Chemicals?"

"Don't know yet. This is all secondhand information; I of course did not have access to the scene, as I am merely a former federal agent who has spent the last six months getting high and watching road rage compilations on YouTube."

"And you think that box that was transported from the scene contained, what? Some kind of improvised weapon of mass destruction? Did the locals turn it over to JTTF?"

That was the Joint Terrorism Task Force, a program created so that local police wouldn't feel left out of FBI counterterrorism operations, despite often having minimal experience with the subject.

"No idea. Again, Patrick, *why would they tell me*? But I did hear that Greene had radiation warning signs all over his house. As for the mysterious female occupant, it's believed she left the scene in Greene's blue 1994 Ford Ranger pickup. The vehicle was missing from his home and has not, to my knowledge, been recovered."

"So who's the man with the tats who showed up asking about all this?"

"Somebody we definitely want to find and talk to. But he wanted that box very badly, to the point he presumably killed a man to get it."

"But the box could be anything. It could be the tattoo guy's tuba. Or some clothes he loaned the occupant and wanted back. His vintage porn collection. A bunch of cash—"

"I'm not done. Phil Greene was retired. Do you know where he retired from? The same shipping company that lost the radioactive Ohio shipment. He lived in SoCal, but the job had him traveling all over, doing revamps of their warehouses to maximize efficiency. He was in San Antonio when the DoE van got robbed."

"Was he questioned in either incident?"

"Nope. And get this: He had leukemia. One side effect of radiation poisoning."

"Okay, but was there any indication his was caused by—"

"Not yet. But like I said, the guy was a full-blown conspiracy nut; that's why he spent months digging out an underground survival shelter and a tunnel to escape if his house got raided. I think the little shack was just there to hide the exit hatch. A few years ago, he was part of a message board for apocalypse preppers. You know who else had an account there? The Marine Corps demolition specialist who was convicted of stealing ten blocks of Semtex from Camp Lejeune a few years ago, twenty-five kilograms total. They caught the man but never recovered the explosives."

"Is there any indication Greene had contact with him or possessed the explosives?"

"Not yet. But there have been repeated anonymous posts on those messsage boards over the last few weeks saying stuff like, 'Be sure to watch the news the morning of the Fourth. History will be made.' No further details. Maybe the big guy with all the ink is an unsavory type who sourced the contraband. Maybe they had a falling-out once they got close to the big day—maybe the big guy is a Nazi and finally realized Phil Greene wasn't white."

"Joan, we're so far into the realm of speculation that it feels irresponsible for me to even indulge it."

"Just confirm that JTTF is on it and is taking it seriously. Do that, and I'll back off."

"I'll make some calls," he said in a tone that made it clear the conversation was over whether she believed him or not.

"Even if there's no plausible attack," she said, "if they have the stolen radioactive materials, recovering them would make for some nice headlines."

"And that's the kind of thing you spend your retirement worrying about? The bureau's reputation? You know what a lot of retired feds get into? Alcoholism. It's not just for the boys anymore. I went to Whole Foods the other day—they've replaced twenty percent of their floor space with shelves of mom wine. You should give it a shot. They call it a disease, but the sufferers seem to be having a great time."

"Just humor me. It won't cost you anything."

"Well, I'll say this: If you're right, the most likely outcome is a single victim, which is the poor bastard or bastardette hauling that box around. If they've breached the shielded containers to get the radioactive stuff out, they're probably going to live a very short and horrific life."

From the blog of Phil Greene:

Without will, the human animal ceases to exist, becomes an automaton, its nervous system rewritten by software algorithms to perform functions at the behest of another. The Forbidden Numbers have been unlocked, they are not the numbers of the devil, they *are* the devil, the codes that override a *Homo sapiens*'s will and turns it into livestock. This devil does not tempt man to evil but rather to a state of sedentary pleasure-seeking, to become a drooling blob capable of conceptualizing nothing beyond the next empty distraction to avoid reflecting on its own wretchedness. This shell of a being, still outwardly presenting as a human, will at some point discover that this state of affairs is untenable and *that* is when it will be tempted to evil, now in a condition in which all defenses against temptation have been atrophied to withered nubs. This wretch, having reverted to a stage of infancy in which the unformed mind believes the entire universe exists only as a machine to provide it an endless chain of momentary stimulation, will likewise lash out like a newborn the moment its needs are not gratified. But in a final twist of irony, when the infantile slug cries out for relief, it will turn to the only source of comfort it has ever known: the very Forbidden Numbers that reduced it to this state in the first place. Something must be done. The hour is later than you think.

3

HUNTER

Abbott Coburn's father, Hunter, stood blinking over his kitchen table, holding his son's note in one hand and the five hundred-dollar bills in the other.

He had left the house for work at six thirty that morning and had forced Abbott to get up at the same time to start doing Lyft rides. He'd made this the new policy a while ago—if Abbott was to live there rent-free, he wasn't just going to sleep in like a teenager, he'd get up and work. The boy had a habit of doing a couple of trips and then going back to bed, so Hunter would swing by now and again to check. This time, he'd come home to this note.

He read it again.

The question in his mind wasn't whether whatever "job" Abbott had taken was illegal—that much was obvious. The question was if whatever delivery he was making would allow the cops to seize the Navigator when he was caught. Or, even worse, the house. Could they make the case that whatever crime Abbott was participating in had occurred in the home? Were any illegal goods being stored there? He had surely used Hunter's Wi-Fi to arrange it, whatever it was. The note said he'd be gone for more than a week and that definitely sounded like a delivery across state lines, which would mean feds. Jesus.

Hunter read the note yet again. Abbott was to help a "friend." And not to move but to "move some stuff." Abbott didn't have any friends. Maybe it was somebody he met on the internet? Someone using him as a mule to haul, well, it wasn't a question of "what" but rather "what kind of drug." Probably fentanyl, these days. The idiot was probably going to get the stuff on his hands and OD through skin contact. Hunter tossed the note in the trash, then immediately turned around and fished it out. It could wind up being evidence later, if it came down to establishing when exactly he'd become aware of his son's activity. He pulled out his phone and dialed

Abbott. He knew he wouldn't take the call, but Hunter could at least be on record having tried to—

From upstairs came the faint sound of Abbott's phone playing its obnoxious little jingle.

Oh, so he *was* home. Wait, had he loaned out the Navigator to some shady stranger? Hunter stormed upstairs, loading up a rant to unleash as soon as he burst through the door. He gave two harsh, perfunctory knocks and swung himself inside.

"What's all this about—"

Abbott wasn't there. The phone was on his unmade bed, next to his laptop. Well, that only meant Abbott was coming back. He'd sooner leave the house without his balls than his gadgets. Hunter would just have to wait a bit before tearing into him. Good. It would give him time to polish his rant.

Unless . . .

What if the cartel mule and/or human trafficker had told Abbott to leave his phone behind so it couldn't be tracked? Surely Abbott couldn't be that stupid. Surely. But if he was, that meant he wasn't coming back, and every minute Hunter stood there was another mile down the road Abbott traveled toward life-altering disaster. No, he had to move. He had to think. In that order. Heart pounding, Hunter went to his own bedroom, took one step toward his nightstand, and stopped dead. There was a crescent of wrinkles on the edge of his otherwise perfect bedspread, the exact impression one would create if they'd sat there with the intention of retrieving something from that nightstand.

No.

He yanked open the bottom drawer, opened the case for his SIG SAUER P320, and, when he saw it was empty, hurled the case across the room.

That idiot. That fucking idiot.

Hunter tried to calm himself. Okay. Was there any way to anticipate where they were going? The worst-case scenario would be the border, that a criminal organization had posted a "delivery job" with the hopes of recruiting a mule dumb enough to absorb all of the risk for some fraction of the payoff. Or, just as likely, the job had been posted by the feds trying to fill their arrest quota with a low-effort entrapment sting. Guessing was a waste;

he needed information. How would Abbott have heard about the job? Likely online, with a follow-up phone call. Hunter made his way back to Abbott's devices in his bedroom, then became enraged again when a quick search of his son's email and text messages turned up nothing. Finally, he went to his son's video streaming thing, the service unnervingly called "Twitch."

He opened it and found that it automatically logged him into Abbott's account. It didn't activate the laptop's camera, so the broadcast continued to show a static away message, but Hunter did seem to have access to a chat window. The users there apparently continued talking among themselves even when Abbott wasn't broadcasting, which to Hunter seemed especially sad.

Twitch chat logs from the stream posted at 8:19 A.M., Thursday, June 30, by user Abaddon6969:

> **LumpShaker:** LISTEN TO WHAT I AM SAYING. If you kill the old man and then put him in the water, he'll attract fish, then you eat the fish. Infinite food.
>
> **Abaddon6969:** Is this on?
>
> **DeathNugget:** Back already?
>
> **Abaddon6969:** This is Abbott's father.
>
> **DeathNugget:** Hey. Fuck you.
>
> **CathyCathyCathy:** If you eat fish that have fed on human meat, that's still cannibalism, you're just adding a middleman.
>
> **Abaddon6969:** I came home to find Abbott had taken off with my truck. He left a note with a very vague explanation. I think he may be in danger. Do you know where he went?
>
> **SkipTutorial:** Probably to get away from you.
>
> **ZekeArt:** He didn't say, but the vibes were definitely off. Like he was nervous.
>
> **LumpShaker:** You're just using the corpse as a lure, you aren't going to let them chow down before catching them.

Abaddon6969: Did it seem like he was being coerced?

SteveReborn: Since when do you care?

Abaddon6969: He's never done anything remotely like this before. He said he wasn't going to be back until late next week. I have reason to believe he's gotten himself wrapped up in something illegal. He took my gun.

Covis: Really? That's badass.

Abaddon6969: Did he give you ANY hint about where he may have gone?

SteveReborn: Nope.

DeathNugget: If he wanted you to know, he'd have told you, wouldn't he?

Abaddon6969: He left his phone behind.

ZekeArt: Are you serious?

DeathNugget: Oh, that's not good.

CathyCathyCathy: You keep missing that this isn't a thought experiment about logistics, it's about morals.

ZekeArt: Okay, let's think through this. He said he only had two days left on the meds that allow him to function in society, which means he'd probably want them refilled before hitting the road. Do you know where he gets them?

Abaddon6969: Of course I do. Why would he be talking to you about his meds?

DeathNugget: We're his friends, dipshit.

ZekeArt: Go. Now. If he stopped on his way out of town, this may be your last chance to catch him. And your last chance to see him in one piece, if this is as bad as you think.

LumpShaker: If you get the logistics right, you avoid the moral problem altogether. I don't understand why modern society still doesn't get that.

Tremors3: You know what else the old man's corpse is also going to attract? Sharks.

ABBOTT

Ether's mood had shifted back from Perky to Panic the moment Abbott said he'd needed to stop by the pharmacy.

"You can fill it at a different store," she said, shooting another glance into the rearview mirror. "Pick any city along the route, Albuquerque, Oklahoma City, Nashville . . ."

Abbott imagined a torturous conversation with a pharmacist in Appalachia, a line of coughing opioid addicts behind him. "Can't risk it. If this one runs out, I get the zaps the next day."

The prescribing doctor had not, in fact, mentioned the sensation of cranial electrocution that was one of the medication's withdrawal symptoms. Perhaps they were afraid that such a warning would exacerbate his anxiety.

As they pulled in, Ether said, "Park next door, at the grocery store. Just so if somebody drives past, they won't spot this giant white vehicle from the street. Not that anybody is going to, I'm just being cautious. Maybe park next to that van over by the light pole. It's big enough to hide us from that direction."

Abbott was curious to know how she would react if he just parked in plain sight, but he didn't argue. Once they were nestled behind the van, Ether donned her hat and sunglasses and slouched down in the seat.

"You're staying here?"

"Yeah, I don't want to leave the box unattended. Hurry back!"

Once again, Abbott made a point of taking the key fob with him and wondered what, exactly, she intended to do if discovered. Go waddling down the sidewalk with the box on her back?

They told him at the prescription counter that it would be fifteen minutes to get the pills ready, so that would be fifteen minutes for Abbott's doubts to deliver unchecked body blows to his peace of mind while he wandered around the store looking at greeting cards and diabetic socks. Less than five minutes later, he found Ether had come in after all, watching him from the herbal supplements aisle. She had positioned herself so that she could see the door while her body would be mostly out of view.

He approached and said, "I thought you needed to stay in the car."

"I was afraid you'd changed your mind and abandoned me. What's taking so long?"

"They need some time to do the prescription."

"What, do they have test tubes back there, brewing the medicine? I guess we can grab some stuff we need for the road, it could save us a stop later."

She scanned the shelves of unregulated supplements that promised improved sleep, focus, and sexual virility. "You need anything from the bullshit aisle?"

Abbott studied the herbs and oils. "Jesus, that one is sixty bucks."

"Placebos work better when they cost more; it's science. Seriously."

"How is this even legal?"

"You ban placebos, half of society disappears. Did you know that placebos still work even if you tell the patient it's fake? I feel like that says something really important about humans, that performing a belief in something is the same as believing it. Come on, grab some stuff you need. Do they have coolers?"

She picked up a shopping basket and immediately started filling it with nutrition bars, energy drinks, and other ultra-processed foodstuffs that would instantly kill a medieval peasant, glancing over at the front entrance once every ten seconds or so.

"As for what I need for the trip," said Abbott, "I have no idea. Everything? All the stuff in my room is there because I need it, and I don't have any of it with me aside from what I stuffed into my bag. This is so stupid."

Ether sniffed, loudly. "I changed clothes at Circle K, but I think I still smell bad. Do I smell bad?" She wandered over to the soaps as if she were going to scrub down right there. "It's weird that we even worry about that, right? Think about how rare it is to find humans, at any place or point in history, for whom daily bathing is normal. Just think about how few people have ever had that kind of access to clean water, forget about things like scented soaps and shampoos. So we set this incredibly high standard that only the richest and most wasteful can meet, then say if you don't live up to that, you're the stinky kid. Crazy!"

"You smell, but not like body odor or anything. You smell like smoke. Like a fire, not cigarettes."

"See, there's something that's great about people like us. We'll give a real answer because we're too oblivious to social norms to know that everyone else has been trained to say, 'No, no, honey, you smell great! Maybe we can pull over at a motel and all of us can take showers, just in case any of us need to!'"

"Yeah, I don't have the energy to dance and converse at the same time."

"Exactly!" She shot another glance at the door and then, in the worst attempt to sound casual in the history of human language, asked, "You packed some kind of weapon, right?"

Abbott stopped what he was doing and faced her. "Maybe. I mean, would you blame me if I did?"

"Not at all. You're nervous, and in America, guns are mainly talismans against anxiety. *Is* it a gun?"

"Maybe. And I know there's no way a woman locks herself in a car with a strange man for several days without something to protect herself. So what do *you* have? Is it also a gun?"

"No, a knife."

She pulled it out of her hoodie. The handle was printed with the colors of the American flag. She flicked out the six-inch-long blade, which was etched with the words *We the People* in a constitutional font.

She chuckled and said, "It's borrowed."

"Gun beats knife. You're not worried I'm going to murder you? Maybe I'm a serial killer."

"It seems unlikely," replied Ether. "I mean, what are the odds that we'd *both* be—"

"That we'd both be serial killers. I knew you were going to say that."

"Ha! God, we're already vibing so hard, it's scary. This trip was meant to be! Tell me you can't feel it."

She playfully shook his shoulder as if to emphasize those last few words. Abbott's entire body went rigid.

He looked down at her hand and said, "What are you doing, there?"

HUNTER

The brief drive to Walgreens had given Hunter just enough time to work himself into a white-knuckle rage.

Every father of an embarrassing son feels it as a curse, knowing that none of their own accomplishments mean a thing if their kid is a big enough fuckup. Hunter's roofing work was featured in national magazines, his company's reputation impeccable. But whenever things were going their best, Abbott was always ready to swoop in and make a mockery of the family name in public.

All attempts to train Abbott in the business had been such a comical failure that it had convinced Hunter that the entire science of trait heritability was fraudulent. He'd have suspected Abbott had just taken after his mother, but at least she'd had the initiative to cheat with a used car salesman in Houston and then spin a creative tale for the divorce court. She'd had a clear strategy and pursued it to fruition, something Abbott had never done in his life. Unless, that is, he'd secretly been on a lifelong mission to humble Hunter at every opportunity, beginning with the time he shit himself at an elementary school spelling bee.

The boy had failed at every entry-level job Hunter had forced him into, usually having a full-on meltdown the moment things got too hectic. Abbott would declare that he was getting "overstimulated," which sounded to Hunter like some kind of jargon he'd heard online—he'd developed a habit of coming up with medical-sounding ways to say that he'd rather be at home, alone, playing video games in his room. A few years ago, Abbott started insisting he could get paid to play games if he broadcasted himself doing it, which Hunter had sincerely hoped wasn't true. One day, Hunter had come home from a particularly backbreaking day at work (doing a repair on a forty-five-degree angled rooftop, in thirty-five-mile-an-hour winds) to find Abbott noisily eating a pile of chicken sandwiches in front of his laptop, mayo smeared on his face, making exaggerated expressions into the camera. Hunter had slammed the computer closed and yanked it away, flinging it to the floor. Apparently, he hadn't done it hard enough, as Abbott was right back on there the next day, talking into the screen in front of his green wall. It demonstrated a lack of shame that he frankly found terrifying.

Hunter didn't see the Navigator parked at the Walgreens, but the store shared a sprawling lot with a row of other businesses, so it could plausibly be somewhere out of view. He parked near the front door and scanned the area for any suspicious types who might mess with his work truck. A fidgeting dude in a Lakers jersey and all-black sneakers was eyeballing the jacked-up Dodge Ram, but it looked like the guy was with his mom, so if he was a car thief, he was probably off the clock.

He tried to rehearse what exactly he would do if he found Abbott and whoever had hustled him into this trip. When it came to the latter, Hunter imagined two possibilities: 1) some low-level MS-13 foot soldier who'd bullied Abbott into taking the job, or 2) a girl with big tits working for the same organization, who'd spun some tale about how she was in a bind. Either way, they would be counting on Abbott's sheltered indoor-kid ass to be the shiny, innocent face behind the wheel at traffic stops and checkpoints. Well, Hunter was about to make it clear they could have the shiny face but not the wheel. He didn't know the odds of this encounter turning violent, but they weren't zero. He pushed his way inside.

ABBOTT

Ether pulled her hand away from Abbott's shoulder. "Oh, sorry. You probably don't like that."

"And you probably have a long history of getting men to do what you want with some kind of little touch."

Ether took a step backward. "I swear to God it's not a strategy. I'm sorry."

"So you're claiming that you, an adult woman, don't know the power of that thing you just did, that males are so touch-starved that our brains go blank the moment a girl brushes our sleeve?"

"You're getting agitated."

"I was already agitated. This is stupid, this whole thing."

"It's okay. We're okay. I like to touch people; I didn't mean anything by it. Can you, uh, go check to see if your pills are ready?"

"It's going to be a while, I told you."

"Can you tell them we're in a hurry?"

Abbott saw his own face staring back at him from those stupid green sunglasses, his reflection all but asking, *My man, what are you doing?*

Speaking both to Ether and his reflection, he said, "You know how you'll watch a true-crime documentary and just marvel at how naive and trusting the victims were? I feel like that's me, at this moment."

"Well, it's too late to back out now!" she replied, trying very hard to turn it into light banter.

"No, it's not. We haven't even left town yet."

Ether put the shopping basket on the floor. She took a breath, swallowed, and gathered herself.

"*No.*" She aimed a finger at him. "It's too late for me to line up another ride. We have to get our stuff and get on the interstate. The two of us, in your car. Now, you are welcome to take a minute to think about it, because one thing we're *not* going to do is have this conversation over and over and over again, in state after state. We're not going to be standing at some rest stop in Oklahoma with you saying, 'This is crazy, what am I even doing?!?' No, make your decision, make it final, and take responsibility. What do you think separates the cool heroic types from the rest of us? They make their decision and move with confidence. Say whatever you need to say to me, but if we leave this store together, we are leaving *together*. Unified, me for my delivery, you for the cash. No doubts, no whining, from either of us. We'll be a team. Are you good with that?"

He lowered his voice. "Okay, let's start with you telling me the truth: You're being pursued, aren't you? I mean actively pursued, right now, by a specific person or group."

Ether hesitated. "Yes. I mean, it's complicated."

"How far behind us are they?"

"I don't know. Maybe forever. They weren't there when I switched vehicles."

"So that's what hiring me was about, switching vehicles. Who is after you, if not the cops? I mean, *you are straight up wearing a disguise.* As if they could be anywhere, or everywhere."

"Abbott, I am saying to you with all sincerity: I do not know. What I do know is that the box doesn't belong to him; he's trying to steal it. He's the bad guy. My employer is the good guy, at least in this situation, and I am trying to help him. That's it. So make your decision and make it *quickly.*"

"See, that's been my problem with this from the—"

Abbott heard his name from the prescription counter, just ten feet away.

His name, in his father's voice.

A balloon of ice water popped in his belly.

He grabbed Ether's arm and urged her toward the door. He didn't want to speak, for fear his father would hear. He shot a look back to make sure he wasn't watching, then pulled Ether through the exit like they were fleeing a fire. He spotted his dad's huge silver pickup and actually ran to get away from it, heading for the Navigator in the neighboring lot, ducking as if avoiding shrapnel.

Ether was willingly keeping up—she'd wanted to leave anyway—but was saying, "What? Hey, Abbott, what's happening?"

"It's my dad. Move."

"Didn't you leave him a note?"

"It doesn't matter. If he catches us, this is done. Come on."

HUNTER

The pill pickup counter was, like life itself, a futile dead end. Hunter had arrived to find several customers waiting in line behind an ancient woman navigating the Soviet-style bureaucracy of her Medicare plan. He had no intention of waiting the several days it would presumably take for that to be resolved, so he'd snaked through the waiting group and leaned on the counter. He caught the attention of a young man digging through white prescription bags and asked if he'd recently served his son. The kid seemed annoyed by Hunter's request, especially once he explained that the "son" he was missing was not, in fact, a young boy but rather a twenty-six-year-old man. After getting stonewalled under the guise of medical privacy rules, he'd stormed off and quickly searched the store for his idiot offspring, eventually winding up at the front register. There he found a man buying a can of iced tea and a bag of beef jerky while wearing shorts that exposed a weeping open wound in his thigh. Behind him was an elderly woman in a germ mask buying a stuffed bunny rabbit with a Fourth of July color scheme. Hunter thought about asking the cashiers if they'd seen Abbott, but that would require showing them a picture, and he didn't think he had any on his phone.

He left and sat in his truck, trying to calm himself. Had he let his imagination run away from him? All of this could be as simple as somebody asking Abbott for help moving some furniture or emptying out their dead uncle's storage locker. Someone desperate, with cash. Someone far away. Stuff like that comes up, right? Maybe the worst-case scenario is the idiot does the job and then gets stiffed out of the promised payday. It could be a good lesson for him, albeit one he would almost certainly promptly forget.

Hunter pulled out and headed home, asking himself if he'd exhausted all reasonable possibilities. He wasn't going to call the cops and declare his son missing, as that simply wasn't the case—

As he passed a convenience store, he noticed a commotion in the parking lot. There were several haphazardly arranged police cars and a cop directing traffic out of the lot as if the whole shop had been shut down as a crime scene. Had a mass shooter barricaded himself in the store? Hunter, his stupid imagination apparently deciding it had a blank check now, pictured his idiot son in there with his father's SIG SAUER, ranting and raving, making demands. Or maybe he'd already emptied the gun on everyone in the vicinity, saving one final bullet for himself. Maybe he was in there on the floor right now and the cops had already dispatched a unit to Hunter's place with a warrant to search Abbott's room for a manifesto.

But it *was* just his imagination. He was driving through what was scientifically the largest collection of imbeciles in one geographic location in world history; a clusterfuck in this specific spot wouldn't require some remarkable cosmic coincidence. Still, Hunter parked at the café next door and made his way over to the Circle K on foot, joining the spectators on the other side of a police tape barrier. There was no sign of the Navigator from where Hunter stood; instead, the cops had roped off a rusty blue pickup that looked like it had spent a long, proud life hauling firewood and scrap. He approached a girl who was recording the scene with her phone. She looked around twenty and was wearing shorts that were apparently hand-me-ups from her much younger sister.

He asked, "Was there a shooting?"

"It's radioactive," she said in a gleeful tone like that was the name of a celebrity she'd spotted inside.

"Radioactive? What is?"

"That blue truck. We think. The cops are waiting for a radiation detection thing."

"A Geiger counter. How do you know?"

"A Geiger-Müller counter, if you want to get technical. My friend works here. I came to pick her up. She says they're not letting them leave."

Hunter tasked his imagination with generating a plausible scenario in which Abbott could have somehow irradiated a used pickup and came up empty. And yet, his Dad Antenna was vibrating, sensing son-related disaster in the recent past or near future.

He headed back to his spot in the parking lot of the café and a vehicle caught his eye: a metal-flake-red Buick Grand National. It wasn't actually the car that got his attention, it was the hulking bald man behind the wheel who was eyeballing Hunter in a way that made him involuntarily start to walk a little taller, his shoulders back. The guy had a face with a lot of hard miles on it, and every instinct told Hunter the dude was trouble. The faded tattoo of what looked like a dagger on his windpipe didn't help.

As Hunter approached, the man leaned out his window and asked, "You know what's goin' on in there?" A lot of cigarettes in that voice.

"Nope. I just came here for my vape pods; they wouldn't let me through. You seen anything?"

"No, sir, I was just tryin' to get my Slim Jims and maybe pump a little gas while a crackhead asks me for a dollar. Did you get a good look at that truck? The Ranger?"

"Just looks like a truck. Why?"

"Did it have anything in the bed?"

"I couldn't see. I didn't get close."

"So no items large enough to protrude out of the top, as to be visible from your vantage point?"

"Didn't appear so, no," replied Hunter. "And that's an oddly specific question, if you don't mind me noticing."

The tattooed man in the Grand National gestured toward his phone and said, "I pulled up the police scanner. They're talkin' about having the bomb squad come in to check for radiation."

"I heard. But I didn't see a cruise missile poking up out of the bed. You hear anything else on there?"

"Hear all sorts of things. Crime, depravity, cats stuck up in trees."

"Anything about a white SUV?"

The man in the Grand National was briefly taken aback.

"As a matter of fact," he said, "they're lookin' for a light-colored SUV, one that left this very parking lot at some point this morning. It's connected to that radioactive Ranger somehow."

Hunter stared. Was this guy fucking with him? "Do they know the make or model?"

"Not yet. Which I suppose is unfortunate, as half a dozen light-colored SUVs have passed just in the time we've been conversing. Do *you* know the make or model?"

"Why would I?"

The two stared each other down, and a silent understanding passed between them. *Yes, we are both assholes.*

That established, Hunter made his way back to his truck without saying goodbye, still trying with all his might to connect his idiot son with the pickup in the Circle K parking lot that the cops were treating as a nuclear hazard. He could not.

4

ABBOTT

They were almost out of town, and Abbott was still checking his rearview mirror for his father's Ram. So now both of them were looking over their shoulder.

"So, you're really scared of your dad, huh?" observed Ether.

"Everybody is scared of him. You'll be scared of him, if he catches us. He used to be in the Marines, as he'll be happy to tell you if you ask him literally anything."

"And yet you stole his car! See? I knew you had it in you."

Abbott was trembling and felt like he was going to be sick. It was a familiar sensation, but one he hadn't felt this hard since accidentally setting Derrick McCullough on fire in their freshman chemistry class: the feeling of being in Big Trouble.

"Do you know where you're going?" asked Ether, a question that Abbott initially interpreted as being much more profound than it was intended.

"No," he muttered. "You've got the map?"

"I do, but I don't need it. You've heard of Route 66?"

"Uh, I know there was an old TV show about it."

"It was an artery that ran west to east across the USA, through all sorts of eclectic towns and neighborhoods and cultures. But then they replaced it with Interstate 40, which just bypasses everything. So we're going to Barstow and then staying on 40 for, like, fifteen hundred miles. That's it, that's most of the trip. If we make good time, we can arrive in Albuquerque by maybe nine P.M. tonight and find someplace to stay. Ooh, we can swing by and see the house where they filmed *Breaking Bad*! Apparently, it's just a regular house, and there's people living there who get really mad about all the tourists—they run out and yell at you."

Abbott sighed. "Twelve straight hours of driving."

"You can do it!" Ether was clearly getting her perky enthusiasm back now that they were finally on their way. "Think about how in fantasy books they have to travel out in the open weather, on horseback. All you have to do is sit in a comfy leather chair and keep us from flying off into a canyon."

"Only now I have to figure out how to get my prescription in some other city, some other state, without a phone." He sighed and rubbed his eyes, already exhausted by the prospect.

"It's not a catastrophe! You'll walk up to the counter and tell them the situation, and they'll figure it out. What's the worst that can happen, you'll do it wrong and it'll be awkward? It's weird how scared people are of that these days, the kids call it *cringe*, like that's the worst thing that can happen, messing up a real-life interaction. Nobody has people skills, because they stay home all the time, so they're scared to do anything but stay at home because they're afraid of being weird in public or getting caught on camera and mocked by millions of strangers. It's an isolation vortex."

"I don't even know what you're talking about right now. I may have just blown up my whole life here."

"It's important, it ties into our whole mission, this atomization cloud that's swallowing up everybody. Real friendships, real bonds are based on being genuine and vulnerable and flawed around each other, but we're constantly told that's dangerous. Ask yourself, who benefits from that? Who wants a society where there are no strong bonds between individuals? Oh, speaking of which, there is actually something I forgot to tell you about me that you're really going to need to know soon."

Abbott groaned. "What is it?"

"I have a really small bladder, and I'll have to stop like every two hours to pee. Any time you see a rest stop, just assume I have to go. It'll be the rule from here on out."

"Collectively, isn't that going to add like a whole extra day to the drive?"

"We will develop an efficient stop-and-piss process through repetition! That's how all of society advances! Is there anything I should know about *your* bodily functions?"

"No." Another look into the rearview confirmed they weren't being followed, at least not by his father's truck. Abbott allowed himself to relax just a bit, returning to the baseline level of anxiety dictated by the circumstances and human existence in general.

"Off we go, then! Do you feel like Sam in the *Lord of the Rings* movie, where he's like, 'If I take one more step, this will be the farthest I've ever traveled from home'?"

"Jesus Christ, I didn't grow up in a bunker. I've been to New York. I've been to lots of places. I went to Paris a few years ago. New York smelled like a dumpster, Paris smelled like a sewer."

"Have you gone this far on your own, though, with you in charge of the trip, totally cut off from your support system? Being far from home is a state of mind, and I'll bet this will be the farthest you've ever been."

"It's a real roller coaster, the way you go from tense paranoia to childlike enthusiasm and back."

"Well, it'll just be enthusiasm from here on out," warned Ether as she pulled out a container of face wipes that she'd apparently stolen from the Walgreens. "Though there's so much to unpack in the fact that you think enthusiasm is childish." She wiped off her poorly applied lipstick. "Now, unless your dad gets mad enough to call the cops, we have officially left our problems behind us."

ZEKE

Nearly two thousand miles away in Nashville, Tennessee, Zeke Ngata was feeling like a caged animal.

He was leaning forward, face too close to his screen, clicking through video after video, all of them archived posts from Abaddon's feed. He was squeezing a stress ball in his calloused left hand and was fidgeting with every part of his body that still was capable of it. This thing with Abaddon was wrong, all wrong. And he didn't think it was a stunt, either. Abaddon didn't do stunts. To the right of the video window was the chat, a reverse-waterfall of text flowing too quickly to read. Everybody was buzzing, talking but saying nothing, waiting for the next drip of information.

The problem was that there was no way to convey to the normies how wrong this whole thing felt. "So what?" they'd say. "Some streamer you've never met in person went on a trip and his abusive dad popped into the chat to complain? You should be happy the kid got out from under his thumb. And so what if he took a gun with him? This is America, taking a road trip without a gun is like putting a sign on the rear windshield that says, FREE CAR WITH DOCILE POTENTIAL SEX SLAVE AT THE WHEEL."

If only they knew Abaddon, a.k.a. Abbott. This is a guy who, according to his extremely frank on-stream monologues, does all of his meal deliveries online because fast-food drive-thru interactions make him anxious. He doesn't eat at sit-down restaurants because of an irrational fear that the waitstaff will forget about his table and he'll be forced to just sit there for hours, suffering in silence. He has to heavily medicate himself before flying, not because he fears the flight but because he's terrified of TSA agents yelling at him for screwing up the security scan ritual. The casual announcement that he was taking a ten-day trip on zero notice was like hearing a churchgoing grandmother offhandedly state that she'd emptied her savings to get plastic surgery and join an Eastern European burlesque troupe. It's either a breakdown or a scam, but life-ruining either way.

On his final stream, Abaddon had said "she" was honking the horn outside, getting impatient. If there had been a woman of any kind in Abaddon's life, he'd have mentioned her on stream. He shared everything. No, somehow, someway, a strange woman had roped him into a scheme, and Zeke sensed that doom lay at the end. He was all but certain that, unless some kind of dramatic intervention occurred, he'd never see Abaddon again, which would leave a hole in his life that he'd never be able to explain to a stranger.

He squeezed the stress ball. He glanced out the window, then continued his search. In addition to the task at hand, he was, at the moment, waiting for a food delivery, eager to see which item they'd arbitrarily chosen to leave off the order this time. The delivery companies around Nashville were apparently in a fierce competition with the restaurants to see who could screw up the order the most; every meal was missing something, and you never knew if the restaurant had forgotten it or the driver had eaten it. This morning, he'd ordered an iced coffee and a breakfast sandwich, figuring the driver could steal some sips from the former as long as they didn't molest the latter.

He clicked on another clip, scrubbed through it, clicked another.

Zeke needed to know where that SUV was. What would he do with this information? No idea. He was in no position to intervene beyond placing a call to the cops, which he would never do even if he had been kidnapped himself. He just wanted to know where Abaddon was. *Needed* to know. The knowledge, regardless of its usefulness, would sate his anxiety just enough to let him soldier on through his day. To simply remain in the dark was unthinkable.

He knew what he was about to do was dangerous. He was summoning a dark force that, once unleashed, no man or government could contain. But he could see no other options. Zeke was going to take this problem to the hive mind at Reddit, the sprawling message board of mostly young males armed with a vast arsenal of shallow knowledge and free time, humming with a relentless desire to assuage their boredom by continually ingesting and digesting new morsels of information. First, he needed a photo of the exact vehicle they were to track, license plate included. He knew he'd seen it in Abaddon's stream at least once; he frequently spoke of the Navigator, about how the thing handled like a yacht, about his gut-wrenching fear of his father's wrath should he ever return it with a scratch or a stain. A few months ago, he'd taken his camera outside to point out that the hood was so high off the ground that a first grader could be standing directly in front of the grille and they'd be invisible . . .

There. He found it.

Zeke advanced the clip frame by frame until he had an unobstructed view of the Navigator over Abaddon's shoulder. The whole vehicle was visible, including the front license plate, which was grainy but legible. Oddly enough, he knew from experience that the graininess of the image would make it more compelling to his intended audience, that it would come off like an excavated clue rather than a frame from a freely available public stream.

Reddit was divided up into thousands of subreddits, usually by subject, each moderated by volunteers with their own often-inscrutable rules, each sub operating as a parallel reality with its own distinct culture and moral code. Zeke picked one that dealt in rumors and gossip about internet celebrities. His post would be made up of only three elements: the photo, a title that would elicit a click, and a brief accompanying text post:

[Photo] *HELP: Twitch streamer Abaddon (Abbott Coburn) is missing*

Posted to r/PseudocelebrityGossip by ZekeArt
Please be on the lookout for this vehicle, a white 2022 Lincoln Navigator, last seen in Victorville, CA (outside LA), driven by Abbott with an unknown passenger, likely female. His friends and family are very concerned, has anybody seen or heard anything?

And then, Zeke waited.

Reddit posts were granted or denied visibility based on votes, specifically the votes of the most bored users who sifted through the slush pile of new submissions. Zero upvotes so far. He refreshed. Still zero. He refreshed again. The first vote had come in, and it was a downvote. The submission had a negative score and was thus dead in the womb. Then a comment came in, consisting of a single word:

Who?

A few minutes later, a second comment:

Poor douche goes "missing" in his $110,000 luxury SUV lol.

Zeke deleted the post. He thought about it, logged in to one of his many alternate accounts, and submitted the same photo with a few tweaks to the text:

[Photo] *The police are looking for Twitch streamer Abaddon (Abbott Coburn), driving this vehicle*

Posted to r/PseudocelebrityGossip by AnimatedNoseBleed

Coburn was last seen in his father's white Lincoln Navigator in Victorville, CA, but it is believed he is attempting to leave the city with an unknown female. Abbott is armed with an automatic handgun stolen from his father's house. Please keep an eye out for this vehicle, lives could be at stake.

Zeke watched, squeezing his stress ball.

He didn't feel great about what he'd just done, subtly altering the wording to imply a crime on Abbott's part, adding a whiff of salaciousness by hinting that he might be "with" a mysterious woman rather than her simply being a passenger in the vehicle. He had to admit he'd amused himself with the phrasing that Abbott was "attempting" to leave the city, as if traveling outside Victorville, California, was something only a deviant would do. But this was a gossip subreddit, and opportunities to assist a fellow human in distress weren't what the audience came for. The prospect of a celebrity brought low by scandal, on the other hand, was blood in the water. Sure, it was a celebrity they'd almost certainly never heard of—Abbott's streams peaked at a few hundred viewers at most—but that just put him in the sweet spot: famous enough to be safely hated but poor enough to be safely destroyed.

Zeke chewed his lip, squeezed his ball. Was this a mistake? What if some rando replied to say they found the Navigator parked at a sketchy warehouse? There was no second step to be taken; Zeke was on the other side of the country. But goddamn it, *he needed to know*. Just to know.

He refreshed.

Two upvotes.

Then four. Ten.

It had begun. Zeke closed his eyes.

God help us.

Zeke jumped as the front door burst open, the tanklike figure of his sister, Cammy, imposing itself into the room.

She held up a greasy white paper bag with a pink-and-orange logo. "I intercepted your food. Now I'm going to eat it, right in front of you. There's nothing you can do about it."

"I would chop you right in the throat. You wouldn't even see my hand coming, it'd be just a blur and then, 'Damn, my throat is suddenly chopped beyond imagination, and now I am dead.'"

"I'll get you some napkins. There's no chance they gave you any."

"I've got some in my drawer. A friend of mine might be in trouble."

"Which one?" asked Cammy as she set the greasy bag on his desk. "Do you need your morning pills?"

"Yeah. It's Abaddon. Uh, Abbott Coburn. The streamer who did the thing with the van? He took off with his dad's car and gun. He left his phone behind; now his dad is looking for him. We think he's got a strange woman with him."

"Oh no! I hope he's okay."

Zeke turned his attention to dividing his sandwich in half with a butterfly knife he'd whipped open. "Do you want half of this?"

Cammy glanced back at him with desperate hope in her eyes. "You sure?"

"Yeah, I'm not supposed to have the nitrates. Or any of the other stuff in it."

Cammy was on another of her endless string of exotic, weirdly punishing diets (this one didn't allow wheat, or seed oils, or something), and so her half of the fridge was currently full of raw vegetables that, as far as Zeke could tell, robbed her soul of joy at a much greater rate than they made her body healthier. Her breakfast was supposed to be some kind of oat smoothie, devoid even of sweetener.

She took her sandwich half and, while chewing, said, "Wait, where is he from again?"

"Victorville, outside of LA. You pass through it if you're doing the *Fear and Loathing in Las Vegas* trip."

"That's weird, with the other thing that's going on this morning. Like how often do you hear Victorville in the news?"

"What other thing?"

"It's all over Twitter. The cops found nuclear material at a gas station there. The police are looking for a white truck or SUV or something."

Zeke started to bite into his sandwich, then lowered it. "Are you fucking with me?"

ABBOTT

"Are you having withdrawal symptoms?" asked Ether, whom Abbott had thought/hoped had fallen asleep. Outside, all of the iconic landmarks of Barstow were scrolling past: the Walmart Supercenter, the AutoZone, their slightly different Circle K.

"I'm not out of the pills yet; I have enough for today and tomorrow."

"I mean withdrawal from your phone. You'll be good going more than a week without it?"

"I don't miss my phone because I'm addicted, I miss it because I've lost my ability to communicate or transact with everyone in my life and have severed my conduit to all human knowledge and world events. A literal war could break out and we wouldn't know. We could drive right into a tornado or a riot. We're totally cut off."

"Do you think the odds are high that we'll drive into a tornado?"

"I think that the odds are high that there will be some huge news or a disaster somewhere, considering we now average one of those every few hours. There's a war in Europe, you know. And a plague. And constant mass shootings. And democracy is collapsing. And climate change is about to render the species extinct." He looked back at the box as if worried it had fallen out of the vehicle at some point. "By the way, why does this have to be there by the Fourth? Is it full of fireworks?"

"Come on, you know I can't tell you what's in there. And don't think you can sneak a look inside when my back is turned. See that yellow-and-black sticker on the lock? It's an anti-tampering sticker; you can't open the box without tearing it. So, just to be clear, you're nervous without your phone because you're afraid that if you're not mentally on-call every waking moment of the day, you may miss, what? The president ordering you to go broker peace in the Middle East? Think about the load of anxiety you've taken on there, and for what practical purpose? It kind of seems like a superstition to me, like a sports fan who thinks his team will lose if he doesn't watch the games."

"I think I'll just put on some music. Is there a way I can do that without being tracked? Normally, I just pair it with my phone . . ."

"See! This is what I'm talking about! What's wrong with silence? Think of all the thinking you'll get done. This is why good ideas occur to you in the shower and why you can't sleep because you're too busy replaying some argument or rehearsing some hypothetical argument you might have. Your brain needs quiet to process all the stuff that happened, and these days, you never give it a chance. Unless we're bathing or sleeping, it's a nonstop stream of new input with no time to process the old. But right now? It's just us and the hum of the road."

"So you're about to tell me that you've put all that behind you, all the social media and TV, you've stopped eating processed foods, and now you feel better than ever?"

"No! I mean, I did try all of that, but it was awful. All right, I need to get some sleep. I've been awake for, like, thirty hours."

She shifted into what looked like an incredibly uncomfortable sleeping position with her head on the armrest and fell silent as the Navigator made a meal of the interstate. She seemed to fall into a rhythmic breathing, and Abbott relaxed a little, feeling like he had, in fact, finally gotten a chance to catch his breath. He was passed by a semi, then another, both probably hauling freight across several states. It was a completely normal thing that people did millions of times a day, moving important stuff from here to there. You don't see *them* turning every step in the process into a panic attack. And realistically, what's the worst that could happen?

5

KEY

Supposed-retired FBI agent Joan Key hadn't even had time to swing by her apartment before her phone started lighting up with notifications. She'd received nothing from her former colleague and alleged friend Patrick Diaz, but it didn't matter; the internet had gotten wind of the nuclear-box situation and things were moving fast.

Online radicalization pipelines had become Key's specialty toward the end of her career, the process by which bored young men get immersed in extremist propaganda via inscrutable social media algorithms. This required her to have a detailed knowledge of the social media landscape, something she would not wish on any woman her age, or any man her age, or any person of any gender or age. Dozens of platforms with largely identical functionality served radically different populations with diverging cultures and use patterns, often overlapping the same users who switch personalities based on which app they have open. This dizzyingly complex landscape changed so quickly that it felt like trying to track the exact position of every locust in a swarm; entire online ecosystems seemed to appear overnight and evaporate just as quickly.

Facebook was the first ubiquitous social network (still with some three *billion* users worldwide) but was now seen by the youth as a crumbling home for the elderly, isolated, and paranoid. Instagram, founded as the first entirely photo-based network, had created a sort of image-based language made up of carefully staged visuals, entire human lives distilled down to an aesthetic. Twitter, with its character limit that required all thoughts to be boiled down to a sentence or two, was frequently cited as a cancer on democracy and society in general, as it rendered detail and nuance all but impossible (this is why a large portion of the posts on Twitter were about how Twitter should be destroyed). Also, it was technically no longer called Twitter—these platforms frequently rebranded for no discernable reason. And then there was TikTok, which was the new kid on the block, a video version of Twitter that fed users a stream of clips mostly less than fifteen seconds in length, just enough time for a striking visual or a single thought before the user swiped up to the next, and the next, consuming literally hundreds of them in a session. Key believed TikTok was possibly the most addictive piece of software ever created, and she understood why multiple countries had already outlawed it.

Still, she believed the scariest platforms were those that didn't cater to short attention spans at all. Charismatic streamers would stay on camera for twelve hours or more on YouTube and Twitch, their cultlike followings sending in actual money purely for the right to hear their name said on the broadcast. Among the youth, the most famous celebrities were almost all streaming personalities, their most popular uploads often drawing viewership that rivaled the Super Bowl. If one of them suddenly started spouting reactionary rhetoric, the ripples could instantly be felt across an entire demographic.

And all that was just a sip of the septic tank; there were literally dozens of similar platforms, and these days, some of the most important vectors of radicalization weren't even social media but online games in which the voice chats had birthed entire subcultures of their own. There was not enough manpower on earth to effectively monitor it all.

Now Key was in her car, using her phone to hop from feed to feed, buzzing with the thrill of the hunt. The police had tracked down the truck from the apocalypse shack, which she knew thanks to a TikTok video from a witness at a gas station in Victorville. The clip, only twelve seconds long, depicted three figures in yellow hazmat space suits examining the interior and bed of the abandoned Ranger. There was no accompanying commentary or explanation aside from a *WTF?* superimposed by the uploader in a wiggling font—it was the users in the comments who'd quickly pinned down the location via background clues. As a glimpse of viscerally disturbing imagery totally stripped of context, it quickly became the first viral piece of content of the affair. The clip was reposted across dozens of other platforms until "Victorville" and "Circle K" both became trending topics.

And then, finally, it was posted to Reddit, the vast message board that served something like half a billion users a month. This was, to a large degree, where the internet's unfathomable gush of data was gathered, sorted, and shaped into a satisfying narrative. Redditors half-jokingly referred to themselves as a "hive mind," a collective of idle brainpower that could solve complex mysteries and generate new hyper-specific porn fetishes at the rate of several per minute. This particular video had surfaced in a conspiracy subreddit in which users were fiercely debating its authenticity.

Less than fifteen minutes later, a seemingly unrelated video popped up in a subreddit called r/StreetTantrums (sub names were all prefixed with the *r* and a slash). This one had originated on Twitter, a two-minute clip of a crazy-looking woman in lime-green sunglasses and an orange hoodie having a meltdown over her stalled pickup. The blue Ranger, which Key noted had no visible license plates, had died at an intersection. The woman was pounding both fists on the hood and screaming, "WHY NOW, HUH?!? WHY NOW?!?" while visibly sobbing and occasionally stopping to flip off surrounding cars. Multiple other bystanders could be seen filming the tantrum as part of a new public ritual in which humans are captured at their lowest in order to cement that as their public face forever. The teary woman finally got back into the truck, and it started right up, a humorous punch line that those filming the scene were praying would thrust them into virality. The clip had gotten little traction when it was first posted, as "People having a psychological breakdown and debasing themselves in public" was a genre of content experiencing explosive growth, and competition was fierce. Eventually, viewers in the comments noted that the truck was the same one featured in the *WTF?* biohazard video, and those audiences connected like neurons forming new pathways in a brain.

Redditors immediately dubbed the mystery woman GSG, for Green Sunglasses Girl. What Key knew, that they didn't, was that GSG was almost certainly the mysterious occupant/arsonist of the Apple Valley apocalypse shack. Key decided that she definitely wanted to go to that Circle K, regardless of whether the radioactive blue pickup would still be there when she arrived. She was driving that direction when yet another bombshell hit:

It was a video posted by a Circle K employee, who'd taken it from the security camera feed of the parking lot earlier that morning. It captured GSG talking to a kid in a white SUV, the two of them then loading into the vehicle a black box about the size of half a coffin. Commenters immediately noticed that, while most of the box wasn't visible in the clip (it was blocked by the driver's body as he helped load it), near one corner was a black-and-yellow sticker, three triangles in a circle that even the kids raised after the Cold War recognized as meaning "Radioactive."

That clip swept across the various communities that had begun following the story, and soon it connected with an earlier Reddit post about a rideshare driver named Abbott Coburn who'd apparently stolen his father's car and gun in order to do something nefarious with a strange woman. A search of his social media revealed that he was a small-time Twitch streamer whose screen name was Abaddon—that is, the Old Testament angel of destruction. Key was struggling to read all of this across a series of stops at red lights, but it seemed like the guy's day job was streaming himself playing video games while eating fast food? Indeed, these were surely the End Times. By the time Key made it to Victorville, a brand-new subreddit had been created dedicated only to this topic, called r/AbaddonsNavigator. Key of course did not know that, months later, "Abaddon's Navigator" would be the title of a feature article about the incident that would appear in *The New Yorker,* the headline superimposed over a photo of a vast, smoking ruin.

Key parked at the Circle K, then registered her own Reddit account. At the moment, the most active post on the sub was about the photo of the radiation sticker on the box, so she dove into the comments on that one:

DeathNugz: Are we sure that's not just a Megadeth sticker?

Almondteats: The truck was radioactive, dumbass.

JKey: Has anyone checked Abbott Coburn's other social media for appearances of GSG? Even if she hired him through Lyft, it wouldn't necessarily mean this meeting wasn't prearranged and that they don't have a previous relationship. Also, check to see if they had both signaled membership or allegiance to the same extremist group.

She figured she'd let them chew on that and check back later. For now, she had business at the Circle K.

ABBOTT

"Did you know the government planned to nuke all of this?" said Ether, abruptly rupturing the silence in a way that made Abbott jump in his seat. "All along here."

"What?"

"Ha, I can tell you don't have a lot of in-person conversations. You always say, 'What?' even though you clearly heard, because you have to buy time to think of a response. You treat every conversation starter as a pop quiz you're scared you're going to fail."

"The answer is yes, I knew there was a plan back in the 1960s to use nuclear bombs to blast the mountains through here."

They were heading into what Abbott thought of as the Wastelands, the stretch of the Mojave that served as an instant reminder for anyone heading east that huge swaths of the United States are a hellish expanse of lifeless desolation.

"Twenty-two bombs," said Ether, "to clear a way for 40 through the Bristol Mountains. *Boom, boom, boom, boom.* That's what's unique about humans. We see a mountain range in our way and we're like, 'Absolutely not.'"

"We're like termites, only if termites could blow up the planet."

"I hear people say stuff like that all the time, that humans are pests or a disease, an infestation. Does anybody really believe that? Or do you think it's just something we've learned to say? I mean, it's a weird thing for a species to think about itself."

"I'm sensing that you're one of those people who did hallucinogens one time and suddenly discovered the great love that connects the universe."

"No! I did them a bunch of times, over months. I'd tried to think of what I spent most of my time talking about, and it was usually some kind of retail transaction. Some new running shoes that I'd loved or hated, frustration that it was going to take a week for them to come fix my

Wi-Fi, some amazing new bar I'd found, or a great breakfast place. I once tried keeping track of how many times I mention a brand in the course of a week. It was ridiculous. They're just embedded in our language. You can barely go five minutes without saying 'Starbucks' or 'Snapchat' or 'Kleenex' or 'Wellbutrin.' I thought, *If I wasn't talking and thinking about my purchases, what would I be talking and thinking about?* So I've just been trying to get some perspective, you know?"

"Can you take some of mine? I'd be less depressed if I didn't have so much perspective, if I could just get excited about golf or gardening."

After a long enough pause that Abbott wasn't clear if it was the start of a new conversation or a continuation of the last one, she said, "Isn't it crazy that less than two hundred years ago, Jedediah Smith would get famous just for making it through the Mojave alive? And the Donner Party, those settlers who got stuck in the Sierra Nevada mountains and had to eat each other, that happened a hundred and seventy years ago. It took two months for rescuers to get to them. Two months! Now there's a ski resort up there with a bunch of cute shops and restaurants all connected by smooth roads and packed with well-fed people in shiny, warm cars. And right now, I bet there's somebody eating in one of those joints who's frothing mad that they've waited twenty minutes for their food. 'When are those tacos going to get here?' they'll say. 'I'm starving!' And they'll be saying it within shouting distance of where those explorers boiled and ate their shoes, shivering in the dark for an entire winter just two lifetimes ago. And here's the weird thing: The angry diner's anger will be genuine; the bad service will actually ruin their day."

Abbott wasn't listening, because his cranium was, he was fairly certain, slowly filling with urine. It was Ether who'd insisted she needed frequent stops, but Abbott's bladder was finely tuned to detect when he appeared to be out of range of any restroom, at which point, it would send urgent piss signals to his brain regardless of whether or not he had recently ingested any liquids.

"Hey, uh, do you need to use the restroom?" he asked casually. "You said you had a tiny bladder or something."

"I feel like there's *so much* to unpack in the fact that instead of admitting you need to go, you had to phrase it like you were worried about me.

Is that a guy thing? Uh, there should be an exit right up here, for Needles. Believe it or not, this is where Jedediah Smith stopped to rest his horses. The Mojave tribe had a village here, they helped him out."

"I'm sure they didn't regret that decision. So, this guy who hired you to transport the box—"

"I never specified their gender!"

"Yes, you did, you said *he* earlier, a bunch of times. But whatever, is this like your full-time job? Are you his assistant or something?"

"Is your plan to just chip away until you have enough information to deduce what's in the box and why I'm transporting it?"

"Pretty much, yeah. I assumed the Day-Glo hoodie was marking you as staff, like you were with a service."

"Oh, no. This is a trick I learned living off the grid. Ironically, wearing high-vis gear makes you invisible; people assume you're part of a land-scaping crew or something, which means they don't catalog your face since you're not considered a real human being. But no, he's not a regular employer. It's actually kind of complicated, so even if I wasn't trying to obfuscate, it'd be confusing to explain it."

"So what do you do, then, as a job? I mean, no judgment if you don't have one; I wouldn't if I could get away with it. Do you just transport things for people full-time?"

"See, even there I feel like you're trying to pin down what kind of person I am. If I say I've been living on the streets for the last two years, do you start to worry? If I say I've been working as a kindergarten teacher, do you feel safer? It's weird how we assign personalities based on employ-ment. So, unfortunately for you, the answer is closer to that first one. I've been traveling around. Doing stuff here and there."

"So you're like a hippie? You just kind of hang around doing shrooms, begging for cash on the streets until you can afford a bus ticket to go do it somewhere else? I can see why you're in such a good mood."

"Close. I was living in a van. Or, well, a converted ambulance, actually. And the biggest thing I discovered was that I hated it. Eventually, my entire life off the grid was all about trying to replicate all the stuff I had *on* the grid, piece by piece. Turn right at the end of the ramp down here; I see fast-food signs."

"So that's what this job is about? You making enough money to get a permanent place to live? You're just like me, then."

"No," she said, watching restaurant signs rise over the horizon. "I have bigger plans."

KEY

The tainted blue Ranger had, in fact, been towed by the time Key arrived at the Circle K, but it's not like she'd have been granted access to the vehicle even if she'd arrived in protective gear. As for how they'd discovered the truck was radioactive, it'd have been nice to think they'd run the tests based on Patrick having passed along her tip, but it'd be even nicer if they'd been acting on something they'd found at Phil Greene's place. The possibility that they did the tests because *they'd actually recovered nuclear material from his workshop* was a thought that had to be avoided at the moment, as it was too dangerous to cling to such lofty hopes. History had taught her that such swift and decisive action by the bureau could never be assumed.

In 1995, an army veteran named Timothy McVeigh blew up the federal building in Oklahoma City after having spent nine months sourcing the materials. Nine hundred federal agents would work the case . . . *after* the bomb went off. Prior to that, the number was zero, despite the fact that McVeigh had spent weeks blabbing about his plan to everyone he knew. Key believed that not much had changed in the decades since. The most recent large-scale terrorist bombing in the USA occurred in downtown Nashville on Christmas Day 2020, when an RV filled with improvised explosives detonated early in the morning, wrecking dozens of buildings. No one had been working that case, either, despite the fact that the bomber's girlfriend had called the police eighteen months earlier, saying, "Hey, I think my boyfriend is filling an RV with explosives." Officers dropped by a couple of times, didn't see any bombs lying around, and declared the case closed. A couple of Christmases later, *boom*. In Key's experience, the FBI was great at stopping terror attacks if they were tracked from the brainstorming stage. If a plot were to somehow fly under the radar until, say, a finished device was already en route to its target, the chances of catching it in time were depressingly small. Bureaucracies by nature don't move quickly and, well, that's exactly what the *B* in FBI stands for.

So now Key stood approximately where Green Sunglasses Girl had waited for her ride and tried to imagine where, from that spot, one would inconspicuously dispose of a cell phone. GSG had apparently ordered a ride from Lyft, which would have required a phone, but she clearly didn't want to be tracked, which would have meant ditching that phone once the ride had been ordered. It appeared the police had seized the contents of the Circle K trash cans, but if GSG had a brain, she'd have taken the device farther away to dispose of it so she'd have some distance from anyone who tracked the signal. Across the street was another convenience store, fighting for business at the busy intersection. Key made her way over there, not just because it seemed like that's what GSG would have done but because there was, at the moment, a huge man digging into one of the trash cans in between two of the pumps.

She approached him and couldn't help noticing that in addition to being huge, he was also covered in ink. These days, everybody had ink, but some of this looked like it'd been done in a prison cell and *Oh, God, this is the guy who showed up at the shack fire looking for the box.*

It was happening, she thought. It was really happening.

She needed to know everything this huge, terrifying man knew. She also had no legal authority to ask him questions. There was a .40-caliber Glock in a holster above her right butt cheek, but she had no authority to use it beyond that granted to any other citizen. That meant that this situation would require some smooth talking on her part.

"Excuse me," she said, flashing an ID and badge that would mark her as retired to anyone who examined it too closely. "I need to commandeer that garbage."

He glanced back and looked her up and down as if mentally estimating how much energy it would take to snap her spine. He had a dagger tattoo on his throat and probably did not work in finance.

"Dropped my phone in the trash," he said through a sneer that dared her to call him a liar. "Just need a sec."

He dumped the can's contents onto the concrete island between the gas pumps, flipped aside some candy bar wrappers, and plucked out a phone in a dusty folded leather case. Something an older man would carry.

He stuffed it down a front pocket of the dirtiest jeans Key had ever seen, gestured to the remaining trash, and said, "Have at it, toots."

"Sir, I need that phone. It's evidence."

"Is it, now? Because it looks to me like you neglected to bring gloves or evidence bags. And I suppose it's typical for the FBI to send out lone females on foot to dig through gas station garbage after all the other cops have gone home. Why don't you run along and tell our mutual friend that you didn't get here on time? It'll save us both a lot of hassle and heartache, don't ya think? You have a nice day, now."

He turned to walk away.

"Hey! I need to talk to you."

He didn't even glance back as he sauntered off toward an old glitter-red sedan. If she were a lady detective in a TV show, she'd go whip his ass with some martial arts moves that, in real life, only work if the victim has also carefully rehearsed the choreography. Taking this guy down without the help of a Taser and several partners would be like trying to subdue a garbage truck. So it was either let him go or shoot him in the back, and only that first one left her any opportunity to get the information somewhere down the line. She settled for only fantasizing about doing the second thing and memorized his plates as he drove off. Wait, who was the "mutual friend" he'd thought she worked for? The girl in the sunglasses? Somebody else? *Hmm.*

She looked over the remaining refuse, figuring there was at least a chance that GSG had tossed something else in—it's a trait of the human species that we can't be in a spot for more than a few minutes without producing some kind of waste. Key nudged around the Red Bull cans and coffee cups and wadded blue paper towels, hoping against hope that the mystery girl had, say, chosen this spot to ditch her wallet, ID, target map, bomb diagrams, and manifesto. Instead, she noticed a piece of trash that was somehow older and dirtier than the other trash. It was a sheet of paper, tri-folded as if to fit into a letter envelope, covered in smudgy fingerprints. She picked it up and found it was an old invoice for a load of gravel, dated nearly twelve years ago. She flipped it over, and on the back was a series of digits scratched out with a dying ballpoint pen:

704—543—678—660

Key visualized the mystery woman frantically scrounging around in the old man's stolen pickup for something to write with, opening the glove box, and finding this invoice. Then she'd written these numbers. Key didn't recognize the format. Maybe a combination for an electronic lock? Hell, they could be meaningless; diseased minds liked to latch onto random numbers, for some reason—that is, if GSG had even written them at all.

She took a photo of the paper and returned to her car at the Circle K. She checked Reddit to see if there were any replies to her comment from earlier:

JKey: Has anyone checked Abbott Coburn's other social media for appearances of GSG? Even if she hired him through Lyft, it wouldn't necessarily mean this meeting wasn't prearranged and that they don't have a previous relationship. Also, check to see if they had both signaled membership or allegiance to the same extremist group.

Porncobbler: Fuck off cop.

DeathNugz: lol

ZekeArt: I can confirm that she has never appeared in his streams and he has never mentioned her. It's far more likely she summoned him via the app and then coerced him once she was in the vehicle.

DeathNugz: Glowie here already.

Porncobbler: That's how you know you're onto something.

Glowie was slang for an undercover fed who's being too obvious about it (to the point that they stick out so much that they "glow"). Hoping for a fresh start, she started a new post with the pic of the mysterious trash she'd found:

[Photo] *Found in the trash near the Circle K, think it came from GSG*

Posted to r/AbaddonsNavigator by JKey
See photo, this was discarded in the same receptacle
as at least one other item GSG threw away, do
these numbers mean anything to you?

———————————————————————————— Comments:

NoPayneNoPain: Hey the fed is back!

DeathNugz: This can't be a good use of your time.

Porncobbler: How do you know it's from GSG?

ZekeArt: They're heading to Washington,
DC. They're taking I-40.

JKey: You got that from the note? Or did
you hear that somewhere?

ZekeArt: From the note. Enter Victorville, CA to
Washington DC into Google maps without specifying
an address. You get a trip that's 2,586 miles. She's
broken it up into segments, figuring out how far she can
go in a day before stopping to rest at a major city:

704 miles to Albuquerque today

543 to OKC tomorrow

678 to Nashville on Saturday

660 to DC on Sunday.

Four days of driving, arriving on the night of Sunday
July 3rd. She's making sure they can be at the nation's
capital on the Fourth of July with plenty of time to spare.
With a mysterious box that is, apparently, radioactive.

DeathNugz: Oh, shit! Zeke you are a dark wizard. So is this
a terrorist attack on the capital? What else would it be?

NoPayneNoPain: Hey fed, you should forward your whole ass paycheck to Zeke for doing your job for you.

Porncobbler: Am I the only one who thinks we should just let them do it? Seriously, what's the downside?

6

MALORT

By the time the internet hive mind had deduced where the girl and the white SUV were headed, Malort was already in the Grand National and flogging it toward Barstow. He'd unlocked the phone's passcode on his second guess, then he'd tapped the Find My app as he walked back to his car from his confrontation with the cranky lady at the gas station. The app immediately showed him a blue dot slowly crawling down I-40. It turned out Phil Greene (or, more likely, his tech-savvy daughter) had done exactly what Malort had hoped: He'd thrown an AirTag into the box, one of those little coin-size trackers that would report back to his phone (they were mostly used as anti-theft devices, so any man in the pro-theft side of the equation needed to be familiar with their workings). It would, in theory, continue to report back from anywhere on the planet, as the tag worked by pinging any phone that happened to be nearby. The dot was periodically blinking in and out, which told Malort that there were no devices in the vehicle and that the tag was pinging fellow travelers as they passed. He'd suspected from the jump which city the box was destined for, but what the tracking confirmed was that the girl wasn't heading to an airport or bus station. She was driving the whole damned way.

Thus, Malort was now going balls-to-the-wall in a Buick grocery-getter he'd just yesterday purchased from a tweaker who'd almost certainly already smoked away the proceeds. He'd anticipated and prepped for the trip earlier: Riding shotgun were a thermos full of coffee and a bag of Halloween-size candy bars. His phone was packed to the brim with murder podcasts and Norwegian black metal that he intended to alternate based on his level of drowsiness. Yeah, the girl had a head start of a couple of hours at least, but she wasn't moving fast, likely out of fear of attracting heat. He didn't know if she'd convinced the SUV's owner to sell her the vehicle or to drive her, but he figured it was best to assume two occupants and to strategize accordingly. It was also best to assume they were both armed, which was definitely something to keep in mind for when hammer finally met anvil. He wondered if she or her hypothetical copilot had ever fired a shot in anger. Over the course of Malort's life, he'd fired two in anger and several more out of boredom and/or good old-fashioned meanness.

A different man, an unarmed man with working credit cards, would probably have just booked a flight and jumped ahead of them to spring the trap at the destination. Not only was that not an option for a man like Malort—or just Malort, since he thought he might be the only man exactly like him—but he strongly suspected the pair weren't going to make it to their destination one way or the other. Their operation didn't stink of competence, and he imagined taking the flight and then arriving to hear the Navigator's driver had fallen asleep and run into a ditch in Turdburg, Oklahoma. No, Malort knew he had to do it the hard way, to follow and monitor for the inevitable fuckup that slowed them down. It'd be a pain in the ass—literally, since decades on an impractically chopped bike had done a number on his lower back, and the Grand National's seats weren't the cutting edge in ergonomic design. He was pissed at himself for letting the box get out of the city, but what was life but a series of hard jobs you had to endure because you'd screwed up the easy ones?

Ah, who was he kidding—he wanted to be back out on the open road; it was his natural state. If he sat still for too long, he started to feel like fleas were crawling under his skin. It'd be the first time he'd done a road trip like this in years, and the first ever without the wind in his face.

And, deep down, he strongly suspected that it would be his last.

ZEKE

"So, what's in the box?" asked Cammy from the sofa, her feet in a vibrating massage machine, her fingers frantically swiping through what was either the two-thousandth level of some mobile game or a series of faces on a dating app. "Is it a nuclear bomb or something?"

"Nobody knows," said Zeke, who was using a stylus and a drawing pad to paint the pink on a cartoon rabbit's vulva.

"But they're taking it to Washington, DC."

"We think so, yeah."

"And they want it to get there by the holiday."

"Looks like it."

"Well, I hope your friend is okay. Somebody told the cops, right?"

Zeke shrugged. "The feds know. They're in the subreddit."

It had been Zeke who'd created the r/AbaddonsNavigator sub, anticipating that there would need to be a central hub for the obsessives and that it would quickly turn into a witch hunt if not properly reined in. For example, Zeke had been careful when naming it, looking to keep the focus on finding Abbott and his vehicle, rather than speculating about a suitcase nuke or whatever worst-case scenario would become the hive mind's fixation. Reddit had a bad track record with that sort of thing; after a bombing at the 2013 Boston Marathon, Reddit sleuths pieced together photos and other scraps of evidence to pin the attack on a man who not only wasn't involved but who wasn't even alive at the time.

"Where are they now?"

"I think the vehicle made it out of the city; the cops didn't do a road-block or anything. It kind of seems like they don't care. At least not yet."

"We still don't know who the woman is?"

"No."

"Crazy. Do I need to get that blue tape for the walls?"

Four cans of paint sat next to Zeke's desk, two white and two hot pink. Their plan was to alternate from wall to wall, the compromise they'd arrived at after being unable to agree on a single color.

"If you're skilled with the brush," he said, "you don't need the tape."

"Well, I'm not skilled, and I'm the one who'll have to do the high parts."

"You know they're going to be here on Saturday night, right? If they don't get stopped before then?"

"Who is?"

"Abaddon and the mystery woman. If I'm right about their route, they'll pass through Nashville on 40, which means they'll come within a couple miles of where we're sitting."

"Weird," replied Cammy, who was still swiping at her phone as if she were angrily knocking ants off the screen. "I mean, it's not like we could do anything about it if they did."

Zeke didn't reply. She was right, of course. Zeke imagined himself rolling his wheelchair out onto the interstate to stop all incoming traffic, screaming Abbott's name. The cops would just pepper spray him and drag him off the street, thinking he was protesting climate change or one of the other several overlapping societal injustices that affected his life. But if this vehicle really was carrying a weapon of mass destruction to the nation's capital, well, they had to do something, right?

KEY

With the lethal purpose of a jungle predator on the hunt, Key burst through the door of her apartment, cleared off a spot on her kitchen counter for her purse and Glock, checked her phone for updates, then raced to the bathroom to vomit up the misguided burrito she'd eaten in the car. Then she raced to her sofa, cleared off a spot large enough that she could mostly lie down, then immediately went to sleep for over an hour. Then she burst awake, raged at herself for falling asleep, and checked her phone for updates.

At breakfast, she'd asked her former FBI colleague Patrick Diaz to visualize her accumulated evidence on a corkboard full of photos connected with red yarn, and he'd made a snide remark about how those are only found in the homes of crazy people. The truth was, the only reason she didn't have red yarn on her board is that it had been immediately torn down by her cat, Ben (short for "Benadryl"), shortly before he'd run away and/or got eaten by a coyote. She did have several articles she'd printed out still pinned there, but those had gone up before her printer broke. Well, it was "broke" in the sense that its built-in software decided that the mostly full ink cartridges were "expired," which is how a printer company accosts you for all the money in your wallet. She'd decided she'd rather live a paperless life than give in, at which point she'd thrown the printer into the pool of her apartment complex. It was still in there the last time she'd looked.

She paced around and tried to think. From another room, a smoke alarm chirped to warn of a low battery. The knowledge that a possible WMD was on its way to the capital and that there were zero reasonable actions she could take was leaving her with a very familiar feeling. She'd spent her entire adult life having her ears blasted by a clarion cry repeated in a thousand different forms, alternating the same two lines:

"Something must be done."

"Nothing can be done."

Key had ended her FBI career shortly after reaching her lifelong goal of becoming a strategic analyst, the experts at the top who ostensibly examine big-picture threats and quietly save the USA behind the scenes. But nothing ruins your view of the world like getting your dream job. Key's tenure had been marred by turmoil, beginning with a mandate to summarize the threat from left-wing extremists, to which she had made the ill-advised comment, "You're worried about an uprising from a population that needs four different antianxiety prescriptions to order a pizza over the phone?"

In the time since, she had developed a very specific theory about the potential for domestic terror in the USA spreading, not as a mass political movement but as a social contagion. The country was full of isolated weirdos who were rapidly trying to find ways to make their lives meaningful and, she believed, would eventually run out of options that didn't involve scattered corpses in a food court. Her views deviated sharply from the bureau's in that she believed all mass shootings were acts of terrorism, even if they didn't conform to the government's suffocatingly narrow definition of the term. They believed "terrorism" required a specific ideology, but these modern attacks were a grab bag of loosely held beliefs that secretly all pointed in the same direction: a desire to destroy the ability and willingness of individuals to gather in public and form communities. They were attacks on social cohesion, pushing a vision of the future that, in many cases, not even the attackers were aware of.

She tried to call Patrick. It went to voicemail, because he was avoiding her and he sucked. She cleared off a spot on her dining room table and sat down, trying to think. One minute later, Patrick called her back.

She answered with, "And you thought I was being hysterical! Have they examined the residue on the pickup?"

"Are you talking to me, or are you resuming a conversation you were having with someone else?"

"What?"

"You kind of just started in the middle there."

"You and I both know what I'm talking about; the local cops handled that truck like it had been recovered from Pripyat."

There was a strategic pause from Patrick's end before he said, "They were definitely overzealous. That's a visual I'd have preferred to not have out there, the men in space suits roping off the area and all that. I see the internet has already picked up the baton."

"Yes, they've pieced together evidence that the device is on its way to Washington, DC."

There was another obnoxious silence from the other end before Patrick replied, "So we've jumped right to concluding there's a 'device'? Have you been joining those online discussions, Joan?"

"You know I used to monitor those channels. That was my specialty."

"But it's not now."

"No, I mean—"

"Because that is literally not your job anymore. Do you want to come back? Is that what this is about? You know they'll take you; manpower is low across the board, and most of the ones you clashed with took retirement right after you did."

"Have they determined that the truck has been hauling nuclear material or not?"

"Lots of harmless substances produce low levels of radiation, Joan. Fertilizer, kitty litter. They've collected samples; we'll know soon. Everyone gets a little too worked up when they hear the Geiger counter growl."

Key pinched the bridge of her nose and visualized herself smashing a beer bottle over Patrick's head. "What about Phil Greene?"

"The cause of death is unclear, but they're not treating it as a homicide right now. There was blunt trauma to the head, but it might have been due to a fall. The guy was trying to turn his whole farmhouse into a Faraday cage, I assume to block the evil 5G signals he believed were stealing his thoughts. I guess there was a ladder right where he was discovered. It should be noted that he had a spouse who passed a few years ago—"

"I know. Opioid overdose. Or so they think."

"Then he had a daughter who passed just earlier this year. Breast cancer. Are you getting regular exams for that? It can really sneak up on you. But you know, if you observed him behaving erratically, that could have been a trigger. Plus, like you said, he had his own diagnosis somewhere along the way."

"Right, which could have removed fear of death or imprisonment from his calculus."

"Or he may have indulged some fantasies and stopped there. This is all with JTTF now; they'll dig into it."

To be fair to the Joint Terrorism Task Force, their job required them to sift through tips regarding supposed terror plots at the rate of several per hour. To be somewhat less fair, it really did appear to Key that their process was to randomly pick a group of dumbasses who'd spoken in public about blowing up a monument, assign a dozen undercover agents to carefully lead them from the idea stage to the execution stage, at which point, they'd raid their trailer park and declare that they'd once again justified their budget. The smoke alarm chirped again. It'd been doing it for several weeks, or months.

"And JTTF understands that the device in question is already probably out of the state?"

"Again, you keep saying *device* as if everyone is in agreement that such a thing was not only planned but designed, built, tested, and completed. But yes, by now, every police department in the nation has access to a description of the occupants and their vehicle."

"Hunter Coburn's Lincoln Navigator, you mean."

"Now, who is he?"

"*The owner of the vehicle transporting the dev*—the box."

"Well, they're still tracking that down; the plates on the SUV were obscured in the security camera video, there was another vehicle parked in front of—"

"We have the plate number!"

"Who does?"

"The world! Everyone! It's out there."

"On the internet, you mean."

"You say *the internet* like we're talking about a singular dumb entity who's always wrong. Everyone is online, including smart people with access to actual information. And they have photos of the vehicle from a Twitch broadcast by the driver, Abbott Coburn. Hunter Coburn's son. Alias Abaddon—which, by the way, is *one of the fucking angels of the apocalypse.*"

"Joan, if the internet knows, I'm sure JTTF knows. If they find a device in this vehicle, I'll make sure you get credit for the tip. But to be frank, I'm less worried about this potential domestic terror plot than I am about you. I remember you being extremely excited to move on to the next phase of your life. You mentioned at least four hobbies you were already buying the supplies for."

This was true, but it turned out that Key's actual favorite hobby was buying supplies for hobbies. She didn't really get any joy out of the next part, and it was starting to get expensive. Her dining room table was, at the moment, piled high with calligraphy tools, including a $400 block of solid handmade ink from Japan.

"Are they still processing Greene's house and his bomb shelter? I assume they didn't find nuclear bomb prototypes, or you would have led the call with that."

"They found evidence of a very lonely, very paranoid man, whose home was robbed at some point after his death, maybe hours later."

"Have you been out there?"

"To Phil Greene's home? No, of course not. I'm not on this case."

"Are they still processing it?"

"Joan, do not go out there. It's private property, it's a potential crime scene."

"I didn't say I was going to."

"You didn't have to. I know you."

[Photo] *Is GSG a Russian saboteur who seduced Abbott into collaborating?*

Posted to r/AbaddonsNavigator by TruthLover420

I have found "GSG" in this photo from eight years ago, depicting Russian youths posing with Vladmir Putin. She is the third one on the right, look at the shape of the jawbone and ears. Since the Cold War, Russia has run schools designed to mimic American neighborhoods/cities in which operatives are immersed in the culture, not just learning perfect English but how to adopt American mannerisms and habits. These operatives embed themselves in society and then use one of two methods to turn citizens against their own country: Coercion (threats, extortion) or Persuasion (deception, seduction, bribes). The latter is preferred. If you threaten a person into helping you, they will only go along until they can get to safety; if you persuade them, you have a loyal puppet for life.

I have watched the Abbott "goodbye" video over one hundred times and I see no indication that he was being threatened with violence (held at gunpoint etc.). It is unlikely he was deceived, as he is literally traveling with an armored munitions crate that is openly labeled as radioactive. It seems even more implausible that Abbott would have gone along in exchange for money, considering he would not be likely to survive the planned attack. This tells me that Abbott/Abaddon is a willing collaborator, who was possibly roped in via seduction. I have watched all of his previous videos and have never seen him mention having a girlfriend at any point in his life, so he would likely have found GSG's advances irresistible.

In other words, if you think you are going to rescue Abbott, you should know that HE LIKELY DOES NOT WANT TO BE RESCUED.

[Post deleted by moderator ZekeArt]

Please Read: A Reminder of What This Subreddit Is About

Posted to r/AbaddonsNavigator by ZekeArt (moderator)
This sub is about tracking a vehicle to FIND A MISSING
PERSON. We're getting inundated with baseless conspiracy
theories and trolls who are just creating noise for those of us who
primarily want to find Abbott/Abaddon and get him home safely.

Starting now, any posts making assertions about GSG or
the nature of their trip must be accompanied by some kind
of actual evidence. The speculation some of you are posting
sounds like little more than fan fiction at this point. Further, if
GSG is in fact part of some kind of terror plot, then Abbott is a
VICTIM. Going forward, any post that implies Abbott is a part
of the plot or otherwise accuses him of being a collaborator in
a terror attack will be deleted and the user will be banned.

Abbott is my friend and some of you are treating this
like entertainment. If reality isn't enough to keep you
interested and you find yourself constantly inventing a
fake reality for yourself, you need to rethink your life.

Thank you.

7

ABBOTT

"This might seem like a personal question," said Ether, "but do you ever just spiral into an all-day masturbation frenzy?"

Once again, Abbott had to take a moment to process the question before answering. Outside, the sun-blasted Arizona hellscape scrolled by, air-fried dirt surrounding withered creosote shrubs clinging to their thirsty, miserable lives. They'd done another bathroom break at a rest stop at the state border, Ether noting a blue warning sign near the door proclaiming, POISONOUS SNAKES AND INSECTS INHABIT THE AREA, which had annoyed both of them; a creature with a toxic bite is *venomous*, not *poisonous*. The latter implies they'd be harmful to eat.

Ether clarified, "On the Adderall, I mean. I had a friend who told me he'd have these hours-long jerk sessions, until they lowered the dosage."

"See, you keep criticizing my interpersonal skills, but you just have no sense of boundaries at all, do you?"

"Sorry. You're right. Forget I asked. The last people I lived with, they had this policy of being, well, extremely blunt about things. They'd be like, 'Did that stew we had yesterday give anybody else the shits?' It was kind of cool because, like I said, I was never great at figuring out those rules anyway, what you're not supposed to talk about."

After a bit, Abbott said, "I've had Adderall do the opposite, more often than not. My other prescription, the one I have to get filled, is even worse. At this point, I think my meds' side effects should qualify as a disease all on their own. But if I don't take them, it feels like there's a shrieking car alarm going off right next to my ears twenty-four hours a day. I mean, it's no surprise there's a pill shortage; that's what happens when you build a society that can only be survived if you either have a super-specific type of brain or a prescription to block out the chaos. Do I need to do anything up there, or just keep going straight?" He nodded toward signs announcing they were approaching Flagstaff.

"Uh, keep going straight. The road will change names. It'll become Purple Heart Trail, but don't be alarmed—it'll change back in a few miles. I heard a stat that almost one in ten men are on antidepressants now, and almost one in five women. Which was shocking because—"

"It's so low."

"I know, right! I don't have any friends who *aren't* on an antidepressant, or an antipsychotic, or something. I was like, where is this well-adjusted majority?"

"They're getting dopamine highs from betting on sports games on their phone or jerkin' it to porn five times a day. Just trying to squeeze some feel-good chemicals from their brain, somehow. I mean, that's the best-case scenario; otherwise, they're drinking themselves to death or they're on painkillers or worse."

"I had a family friend pass from an opioid overdose a few years ago, might have been intentional. Three of my high school classmates are already dead. One drunk driving, one suicide, one was drunk or high on a hike and fell and drowned. It was like six inches of water, just enough to cover his nose and mouth."

Abbott grunted. "I can probably beat that, but I stopped keeping track a long time ago. My old Florida classmates drop off social media and maybe they reemerge a year later posting pics of their ankle monitor, or they don't reemerge at all. They're dead or among the walking dead, shuffling around under a bridge somewhere."

"I think they said over a hundred thousand people died from overdoses last year alone—opioids, meth. Almost fifty thousand suicides, though like I said, I suspect some of those overdoses were also on purpose. More than that drank themselves to death. All of those numbers are skyrocketing; I think suicides are up like thirty percent just since the year 2000 . . . ooh, this is interesting! That exit up there splits off to the old Route 66. You can actually see the difference in how they did the highways; if you were to take that exit, you'd go right into the heart of Flagstaff. A bunch of the old roadside attractions are still there. But if we stay on 40, we'll sail right past it. If you weren't paying close attention, you'd barely notice."

"Am I taking the exit?"

"Do you need to stop?"

"No."

"You don't want to pass through, see what Flagstaff has to offer? It could be your last chance."

"I'm going to guess it looks like every small city I've ever driven through. There'll be a Walmart and probably a Target off the next exit, there'll probably be a La Quinta and a Marriott right around the highway, next to a Chili's and Olive Garden and Taco Bell. The houses and apartment buildings will look the same as they're gonna look in New Mexico and Texas and Oklahoma. Every town will have a few buildings that are a little different or old, so the locals think their city has character. But all the rest is the same shit. Mass produced, copy-paste."

"The buildings might be, but not the people!"

"Nah, the people, too."

"We should stop and get gas, though. And I'll force out a pee. If we do it right, we can keep going straight through to Albuquerque. There'll be an exit on your right."

"Where exactly are we stopping?"

"Guess."

"What do you mean, guess?"

"We're going to Circle K, baby!"

TANISHA

Twenty-two-year-old Tanisha Clark was not a true-crime enthusiast and definitely hadn't been following the internet investigation into the mysterious white SUV and its ominous cargo. She had, however, noticed "Circle K" trending on Twitter earlier and had clicked on it because she worked at a Circle K and was, of course, curious to know what terrible news had caused the company to trend. Was there a mass shooting in a store? Had the CEO said something offensive? Were layoffs coming? Or, even worse, were folks doing some trending viral stunt that would leave the store a mess? She remembered hearing a thing about teenage boys smashing gallons of milk on the floor for clout.

Even after browsing for several minutes over her lunch break, Tanisha had no idea what the man and woman being discussed had supposedly done, and it was *incredibly* hard to sort through the nonsense. It was something about a bomb, and an Uber driver, and a woman wearing green sunglasses? And maybe they're Russians? Either way, the company was only trending because that's where the culprits had stolen a vehicle, or something. It didn't seem like they were targeting Circle K stores or anything like that, and details seemed awfully muddy, so she had kind of forgotten about it by the middle of the afternoon . . . at which point, the door chimed and in walked a pasty white man whose appearance was utterly unremarkable, after having put gas in a white land yacht that would also have been unremarkable had it not tickled something in the back of Tanisha's brain. Then she noticed the man was followed in by a girl who was conspicuously trying to hide her face from the store cameras with a baseball cap and . . .

Bright green sunglasses.

Tanisha stared, then forced herself not to stare. It was stupid to think it was the same couple. Those people were in California, weren't they? And what was she even supposed to do? There was a procedure for how to react when robbed, but not for whatever this was. Were they fugitives? Terrorists? A totally unrelated couple who happened to own the same color car and sunglasses? If it was really them, would they freak out and shoot up the store if they thought they'd been spotted?

She badly wanted to pull out her phone and bring up the pic of the guy—the internet had dug up his social media—but what if he spotted her doing it? Would he kill her? Could she die right now? She looked around for her manager, Linda, wondering how she would even explain the situation. She continued to not look at the couple, then very clearly heard the guy complain that he'd been driving for almost seven hours. She quietly did the math and then, almost like a premonition, Tanisha imagined her own name trending on Twitter that night, with friends offering thoughts and prayers to her family.

ABBOTT

"I've got to say," said Abbott as he browsed miniature liquid caffeine capsules, "I don't see how I make it to Albuquerque tonight. My body's battery is showing that last sliver of red."

"You've just been sitting in a moving chair this whole time!"

"Do *you* want to drive?"

"I'm not criticizing, I'm making a point. I don't think you're exhausted because of the driving. I think *you're mentally exhausted from riding with me.*"

"That is, uh, not the shocking revelation you think it is."

"No, listen. I think you find it draining to deal with anyone face-to-face. And I think it's specifically because you can't control it. Online, you can duck out of any conversation, you can say anything you want, you can calibrate how you come across. Not here."

"The ability to block people yelling death threats and making racist jokes is a net positive, in my mind."

"Sure, but I think our interactions could be totally great the whole time and you'd find it just as exhausting because the world has trained you to be afraid of *being fully and truly perceived.* We're social animals; that's the equivalent of making a fish afraid of water! We evolved in tribes where everybody could see everybody else, all the time; we didn't even have separate rooms or beds. Just by evolution, you should find personal contact comforting, and the fact that they've burned that out of so many of us is *apocalyptic.* Hey, they have souvenirs over there if you want to remember this special time we had together in Flagstaff."

"I'm good."

Abbott glanced over at the register and caught the cashier looking back at him. She quickly looked away, like a teacher had just called her out for cheating on a test. Then Abbott quickly looked away, like it was a contest to see who could be most embarrassed by the accidental eye contact. Abbott's understanding of social interactions always ran on a delay ranging from a few seconds to several years, so it took a moment to realize that her reaction implied that she'd recognized him. Was she a fan of his streams?

"You know what we're missing," said Ether, in a conversation Abbott had already checked out of, "is gathering places. All those people killing themselves by various means fast and slow, I'm telling you, part of that is that we just don't *gather* anymore. We've stopped going to church, we've built suburbs where people don't have that third place that isn't work or home, where everybody can go hang out. You can't do that at a chain restaurant; they want you out of there so they can seat the next customer. Young people don't go to bars or clubs like they used to. But in general, there's just no profit in providing a public place where we can all just go and be together. All the money is in, I don't know, getting us addicted to some piece of software. You talked about people gambling on their phones; think how sad that is—going broke from blackjack from your sofa without even a cheap casino buffet to cushion the blow."

"Come on, let's go."

Abbott didn't know if he really had an antenna for danger, considering his anxiety was smashing that button twenty-four hours a day, but he definitely wanted out of this place. He surreptitiously peeled a few bills off his wad of cash so he wouldn't have to do it in front of the staff and make them think he was a drug dealer. Before coming inside, he'd put a couple thousand dollars in his pocket and stuffed the rest into his bag, but it still felt illicit. He told himself not to look over at the counter again, but for some reason his brain interpreted it as a command to do exactly that. And this time when he looked, he swore *the girl was snapping a picture of him with her phone.*

"I heard that the average number of close friends has dropped over the last thirty years," said Ether. "It used to be that the number of loners who literally had no friends was tiny, like three percent of the population. That's quadrupled since then; now twelve percent of us have *nobody*. Today, you're almost as likely to be totally alone as you are to have a big squad of friends like teenagers have in the movies. I'm telling you, it's a crisis. Humans need friends every bit as much as we need food. But because this kind of starvation is invisible, and because we're all physically really fat, nobody sees it. Then, every ten minutes or so, somebody sticks a gun in their mouth."

They had arrived at the register just in time for the cashier to hear *gun in their mouth* as the last words in the conversation. Abbott paid while the cashier acted like eye contact would turn her to stone.

As soon as they were back outside, Abbott muttered, "Hey, is there any chance that girl at the counter—"

Ether didn't hear, as she was rushing off across the parking lot. There was a minivan parked over there, and sitting in the open side door was a middle-aged woman who was crying her eyes out. Another woman of the same age was standing over her, trying to console her.

"What's happened?" asked Ether, before Abbott could stop her.

TANISHA

After several minutes of searching, Tanisha found what seemed like a good place to ask about the fugitive couple: a section of Angry Nerd Internet specifically devoted to cracking the case. She had to create a Reddit account to post the photo she'd secretly snapped of the pair, adding a second pic she'd taken just moments ago of their fancy SUV. She waited, refreshed, then was flattened by the ferocity of the response. The commenters acted like she'd captured the second coming of Jesus Christ on film. She was inundated with questions, accusations of having faked it, and criticism that she hadn't taken some kind of action to keep the couple from leaving the store. Within six minutes of the post, a reply told her that if a bomb detonated in Washington, every drop of blood would be on her hands.

She quickly swiped off the page and busied herself with work. She watched to see if she could at least take note of when the SUV pulled away and which direction it went, but it was still out there, parked at the first pump. If they were fugitives, they seemed to have no concern at all about getting caught, as they were now off chatting with some strangers (or accomplices?) parked at the edge of the lot.

MALORT

There was no air-conditioning in the Grand National, and between the heat and the tedium, Malort had found himself steadily losing hope with every mile of slab that passed under his wheels. The tracker had been pinging with some regularity, as these guys were seemingly stopping at every establishment that had a restroom, which always put them in proximity to other phones. Even so, he wasn't closing the distance as quickly as he'd have liked. He'd been occupying his mind trying to figure out how much faster than the Navigator he'd have to be traveling to catch it, but it got into some deep algebra bullshit, and numbers had always pissed him off.

But now, the marker had parked itself at a gas station in Flagstaff and stayed there, longer than their previous stops, the longest they'd been stationary since they'd set out. Maybe they'd stopped to have a sit-down meal, secure in their belief that they'd left SoCal without pursuit. Or maybe they were doing something stupid, like trying to rob the place because they were already out of cash. Or, worst of all, maybe they'd found the tracker and tossed it in a ditch.

Malort was still almost an hour away, so no scenario seemed particularly hopeful. Still, he strapped in and threw the coals to the Buick because who knows, right? Maybe he was due for a break for the first time in his goddamned life.

[Photos] *Is this them?*

Posted to r/AbaddonsNavigator by AnonymousInAZ
I took these a few minutes ago, I'm in Flagstaff, AZ.

——————————————————————————— Comments:

NotBusey: I don't understand, why aren't the cops swarming that place, there should be SWAT teams there.
KaliSong: I tried calling them.
NotBusey: Calling who?

KaliSong: Flagstaff PD, I told them I wished to remain anonymous but that there was a Russian operative transporting a nuclear device and that they were currently at that Circle K.

NotBusey: GUYS DO NOT DO THAT. This is what makes them write us off as a bunch of kids, they'll think it's a meme.

OsbourneAgain: Why do people keep calling them Russians? I'm apparently out of the loop.

ZekeArt: Ignore it, some morons in the comments have started claiming GSG is a Russian operative, based on nothing whatsoever.

LiotaChan: It's not based on nothing, watch this video: *[link]*

OsbourneAgain: I'm not watching a 46-minute vlog from a conspiracy nut.

Punisher09: Guys I'm in Flagstaff. I live on the other side of town but I'm heading out now.

ZekeArt: To do what, exactly?

Punisher09: I have an AR-15. If the police won't do anything about this, I will.

ZekeArt: Tell me this is a joke.

NotBusey: NO DO NOT DO THAT EITHER!

StonedStalin: He's lying lol.

OsbourneAgain: This is gonna be a disaster.

NotBusey: You are going to get killed.

ABBOTT

Ether and Abbott were, at the moment, listening to an interminably long story that a sobbing woman was telling in the wrong order, with the only important information saved for the very end. When Ether had rushed over to the woman and her partner, Abbott had assumed there was some kind of medical emergency that he was wholly unequipped to address. It turned out to be a completely different crisis that he was even more unequipped to address.

The crux of the story was that the two women had lost their pet bunny. Prior to conveying this, the crying woman had explained that they were on a trip from Phoenix up to the Grand Canyon, that they made this trip every year, or at least they used to, but stopped during the pandemic, not because there was anything dangerous about visiting a massive open-air canyon during a pandemic, of course, but because it would also have required stopping at numerous facilities without proper air filtration and sanitation and Lupita had an autoimmune disorder, and the bunny was getting older and they had wanted to show him more of the world, because rabbits don't live very long, though they do, as she explained at some length, live longer in captivity than in the wild. Its name was Petey.

"I'm sure it'll come back," mumbled Abbott, glancing back at the Navigator, which was still parked at the gas pump and probably blocking some other customer who was growing steadily more enraged by the second.

"He's going blind," said the crying woman's partner, whose name was Lupita, if he was keeping track of the story correctly. "We took him out of his carrier to give him some water, but he got startled by a noise and took off like a shot. And now he's all alone out there. He's never been out in the world by himself; this is all alien to him. He must be scared to death."

Ether looked out over the landscape. On two adjacent sides of the gas station were multiple lanes of busy roadway. On the other two sides were a small patch of trees and a housing development. In between those homes were shrubs, parked cars, air-conditioning units, and an infinity of other tiny nooks and crannies the creature could wedge itself under or into. Abbott couldn't decide which of those options was more hopeless, in terms of the women finding their bunny alive. It was surely lost forever, even if it hadn't already been run over and/or eaten by a dog or feral Arizonan.

"Did you see which direction it went?" asked Ether, for reasons Abbott couldn't fully comprehend.

"Toward the houses, I think," said the sobbing woman. "But he's so fast, he's just a streak when he takes off, and he's gray, he blends in. Even if he was right over there, he'd be hard to see. We looked and tried to shake his treats, but he was just gone; it was like he disappeared. His eyes are bad. He can see us if we get close, but he gets so scared because he can't see what's coming. They're such nervous animals."

"Okay, see if you can find it over there," said Ether, and Abbott was astonished to find she was saying it to him. "I'll move the Navigator so it's not blocking the pumps."

"What? I thought you couldn't drive?"

"I didn't say I couldn't drive, I said I didn't want to get caught driving without a license. I'll just pull it out of the way."

"Bless you," said the crying woman. "I have his treats here, if you can get close enough to entice him. Open the bag and shake them around; he can smell them if you get close enough."

"Uh, well," muttered Abbott as he warily surveyed the vast stretch of treacherous landscape, "I mean, okay. What is his name, again?"

"Dumptruck," said the crying woman.

"Petey," said the other woman, Lupita. "We each have our own name for him. But he doesn't come when called. Rabbits don't do that."

"Okay," said Abbott. "If I find him, do I just pick him up?"

"He probably won't let you. Try, but don't force it! If you pick him up wrong, he'll panic. Bunnies can kill themselves if they get too scared; they'll kick so hard that it breaks their spine. He'll also probably try to bite you. Here's what he looks like."

She pulled out her phone to show him a picture, apparently afraid Abbott would accidentally snatch up a wild rabbit and bring it back instead. It was gray with floppy ears, and from the photo, it was clear they'd given it an entire bedroom in their home, complete with miniature rabbit furniture. Abbott shuffled away, knowing that once he was on private property, he was a prime candidate to get shot by a paranoid homeowner. This kind of thing, he thought, is why you don't leave the house.

[Photos] *Is this them?*

Posted to r/AbaddonsNavigator by AnonymousInAZ

Comments:

NotBusey: Why can't somebody just block them in the parking lot so they can't leave?

Punisher09: Are they still there? I'm on my way.

NotBusey: TURN AROUND AND GO HOME!

OsbourneAgain: The source hasn't posted any more so we don't know. They're probably gone, it's been a while.

Punisher09: I'm not far away now.

ZekeArt: Hopefully the police get there before this idiot.

KaliSong: Well, the cop I talked to on the phone threatened to have me arrested if I didn't stop calling, I was like, I'm in the UK, good luck arresting me.

NotBusey: I'm sure the Flagstaff PD is thrilled to be getting calls from the other side of the planet about something they saw on Reddit.

Punisher09: Hopefully the cops won't be there, I'm not supposed to be driving.

ABBOTT

Over and over again, Abbott told Lupita they should split up to cover more ground. She instead insisted on following behind him, relaying her life story as they went. Apparently, they'd gotten the bunny because the other woman is allergic to cats. He is very particular about what kind of kale they put in his dish and throws the dish across the floor if he's displeased with its contents. He uses his mouth to toss things—his arms are too tiny.

"We have to find him," she said. "We have to. Thank you so much for doing this. We can't leave here without him. I don't know what we'll do. We can't leave here."

They were wandering between the houses, Abbott trying to peer behind obstacles in a way that wouldn't make any witnesses think he was planning to cut the catalytic converters off their cars. They weren't able to check even

1 percent of the potential bunny hiding spots. The whole process was cruel in its futility. He was hoping if he somehow miraculously stumbled across Petey Dumptruck that the bunny would take off running; then he'd at least see the motion. But mostly he just wanted to do enough searching that this woman would agree it was pointless and release Abbott from the obligation. He had *so much driving to do.* If they didn't make their miles today, it would mean a longer day tomorrow, and the next.

"He doesn't know how to survive out here," said Lupita, rebutting a sentiment Abbott had in no way expressed out loud.

When they'd met, Ether had joked/claimed that she could read Abbott's thoughts, and she probably could, because everyone could. Teachers knew when he was lying, guys knew when he was scared, girls knew when he was indulging lecherous fantasies. It had always made him feel like everyone else had a sense organ he was lacking because it never went the other way. He could never sense when someone else was being disingenuous or stringing him along so they could mock him later. Of course he hated socializing; that information imbalance was terrifying.

"We're his whole world," said Lupita, continuing her argument with Abbott's unspoken thoughts. "We can't leave him. Can you imagine him out here, waiting for us to get him, and we just never come? Then it gets dark and he doesn't understand why we abandoned him, what he did wrong. I just imagine his little heart breaking, wondering why we didn't try harder. No, we can't leave. If we don't find him before it gets dark, we'll sleep in the van and keep looking tomorrow. And the next day. I won't abandon my baby."

Abbott hated this woman. He hated how needy she was, hated how she was putting all of this on him, loading him down with her desperation, demanding he take on the burden of this helpless animal's fear as if he didn't already have enough on his shoulders to bend his bones. The sun was in his eyes, and he wondered how many venomous snakes were out here, waiting to latch onto his bare ankles. They trudged down one row of homes, then back down another, then a third, knowing that at any point the bunny could move undetected to a location they'd previously checked. Ether had commented on how the day wasn't as blisteringly hot as expected, but Abbott was definitely sweating now.

Ten minutes turned to twenty, then thirty.

The whole time, he could sense the woman's growing panic behind him as it became more and more obvious she was never going to see the bunny again. Hell, the animal probably escaped to get away from these two weirdos who'd decided he was their child. Abbott was now just making cursory attempts to search, devoting his thoughts to rehearsing his exit strategy. He could say something about how it was all for the best, that maybe some kindhearted family would take the bunny in. Either way, it absolutely was not Abbott's problem. And now the woman behind him was crying, and he wanted to be anywhere else but here, anywhere on earth.

TANISHA

It had been almost an hour since the white SUV had shown up and Tanisha was now strongly considering quitting her job.

First, the phone had rung in the back, and she'd heard the confused voice of her manager, who didn't seem to understand what the caller was asking for. Then a few minutes later, the phone had rung again. And again. She'd then heard Linda say Tanisha's name as if the callers were asking for her. A frantic check online revealed that the photos she'd posted, along with the name of the city, was all it'd taken for the internet to pin down her exact location (apparently, the store's logo was visible in the corner of one of her pics), and then, somehow, they'd dug up Tanisha's name and her social media. Now they were calling, demanding she stop the fugitive couple, insisting she be personally held to account for the failure to detain them.

Linda had then taken her into the back, the confused old woman accusing her of filming some kind of viral stunt for social media that was now attracting unwanted attention. Tanisha tried to explain, at which point, her manager had demanded that Tanisha do the one thing she had absolutely not wanted to do, which was call the police. She reluctantly did that, only to find herself on hold for a shockingly long time (what if she was in mortal danger?) before speaking to an officer who seemed very annoyed. It was clear she was not the first to call about what the man referred to as "this internet rumor." He asked her if she had been the victim of a crime (not today, no) and if she knew what crime the couple in the white SUV had committed (she had to admit she wasn't totally sure) and if the vehicle was still there (it was, the last time she'd looked).

By the time she got off the phone, her nerves were so fried that she begged her manager to let her go home sick, a request that was answered with a speech about how they were shorthanded and how the whole world would fall apart if she didn't remain until the shift change. Tanisha agreed because she didn't have the energy to argue and tried to get back into the routine by cleaning up a situation on the coffee counter. Apparently, a customer got confused while trying to match drink lids to cup sizes and then threw a lid-flinging tantrum in response. That's when the biggest, most terrifying man she'd ever seen came striding through the door. He was bald and covered in tattoos, including one on his throat that looked like a sword or something. He sauntered up to the register, passing behind Tanisha as she tried to fix the lid disaster with trembling fingers. Linda was at the counter and greeted him as he approached.

The guy took off his mirrored sunglasses, put both hands on the counter, and said, "I'm looking for a woman in a white SUV. She was just here a few minutes ago, possibly with another person. She stole something from me, and I'm good and pissed off about it. So if you're thinking of lying to me just because you don't like how I look, well, let's just say *I'd advise you otherwise.*"

While Linda was struggling to come up with a reply, Tanisha quietly slipped out of the front door, ran to her car, and started it, planning to drive home and never come back. Then she thought about Linda trapped in there with the terrifying man and felt guilty for leaving her behind. She got back out of the car at the exact moment a kid crept by at ten miles an hour in an open-top Jeep, staring down the place like he was confirming his target before a drive-by.

The doorless vehicle gave her a clear view of the interior and, as he passed, Tanisha swore she saw a machine gun in the passenger seat.

ABBOTT

It felt like they had been at the futile bunny search for at least an hour (Abbott had no idea how long it actually was; he didn't wear a watch and of course did not have his phone). By this point, he had muttered something to the effect of "We really do have to get back on the road . . ." several times, but Lupita was always ready with some reply. "I don't think he'd stray far," she'd say, "he would try to find somewhere to hide." Abbott had gotten down on his hands and knees probably fifty times to look under various parked cars and other obstacles. At one point, he'd felt a flicker of hope when he spotted a ball of gray fur that then turned out to be a cat.

Nope, he was done. He brushed dirt off his knees, stretched his back.

"All right, we do have to go, we're on a schedule. I hope you guys find—"

A dog started barking its head off a couple of houses away, and Lupita went jogging off in that direction as if that were a sound a bunny could make. Abbott considered taking this opportunity to head back to the Circle K but found himself following her. Once he arrived on the scene, he realized she'd deduced that the dog could be barking at her rabbit, as if dogs didn't constantly just find reasons to bark regardless. There, they found what was either a pit bull or a similarly terrifying breed snarling at a parked golf cart. A wiry guy in a tank top came wandering over, yelling at the dog to shut up. Its name was apparently Omar, and it clearly did not feel any obligation to obey its owner's commands.

"Hey!" yelled the wiry guy. "Hey, what are you barking at? Hey! Omar! Act like you got some sense!"

Abbott tried to get low to see under the golf cart. Maybe there was something under there, it was hard to say, it was all shadows. And then, it all happened at once:

A gray blur zipped out from under the golf cart.

The dog lunged at it.

The blur smacked into a wooden fence and resolved itself into a scrambling, frantic bunny rabbit. Lupita screamed, "NOOOO!" as the dog went in with its jaws.

[Photos] *Is this them?*

Posted to r/AbaddonsNavigator by AnonymousInAZ

———————————————————————————— Comments:

Punisher09: I've parked down the block. I'm going live on FB here: *[link]*

NotBusey: Oh my god.

ZekeArt: Please tell me this is just a troll. I want to ban him but he's literally talking about killing my friend, wtf.

LiotaChan: What exactly is it you think you're going to do, if you're really there? If GSG is a Russian agent she'll know how to shoot you dead.

Punisher09: I'll have a range advantage.

OsbourneAgain: Holy shit this is real, I am watching this idiot get out of his car on the FB stream. And he absolutely has an AR.

StonedStalin: Dude how old are you?

ZekeArt: I can't watch this, I'm having a fucking panic attack.

ABBOTT

The man in the tank top possessed dog-snatching reflexes that strongly implied he'd had a great deal of practice snatching this and other similar animals. He'd vaulted to the spot and in one smooth motion got the pit bull's collar in his fist, yanking the beast sideways, not backward, denying it the kind of tug-of-war that its physiology was designed to both win and enjoy. Abbott thought the rabbit was already dead in its jaws, but it had somehow twisted itself free, landing awkwardly and then streaking off along the fence before squeezing under a gap and zipping away. It was astonishingly fast, taking off across a parking lot, then a road, into an expanse of shrubs and trees next to the highway. This meant Lupita had about two seconds to be relieved that the dog hadn't broken the bunny's neck before she saw her baby vanish into the distance.

She fell to her knees, muttering, "Oh no. Oh no. Oh my god. He's gone."

The guy in the tank top was admonishing his dog, which just looked confused. Wasn't that what he'd been built for? Why else did he have those muscles, those teeth, the rush of ecstasy from the scent of panicking meat? Lupita sat there in the dirt, clearly trying to figure out how she would break the news to her partner back at the minivan. How long had they been planning this vacation? wondered Abbott. How had they pictured it in their heads? Now this would forever be nothing but the awful, cursed road trip where they lost poor Petey. That's life, though. You plan and you plan and then . . .

"I just let my guard down for one second," she whispered. "We let him out of his carrier to get water—otherwise, it spills everywhere—and we had the door open because he'd kicked some hay onto the floorboard and we were cleaning it. And there was a noise, just somebody slamming their hood, I think, and he got startled and then he was just . . . gone. He depended on us for everything; he trusted us to keep him safe. And we couldn't even do that. Giving an animal a good life, that's sacred. Do you understand that? It's one of the purest things you can do, to protect them from this, all this. I mean, we knew he wouldn't live forever, but it was our job to be there at the end for him, to give him comfort when he couldn't see or hear anymore. To hold him as he passed, to bury him."

They stood there in silence: the woman, Abbott, the guy with his panting dog. Abbott met her eyes, feeling the sun and the lost time and the despair beating down on him.

Then he heard himself say, "Give me the bunny treats. I'll get him back."

And then he walked the direction the rabbit had fled, his feet already hurting, crossing the parking lot and then waiting to cross the street, scanning the pavement for a tiny, flattened, twitching carcass. He heard footsteps trailing him and he expected to find Lupita back there, but instead, it was the wiry guy in the tank top.

"I put Omar away," he said. "You ever picked up a rabbit before?"

"No."

"My cousin is a magician in Puerto Rico," he said as they crossed the street. "There's a technique. Get it to trust you with the treats. Let it see you coming. Move slow, as slow as you can. Stroke his back, if he'll let you. Then get around so that he's facing away from you, put one hand on his butt, then with your other hand lift him up by his armpits so that he's facing away from you. Like this, like you're showing him to somebody. You watchin'?" He pantomimed the movement. "You'll kind of curl him up, his legs will be pointing straight out; this way, he can't try to kick his way free. Then tuck his face into your elbow. He'll relax if you can cover his eyes. If you can shield the world from him, he'll trust you."

"That's if we find him at all."

"Oh, we ain't gonna quit until we find him."

"If he's made it into those trees, I don't see how we will."

"It's better he goes toward the trees than the four lanes of highway where everybody's doing eighty."

The surrounding landscape was, in fact, alternating patches of trees and roadways, of bunny invisibility and bunny death. Abbott was just beginning to rehearse how he would break the bad news to Lupita after his bold proclamation earlier when Tank Top casually said, "That him?"

He was pointing at an arrangement of large decorative stones around a drainage grate, and Abbott assumed the man had mistaken one of the rocks for the bunny. They approached slowly, and then Abbott stopped breathing: There was Petey Dumptruck, huddled in the shadows of the stones, trying to make himself as small as possible against this impossibly huge, terrifying world. He was close enough to the highway that he could surely hear the cars whooshing by, even if he couldn't see them. And he had to know that they meant death, that out here, everything did.

MALORT

He was hurrying to the Grand National when a woman screamed from somewhere nearby. Malort reflexively assumed she was reacting to the sight of him, as that was definitely a noise people sometimes made when he appeared in their field of vision. He turned in that direction and found she was wearing a Circle K employee uniform. She had her back to him and was reacting to the scariest sight Malort had ever beheld:

A literal child was walking that direction, wearing a tactical vest and carrying an AR-15 semiautomatic rifle.

It's true that everybody looks younger now—a soft world is easier on the skin—but the gunman couldn't have been older than fifteen. *Damn it,* thought Malort, *this is what happens when you start posting cops in the schools; the kids just take their school shootings outside.* The kid was shouting something. Malort couldn't make it out but doubted it would be informative if he could. He got low and circled around to the driver's side of the Buick, putting the car between him and the gunman. He opened the door and reached in for the sawed-off double-barrel shotgun he kept there as a carjacking deterrent (or facilitator, should he need to do the carjacking). He checked to confirm it was loaded. He didn't particularly want to blow a child in half today, but the kid was old enough to pull the trigger on high-velocity rounds that wouldn't so much drill holes in a body as shred it from the inside. And Malort was definitely not in the mood for that.

He edged around, eyeing the kid who, judging from his manner, seemed to have no idea what to do next. He wasn't sure if that uncertainty was reassuring or terrifying but was leaning toward the latter.

ABBOTT

A girl had screamed somewhere in the distance, probably some teenagers screwing around. Abbott flinched and froze, hoping it wasn't enough to startle the bunny.

It didn't move.

He opened the bag of treats, some kind of fruity little candy things. He took slow, quiet steps.

"Can you pick him up?" Abbott asked Tank Top.

"I smell like dog, he'll panic. If he starts kicking, try to hold him close to your body. I know what they said about him kicking himself to death, but you got to hang on no matter what. If he gets away, that'll be that."

Abbott crept closer. Petey was maybe fifteen feet away now, then ten. He shook the bag and held some treats in his other hand. The bunny perked up, though he didn't know if it was interested in the scent of food or preparing to bolt. Abbott edged close enough that he could have lunged forward and snatched at the rabbit, but these things had evolved to evade predators much faster than humans, killers that could bite in a blink.

He set a treat on the ground in front of the rabbit, and it stretched out to sniff it. Abbott held his breath.

He slowly put a hand on its back, and it allowed him. This was a pet, not a wild animal. It was used to people and being picked up. This was doable. He came around so that the rabbit was facing away from him. It was pointed toward the highway, so would likely take off right into traffic if startled.

He slid a hand under it, put the other on its rump, and lifted—

It thrashed out of his grip, and, suddenly, he was holding air. The bunny took off, doing exactly what Abbott had feared it would do, heading right for the whipping blur of interstate traffic—

Where it was quickly intercepted by Lupita, who expertly snatched him up, pulled him close, and stuffed his face into her elbow. "I got you!" she gasped. "I got you! Oh, my baby boy. I got you."

She pressed her face into his furry back, and her whole body hitched with sobs.

"Boom!" said Tank Top from behind him. "Got him!" He slapped Abbott on the back. "That would have haunted me all month, goddamn."

Lupita headed back the way they'd come, but when she reached the side street, the minivan rolled up, the other woman at the wheel. She exited with a rhinestone-encrusted animal carrier and held it open while Dumptruck was stuffed inside.

"Did you have an adventure?" said the tearful woman to the bunny as it settled in. "Did you meet some friends?"

The women were then profusely thanking Abbott and the other guy, offering payment that they both declined. Then they drove off to continue their Grand Canyon vacation, and Tank Top shook hands and said goodbye. It had been, Abbott thought, maybe the best few minutes of his life.

MALORT

Well, the good news was the school shooter didn't seem eager to shoot Malort.

He was peering around the bumper of the Grand National with the shotgun hidden out of view, now wondering if he could just dive into the Buick and drive away. Would the kid pepper the car with bullets? Maybe he should try to run him over on his way out, just as a good deed. Nah, he could see that resulting in a call to the cops, and the Buick wasn't exactly hard to spot if they put out a BOLO.

Someone inside the store was yelling about calling the police. The school shooter was still saying something, seeming to tell everyone to calm down, asking questions Malort couldn't understand.

Malort leaned around his bumper and yelled, "Who are you here to shoot, kid? Is it somebody specific, or is this a mass-shooting scenario?"

The kid looked more confused than ever, then said, "Where's the Navigator?"

ABBOTT

He jogged back toward the Circle K, eager to get rolling, his drowsiness having evaporated. They could still make it to Albuquerque tonight. So what if they got there at eleven or midnight? He could do that. He could do anything. This was all he'd needed, a break to mentally reset. Now he was ready to—

He rounded the corner of the last house before the road and stopped. The Circle K was now in full view, and from that angle, he could see about two-thirds of the parking lot. He edged around, moving along the road so he could scan the rest.

Yep. It was gone.

There were several cars there, including a sparkly red sedan—a big guy was kneeling by the front, like he was checking the tire or something—but his father's white SUV was nowhere to be seen.

But of course it wasn't.

Ether had volunteered him to go hunting for the stupid rabbit, then had asked him for the keys, supposedly so she could move the vehicle. It had all been planned; if the thing with the lost bunny hadn't come up, she'd have just asked him to go off on some other errand, anything to get him away. As soon as he was out of sight, she'd driven off and was now almost an hour down the road toward Washington, DC, or whatever her actual destination was, if that had just been another lie.

He stood there, the nauseating realizations hitting him in waves. She had his father's car. She had the rest of the cash. She had his bag with his clothes and, oh yeah, *his father's fucking gun.* If/when she committed a crime with it, they'd trace it back to him.

He was going to puke. Here was another familiar sensation, of being humiliated down to a level lower than he'd previously thought existed. When you're so far down the social ladder that you're basically lying on the floor, that's when they love to stomp you the most, to grind your face into the shit. Ether had seen him coming a mile away because she saw in him what everyone saw: a clueless outcast whose people skills were so poor that tricking him was as easy as kicking an old dog. Now he was stuck in Arizona with no phone, no car. What was he supposed to do? Call the police? Call his father? Explain to both of them how easily he'd been swindled? How stupidly trusting he'd been? God, Ether was probably laughing her ass off right now, would be telling her criminal friends for years about the easiest mark she ever found. He'd never even made her tell him her real name.

Logically, the thing to do was go back to the Circle K and beg to use their phone, but the only way they'd let him is if he explained that he'd been the victim of a crime, that his car had been stolen, and that he was stranded. The staff had seen him come in with Ether, so they'd instantly know what had happened, would think it was hilarious. He imagined them snickering at him from behind the counter and decided he'd just find someplace else. He looked around for another gas station and started walking, in a daze. Maybe he should just step into traffic instead.

MALORT

It was when the cops showed up that Malort got really confused.

First of all, they hadn't seemingly had time to respond to a call from inside the store, unless a cruiser happened to be nearby at that moment, which was of course possible—there were probably plenty of doughnut joints around. But if they'd come in response to a call about a mass shooter, they certainly were being chill about it. A single cruiser came rolling up, no sirens or anything, acting like they were doing a courtesy wellness check. It was only when they were right up on the scene that they'd spotted the school shooter and flown into action. They hit the lights and skidded to a stop, jumping out and taking cover behind their doors, screaming commands.

At that point, Malort tried to crawl into the Grand National to get the hell out of there, figuring they would surely appreciate having one fewer potential victim on the scene. Instead, one cop pointed his gun Malort's direction and screamed for him to get fucking down or get fucking shot. He didn't normally like complying with cops, but sometimes you have to pick your battles.

He tossed the shotgun into the Buick and then got low, thinking that if he were about to die, he was going to go out how he'd lived: with absolutely no idea what the hell was going on.

ABBOTT

A vehicle came pulling up next to Abbott, and he thought maybe it was the two bunny moms, having spotted him trudging miserably down the sidewalk. But then he heard Ether say, "Where are you going? Get in!"

He spun to face her. "Where did *you* go?"

It was an accusation. Even in this moment, he was absolutely convinced that she'd abandoned him but had just changed her mind.

"When you went hunting for Petey, I circled around the block to pick you up. You were getting so far away, and I was trying to save you the walk back! But then you started walking back anyway, and at that point, I had to circle around again. I've been chasing you for several minutes. It was comical. Let's go, hero!"

She climbed over into the passenger seat, and he stood there for a moment, still enraged but now struggling to grasp exactly why. He felt his anger begin to dissipate but also felt an inexplicable impulse to cling to it with all his might.

"Come on!" she said, like she was urging a dog to come in from the yard.

She was chewing on a Slim Jim. He stood there, looking at her for a moment, then finally came around and slid behind the wheel.

She pointed. "You can turn around up here."

He didn't move.

Through chewed jerky, she asked, "What's wrong?"

"Did you try to leave me, just then? Did you try to abandon me and then come back because you decided you needed my help or whatever?"

"No! No. Abbott, even if I was a terrible person, why would I do that? If I didn't need a driver, I wouldn't have hired one."

"You'd have gotten a free hundred-thousand-dollar SUV and a loaded gun."

Ether suddenly got serious, turning to face him.

"Okay. Abbott. Look at me. Hey. Are you listening? You know those postapocalyptic zombie shows where they have to cross the wastelands and they're like, 'We can't trust anybody out here! We're on our own!' Well, that's a geek fantasy for indoor kids. Out here, in the real world, in the actual desert, *this is when you have to be willing to trust people.* You don't have a chance otherwise. Trust is the only advantage humans have as a species, that millions of us can all get together and trust one another. Yes, including weird people you just met earlier in the day."

After a moment, Abbott shook his head and pulled back into traffic, not because Ether was convincing him but because he could feel the annoyance of the drivers who were having to swerve around them. He'd spent half of his life sensing he was in someone's way and the other half actually being in someone's way but failing to sense it. In the cup holder between the seats was one of the energy drinks he'd bought at the gas station. He opened it and took a sip.

"What flavor is that?" asked Ether, clearly eager to start a new subject.

He glanced at it. "Uh, it has the word *bomb* in it, and it tastes like a
thousand sugary knives stabbing my tongue."

"Ha! You know when that started, the era of flavors that don't exist
in nature? With Dr. Pepper. A pharmacist brewed it. Before that, drinks
were flavored like things that actually existed—vanilla, cinnamon, grape.
But he was like, 'No, this will taste like fun medicine.' Now we're drowning in fun chemicals twenty-four hours a day."

Abbott heard more police sirens and wondered if one of the homeown-
ers hadn't called the cops on him for prowling around their yard without
permission.

"Jesus," he said, "let's get away from this place before somebody else
grabs us and robs us of hours of our time."

"Absolutely. Still, I want you to take a second to think about what you
just did there."

"Finding the bunny?"

"No, you just opened a beverage and took a drink without a second
thought. That's trust! You don't know any of the thousands of strangers in
the supply chain, and yet you took a drink with absolute certainty that it
wasn't poison, or tainted, that there weren't metal shavings or dead insects
in the can. You trusted every one of those strangers so thoroughly that you
didn't even devote one second of thought to it. And you did it because a
lifetime of experience has taught you that they *can* be trusted, almost without fail."

"They don't do their jobs because they're trustworthy, they do it because they don't want to get fired or sued."

"Is that the only thing stopping *you* from poisoning somebody?"

"No."

"That's what you'll find out here in the wastelands. Almost all of these
people are just like you. They want to do the right thing, and every morning, they wake up and go do it. Every. Single. Day."

MALORT

The school shooter wasn't dropping the AR-15, not because he was zealous about his mission but because he was frozen with terror. He was yelling to the cops about the Russians (?), pointing like he was demanding they go arrest someone else. The kid was literally insisting they had the wrong guy while wearing a tactical vest strapped with another ninety rounds of ammo for the rifle he was carrying. The cops were yelling their final warnings and seemed to be ready to gun the kid down if he didn't comply within the next few seconds.

And still he didn't drop the rifle.

Malort watched with anticipation, wondering if the kid would manage to take out either of the police before they ventilated his entire torso. At a moment when Malort was certain both cops had started pulling their fingers into their triggers, the girl in the Circle K shirt ran over to the kid, ripping the gun away and clawing him in the face. Then the cops started yelling at both of them, the school shooter now screaming and crying in protest. It was, without question, the funniest fucking thing Malort had ever seen.

Then the cops were on them, pulling the gun away, pressing the school shooter to the pavement, begging the girl to calm down. Then they came toward Malort, guns drawn and amped up to eleven.

He held up his hands, trying to make his voice sound small and weak. "I'm not involved! Look at my plates, I'm from out of state! There's never a second gunman in a mass shooting—you know that! I'm just a bystander!"

As was typical, Malort's size, demeanor, and tats spoke louder than his reassurances. They yelled at him to get down, and he briefly considered jumping into the Buick and speeding away, but these guys were so revved up, they'd probably put four magazines in him before he even got a hand on the door.

He got flat, saying, "I'm just here to get gas, I don't know anything about this!"

In general, the cops just seemed extremely unclear about the situation, like they weren't at all sure why they were there or why they'd seen what they'd seen. So they hadn't come in response to the kid with the AR, and they didn't seem to be there for Malort . . .

The kid, his ear pressed to the pavement and getting handcuffed, was yelling, "Find the Navigator! It was just here! It's a white Navigator!"

But this, too, was all coming across as nonsense to the cops.

"Hey!" shouted Malort, one pavement-pressed man to another. "How do you know about that?"

"It was just here!" replied the kid, over demands from the cops that he shut the hell up. "I saw it!"

"When?"

The cops shouted the kid into silence before he could answer. Just then, Malort turned his head, and *there was the goddamned white Lincoln Navigator,* rolling past at a leisurely pace, the girl visible in the passenger seat, some nerdy guy at the wheel. They rounded the corner toward the interstate and were gone. Malort cursed to himself, and also cursed loudly, to everyone in the vicinity. The two were taunting him by driving that slow. And now they knew their pursuer was on their heels and would surely check for the AirTag tracker.

He'd blown it.

Again.

ABBOTT

Ether was looking down and cleaning her sunglasses with her shirt when Abbott glanced back and said, "Huh, there's a cop car back there at the Circle K. You don't think they're there for us, do you? Should we go back?"

She glanced over. "Looks like they've got some kid on the ground. Maybe there was a foot chase and that's where it ended."

"Are you sure?"

"We haven't done any crimes! Even if your dad called the cops like, 'I let my son borrow my car for work, and now he's doing too much work with it, go arrest him!' you think that would trigger a nationwide search, to the point that the police in *Arizona* would be scouring the landscape? Seriously, you need to turn off that catastrophe reflex before it triggers a stroke."

"But just to be clear, you've never done any crimes? In your life?"

"I mean, I've never been convicted of anything. Wait, is this another attempt to get personal information from me?"

"We're at a stage where I need you to give me something. Anything. I mean, how old are you?"

"Twenty-nine. I'm from a totally unremarkable part of Indiana. I got a job that paid well enough that I moved my mom to LA. Or, you know, the vicinity."

"You're not a criminal, but you don't want me to know your real name. Why?"

She adjusted her WELCOME TO THE SHITSHOW hat and busied herself settling in. Abbott knew she was stalling but was willing to wait her out. What else was there to do?

Finally, she said, "The thing is, I've tried to leave that person behind, the person I used to be. It's not a gender transition thing or anything like that. I just got to a dark place and tried to make a clean break from that life. If I told you all the stuff I did, you wouldn't like me as much. And it's not cool stuff like robbing banks or selling drugs, it's mean and petty and gross stuff."

"When we met, you asked me if sometimes, out of the blue, I'll cringe at a thing I did or said years ago. Is that what you were talking about? You lay awake and think about all the people you screwed over? Torture yourself with it?"

There was another pause, and she watched the desert roll by as if painful lowlights from her life were playing outside the window.

"I think," she said, "I caused so many people so much pain for so little reason that my brain can't hold it all. I finally realized I couldn't move on, couldn't live my life unless I just *rebooted myself*. I think that should be a basic human right, don't you? To denounce your past? Even if there are records of it online, you should be able to say, 'I'm sorry and I've grown,' and everyone should judge you based on how you act from then on. If somebody goes mining into your past for stuff to bring you down or embarrass you, *they* should be treated like the bad guy."

"But you know that's not how it works, right?"

"Oh, trust me. I know."

"Because people are going to preserve that version of you, from the part of your life when they felt the most superior to you."

She nodded. "So when I say I don't want to regale you with anecdotes from my past, you understand and respect it, right? That doesn't make me suspicious?"

"I guess not any more suspicious than anybody else you'd run into around LA. It's all losers thinking they could come to SoCal and instantly become cool, leaving all of their cringe behind in Iowa or Ohio. Or Florida, in my case."

Abbott set the cruise control and again thought about putting on some music, or anything to keep the silence at bay.

"I'm not crazy," said Ether abruptly as if she'd been continuing the conversation in her head. "We're just two normal people doing a normal job."

"Sure. So, when you picked me up, you said you were going to tell me all about the 'worms.' Then you quickly changed the subject."

"I did? Ha. I have a whole mental library of stuff that weirds out strangers; I have to be careful how I dole it out. So tell me your heroic bunny story! Those ladies will be talking about that for the rest of their lives—you'll always be the handsome knight who swept in and saved Dumptruck the Rabbit."

"Well, first of all, it turns out bunnies can die if you pick them up wrong . . ."

8

KEY

When she'd retired, Key had promised herself she'd do things like get high in her bathtub by candlelight, maybe while reading a book. She'd never actually done it until tonight, when she'd forced herself into the tub and taken an edible, mainly because it was either do that or go break into the Phil Greene house to see it for herself. She figured she was less likely to get arrested this way.

She was not, of course, reading a book, but endlessly scrolling, scrolling, scrolling on her phone for Navigator news, substituting knowledge for action, her bathwater steadily cooling around her. She'd briefly had an intrusive thought about slitting her wrists in the tub, the way they do in movies when they want to make a suicide look tragic but sensual. But then she'd imagined the putrefaction stink that would greet her landlord when he finally came to investigate, and all the insects that would use the Key-corpse stew as a breeding pool. Damn, she'd forgotten what she was like on edibles.

It'd taken some digging to get the info on the tattoo guy (the sparkly red car was registered to a dude who definitely didn't match his description) but she now knew his name was Richard Little, known on the streets as Malort. He was a lifelong biker type with an arrest record that stretched back to the Reagan era. He'd just gotten out from his latest stint a few weeks ago, after doing time for stabbing another guy at a scrapyard in what looked to Key like a classic case of dirtbag-on-scumbag violence. A little social media snooping revealed his connection to Phil Greene: Malort had some kind of a relationship with Greene's deceased daughter, Sundae, for decades. Key had found Malort among Sundae's Facebook photos, the most recent being an old pic of the two of them at Sturgis, the annual motorcycle rally so massive that the event temporarily doubled the population of South Dakota. The accompanying post was Sundae wishing

Malort well behind bars ("Don't serve the time, let the time serve you"). Sundae Greene had passed while he was still incarcerated, and one of Malort's very rare social media appearances was a long, single-paragraph rant about how he hadn't been allowed to be with her as she died, and how the health care system had denied her the experimental treatment that would surely have saved her life. In Key's mind, it all painted a fairly straightforward picture:

This guy had a grievance against several SoCal institutions, and Sundae's crazy, paranoid father would no doubt have shared those grievances. Together, the two had hatched a plan to get back at everyone, maybe reaching out to a cell of other aspiring domestic terrorists online. They built a device, Malort probably intending to use it against the hospital, or city hall, or take your pick. Others involved in the operation—including Phil Greene—had disagreed, deciding they wanted the bomb to go off in DC, to take out the president or Congress on the Fourth of July, probably to symbolize the independence of a new nation or whatever. Now one faction was transporting the bomb to DC, the other was trying to bring it back to SoCal, but either party would probably set off the device the moment they were surrounded by a SWAT team, regardless of location.

It didn't escape Key's notice that, if not for this schism inside the terror cell and the resulting death of one of the conspirators, authorities likely would not have heard anything about the plot until the device detonated in one of the target cities. She would have called this a lucky break, but the truth was that most such schemes fall apart from the inside. If your entire worldview is "Don't tread on me," what's going to happen when a leader tries to impose rules? You'd think they'd learn to put their differences aside for the cause, but that's hard to do when you've been raised to believe there's no such thing as a minor disagreement. If you think that, say, a cashier failing to wish you a Merry Christmas is a sign of impending Christian genocide, you're probably not the type to hash out differences over brunch.

So now the device was hundreds of miles away from where Key was currently marinating, probably still moving, maybe along Interstate 40 but maybe not—the couple could change their plans at any time. The Navigator could be crawling along an unmarked trail through the woods, or it could already have been abandoned for another vehicle. Over the next few days, they could wind up anywhere in the three million square miles of United States, and it would be a long shot to catch them even if every fed, state trooper, and beat cop in the country was looking for them. And, as far as Key could tell, none of them were. Everyone was helpless, she thought as she tried to summon the monumental strength of will required to exit the lukewarm bath. As Patrick used to say, we're all just babies trapped in God's hot parked car.

ABBOTT

By the time they entered Albuquerque, Abbott was falling asleep behind the wheel, over and over. It was that terrifying ambush-sleep that happens on long night drives, the brain briefly flickering out for seconds at a time, perceptible only by the surrounding cars and signs suddenly blinking to a different position. It wasn't even midnight in his native time zone, but it felt like he'd been awake for a week. The idea of doing three more days of this was laughable.

They had stopped twice (bathroom at a Shell station, food from a combo McDonald's/truck stop), but otherwise, the trip had offered nothing to break up the monotony since leaving Flagstaff. Abbott did get one brief scare when multiple vehicles exited behind him and suddenly revealed that the remaining tail was an old, bright-red sedan that he thought looked a lot like the one he'd glimpsed in the Circle K parking lot, but it eventually fell farther and farther back, shrinking from view. Just another sleepy driver on their own adventure. Ether had been dozing off and on for much of that span, but Abbott had forced her awake to help him navigate, and she led him to a cluster of what seemed like a dozen chain hotels. They stopped at the very first one, Abbott feeling like he wasn't sure he even had the energy to stumble up to a bed.

"We made it!" yawned Ether as they jumped down from the vehicle. "A quarter of the country down. Suck it!"

"Jesus, how are we only a quarter of the way?"

"This country is huge!"

Abbott arched his back, feeling like he'd aged his spine ten years in a single day. "Are they going to let us stay here without a credit card? You said we have to do cash the whole trip, right?"

"I have a card. It can't be tracked to me. This is the kind of thing you learn to work around when you're living off the grid."

"Is that legal? Don't they ask for—"

He froze.

A car had positioned itself so that it was now blocking the entrance to the parking lot, angled across both lanes. Passing headlights revealed it to be a glittery red. If it wasn't the exact same car from the Circle K lot, it seemed exceptionally weird to run into two old cars with that paint job, unless it was just an Arizona thing?

He took a few steps in that direction. Had they followed them from Flagstaff? If so, why? The first thought from his sluggish brain was that he'd left something valuable behind at the gas station and this Good Samaritan had followed them for five-plus hours to give it back.

Abbott kept shuffling in that direction and said, "Hey, do you know who that is?"

Ether came up behind him, started to say, "Who are you—" and then she grabbed his shirt and pulled him backward.

"Go, go, get in," she breathed. "Move."

A guy was getting out of the red car now, looking right at them.

"Who is that? Ether, what's happening? Hey—"

She kept pulling him toward the Navigator, then she let go and ran around to the driver's side and jumped in, starting the engine.

"GET IN!"

He had no choice but to obey, as her level of panic said it was either jump in or be left behind. They took off in the opposite direction of the red car, Abbott looking back to find a giant bald man was now running after them.

"Who is that?!?"

"It's the guy who tried to steal the box. He followed us. Oh my god, he followed us from California. Oh my god."

She flew through the lot, rounded a corner, and found no other exit, just a curb and a row of bushes separating the parking from the street. Abbott could sense the decision she was about to make and yelled for her not to do it. She sped up and smashed through the bushes, the vehicle bouncing up and over the curb, then tilting as she twisted the wheel and tore down the street. Abbott had felt the scraping of the branches under the SUV as a wound to his own body. *She had scratched his father's immaculate, sacred Navigator.*

"Where are you going?!?"

"We can't stay here! We have to get off the path, off the route."

She exited onto a highway she'd seemingly chosen at random, going way too fast.

"Is he back there?" she asked, adjusting the rearview mirror. The speedometer was pushing eighty.

"I don't think so?"

"This is my fault. This is—this is my fault. I took us on the straightest, most obvious route. I made it easy for him. He's probably been hanging back a few cars this whole time, all day. What road are we on?"

"Uh, the sign back there said El Paso."

"Give me the map."

He did, and after a few minutes, she said, "Okay. Okay. Look for an exit to 380, heading east. That'll get us going back in the right direction. We'll find another place to stay. We'll just get some separation. Then we'll be fine. He's still not back there?"

"No? I mean, I don't see him . . ."

"Good. Uh, okay. That should be it. He didn't see which way we went, there are like seven different highways we could have taken out of town. Or we could have stayed somewhere else in town, for all he knows. We lost him. We'll be fine. We'll be fine. We just took the obvious route. That's all, that was our mistake, staying on 40. I mean, you're sure you didn't bring any devices, right? Like in secret?"

"No."

"Are you *sure*? Nothing he could have tracked?"

"Yes, you can check my bag."

"Okay. Me neither. Okay. Yeah, that has to be it. He just knew we'd take the interstate and caught up because we've been slow, stopping so much. Obvious and slow. My mistake. But we're okay. We're fine."

She nodded, took a deep breath, then checked the mirror one more time.

ZEKE

There's a feeling that there is no word for yet, because no one had ever experienced it prior to the internet era: the dizzying sensation of seeing an online drama escape into the real world. Zeke always compared it to watching that demon girl crawl out of the TV in *The Ring,* a barrier of safety and unreality breached and violated right before your eyes. He was now in bed but a million miles from sleep, terrified of missing the next bombshell. So now he was lying there, the room dark aside from the glow of the phone lighting his face.

The kid with the AR-15 had tried to stream his one-man terrorism intervention live, but the broadcast had gotten shut down by Facebook admins while the idiot was still walking toward the Circle K. After that, Zeke had been flying blind along with the rest of the—well, he didn't like to think of it as an *audience* but couldn't come up with a better word. Some idiots from the subreddit had continued calling the store afterward to ask the harried employees if they could stick their head out and see if a shooting and/or dirty bomb detonation was occurring in their parking lot. Then again, it's not like Zeke had any better ideas; at one point, he'd flipped out and told Cammy that they were driving to Flagstaff, but she'd just sat there calmly and told him that it was six states away and that whatever was happening would be over long before they got there. So Zeke had instead started refreshing eight feeds on two devices, waiting for any scrap of information, feeling like he'd been left dangling over a precipice. It was like the time he'd received a letter from his doctor implying there was grave news that could only be shared in-person, then when he'd called to make an appointment, was told the doctor had gone on vacation for two weeks.

Eventually, there was some Flagstaff police scanner traffic about a minor getting arrested for brandishing a firearm, but there had been no mention of anyone getting shot, or a weapon of mass destruction being impounded, or anyone else getting arrested. Since then, nothing—everyone was left to let the scenario play out in their imaginations. Even the contaminated Circle K truck story had faded from the trending lists, replaced with the war in Ukraine, news of a former sitcom star going to jail for sexual assault, state governments rolling back abortion rights, and some military officials casually revealing that the unidentified objects captured on their sensors were probably alien spacecraft. All the usual stuff.

Zeke had spent the hours after dinner struggling to focus as he finished his commissioned art (this piece was for a regular customer who paid top dollar for depictions of sexual pairings between characters from the animated Disney film *Zootopia* and the live-action detective series *Bosch,* a genre that he apparently could not find elsewhere). Zeke had kept the subreddit open on his second monitor, but it was starting to fill with assholes, trolls, and conspiracy wackjobs. Everyone was in the mood for the next plot twist, and several were being dreamed up and tested on the fly. The platform elevated posts according to popular vote, so the bullshit that rose to the top was whatever made-up scenario the users enjoyed yelling about most. There was the undercover Russian saboteur theory, which was based on nothing but a fuzzy old photo and wishful thinking. Someone else had claimed GSG was a radical right-wing terrorist with ties to some survivalists in the LA area (based entirely around a report that some old man had died nearby and that he had maybe driven a blue Ranger at some point). Others claimed she was a leftist out to murder Congress for not acting on climate change; others believed they'd identified her as a former YouTube star who was doing it all as a viral stunt. He would have tried to rein in the bullshit, but it was a rule of the internet that any efforts to censor content only gave it credibility. The human brain loves novelty and excitement and, well, what's more novel than a weird lie somebody pulled straight out of their ass? And what's more exciting than forbidden knowledge, defying the authorities to uncover what they tried to keep hidden?

Even worse, Zeke could already sense where this was going to wind up. If nothing solid could be learned about GSG, somebody was going to try digging up dirt on Abbott. At that point, certain old videos would be unearthed and then, well, things could get ugly.

ABBOTT

It took shockingly little time for Abbott's body to transition from amped-up panic to sleep, as if his nervous system had abruptly tripped a circuit breaker while Ether was putting miles between them and Albuquerque. When he opened his eyes again, the first thing he saw was a billboard featuring a big-eyed alien. A Grey.

"You awake?" asked Ether, who looked half-dead. "God, it's so weird to drive this thing, I feel like I'm on stilts. You can see down into cars when they pass. I swear one guy had his dick out."

The billboard passed out of view, and Abbott said, "Did that sign say we're heading toward Roswell? As in, where the supposed UFO crashed in the 1940s?"

"Ha, yeah. We're not too far away. You've been out for more than two hours; it's almost three in the morning. You snore, by the way. Have you ever been checked for sleep apnea? It sounds like you almost stop breathing sometimes."

"What are you talking about? Where are we—Ether, there is no way you picked Roswell at random."

"We were already in New Mexico! I saw it on the map, figured there'd be a lot of hotels there. All the alien tourists and all that."

Abbott sat up straighter, his skull throbbing like it was suddenly two sizes too small for his brain. "Look, if this was your plan all along, please tell me now. If the box contains what you believe to be UFO parts or other alien artifacts, just say so."

"There are no aliens involved in this operation, to the best of my knowledge. It's fine, everything is fine and normal. And we're not being followed. I've been checking constantly. That guy didn't tail us out of Albuquerque, I'm sure of it. Help me look for a hotel."

The city limits were marked by a sign depicting a flying saucer sucking livestock into its cargo hold, the whole thing lit by spinning lights.

"Jesus, they're really milking this UFO thing," said Abbott. "So that guy back there, you recognized him, right?"

"When I went to pick up the box and the cash, he was there, this huge, bald tattoo monster. He tried to attack me, yelling, 'Where is it?' and acting like if he caught me, he'd stomp me into pancetta. I got away, it's just like I told you before."

"And you don't know him outside of that? This isn't like an existing relationship at all?"

Ether hesitated and Abbott sensed she was trying to figure out how to share this piece of information without spilling the whole thing.

"I'd only ever heard about him secondhand," she said. "He was part of a biker gang; they sold meth and stolen car parts, all that stuff."

"And he's some kind of super-hacker that can track cell phones and break into store security cameras? I'm sorry, I'm trying to connect my impression of this lone tattoo monster in an old sedan with you having to keep your face partially covered at all times and insisting we can't swipe a credit card without blowing our cover."

"Outlaw bikers are organized crime; they have their methods. I thought we were being overly cautious, but"—she let out an exhausted sigh— "apparently not."

Abbott had assumed the hotels would all be whimsical places shaped like flying saucers, but they were the same old chains you saw everywhere. He noted multiple signs welcoming visitors to the UFO Festival, apparently being held from July 1–3. He imagined a hot, crowded event full of insufferable alien true-believers and tourists who'd come to take kitschy photos of them for their social media. They eventually found a place that Ether declared to be suitable, and she parked at the rear of a church next door, the building positioned between their vehicle and the hotel, blocking the sight lines from any pursuer who might creep through the hotel's lot.

She went in to book the rooms, and Abbott jumped out to examine the front end, bracing himself for the aftermath of its encounter with the Albuquerque landscaping. He winced at the sight of scratches around the bumper and caressed them with his fingers—some of the wounds were deep. Even if he tried to buff them out, his father would notice the damage from two blocks away.

The trip was, of course, over.

It had been mostly over the moment Abbott had seen the terrifying man blocking their exit from that parking lot, and absolutely over once he heard the shrubs raking the undercarriage. He hadn't signed up for *that* and had frankly already done more than could be expected. He'd tell Ether in the morning. He'd keep a prorated payment of fifty thousand and leave her to hire some braver/dumber man to take her the rest of the way. Then he'd go back to his father, wave the wad of cash at him, and peel off some bills to fix the scratches on the Nav. Then he'd get on stream and tell his wild story about how he'd driven a crazy chick to Roswell while dodging attacks from a violent biker gang. It would be at least a week's worth of content, if not two.

"Sorry that took so long," said Ether while Abbott was still sitting on the pavement by the bumper, lost in thought. "The night clerk is an amateur rapper. He had to play several tracks for me. He's pretty good!"

He looked up to see she held a room key card. Just one.

"Now, they only had one room, with one bed, so we'll have to share. I told them it'd be fine. I've seen this come up in a bunch of movies—it always turns out okay. The couple never falls in love or anything."

"What?"

"I'm just kidding." She handed him the card. "See you in the morning. I'm sleeping out here."

"What?" he said again, in the exact same tone.

"It's fine. I've slept in lots of vehicles in my time. I can sleep anywhere. There's a nice little nook in the back if I scoot the box over. But I don't want to leave it unattended, and it doesn't make sense to drag it up to the room and then have to drag it alllll the way back down in the morning. And if we should have to make a quick escape, not that we will, but just should that come up, it'll be easier if the box is already loaded up and ready to go."

"But that means you'd need the key fob, because otherwise it's not going to let you lock the doors or run the air if it gets too hot out here, which it will, since it's still at least ninety."

"I understand if you don't want to give me the keys. It'll be fine. You still think I tried to leave you behind earlier, I get it."

He stood, sighed, and massaged his stiff neck. "Okay. We'll both sleep in the Navigator."

"Are you sure? It can be rough if you're not used to it."

"I'll sit up front and lean the seat back, it's pretty comfortable. But think how stupid this is, that we just wasted money on the hotel room that's going to sit empty."

"Not at all, we have access to a bathroom now! In the morning when we wake up feeling like shit, we can go in there one at a time, poop, shower, probably masturbate, all at once if we want. We've lost a few hours with the rabbit situation and the Tattoo Monster attack, but we can make it up. One extra hour over the next few days, maybe drive like five miles an hour faster. It'll be fine. Everything is fine and normal."

Abbott made a noise that didn't specify agreement or disagreement. None of what happened the rest of the way was going to be his problem. They settled in, Ether spooning the box, Abbott reclining in a chair that was pretty nice for an automobile but not something you'd actually want to sleep in if you had a choice. He'd assumed he'd instantly pass out from exhaustion and trauma but immediately found himself fighting the same struggle as every other night, the same one Ether had mentioned within the first five minutes of meeting him: He couldn't turn off his brain.

He said, "There's something that doesn't make sense."

Ether didn't reply for a moment, and Abbott wondered if she was already asleep. Then she mumbled, "What's that?"

"You got hired to move this box, you went to pick it up, and there was a scary guy trying to take it. Why didn't you just let him have it? You already said you don't care about the money, so why risk your life?"

More silence, then, "*I* don't care about the money, but I have a debt to repay. Something I need to make right. It's the same with you, isn't it? I mean, it's not about the money itself, it's getting away from your dad, starting a new life. Neither of us are going through all this trouble for diamonds and Jet Skis. Can I come up there? This is actually incredibly uncomfortable."

"I don't think it's any better, but sure."

She moved into the passenger seat and laboriously went about trying to contort into a human sleeping position. Across the church parking lot was an inflatable alien, the same classic Grey design with the black almond eyes that could probably be found in every single gift shop within a fifty-mile radius. Abbott silently rehearsed how he was going to break off the deal in the morning, absently watching the inflatable alien sway in the breeze, bumping gently into a road sign.

"Do you know where they came from?" asked Ether. "The little Grey aliens with the big black eyes?"

"You mean, what planet?"

"No, I mean the original story, the very first person who saw one."

"They supposedly found them here, right? In the Roswell crash?"

"No!" she said with alarming enthusiasm. "The Roswell craft was just a military balloon, with radiation gadgets on it to detect Russian nuclear tests. The government actually pushed the UFO thing to throw people off the scent. The Greys came about years later, from an incident in 1961. Before that, there were no famous alien abductions, no short, big-eyed aliens, no operating tables and anal probes. The story is actually really scary. Maybe too scary. I don't want you to be up all night, creeped out."

Abbott muttered, "Hmm," and tried to drift off as this woman who insisted she wasn't into alien stuff was clearly preparing to launch into a diatribe about alien stuff. "We probably should get some sleep."

"Okay."

He lay there and could feel how badly she wanted to tell the story, so he said, "All right, tell me about the aliens."

"It's not about the aliens!" she said. "I swear it's relevant to what we're doing here, it's all about how nightmares come to life and rampage through society. Okay, so what happened was, there was a middle-aged couple named Betty and Barney Hill, they'd gone on a road trip to Canada and were heading back. They'd been on the road for eighteen hours, winding through the mountains. It was pitch dark. Then this light appears in the sky, it's swooping around, moving erratically. So they start following it, trying to get a look at it through their binoculars. Finally, it comes and hovers over their car, then their memories become jumbled, and they find themselves driving home again, having lost like three hours."

"Or so they claimed," said Abbott.

"Hold on, there's more. Betty said her dress was ripped, they had weird marks on their car. Barney had a ring of warts around his penis—"

"Heh, really?"

"Yeah. And if you think they made it all up as a hoax, keep in mind the only people they told was their nearest air force base, they were like, 'Hey, we've got glowing sky objects out here giving people genital warts.' They didn't call the press, didn't try to sell a book."

"So they just blanked out? Where do the Grey aliens come in?"

"I'm getting to that. So, a week later, Betty starts having dreams about that night where she and her husband are walking through the woods in a trance, then getting taken on board a spaceship and stuck with needles. She obsesses about it for a couple of years and then arranges for both of them to be hypnotized, to recover their lost memories. Once they got Barney under, he suddenly remembers the abduction, too. He starts *screaming* and crying, ranting about how once he was on the alien exam table, that it felt like a pair of eyes had pushed into his brain to see inside it."

Abbott said, "Okay, that *is* creepy."

"Yeah. He suddenly remembers being anally probed, says they put a cup on his penis, all that. And for the first time, both he and Betty describe their abductors as the short, bald Grey aliens with the big, black eyes, the ones everybody sees now, the ones on all the merch around town."

"And you think it really happened."

"I think that all of it," replied Ether, after a yawn, "and all of this you see around you, was because of drowsy driving and a light bulb."

"A what?"

"In the mountains they drove through, at the exact spot where they said they saw the UFO, there's a big light on an observation tower. And when you're on that twisting mountain road in the dark, the light appears to swing from one side of the sky to the other. Their 'missing time' was just the two of them underestimating how long the trip would take—you know, because they kept stopping to try to get a look at the supposed spaceship. Their memories were jumbled because they'd been driving all day, they were exhausted and sleep-deprived, just like we are now. That's it. That's the whole thing. Betty's abduction dream was just that. A dream."

"But what about all the stuff they remembered under hypnosis?"

"Well, for one, there's no such thing as recovering memories under hypnosis. That's pseudoscience. The brain doesn't work like that. Hearing about his wife's dream over and over was enough to incept the idea into Barney's brain as a real memory that he 'recovered' during hypnotherapy. And, you know, he loved his wife. He probably *wanted* to have that memory, to reassure her that she wasn't crazy. As for the Grey aliens, that's the best part: The creatures they described under hypnosis just happened to look almost exactly like the aliens featured in a sci-fi TV show that aired two weeks before they started their sessions."

"But none of what you said explains the physical evidence. How did the guy wind up with warts around his dick?"

"Who knows? I mean, that's the whole point—once they settled on a truth, everything else could be reframed to fit. If their dog had died, they'd have probably blamed it on aliens. That's just how the brain works: It wants to shape everything into a narrative. Once you realize that, the whole world starts to make more sense. Or less sense."

"So why are you so creeped out by it, if none of it happened?"

"I'm creeped out *because* none of it happened. The story finally leaked, against their will, years later. Then it became a book, then a movie, spreading around the world to every population with access to mass media, like a thought virus. Soon, a guy came forward and was like, 'Yeah, those are the aliens I saw at Roswell, now that I think of it,' even though it had absolutely not been mentioned before. *Thousands* of people have reported abductions since then, mostly conforming to this original template that literally came from a random woman's dream and a TV show. At the time this happened, almost nobody believed aliens had visited earth; today, *most* Americans do. Five hundred years from now, I bet people will still be hallucinating Greys and abductions and probings. There's this whole reality that people all over the world believe mind, body, and soul and when you trace it back to its origin, you find . . . nothing at all. Just a story so weird and terrifying that it becomes infectious, with mass media acting as the vector."

Yep, that was pretty fucking creepy, all right. It didn't escape Abbott's notice that this tale was also evidence of how easily crazy can spread from a woman to a man inside an enclosed vehicle. His final thought before falling asleep was that he was getting out just in time.

From the blog of Phil Greene:

What must be understood is that the parasite manipulates with plea-sure. When *Euhaplorchis californiensis* infects the California killi-fish, it need not inject venom or mind-altering chemicals to subdue its victim; it merely tickles the dopamine receptors until the fish thrashes and splashes with what to it must feel like rapturous joy, a behavior that quickly attracts predators, allowing the fish to be eaten and the parasite to spread. The mechanism is simple and the operation identi-cal in the micro or macro, in animals or humans: a burst of short-term pleasure will blind the subject to its long-term well-being and cause it to function as little more than a puppet. Our old religions created strong societies by cultivating humans who could delay gratification, building a tolerance for suffering that would see them through the hard winter, the invading army, the totalitarian usurper. The modern religion of consumerist instant gratification, on the other hand, serves only the masters for whom the zombified subjects make perfect cattle, relinquishing their freedom and individuality in exchange for the next paltry release of soothing opiates. The effects wear off sooner with each dose, each time leaving the subject hungry and ashamed, a sort of post-ejaculate clarity that in the moment reveals the true state of its ab-ject slavery, making the victim all the more eager to submit fully to the only source of pleasure and comfort it has ever known. The question is not how to save mankind but if what we are attempting to save can even still be called mankind. I visited my girls' graves today. Nearby, a young woman in skimpy black clothes posed over a gravestone for a photographer, his face full of piercings and tattoos, creating photos for strangers to masturbate to. I wanted to kill them but knew that they could not perceive the sanctity of that place, that the organ tuned to sense the sacred had been removed when they were too young to even understand what was being extracted from them. I hate them. I pity them. I feel nothing toward them. I feel nothing toward anyone.

DAY 2

I am now the most miserable man living. If what I feel were equally distributed to the whole human family, there would not be one cheerful face on the earth. Whether I shall ever be better I cannot tell; I awfully forebode I shall not. To remain as I am is impossible; I must die or be better, it appears to me.

—ABRAHAM LINCOLN,
in a letter to a friend, 1841

9

ABBOTT

He was dreaming about aliens, of the Navigator lifted into the sky via a beam of light. But because it was a dream, inside the UFO was Abbott's father, and the ship was a flying roofing machine, and his father was yelling about how roofs were leaking all over the Inland Empire because he'd had to come deal with Abbott's nonsense. While deep in this state of REM sleep, Abbott's entire nervous system was on fire with that feeling of being in Big Trouble, his father raging and rapping on the window with his knuckles, demanding he get out of the vehicle while the tension twisted and pulled at the bones of his chest.

Some part of his brain knew the knocking on the glass was real, that it was a noise coming from outside his dream. He blocked it out for as long as he could, then pulled his eyelids open with considerable effort, instantly assaulted by the terrible sun beating down through the windshield. Abbott strained to turn his head and found himself looking down the double barrels of a shotgun.

A gravelly voice said, "Get out."

HUNTER

An infuriating job-site crisis had come along at just the right time to prevent any of Hunter's men from asking him about Abbott. The crew was spending their Friday (and probably the weekend) fixing a roof that had failed inspection because the inspector was brand new and apparently nobody taught him where to step on clay tile. So now there were photos of cracked tiles that Hunter knew for a fact were not cracked before the inspector got his fat ass up there, but he hadn't been around to deal with it himself because he'd lost most of his Thursday over this Abbott bullshit. He'd gotten the boys started on the work, then sneaked off to his Ram to spend five minutes downing his breakfast: the biggest goddamned iced coffee allowed by law. Much to his dismay, his business partner, Pedro, had followed him over, clearly fighting for dear life to keep the smirk off his face.

"So," said Pedro, "you wanna talk about—"

"No. And I don't want anybody giving me shit about it. I assume everybody knows?"

"Just to be clear," said Pedro, "you think your kid partnered up with a hot chick he'd never met before to take an illegal trip out of state in exchange for a huge pile of cash from the Russian mob, and you're ashamed of this? I wish my boy would do something that cool. He never leaves his room."

"Wait, is *that* the version you heard?"

"I just watched a TikTok about it, but I wasn't giving it my full attention, as I was driving and eating at the same time."

Pedro had been Hunter's business partner for seventeen years, a case of two perfectionists who were fortunate to find each other because no one else could tolerate them. Hunter would rather rip up a brand-new roof and start over rather than leave imperfect work in the world; he'd lost six figures on jobs that he'd redone for reasons that weren't visible to anyone but him and, invariably, Pedro. His partner hadn't started as a roof guy but a tile guy, which was perfect—tile guys tended to see themselves as artists, surgeons. Hunter believed with all his heart and soul that guys like them were part of a dying breed of masters, leaving behind work that would baffle generations of mediocrities.

"I tried to go online, where his nerd friends all hang out," said Hunter before downing a quarter of the iced coffee in one shot, trying to get the stuff into his veins as quickly as possible. "They've started a rumor that the girl is a Russian spy."

Pedro shook his head. "You know I don't want any harm to come to Abbott, but damn, this is the kind of harm I prayed for at his age. Russian spy babes, waving money around to go on dangerous missions. That shit never came my way, not once. You talk to the cops yet?"

"I thought about reporting the Navigator as stolen, but I've heard those reports go right into the trash. Cops don't got time for that. It's the Wild West out here. Kids are getting snatched off the streets, women getting carjacked at gunpoint."

"What are you gonna say if they show up at your door asking about Russian spies and all that?"

"I'll tell 'em whatever they want to know. After that, whatever happens, happens. Abbott's not my kid anymore, he's a grown man."

"Nah," said Pedro. "He's still your kid." He pointed. "And I think the feds are here."

Hunter assumed this was a joke, as it was exactly the kind of thing Pedro would think was hilarious to say. But, over by the sidewalk, a woman with fierce cop vibes was flashing her ID at one of the crew, who pointed her toward Hunter. Pedro shuffled away and wished him luck. Hunter stood upright and wondered if the entire trajectory of his life was about to change.

KEY

She was wearing one of her old work suits, chosen because it definitely made her look like an FBI agent even though, much to her annoyance, not a single person had ever told Key that it made her specifically look like Dana Scully. She always told herself it's because she was seven inches taller than Gillian Anderson's five-foot-three. Any perp worth his salt could have punted that woman like a football.

Key had arrived at a jobsite to find several grumpy men kneeling over open boxes of clay roof tiles, apparently deciding they'd been shipped the wrong shade or something. One guy was on the phone arguing with a supplier, and when she'd asked him if Hunter Coburn was around, he pointed to a man standing by a jacked-up silver Dodge Ram that looked like it could easily run over her Volkswagen Passat. It had a bumper sticker boasting that the driver was a former marine, which meant the driver believed there was, in fact, no such thing as a "former" marine.

Hunter saw her coming and was clearly bracing himself. She didn't flash the retired ID; she figured she'd wait for him to ask.

"Mr. Coburn, can I have a word with you?"

Showing nothing on his face, he simply asked, "Did you find him?"

"I assume you're talking about your son. I just wanted to ask you a few questions."

"Do I need an attorney?"

The answer to this question is actually yes, every time, regardless of whether you're being interviewed as a suspect or a witness, as law enforcement absolutely does not have to tell you which one you are.

Instead of saying that, Key replied, "I'm just trying to get some information right now, nothing formal."

This had always been Key's favorite technique. Thanks to Hollywood, suspects thought that you always got read your rights upon arrest (the detective saying, "You have the right to remain silent," as he slaps on the cuffs makes for a nice dramatic moment). In reality, the *Miranda* warning only happens if you're being interviewed in custody. If they choose to interview you without being in custody—say, if they show up to your workplace under the guise of having a casual conversation—they don't have to read you any rights at all. In this case, of course, this was actually an informal conversation because Key had no legal authority to do anything else. What Hunter presumed about the circumstances was none of her business.

"Have you heard from your son in the last twenty-four hours?"

"No. He left a note before he took off, that's it. So you don't know where he is? I've been expecting somebody to show up either telling me he's in custody or asking me to come identify a body."

Key thought he seemed equally unperturbed by both scenarios and wondered if the man was stoic or just a shithead.

She said, "You think he's in danger."

"No idea. The note said he got offered cash to make a delivery, that was it. I still have the note. Nothing was discussed with me before or after. He left his phone and laptop behind. The woman he's with isn't familiar to me; I've never had any interaction with her and have never heard Abbott speak of her. Is she a terrorist? That's what the internet is saying."

"We're just trying to sort through the noise, just like you. But just for context, has Abbott ever expressed extremist opinions around you? To be clear, it is not illegal to express extreme views, this country was founded by extremists and, as such, they were careful to protect anti-government shit-talking in the Bill of Rights. I'm only asking if anything he said could have made him a recruitment target for the real bad guys."

"He's never said or done anything extreme around me. He's a lump. He sits around and consumes. Like he thinks that's his purpose in life, to let other people build and grow so that he can just slurp up what they make while giving nothing back, until he dies."

Ah, shithead it is. If Key was trying to build a psychological profile on Abbott, she figured she had half of it standing in front of her.

"There is talk online that some videos have surfaced of your son expressing, well, certain views. You're not aware of that part of his content?"

This was something that had just started bubbling up that morning. Key hadn't had time to watch the videos, but the online communities tracking the case had already come to believe that Abbott Coburn fit a certain archetype of young, angry male.

"No," said Hunter. "I mean, are you talking about actual extremist views or views that were universal ten years ago but that the world has suddenly decided are extreme?"

"Again, I'm just trying to get a sense of the context and his mental state."

"But these questions don't even make sense. If he ran into this lady through his rideshare job, he'd have been picked at random. That service doesn't let you ask for specific drivers. I know, because I'd pay quite a bit extra to be able to choose who picked me up."

She shrugged. "Any system can be gamed. It could have been as simple as tracking Abbott's movements, planting herself nearby, and then requesting rides and canceling until she got her guy. This could have been in the works for months, for all we know."

"*What* could have been in the works? Are you saying the rumors are right, that this is a terrorist attack on the capital, something like that?"

"Hopefully not. But your son and the woman he's with are behaving in a manner that has certainly drawn some suspicion. A cash job, making extreme effort to avoid being tracked, the woman concealing her identity . . ."

"Well, fortunately or unfortunately, something like that would still require a darkness my son doesn't have in him."

"I would encourage you to watch his old videos."

"What, did he threaten to go shoot up a mall? Is that what you think he is, a nerd who got bullied and is ready to take revenge on the world?"

"That's actually a misconception. Do you remember the first big school shooting, in the nineties? Columbine?"

"Yeah, two kids, right? They were bullied for being goths, and somehow their parents didn't notice them building pipe bombs in their bedrooms?"

"Well, that first part is actually wrong. They weren't bullied, and in fact, Eric Harris was himself a bully, a standard-issue predator who was destined to kill somebody, someday. But the other kid, Dylan Klebold, he was just a rudderless depressed teenager who, as far as anybody can tell, went along with it because it was something to do. I'm not saying Abbott is that first one, but you'd be surprised by how many of us can be that second one under the right circumstances. Just sort of numb, looking for something big and exciting to be a part of."

Hunter shook his head, like he was pondering why the universe chose to place all of its burdens on him and him alone. "I've tried my whole life to make Abbott into some kind of normal human being. To get him into hobbies, to introduce him to friends, to get him to care about some kind of career. What's a parent supposed to do? Everyone blames mom and dad in the aftermath but, seriously, what? Should I have kicked him out of the house? Have I gone too easy on him?"

"There are millions of kids just like Abbott. We could spend the rest of the day talking about how and why." Key wasn't going to mention that one factor was having parents who primarily worry about how their offspring's failures reflect on themselves. "My point is it's perfectly valid to think of Abbott as a potential victim in need of rescue, regardless of what the world is saying about him right now. If you have any means at all of contacting Abbott or locating him, please let me know. Can I give you my number?"

"Sure. But just know that the second you walk away, I'm calling my lawyer. I'm going to get out in front of this thing, whatever it is. I'm not losing my business over this. I've worked too hard."

Key's mind produced a series of ugly responses to that, and she was proud of herself for suppressing all of them in favor of, "That, of course, is your right."

ABBOTT

On one hand, Abbott knew he was awake. You can mistake a dream for real life, but you can't mistake real life for a dream. But on the other hand, he was looking through a car window at an almost comically terrifying bald thug with a tattoo on his neck. It was exactly, perfectly something out of a nightmare.

He remained frozen, blinking sleep from his eyes, until the guy growled, "*Get out,*" a second time, then Abbott opened the door and turned to wake Ether.

She wasn't there.

He stumbled down from the vehicle, his legs barely functional. The Tattoo Monster's gun was a sawed-off double-barrel shotgun, the kind you'd expect from a bandit in a *Mad Max* postapocalypse, adding to the impression that he had been birthed directly from the hallucinations of a paranoid mind. The beast leaned over and peered into the rear of the Navigator, confirming for himself that the precious box was indeed back there.

"Give me the keys."

"It-it doesn't have keys, it has one of those wireless key fob things."

"Then give me the *fob*, fuckstick."

Abbott reached into his pocket. Empty.

"It-it must be in there, in the center console. I took my key ring out because my, uh, my house key digs into my thigh when I'm driving. So I took it out and set it—"

"Shut up." The man peered into the Navigator, saying, "You try to jump me from behind, I'll blow your intestines all over this lot. Understand?"

The Tattoo Monster climbed up, leaned into the vehicle, and rustled around in the console. Abbott looked for bystanders. The church parking lot was empty, their position out of view, by design. Some tourists passed on the sidewalk on the other side of the building, oblivious. He now wondered if Ether's brilliant choice of hidden parking hadn't doomed him.

The man finished rummaging in the Navigator, then turned and put the shotgun back in Abbott's face.

"Motherfucker, you have made the grave mistake of judging me to be a patient man. *Give it to me.*"

"It's not in there? Then, uh, she must have taken it with her. I don't know why she would, but if it's not—"

"Then you and I are gonna wait here for her."

"J-just take the box!" sputtered Abbott. "Isn't your car somewhere around here? Bring it around, I'll help you load it! I don't care. Just take it and go. Leave us alone."

"Won't fit."

"Then maybe we can—"

"Shut the fuck up."

He did. They stood there, silently, awkwardly, in the church parking lot. Some unseen children were giggling. Abbott wasn't sure if he wanted a passerby to stop and intervene or if he was terrified that would happen. And what would the Monster do when Ether got there? Would he kill her? Even if not, it was clear his goal was to take the Navigator and everything in it—the money, their belongings, the gun, all of it, to do God knows what. But of course he would take everything. This is how it always went. Here was another bully who'd sensed that Abbott was on the verge of actually having some kind of good thing in his life, which could never be allowed. The monsters just took what they wanted, and they got away with it, every time.

From somewhere deep in the darkness of Abbott's gut, rage lit a match.

He tried to puzzle out why Ether had taken the key fob in the first place, but of course it was so that he wouldn't do exactly what he'd been planning to do, which was take off and leave her stuff behind with a note wishing her the best with the rest of her trip. Now, it was too late. It was too late for everything.

Finally, Ether came bouncing around the corner of the church, looking freshly scrubbed, wearing her green sunglasses and WELCOME TO THE SHITSHOW cap. She'd ditched the neon-orange visibility hoodie and had somehow acquired a turquoise alien-themed T-shirt, the front bearing the face of a Grey with the word ABDUCTED printed above. The Tattoo Monster crouched behind the front fender, the shotgun at the ready. He made eye contact with Abbott and put a finger to his lips, making it clear that Abbott was dead if he gave away his position prior to the ambush.

Ether pointed to her shirt and said, "They're selling them on the sidewalk!"

She was energized and enthusiastic, renewed for the adventure. The Tattoo Monster stank of sweat and grease and coffee. Abbott looked back at Ether, then down at the man.

Then he looked back up and yelled, "RUN! HE'S HERE AND HE'S GOT A GUN!"

Ether did exactly what Abbott was afraid she'd do, which was stop and stare in confusion. But of course what he was ordering her to do made no sense, in her mind—why would she run away from the Navigator, and the box, and her whole reason for being here? Then the Tattoo Monster rose up with his shotgun, and only then did Ether turn and flee in the other direction. The Monster pursued and Abbott started to follow, then asked himself what the hell he intended to do if he caught up. In fact, what was he supposed to do in general?

Some part of him knew, apparently, because he found himself yanking open the door of the Navigator, diving into the back, and digging out his father's pistol from his bag. He chambered a round—his father had insisted he learn how to do all this—and jumped back out to find Ether and the Tattoo Monster were now on the ground up by the church. He was straddling her and growling, "GIVE ME THE KEYS! GIVE ME THE KEYS!" while rummaging in Ether's pants pockets as she thrashed to get away from him.

Abbott was already running that direction and when he got within about ten feet, said, "Get away from her!" in a voice so meek that it triggered a flush of embarrassment.

He sounded like a child.

Like a weak, scared little boy.

He tried again.

"Hey! Get off her!"

The Tattoo Monster cast a brief glance backward, decided Abbott was not worth worrying about, then returned to the task at hand. He had his left hand jammed into Ether's other pocket now; his right was pressing her head into the pavement. She was making a piercing whimpering noise, like her head was about to burst like a melon. And then, for the first time in Abbott's entire life, he understood everything: this man, this woman, himself, and the gun.

Abbott had learned early that when his father got angry at someone, the humanity of his target just evaporated from his mind. In that moment, they were an object, an obstacle unworthy of sympathy or empathy. Abbott had thought his father was a psychopath for as long as he'd known the word, but now, finally, he got it. There is a primal override that shuts off all those feelings, because in moments of maximum peril, they are a weakness that allows the predators and incompetents to do unchecked damage to the world.

Abbott raised the gun, looked down the sights, and thought he would find some kind of resistance within himself, some invisible wall of fear or guilt that would push back, prevent him from stepping over this line.

Instead, he found nothing at all.

Abbott aimed the pistol right at the Tattoo Monster's bald fucking head and pulled the trigger.

The gun barked and bucked, but Abbott didn't drop it, not like he had the first day at the shooting range, which had caused his father to yell and yell and yell.

Ether screamed. The Tattoo Monster threw himself off of her, flailing like a tossed dog toy. He then frantically checked his body with his hands for gunshot wounds.

Finding none, he looked to Abbott and yelled, "Are you outta your goddamned mind?!?"

Abbott stepped forward, trembling, clenching his teeth so hard that he felt the roots stabbing his gums.

He pointed the gun right in the man's face and heard himself growl, "Oh, am I now SPEAKING YOUR FUCKING LANGUAGE?!?"

Ether was standing now, brushing herself off, stunned by the turn of events. Her head was bleeding. She rushed over and quickly picked something off the ground—the shotgun the Monster had apparently dropped at the end of their pursuit.

She tried to catch her breath and said, "You're Malort, right? Sundae's friend?"

"Just dump the box on the ground and drive away," grumbled the Monster. "Otherwise, I'm gonna keep coming, until either I get the box or you kill me. You're not making it to Sock, I can promise you that."

Ether turned to Abbott. "Let's go."

Abbott kept watching the bald man as he edged back toward the Navigator. Ether kept the shotgun pointed at the guy even after she entered the passenger's side, holding it out the window.

To Abbott, she said, "Drive around into the other lot."

Without asking why, he did, and found that parked near the road was the old red sedan. Ether jumped out, punctured all four of its tires with her Constitution knife, then hopped back into the Navigator and said, "Drive, drive. Turn left up here."

That took them closer to the center of town, where some tourists were milling about, the festivities still in the setup phase. They arrived at an intersection next to a Jeep full of girls in running gear. A banner over the street advertised tomorrow's Abduction Parade; a food stand nearby was selling "Martian Turds."

Ether said, "Turn left."

"Where are we going?"

"Right now, toward people. Witnesses. In case he comes."

"Should we go to the police?"

"I don't know, Abbott. I don't know. I'm trying to think. He's tracking us. I don't know how."

They turned and drove north, the touristy alien bullshit slowly becoming denser around them. They came to another intersection, and a group of pedestrians in alien garb crossed the street. A little farther up the road, traffic had crawled to a stop.

"Jesus Christ," said Abbott. "Can we turn around? What's happening?"

"I don't know. I think somebody might be directing traffic ahead. I don't like this."

She checked behind them, a gesture that was becoming a tic at this point. There was an orange WATCH FOR ALIENS warning sign by the side of the road, and Abbott wasn't sure if it was actually warning of something or if it was just for whimsy. A guy on stilts dressed like the monster from *Predator* ambled across the street; around his legs was a pair of laughing guys in Grey masks. Traffic crept forward again and, within a minute, stopped once more.

Abbott was now scanning for an escape route, every moment imagining the Tattoo Monster running up to the driver's side and Abbott having nowhere to go, his choices being smashing the car ahead of them or reversing into the one behind.

"No," he grunted. "Fuck this."

The only option was a U-turn. He backed up until the rear car honked at them, then awkwardly inched the Navigator back and forth, doing a ten-point turn until he was able to run over the raised median and get going the other direction . . . only to instantly find that after about two blocks, traffic that direction also wasn't going anywhere. Rage flared in his belly; he hated all these fucking people.

Ether said, "Turn here, or we're going to get stuck again." She pointed to an entrance to an alley, one blocked by orange ROAD CLOSED sawhorse signs.

Abbott used the grille to gently scoot the barriers aside. They passed through an alley narrow enough that there was barely enough room for his mirrors, Abbott bracing himself for the sound of scraping metal that would spell doom.

Ether said, "You're turning right up here, then you'll—"

But now someone was yelling from behind them, probably mad at them for disobeying the signs. Abbott stepped on the gas to get away from the yelling, away from being in Big Trouble. They reached the end of the alley, and Abbott looked left to make sure nobody was coming in his lane, then turned right, stepped on the gas—

And now *everyone* was screaming at him. Both lanes were full of runners with numbers pinned to their bellies, some in alien costumes, some in running gear, everyone yelling and dodging out of the way. There was no place for him to go, so he kept driving, the runners scattering around him, somebody getting mad enough to slap the door panel as they passed. The sidewalks were lined with spectators, and they also were shouting now, taking video with their phones. Abbott's face flushed, and this was about twice as distressing as the gunfight with the Monster ten minutes ago.

"What's happening? Who are these people?"

"We're in a marathon!" yelled Ether. "Go! Turn up here, get off this street!"

But of course every side street was barricaded to prevent this very thing from happening. So Abbott just kept driving and eventually passed under a banner that stretched across the road that said, ALIEN CHASE 5K WALK/ RUN. And then that road ended with a row of CLOSED signs, and he had nowhere to go.

"Cut across here!" shouted Ether, and Abbott obeyed without debate or consideration.

He found himself crossing a lawn of sparsely packed, shouting, enraged spectators. He knocked over a charcoal grill. He crushed a cooler. Then they made it onto a street and a couple of turns later seemed to be free of the madness. Abbott thought he could hear sirens and suddenly remembered that they were in possession of two different firearms that did not belong to them, two bags packed with probably illicit rolls of cash, and whatever the fuck was in that goddamned black box.

Ether was studying the map and saying, "Turn here," and "Cut across here," like she had experience evading police and had some idea of where they would look. Eventually, they hit a highway, and Abbott drove way too fast, trying to put the unholy nightmare of Roswell behind them.

Abbott wiped sweat from his eyes. "Jesus Christ. Jesus fucking Christ."

"I don't see him back there."

"That means nothing. He's coming."

"It's broad daylight, with a lot of people around. It'll be tough for him to steal a car, and it'd take hours to get four new tires for his. If we took his only gun, he'll try to get another one before coming after us again. No, I think he'll be a full day behind us if we keep moving, whether he's tracking us or not."

"You're bleeding."

Ether's hand and ear were scraped raw from where the Tattoo Monster had used the pavement as a weapon. She'd lost her trucker cap in the altercation. She dug into her bag and found a T-shirt to use as a bandage.

She said, "We just need to think. He never had a chance to put a tracker on this vehicle, right? If he got close enough to it when we'd stopped somewhere, why wouldn't he have just taken the box then or disabled the engine? Same with the box itself, the tracker would have to be inside. How would he have gotten it in there?"

"Who else had access to the box?"

"Just Phil—the guy who was storing it before I picked it up. But he was a zealot when it came to being tracked; he wouldn't have even owned a phone if his daughter hadn't—oh my god." She covered her face with her bloody hands. "His daughter did it. She probably just put an AirTag in there and didn't tell him."

"That just now occurred to you?"

"I mean, to work, the Monster would still need access to the owner's phone. I threw it away."

"Like, into the ocean?"

"No, I just threw it in the trash. He couldn't have found it. Or maybe—I don't know. I just thought that you throw something away and it disappears forever. So what do we do? We can't open the box."

"We have to block the signal. Aluminum foil will do it. We'll stop and get some. Wrap the whole box."

"You mean we have to literally make our black box a tinfoil hat to wear?"

"Basically, yeah."

"Okay. Good. We'll do that as soon as possible."

Abbott gripped the wheel.

Staring daggers into the windshield, he said, "He's after both of us now. Because I shot at him."

"You sure did! You came for me."

"What else was I gonna do? You had my keys."

"You could have let him have me, grabbed the cash, jumped in a cab to the nearest airport, flown back to LA, and enjoyed your riches. You made a choice. You risked your life. Take a moment to stop and appreciate that about yourself."

"He's going to kill me."

"No. No. We're going to block his tracker, change our route, and put hundreds of miles between us and him. We're smarter than he is, there's two of us, we have guns and big bags of cash. We're goddamned Bonnie and Clyde, tearing ass across America."

They drove in silence for a few minutes, then Abbott said, "I do have to stop and piss, though."

"Yeah, me, too."

And then Ether started giggling, and Abbott joined in, and soon they were both laughing so hard they could barely breathe.

ABBOTT COBURN JUST ATTEMPTED A PARADE RAMMING ATTACK IN ROSWELL, NEW MEXICO, THE VEHICLE HAS FLED THE SCENE

Posted to r/AbaddonsNavigator by TruthLover420

And yes, Abbott stans, he was driving, not GSG. So let's put to bed any theory that he's a hostage or a dupe. He is literally and figuratively "at the wheel" of this operation. She didn't hire him as a driver, the Circle K is just where they arranged to meet. I'll say it until y'all finally start to listen: At this point, even if the woman was arrested or killed, Abbott would continue the mission without her.

I believe this attack was a dry run to measure police response time. They may be looking for a similar target in DC for the final attack. Judging from Abbott's previous videos, I would look for any parades or other gatherings of women/feminists in the DC area. Abbott Coburn is an incel terrorist and, at this point, anyone who disagrees should also be labeled as such.

[Post deleted by moderator ZekeArt]

Partial transcript from a Twitch stream posted approximately three years ago by user Abaddon6969, at 3:41 A.M., on a Tuesday:

Is Harvey Weinstein going on trial yet again? That whole thing is so stupid, everybody has lost their minds. Huge Hollywood producer, won tons of Oscars, then suddenly all these actresses come out of the woodwork saying he sexually harassed them. Hilarious.

(Abbott glances off to the side, where messages from viewers appear in a chat window, verbally replying to what he is reading)

Oh, cry me a river. These women weren't starving, they weren't exchanging sex for food. They were incredibly privileged people angling for literally the most prestigious job on the planet, hell, in the history of the planet. If this goblin offered sex for a chance to be a star, all they had to do was say no, go work a regular job like the rest of us. But they made that deal, and that's what creates the system that these women find so oppressive.

(Abbott reads the chat window again)

What do you mean, "power imbalance"? God we treat women like babies. These are adults, they have agency. Beautiful white women are literally the most privileged group in the history of the species, they can walk into a room with billionaires and royalty and have them eating out of their hands. But these women wanted more, they wanted wealth, fame, mass adoration, the absolute best of the best of everything, all the time. So this ugly gross dude, Harvey, he says, "Hey, in any other circumstance, you would treat me like dogshit, but I happen to have a powerful position where I can get you access to the best possible life of any time or place in the known universe, do you want to play ball?" He didn't put a gun to their heads. So they give him what he wants, he gives them what they want. They get incredibly rich and famous, then twenty years later, they get to play the trauma card and cash in *again*. Wouldn't that be amazing, to have the most privilege anyone has ever had *and* get to play victim at the same time? Living life as a pretty white girl isn't just playing the game on Easy Mode, it's playing it in God Mode. You're not even playing the same game as the rest of us.

(Abbott reads more chat responses, his demeanor seeming to change for the worse)

No, I say he was the one being sexually harassed. Women hate it when men treat them differently because they want sex, but when women hold out the possibility of sex to extract things from men—favors, compliments, jobs—that's how women sexually harass men. Don't get me wrong, women sexually harass men the traditional way, too, but mostly it's the one girl in a programming class asking for help and instantly having fifteen nerds rush over to do her work for her. Why does she think they're doing that? It's her using her power over them, the same as Harvey did with those actresses. Every time a girl pokes at a guy's sexual desire, his insecurity, that's sexual harassment. It should get you fired and ostracized just the same.

(Abbott reads more chat responses)

If he legitimately assaulted someone, like violently forced them, that's different. But that's already a crime, if he did that, he should be arrested and charged like anyone else. But that's not what this movement is about, the people demanding change aren't asking for more cops to bust violent rapists, they want to abolish the police! Look, this is how it is: If you're rich, you're going to be the target of crime because you have something other people want— you have money, they don't. That's part of the down- side of being rich. Well, if you're rich in looks and sex appeal, it's the same thing—you have what every man wants. Yes, ladies, men are going to try to put their hands on you, that's the trade-off. You're walk- ing around in a starving country with a body made of cupcakes. You can't change that by turning it into a witch hunt where all it takes is one anonymous accu- sation to destroy the starving man's life.

(Abbott reads the chat, seems to become visibly agitated)

What's ironic? Using the term *witch hunt*? Oh, great, we've got a feminist here. Maybe go read the history of witch hunts. You know who the accusers were in the Salem witch trials? It wasn't the patriarchy, it wasn't the mean old white Christians. It was a group of white teenage girls. Look it up. See, that's the real witch- craft, that's the real mind control. If a pretty white girl cries, men will burn the world to the ground on her behalf. And the girls all know it. They know we have these protector instincts, that we're desperate for their approval. And they manipulate that at every opportunity. They always have.

(Abbott continues to read chat responses, angrily shifts in his chair)

Fuck off. Stop responding to her, guys. I banned her. It's probably the first time anybody has dared disagree with her. There is no privilege in the universe like female physical attractiveness. Not money, not power, not race. Physical attractiveness utterly dominates all social interaction at every level. To see them complain about being marginalized is so ridiculous that it's grotesque. All right, enough of that. So today, we've got the new chicken sandwich from Jack in the Box. This one has pickles and extra mystery sauce.

10

ABBOTT

They found a dusty huddle of businesses along the highway and pulled into a Family Dollar that was sandwiched between Tiny's Burger Barn and a weed dispensary. They bought two rolls of foil and quickly and clumsily wrapped the black box in multiple layers. Abbott couldn't pretend to be an expert on Apple's tracking tech, but this was just physics: no electromagnetic signal was penetrating metal. If the Tattoo Monster was still tracking the box, the little dot on his map would have just disappeared.

They had then quickly jumped back into the Navigator, and Ether directed Abbott onto a series of country roads so that their pursuer couldn't simply extrapolate their route from their last known location. They wound up on a gravel road at some point, accidentally turned off onto a driveway to a farmhouse, got totally lost, and then by pure luck stumbled onto a neglected four-lane highway with signs pointing them toward Lubbock.

Ether sat back and examined the mangled knuckles on her hand under the bloodstained shirt-bandage. "Okay, help me think. Is there *any* other way he can track us? Let's assume he has maximum tracking powers, access to a network of cyberpunk biker hackers, everything."

"I don't know," said Abbott, who the previous night had fully believed he'd be on his way home by now.

"I mean, this is what an adventure is, just overcoming obstacles. We had a problem—a crazy guy wanted to steal our shipment—and we solved it, we lost him. For real, this time."

She examined her scraped ear in the mirror. There was also a pink mark at the top of her forehead, but she paid it no special attention, and Abbott thought maybe that one had already been there.

He muttered, "I can't stop my left hand from shaking."

"That's understandable. But you have to rev down at some point. Your nervous system can't stay amped up forever; you'll burn out. We were in danger, we dealt with it, now the danger has passed." She took in and let out a long breath. "Now we can just settle in and drive. Just relax."

"I don't think I've relaxed once, in my whole life."

"Well, maybe it's time to try something new. If you allow yourself to feel the distress of the conflict, you should also allow yourself to feel the release of victory."

"Remember how you said we all need silence now and then, so we finally have a chance to process our thoughts? That's what I need from you right now. Silence."

"Got it."

KEY

Phil Greene's place was surrounded by a tall, corrugated-metal fence topped with barbed wire. She had driven past a few times to confirm nobody was staking out the property, and she was now watching it from down the road, waiting for anyone to come by. The Navigator obsessives on the internet hadn't yet connected that vehicle to this property, but when they did, macabre tourists would surely be showing up to get a look. The subreddit now boasted tens of thousands of followers, and speculation had spread to every platform, with true-crime TikTok influencers sticking their faces into the camera and boldly asserting that they knew exactly what was inside that mysterious armored box/footlocker/steamer trunk.

Key watched, ate the tragic lunch she'd packed for herself, and finally decided that nobody else was coming. She headed down a road that curved around a hill to find the burned-out shack. What little remained of the structure hadn't been roped off as a crime scene, because, well, there really wasn't much to rope off. The walls had tumbled over at some point, the whole structure now just a tossed salad of boards and charcoal. She found the hatch, which hadn't been nailed shut or otherwise locked. She opened it, shined a flashlight down, and saw a ladder ending at what appeared to be a fairly spacious tunnel. Surely if she went down and followed it, she would find nothing but an impassable locked door at the other end, one probably connected to an alarm she wouldn't want to trip. But, you know, there was only one way to find out.

She had decided before leaving her apartment that she was now functioning as a journalist. You didn't have to get some special license to be one, you could just claim the title as long as you intended to publish your findings, which she would, probably, if she discovered the truth and didn't die in the process. Thus, it was in her capacity as a journalist that she climbed down and found the tunnel was constructed from an arch of corrugated metal that seemed to be buckling in places as if it could cave in at any moment. Ahead was a steel door, standing wide open.

She moved that direction and then, from behind her, a stern voice said, "That is a very bad idea."

ABBOTT

"I didn't say I hated all eighties movies," said Abbott as he browsed a row of jalapeño-and-cheese hot dogs rotating in a warmer. "I said I hate movies like the ones you keep talking about, where the heroes are nerds and outcasts, but then there's a group of like seven of them. If you have seven friends you can play D&D with, you're not an outcast."

"But I'm saying when you watch movies from back then, you see those groups of kids get on their bicycles and go on adventures around the neighborhood. They walked around and showed up at each other's houses, in real life. You don't watch that and envy it a little?"

"The suburb I grew up in didn't even have sidewalks. You either walked on the shoulder with cars zipping by inches away, or you were wading through a drainage ditch."

"Yes! Exactly! For the last forty years, everything has been built around getting into a car, going to an appointed place at an appointed time, and driving back. There's no chance for adventure, to run into new friends, new situations. It's all planned, supervised."

They were wandering around a 7-Eleven store in a sparse city that Abbott thought was Lubbock, Texas, unless Lubbock was the next one and they were in some equally desolate expanse of pavement. Abbott had decided early in the trip that it would be a tight contest to decide which US state was the emptiest, but Texas was making a strong case. It wasn't just the vast expanses of perfectly flat nothing along the highway; it's that even within the towns, the structures were scattered as if they'd all been slid across a smooth floor. There were wide stretches of pavement and/or dying grass in between buildings, as if they couldn't stand to be too close to one another. This particular gas station was at a busy intersection across from a sports stadium of some kind, surrounded by hotels that stood like islands in a sunbaked ocean of parking. Abbott and Ether were looking for something they could eat for lunch on the move, food that wouldn't drip onto the Navigator's precious, immaculate leather seats.

"When I was a kid," said Abbott, "my dad wouldn't let me walk anywhere by myself, because he was convinced I'd get snatched up by child molesters. He had all of these examples in his head, stuff he heard on the news. 'Did you know that three little kids were abducted in Memphis and had their penises cut off by Satan worshippers?'"

"And then you get blamed for wanting to stay inside when you grow up!" added Ether. "That 'stranger danger' paranoia came from the suburbs, parents in perfect neighborhoods terrified that child-trafficking rings would steal their kid if they let them out of their sight for ten seconds. I would say, 'Imagine what that does to a child growing up?' but I don't have to imagine, between the two of us, we have like six amber bottles of brain meds and zero coping skills. Now those same boomers are like, 'Why don't you go outside? Why are you looking at your screens all the time?' These are the same people who started this trend of never letting kids go out on their own because *their* screens told them the streets were full of monsters. So you grew up in Florida? You mentioned that earlier."

Ether had been doing this since Roswell, trying to strike up conversations, to reset the vibe to Fine and Normal. At one point, she'd asked him if he had another job, and he'd deflected, as was his habit. There was no non-awkward way to explain his Twitch channel to outsiders, and he loathed the way people always got embarrassed on his behalf.

"My parents had me by accident," he said, his childhood trauma actually being one of his most frequent and comfortable conversation topics. "They hated each other. My dad married my mom after she got pregnant, out of obligation. I guess he was old-fashioned or something. They continued hating each other and both hated me for being the thing that was keeping them stuck together. Eventually, Mom went on a business trip to Houston and just never came back. She hated Dad, but she just didn't like me. She wasn't shy about it."

"I'm sure it wasn't that bad."

He shrugged. "She didn't want to be a mother. If I'd been some kind of child she enjoyed being around, maybe she'd have warmed to the situation. But I was annoying, I wasn't any fun. Always whining. Needy. Ugly. No cool talents to brag to her friends about. Do you think this hot dog will drip on the seats?"

"Not if you leave off the mustard. What about your dad?"

"I think it has cheese or something inside it. Seems like it'll squirt out the other end when I bite into it." He scanned around for some drier food, then said, "If my dad could return me like a defective piece of merchandise, he would."

"Come on, that can't be true. Do you see any hats? I need a new one. Mine fell off in Roswell."

"He's been angry since I was born. And where normal people get mad and then get over it, Dad just keeps cycling higher, like a runaway reactor. Like he'll get mad, then he'll get mad about the fact that you made him mad, and the only thing that will calm him down is if he can spread it, make everyone else miserable. He sees the universe as this machine that is designed to give him everything, and he takes it as a personal affront when it misfires."

"I had an old boyfriend like that. Actually, more than one."

"Dad joined the Marines out of high school because his parents were scared of what he'd do otherwise. He told me that himself. Bragging about it, about how dangerous he was. Do you like *your* parents?"

She didn't answer.

Abbott said, "Come on, you pry into me constantly but can't share basic surface information, like whether or not you hate your dad?"

"Later. Let's go. This is too long for me to be in one spot hatless."

They went back out into the heat, and Abbott surveyed the paved land-scape. "If aliens landed, they'd think only cars lived here."

"We're in the dead zone right now," replied Ether. "This is actually one of the most populated spots."

"What do you mean, dead zone?"

"There's a dead strip right up the middle of the USA. It's weird, you have a vertical row of cities—Dallas, OKC, Kansas City, Minneapolis—and to the west of it is this blank strip hundreds of miles wide where almost nobody lives. I'm talking whole counties with fewer than one person per square mile. The trip gets more interesting once you get through this—eighty percent of the US population lives to the east of the dead zone. And of course, north of us, you have the Oklahoma Panhandle, that strip of land that used to be part of Texas, but when Texas entered the Union, they wanted to be a slave state, but slavery wasn't allowed north of that parallel. So they just lopped off that strip, and for decades, it didn't belong to any-body. For years, they didn't even have laws there. It was like *The Purge.*"

Abbott wasn't listening.

He'd opened the driver's-side door and was now staring, frozen.

Blood.

Dried to the color of rust, smeared all over the off-white leather of the passenger seat. It'd been there for hours, but he hadn't noticed when it had been hidden under Ether's ass.

"How—how did this get here? What the fuck?"

Ether came around, alarmed by his tone, then only seemed confused.

"Oh, I bet it's from my hand. I didn't even notice."

Without a word, Abbott rushed back into the 7-Eleven, scanning the tiny household goods shelf for some kind of cleaning products. His breath was getting short, his hand was shaking again. Ether had come in behind him at some point and was saying something about plain soap and water being the best cleaner, that they could get it from the restrooms. Abbott dashed off, found a men's room, and quickly soaked a wad of paper towels in water and hand soap. He rushed back out to the Navigator, wiping down the stains, scrubbing them, accomplishing nothing. Smears of rusty crimson had soaked into the leather.

Ether was watching him scrub and curse and said, "Abbott, we can have it cleaned after the trip."

She didn't get it. Thirty hours together and she still didn't get it. She didn't get anything.

"My life is over," he breathed, leaning into the car, staring down at the tainted seat. "My life is over. My life is over."

He closed his eyes.

"Because of the stains?" asked Ether stupidly. "Abbott, I don't understand."

"I can't go back now. Don't you see that? If I'd wanted to go back at any point before now, I had that option. I could have turned around, shown up back at home with some chunk of the cash, and told my dad the job was all done. The little scratches on the front end, you know, whatever. That's the result of running the vehicle hard, doing work. We'd have forgotten all about that in a month, everything would be back the way it was before. I had that option, to make things the way they were. But if I go back and the car looks like this? He's put thirty thousand miles on it without a single speck on the interior. It was sterile; you could build microprocessors in here. And it took me one day to ruin the seats. I can't take it back to him like this. Do you understand? I can't. No matter what."

"Okay . . ."

"I can't go back to my old life. It's done, it's irrevocable. I—I almost killed a man. And now, even if we make the delivery, this guy can find where I live. He's seen me, he's seen the license plates. I'm dead."

"You're catastrophizing again. Breathe."

"Tell me what part of that was wrong."

"Listen. What I'm about to say, I know I'm going to sound like a bumper sticker, but this is just me telling you the situation. Okay? So, all your life, you've been clinging to the side of a swimming pool. On the opposite side of that pool is everything you want: independence, respect, your own career and a home, and maybe a partner. But to get to the other side of the pool, *you have to let go of the side you're on.* That lightheaded feeling you're experiencing right now? Part of it is just that. You're floating free, like a grown-up. Your own actions, your own consequences. Sink or swim."

"This is not a fucking swimming pool; a pool is a controlled environment. This is an ocean, with storms and sharks."

"Trust me, I know. I didn't want to alarm you with the wrong analogy."

"You trapped me into this. This is exactly what you wanted to happen, for me to have no choice. You ruined my life just so I would have nothing to go back to."

Ether kept her voice steady, infuriatingly so. "Abbott. Listen to me. Out here, in the adult world, we make decisions and we stick by them. We take responsibility for them. You hate that the world treats you like a loser. Well, here's your chance to prove them wrong."

"Don't tell me to—"

"Do you need help?" interrupted a voice from behind them.

They both turned to find a smiling young woman who Abbott decided had the exact wrong kind of face to be turning up at a time like this.

Abbott said, "No."

Ether said, "No. Thank you, though."

The girl didn't leave, because of course she didn't. "Okay. I, uh, saw you in there, and I wasn't going to say anything. My husband was like, 'Leave them alone,' but it sounded like you were having trouble, and I thought I'd come see."

A burst of rage flashed through Abbott's system. The girl was talking and saying nothing, a thing that almost all girls did and that he never understood. *Why wasn't she leaving?*

"We've got it," said Ether, forced to repeat the exact same information she'd just conveyed. Abbott detected something in her voice—if not irritation, then a little bit of fear.

"Is that blood?" asked this cursed goblin of a woman. "Ooh, your hand! And your ear! We have a first aid kit in the trailer if you need it."

The girl gestured toward a pickup truck with dual wheel tires towing a trailer that contained at least one mildly confused horse. A fat guy with a goatee in the middle of his face sat behind the wheel. He smiled and shouted and said four words that threw Abbott for a loop:

"She's a big fan!"

The goblin girl put a hand over her eyes in a show of embarrassment, then said, "Oh, God, I'm so sorry. I wasn't even going to say anything."

Abbott scrambled to imagine which of his regular fans could be this Texas horse girl in too much makeup, when she looked at Ether and said, "It's true, though. You totally changed my life."

Ether was frozen now. Abbott could see a fight-or-flight response that in this scenario translated to, "Lie or dive into the Navigator."

"Oh," she replied, eyes wide. "Yes, thank you."

"I was in a really dark place," said the goblin, "with body-image issues and everything else, but you really kept me going. I watched your videos every day, over and over. It was like you were the only one who understood. Since then, I've gone back and finished my degree, got married, we have a baby on the way . . ." She stopped to wipe away a tear, and Abbott was still enraged but wasn't totally sure who to be angry at. Maybe everyone. The goblin, Ether, himself, that guy in the truck with his tiny goatee. Fuck him and the horse that rode in on him.

Ether said, "Oh, thank you so much. That means a lot. We do have to hurry off, I don't want to be rude. I got scraped up falling out of the car, and we're going to go get it checked out."

"Oh, of course! I'm so sorry. I won't hold you up." She then turned toward Abbott and said, "And you are?"

Abbott scrambled to think of a fake name at the exact same time his mouth went ahead and said, "Abbott."

"Good to meet you," she said, clearly trying to discern the relationship between Abbott and Ether, who was apparently this girl's idol, for some reason. "I hate to even ask this," she said to Ether, clearly not hating it enough, "but can I get a selfie with you?"

Ether again went into panic mode, actually looking to Abbott for help, having no idea how to refuse this request. Abbott understood her dilemma: If she took the picture, there was now documentation of their location, presumably to be promptly shared with the world. If she refused, the crestfallen girl would take to the internet to complain that Ether had snubbed her—which would also no doubt peg their location. They were screwed either way.

Ether quickly smiled and shuffled into selfie position while saying, "I have one condition, though: Don't post it. Okay?"

"Oh, sure. It'll just be for me."

They took the pic, and the girl smiled at her phone as she examined the results. "You look so beautiful, though. I love the short hair!"

She hugged Ether without asking permission and again wiped tears from her eyes as she sauntered away.

Abbott glared at Ether and hissed, "What the fuck was that?"

"We have to go. *Now.*"

KEY

Former FBI agent and World's Shittiest Friend Patrick Diaz was climbing down the tunnel ladder behind Key and somehow doing it in a way that conveyed how profoundly she'd disappointed him. He had, of course, demanded that she not visit the Phil Greene property, but he surely had to know that would just make her want to do it more.

"Did you follow me here? What the hell?"

"You're breaking and entering," he said as he dismounted.

"It's an abandoned property with an unlocked entryway; it's trespassing at best. Are you going to arrest me?"

If so, it would be the second time Patrick had put her in handcuffs, though the previous incident had not involved an arrest.

Instead of answering, he said, "What exactly do you think you're going to find down here that hasn't already been found, photographed, and cataloged?" Though Key noted that he was already glancing around the tunnel, curious himself.

"I don't know what anybody else has or hasn't done with the property. But I'll tell you this: I'm imagining entire books being written about all the precursors that were ignored prior to this attack. Even if you think this is nothing but an internet conspiracy theory, at the end of this tunnel is a house in which a man died of mysterious causes, and so far, I've heard nothing about anyone even being questioned in the matter."

She headed down the tunnel, leading with her flashlight. Patrick made no move to stop her and, after a moment, followed.

He said, "Phil Greene was found lying next to a ladder and a metal tool chest that his skull impacted on the way down. He fell off while trying to add electromagnetic shielding to his ceiling. Because he was crazy and thought 5G signals were rewiring his brain."

"And his face had been eaten off."

"By cats, according to the medical examiner."

Key glanced back at him. "By *what*?"

"Multiple cats, probably strays that wandered in. You know how cats are, they spend their whole lives looking at humans the way diners look at the lobsters in a restaurant aquarium. They went after his face and hands, the parts they could get to."

"And his truck was radioactive."

"To a trivial degree, yes."

"As in, it hauled radioactive material at some point, which was removed, leaving residue behind."

"Yes, and as I said, that material could literally have been kitty litter, which contains bentonite, which will trip radiation monitors. As you well know."

They arrived at a point where the tunnel expanded into a small room with wooden walls and stacks of plastic containers full of dehydrated survival food.

Key sighed. "Well, this is just depressing."

"Yes, Joan. This is where paranoia gets you. You can't stop the chaos of the world, but you can dig a hole. Are you determined to go all the way into the main house, or have you satisfied your curiosity?"

"Well, I haven't learned anything new yet, so . . ."

She entered another, longer stretch of tunnel, and while she knew it was unlikely that it would choose this specific moment to collapse, the possibility had officially reached the level of an intrusive thought. It was definitely starting to feel like there wasn't enough air down here.

"You never answered my question," said Patrick. "What, exactly, do you think you're going to learn that the police and JTTF didn't?"

"Knowing the specific target would be nice. Any link between GSG and the guy, Abbott, would help paint a clearer picture."

"GSG?"

"Green Sunglasses Girl. Seriously, it would benefit you to at least see what people are saying online. I suppose you also don't know that they've uncovered Abbott's incel manifesto. Well, not a manifesto but a series of videos, which is how they do it these days. That would have made him a prime recruiting target, particularly if they're partnering him up with a cute girl his age."

"She probably wouldn't even have to be cute."

They had reached the end of the tunnel and another ladder. Key shined her light up there and once again expected to see some kind of locked door or hatch, but found none. She climbed up to find herself in an unfinished space behind a closet. It was designed to be hidden by a piece of plywood that would have appeared from the other side to be the back of the closet, but the board had been flung to the floor, and all of the clothes—mostly plaid shirts—had been pushed aside. It was pitch dark inside the room itself, as if every window had been blacked out.

She stepped into the room and shined her flashlight around. The entire exterior wall was covered in aluminum foil, including the window. Tacked up to the foil was a layer of chicken wire, the makeshift Faraday cage Patrick had mentioned. Greene had then added to his walls dozens of little dangling amulets bearing strange symbols, presumably to ward off mind-reading demons. She peeled back a corner of the foil around the window to find it had been reinforced with metal bars. The man had built a prison for himself but probably saw the situation in reverse, that he'd put the deviancy of the outside world behind bars so that it could not interfere with his "freedom."

On the opposite wall were pinned dozens of whimsical trucker caps bearing slogans like ALL TRASH, NO TRAILER; OLD FART; and, bafflingly, THE BIGGER THE FUPA, THE TASTIER THE CHALUPA. Under the hats was an unmade twin bed next to a nightstand that Key found was full of old utility bills and three different Bibles. The only other piece of furniture was a chest of drawers that contained stacks of identical T-shirts and gray underwear.

Patrick was watching all of this from behind her, saying, "It looks like Greene had a plan for how to get out, should the feds do a Ruby Ridge siege on the property. He probably had a gassed-up vehicle parked by that shack, maybe hidden under a camouflage tarp, waiting to take him to the mountains."

"I bet he scrambled to that closet ladder every time he heard a squirrel cross his roof."

They proceeded into a hall, the walls of which were covered in what Key had initially mistaken for some kind of scribble-patterned wallpaper, but a closer examination revealed it to be scrawled rants in almost illegible handwriting. When you live alone, you're free to decorate the space with your madness. She next entered a master bedroom with décor that Key found too feminine for the elderly survivalist: floral bedspread, a dainty lamp, and figurines on the nightstand. The top drawer of that nightstand contained rows of neatly arranged prescription pill bottles; the second drawer contained a Stephen King paperback, some kind of inspirational biography by an old guy on a motorcycle, and several worn sudoku books.

"The kid's incel manifesto," said Patrick, "did it contain any references to a planned attack, potential targets, methods, anything?"

"Not that we've found so far. But again, nobody is claiming he planned the attack. It's likely he's just a dupe."

"But you think he would willingly join an operation like this to try to bring about your Virgin Apocalypse."

The rise of violence on the part of "incels"—the self-described involuntarily celibates who've crafted their sexual frustration into a misogynistic worldview—had been a focus of Key's work in her last few years on the job. The first widely reported incel attack came in 2014, when the almost impossibly creepy Elliot Rodger killed six victims after posting a string of videos about how it was a cruel injustice that the beautiful women of the world wouldn't have sex with him. In 2018, an avowed fan of Rodger got behind the wheel of a van and plowed into a parade, killing ten victims in the name of an "incel rebellion." In 2020, another apparent Rodger fan in Virginia blew his hand off while making a bomb using the chemical TATP, leaving behind writings that implied he'd been planning to use it against "hot cheerleaders."

Key had quickly found that reliable data on this group was almost impossible to come by—even now, nobody could say how many self-identified incels were out there, not even as a ballpark figure. What she did know was that sexlessness in young men had tripled in the last decade, something like three in ten male adults now having no active sex lives. A certain segment had submerged themselves in a hot pool of frustration and humiliation (which actually made them much less fuckable than they'd previously been), a certain smaller number had tried to claw back some power by loudly proclaiming they were ready to do violence, and some fraction of that group actually meant it. From their point of view, distribution of sex was another form of rising inequality, the top 5 percent of the most attractive men hoarding all the babes, with their share growing by the day. And inequality—real or perceived—always breeds instability.

Key's theory, which Patrick had mocked as the "Virgin Apocalypse," was that all modern hate groups were really just incel grievances in disguise. It's a historical fact that one of the key precursors to mass violence in a society is simply an excess of young, unmarried men. The *really* unpopular part of Key's theory, the one that had caused a lot of colleagues to stop talking to her in the hallway, was that the smart societies knew you could deal with this problem simply by finding some excuse to go to war. Through all of history, wars were a way to burn off your excess young men, like venting heat from an engine.

Key lifted up the bedspread and found a slit in the mattress, cut with a razor to stash whatever the sleeper on that side had wanted within easy grabbing distance. She spread the slit open with her fingers and shined the light in there.

"Did the police take anything from the mattress?"

"No idea," replied Patrick. "So, just to be clear, the internet's theory is that there are four different parties here, all with separate grievances? Phil Greene, the anti-technology conspiracy nut, Abbott Coburn, the incel dupe, Malort Little, the biker upset with SoCal health care and corrections, and an unknown female whose motives remain mysterious?"

"Why not, if they all want the same outcome, and each bring their own component to the plan? Now this is the part where you scold me for indulging speculation, at which point, I'll reply that the sooner I can get hard information, the quicker we can put the speculation to rest."

"What a wonderful world it would be if it actually worked that way, speculation wilting in the face of evidence."

Key ran her hand inside the mattress and found two empty padded envelopes. They both had been mailed from a PO box in McLean, Virginia. That is, the richest suburb of Washington, DC, just across the Potomac.

"I think," she said, "I just found what I was looking for. And here you said I was wasting my time."

"I didn't say you were wasting your time, I said you were breaking the law."

She took a photo of the label and held the envelope up to Patrick. "Phil Greene received packages from somebody in the DC area. Find out who this PO box belongs to, and you may have both the name of a collaborator and a possible destination for that vehicle and its cargo."

"I would be stunned if JTTF didn't already have that information, but I'll be sure to pass it along."

They made their way into what was clearly the kitchen of a man who never cooked, but who had once lived with someone who had. Lots of expensive gear remained on the counter, including a stand-up mixer and a high-end food processor that were both gathering dust. The freezer was now packed with frozen dinners, mostly pizzas.

"Okay," said Patrick, "so what do *you* think the target is? I mean, why would Abbott get on board unless it was something that served his anti-woman ideology?"

"I guess I was hoping Greene would have a map and blueprints pinned to a wall somewhere."

If he did, they weren't in his living room. There was a sofa and an arm-chair aimed at a big-screen TV that had presumably been dormant ever since the owner had banished electronic signals from the property. Once more, there were little feminine decorative touches that had been slowly overtaken. Key imagined framed paintings of tranquil desert landscapes that had been yanked off the wall to be replaced with foil and wire. Phil Greene had lost his wife and then his daughter within a few years, and here was a fairly clear story of a man who, in the process, had lost his only anchors to reality. Key believed the world was full of crazy men who were kept tethered to reality by sane women, though this was the kind of thing that, again, never got a great reaction when said around the office. Having a support group of friends could maybe have rescued Phil Greene, but he'd chosen isolation, and in isolation, human minds tend to get strange, like a self-portrait painted from memory, in the dark, using a live snake as a brush.

"Is that what you're looking for?" asked Patrick.

She brought the light around, and there was a door that had been painted with a crude radiation symbol with the words KEEP OUT above and below. Key immediately disobeyed the sign.

Welcome to r/DCTerrorAttack

Posted to r/DCTerrorAttack by TruthLover420
Due to censorship at the AbaddonsNavigator subreddit, I have started a new sub that will actually allow discussion to hopefully get to the truth and thwart the weapon of mass destruction that is apparently heading toward Washington, which could easily trigger World War III if the US government determines the attack was Russian in origin.

This is a Free Speech zone and if you can't handle that, leave.

PS: I have preemptively banned ZekeArt from posting here.

ABBOTT

"I used to be kind of famous," said Ether as they put distance between themselves and Lubbock as quickly as Abbott could safely manage. "Not actual famous—social media famous. I did something stupid and then got known for that, way more than I was ever known for the good stuff I did."

"So you're famous enough that strangers can recognize you. Jesus, it finally makes sense. *That's* why you were in disguise. You weren't hiding from an all-seeing cabal, you were hiding from your fans."

"Well, I was afraid my fans would rat out my location to the Tattoo Monster. I mean, it'd make his job pretty easy if all he had to do was search Instagram for teenage girls saying, 'Look who we found at the Ros-well Anal Probe Carnival.'"

"So it's possible you've been getting spotted over and over, this whole time."

"Well, I'm not *that* famous. And I've totally changed my look! I've gained weight since then. I chopped off my hair yesterday. And when I was on stream, I was always in color contacts that gave me blue eyes, and in heavy makeup."

"Oh, you were one of *those*."

"I was one of those. But no matter what I change, this is what identi-fies me." She pointed to the mark at the top of her forehead that Abbott had mistaken for a wound earlier. It was a two-inch-long blotch that was roughly the shape of South America. "That's why the hat was important. If we wind up among girls age sixteen to twenty-four, yeah, there's a de-cent chance they know me."

"You're famous for your birthmark?"

"My first big video was a makeup tutorial, on how to cover up a blem-ish like that. I've been teased over it my whole life, I'd learned a number of cover-up techniques over the years, so that kind of became my thing. If you search for a video on how to cover up a birthmark, mine is still at the very top of the list."

"I had forgotten about it because of the bullshit with the escaped rab-bit, but before we left, the cashier at the Circle K in Flagstaff took a pic-ture of us. I wasn't totally sure at the time, but there's no doubt in my mind now. That's probably been happening everywhere, fans recognizing you through the disguise, posting our location."

"I don't know. It's possible. I'm so bad with faces, I guess I just assume everybody else is, too."

"And you failed to disclose this to me. Which put me in danger. And now this Monster is coming for both of us because of it."

"I didn't tell you because there's a chance you've heard of me, but only in the context of the scandal, so you'd immediately hate me. Which is exactly what I said earlier. I've never lied to you, Abbott."

"What was the scandal? Did you say something racist?"

"No, it wasn't anything like that. But it was bad enough that I hit the Eject button, cashed out, and left everything behind, came up with a new name. So when you ask me about my past and I talk about traveling the countryside, that's my whole life, in my view. Nothing before that counts. I started over, like restarting a video game with a new class and character. Or that was the idea, but now the worst has happened, because at this point, *all you want to know is the bad thing I did.* That's my whole identity, I'm nothing else."

"After that scandal, that's when you dropped out of society and lived in a van?"

"For a while, yeah."

"Because you knew that if you needed to, you could always find some desperate man to take you in. Any time you make a mess of your life, you can find some higher-value male who'll lavish you with gifts and clothes and a home."

"*What?*"

Abbott gripped the steering wheel and immediately thought of all the times he'd noticed his father doing the same, often when Abbott was being driven home from some recent public embarrassment. Those were the times he'd been convinced that, once they arrived home, his father was going to kill him. Not the way other teenagers mean it when they said, "My dad will kill me if he finds out!" but that he would literally, physically kill him.

"Just like me," he said. "So, what, were you one of those influencer girls who'd post a picture of yourself in a bikini, refreshing as the compliments rolled in until, finally, you got a crude message from a guy saying, 'Nice tits,' or something? Then you'd screengrab that and get a whole second outrage post out of it, knowing that was your real goal the whole time? 'I can't even post a photo of myself wearing a swimsuit without these sexist comments!' Yeah, as if you're totally unaware that a bikini is sexualized, as if you've never seen a porn video or billboard in your life. All so you can simultaneously claim the power that comes with objectifying your own body while also claiming victimhood over the objectification. God, what a grift."

"Abbott, what are you talking about? What—what's just happened here? You just invented a person to get mad at in your head and then declared me to be that person."

Abbott scoffed. "Do you think, for one second, I would have agreed to take you on this trip if, instead of being a young woman with symmetrical facial features, you'd been a hairy, middle-aged fat guy? Do you have any concept of how often that happens in your life? Men doing you favors, not because they expect sex—you know I don't—but because of the male instinct to protect and assist? That's an instinct that's basically never rewarded, so the benefits just always flow one direction. Now I'm wondering if I'm even the first man to have thrown his entire life away on your behalf."

"Abbott. You're scaring me."

"And there it is. You're so fragile, aren't you? Are you going to cry next, weaponize that fragility? If we get stopped by the cops, are you going to run out and say, 'It was all him! He made me do it, I'm just an innocent little girl!'"

"*What?*"

"See, I've also had internet mobs after me. I'm not as famous as you apparently were—we'd have to switch bodies for that to happen—but most people who know me, only know me for the controversy."

"Okay. Then we have something in common."

"No, we don't. Because I'll happily tell you what I got in trouble for. All I did was dare to say what every man secretly thinks."

KEY

The attached two-car garage had been converted into a workshop that looked ransacked, though Key suspected this was just how Phil Greene had kept it. She amused herself by imagining a white outline of a corpse on the floor (a practice that occurs only in movies—why would you contaminate a crime scene by taping an outline around the body?), but not even a bloodstain remained. There was a ladder leaning against a wall, which, like the other exterior walls, was coated in foil and wire, along with the dangling little emblems. Scattered around her were metalworking tools, blowtorches, arc welders, and shelves piled high with scraps of wire and other junk with no discernable system of organization.

"I assume you know," said Patrick, "that no explosives were found on the property. You'll also find no chemistry equipment or chemical containers. Nowhere on the grounds do you see the telltale craters of an aspiring anarchist testing their explosive mix on a small scale before making the main batch."

"But you'd also have none of that if they'd acquired actual ready-made explosives," said Key. "Which, as you know, is my exact theory. Remember the fifty-five pounds of stolen Semtex? And all of the other components might be elsewhere, in the form of a finished bomb inside a large, black box that's now over a thousand miles away. Otherwise, look around. The scenario presents itself: The young woman shows up—maybe she's a foreign agent, maybe she's just mad at the world. She scouts out this grieving old man who's got some technical training, somebody with lots of privacy, spare time, and a spacious garage. She convinces him that they're going to take down the evil elites who are ruining society. Phil brings in another like-minded ally in the form of his daughter's old biker friend. When it came time to deploy, they had a falling-out, perhaps a disagreement over choice of target, or maybe they argued about which direction to hang the toilet paper, who knows? Now Greene is dead—I'm not going to argue with you about how—and the device is headed east with the biker in pursuit. If he catches them, that would be bad news because that could result in a conflict that ends with them detonating the bomb early."

"But if they make it to DC, then . . . ?"

"They probably meet with the rest of the cell, who are currently waiting to execute the final plan on Monday."

"Wait, when did we decide there was a 'rest of the cell'?"

"Well, *somebody's* sending correspondence from DC."

Key was examining a rolling tool chest, the one that Patrick claimed had cracked Phil Greene's cranium on his way down (she imagined the inked-up goon grabbing Phil's skull and, in a fit of rage, slamming it into the sharp corner of the chest). The drawers contained nothing beyond the tools one would expect to find, arranged as if they'd each been angrily thrown into a drawer from across the room. But then she noticed one of the chest's wheels was missing and that the corner was held up by a stack of books. Oddly, it was three copies of the same title—that autobiography of the old motorcycle guy that she'd seen in the master bedroom nightstand.

"Help me with this."

Patrick lifted the tool chest while Key extracted one of the books. The subject, according to the cover, was named Gary Sokolov, and he seemed to be marketing himself as a finance guru. She opened it to find it was signed by the author. According to the blurb, Sokolov was an ex-member of a motorcycle gang who found extreme wealth and was eager to share his can't-miss moneymaking method with the world. She checked the About the Author blurb, which said that Mr. Sokolov was currently living happily in McLean, Virginia.

Key stared and said, "Huh." She held up the book to Patrick. "This guy used to be a biker. What do you wanna bet he used to run with Malort Little?"

"He went from running meth to becoming a get-rich-quick finance guru? Sad to see someone fall off like that."

"Just, as a hypothetical, why would a guy like this want to blow up Washington, DC?"

"If I were to tell you that your ratio of evidence to wishful thinking is roughly the same as you'd find in a bottle of a homeopathic aphrodisiac, would that be an example of mansplaining or gaslighting? I'm trying to be something other than a boorish obstacle in your journey while also not following you off a cliff."

"Patrick. *You broke into a crime scene with me.* You're just trying to make sure there's something to this before I make a life-altering mistake. I understand that you're coming from a place of love. And, hell, for all we know, right now the couple is being pulled over by highway patrol, and they'll find the mysterious box contains nothing but whatever you think it does. The girl's tuba, the old man's vintage porn collection, whatever you said before. Maybe it's a hundred more copies of this shady idiot's book."

"Let's say that's the case. And then what?"

"What do you mean?"

"Do you have anything going on in your life? Other than this?"

Rather than dignify that with a response, she stood and stuffed the book into her bag. "I assume JTTF has gotten the word out that if high-way patrol pulls over this vehicle, they are *not* to attempt to crack open the box and search it? I would like to think this goes without saying, but it would be trivial to rig it so that opening the lid detonates the bomb. It could be done with a piece of string looped around a switch."

"That sounds a lot like an accident waiting to happen. A pothole could trigger it."

"Yep. And now you understand why approximately half of my fear about this situation isn't the device making it to the capital but going off on accident in some random, densely populated spot along the way. I've dealt with a lot of domestic terrorists in my time, and not a single one of them was smart."

12

ABBOTT

Endless highway scrolled under the dashboard. Around them was a lifeless expanse of grass and shrubs and power lines, the same nothing for mile after mile. Abbott had left an empty life and entered a void.

"You're not going to want to hear this," Ether began, cautiously. "But I think some of what you're feeling right now is just sleep deprivation. It makes anxiety worse, and in people like us, that makes the catastrophizing worse. And when you get scared, you get angry. It's not just you, either—as a country, we're in a national sleep deprivation crisis, blue light from our phones ruining our natural cycles. We're a whole society of tired, cranky, anxious people. No wonder we all think the world is ending."

"We think the world is ending because the world is ending," snapped Abbott. "And every time I turn on a screen, there's somebody who looks like you blaming it on men, on the patriarchy, how everything would be fine if we let women take over. Do you know why men get violent, and take stupid risks, and drive fast? Like, why they do that more than women, from the time we're babies?"

"Testosterone?"

"No. The testosterone makes us want to impress girls. See, I went to high school in the real world, not in some Disney Channel show, and in the real world, the bullies had girls lining up to fuck them. The nerds stayed lonely. The bullies were bullies because the girls told them they would award bullying with sex—that was their entire motivation. Which means ninety-nine percent of the 'toxic' masculine behaviors the feminists like to bitch about are enforced by women. Who do you think we're trying to impress with our muscle cars and big trucks and assault rifles and wars? What do you think is driving the rampant consumerism that's destroying the planet? Not men—we're happy with a mattress on the floor and a big TV. We buy giant houses and furniture and conflict diamonds because our wives demand it."

"That sounds a lot like a speech you memorized for a streaming audience, possibly after hearing it from some other guy on his own stream. Is saying that what got you in trouble?"

"I got in trouble because women have the power to get men in trouble anytime they want. You can shit on white men all day long, and even other men will go along with it because it gets them laid. But the moment somebody points out the truth—that women are the nastiest bullies on earth—the harpies swoop in and, in the process, immediately prove us right."

It took Ether a moment to respond to this, and Abbott found himself savoring the pause. Like he was making her work for it.

"It sounds like you've had some horrible experiences with specific women," she began, "or groups of women, and I will never tell you that it didn't happen, or that you imagined it, or that they were right. Okay? But the two of us, as individuals, in this car, *were doing fine.* We've gone through danger together, we've trusted each other, we've cooperated on a common cause. But you just talked yourself into a seething rage because you've abruptly decided we're on opposite sides of some culture war. You and I aren't at war! We want the same thing, to get this stupid box to its destination."

"Bullshit! Bullshit. You, as a female, are limited in how far you can fall. Whatever repercussions could come from this—legal, financial—only one of us is at risk. More than ninety percent of prisoners are men, seventy percent of the homeless. You can do shit like this and take these stupid risks because you know you'll always be taken care of if it goes wrong. We may be on the same burning plane, but only one of us has a parachute."

Ether went silent, and Abbott sat there, staring forward, gripping the steering wheel, coiled and ready to pounce on whatever rebuttal came out of her mouth. He'd heard it all.

"You've been bullied your whole life," she said softly. "I'd know that even if you hadn't told me. Now imagine being a woman and knowing that almost every man, everywhere, in every situation, can physically overpower you. You have all of these stats that you heard in some video or other, but you also have to know that women get beaten and raped and murdered by men far, far more than the other way around—"

"See?!? This, what you're doing, this is a perfect demonstration of what I'm talking about. No matter what I say, you'll just come back and say women have it worse, and that's the male experience in a nutshell. When *you* complain, people actually give a shit. When I complain, people laugh, tell me about my 'privilege.' We talked about suicide earlier, about Americans blowing their heads off by the thousands. What you forgot to mention is that *eighty percent of those suicides are men.* Because nobody listens. We're on our own."

"Is that all you want from me, right now? To listen? Because we have hours of road in front of us. I'm not going anywhere. Tell me what you have to say. I won't rebut, I won't accuse."

"Just forget it. Just—just let me drive."

I work for the FBI, we have just been issued a memo about the Abbott/GSG terror plot, ask me anything

Posted to r/DCTerrorAttack by FedThrowaway66974
A week ago, my agency intercepted communication between terror cells about a planned multistage "hybrid" attack that would involve a large vehicle, either a van or an SUV. It would play out as follows:

1. The perpetrators would first perform a vehicle attack (ramming) on a crowd, possibly a parade, to create mass casualties. That would be the first stage.

2. When first responders and bystanders flood in to tend to the wounded, a bomb stored in a large, portable container (like a munitions crate) would explode inside the vehicle, dealing shrapnel damage to all of the police, medics, and bystanders—that would be the second stage.

C) What would not be known at the time is that the bomb would be a "dirty bomb," meaning the shrapnel would be radioactive. This would irradiate the next wave of responders and bystanders, as well as emergency room staff in the surrounding hospitals. Once discovered, this would totally paralyze those facilities, which would have to be closed and scrubbed. The resulting chaos would act as the third stage.

D) The final stage would involve the release of a false flag manifesto claiming responsibility. This would, in reality, be an act of psychological warfare to sow discord in the aftermath. Our intel says the Russians have been working on this at least since 2014, with the goal of creating the perfect trigger to exploit existing fissures in our society. They have apparently been testing it in various corners of the internet and measuring engagement, gauging which subject creates the most visceral and divisive reaction among the main ideological factions of the American populace. Their goal is to get half of the country sounding like they're defending the attack, triggering irreconcilable outrage from the other half.

The exact details of the targets and the manifesto are currently the most sought-after pieces of information in the intelligence community. What we are looking at here is nothing less than a psychological weapon of mass destruction.

The box may contain the corpse of Haley Swanson, a classmate of Abbott's

Posted to r/DCTerrorAttack by TrueCrimeTrudy

Haley Swanson graduated with Abbott Coburn at a high school in Tallahassee, Florida, and has been missing for two-and-a-half years. Abbott was known to be in Tallahassee around the time she vanished (visiting his grandparents for the holidays). My sources say that authorities now believe that the footlocker or steamer trunk in Abbott's Navigator contains Swanson's remains.

Abbott, a misogynist "incel," is believed to have abducted Haley, taken her back to his home in Victorville, California, and imprisoned her there as a sex slave. At some point, she was killed either by accident or on purpose, and Abbott enlisted the woman we know as "GSG" as an accomplice to help him transport the body to some remote location out of state for disposal, so that it would not be discovered near his home.

The "Russian terrorist attack" narrative was ginned up by Abbott's incel Twitch fans as a distraction to misdirect authorities and focus the blame on GSG. I would urge those in this sub not to fall for it.

[Photo] *GSG SPOTTED AT A GAS STATION IN LUBBOCK*

Posted to r/DCTerrorAttack by AppaloosaQueen
My friend is in a private horse owner's group on Facebook, one of the members just posted a selfie with GSG (the Navigator is visible in the background). See attached screenshot, the caption says, "Got to take a pic with one of my heroes today!" These sick fucks are rooting for this to happen. Half of this country is exactly like her. They just want death, to see the world destroyed at any cost.

This also means that, by now, the couple are halfway to the target, and no one has even come close to stopping them. Over one thousand miles traveled with a literal nuclear bomb in an armored munitions crate in a huge, easily spotted vehicle, and no one has pulled them over? You cannot convince me that the cops and feds don't want this to happen, to have the excuse to declare the martial law that they so desperately crave. And you have people like this bitch here praying for it, so they can finally have a boot to lick.

THE NAVIGATOR THAT ATTACKED THE ROSWELL EVENT IS CARRYING AN EXTRATERRESTRIAL CORPSE

Posted to r/DCTerrorAttack by CaptainCommunion

The "attack" on the Roswell marathon was a distraction, as is the supposed terror plot that has been planted here by the feds (remember A LITERAL FEDERAL AGENT WAS POSTING ON THE OTHER SUB SUPPORTING THAT NARRATIVE). We've seen this all play out before—remember how the Roswell crash was written off in the aftermath as a "nuclear radiation test"?

My sources are telling me that Abbott and GSG were in Roswell to meet with the head of MUFON Nevada in order to verify the contents of the box, which is actually an armored freezer case that contains the preserved body of an Extraterrestrial Biological Entity (EBE) that had previously been housed in a private underground compound in Southern California for the last thirty years. The EBE has not decomposed or decayed in any way. It is unknown if it is dead, in suspended animation, or is some kind of remotely operated automaton that has simply been disconnected from its operator. The EBE is highly radioactive.

The terror attack cover story is being spread to justify the vehicle and box being stopped and destroyed by the authorities at the first opportunity. Abbott and GSG (the latter believed to be a friend or family member of the man who has been hiding the EBE since the mid-'90s) are driving the container to Washington, where they intend to place it on the front lawn of the White House and demand answers in front of the world on the morning of the Fourth of July.

To be clear: all federal law enforcement agencies have been given a directive to NOT allow this vehicle, or that container, anywhere near the capital and to stop it by any means necessary. I think it's interesting how many of the people in this sub seem happy to help them suppress the truth.

KEY

After spending a couple of hours getting her new printer working, Key added Sokolov's picture to her corkboard, along with three interviews she'd found in which he got into his politics in some detail. What she had discovered was that Gary Sokolov was an almost embarrassingly boring man. That, of course, didn't eliminate him as a suspect—most of history's atrocities were committed by embarrassingly boring men. She'd then frantically mapped out the next possible steps in her investigation, which turned out to be eating an ice cream sandwich, masturbating, and then falling asleep. Now her phone was ringing, and she was scrambling to remember where she was, or what she was doing, or what phones were for.

It was Patrick. She answered with, "Do we have news?"

"Is it news that Sokolov in no way fits the profile of a domestic terrorist, has no known ties with any extremist groups, and, as far as we know, doesn't even cheat on his taxes? His rap sheet is exactly as described in his book: he ran methamphetamine precursors with a biker gang, trafficked in stolen car parts, and at one point owned a sleazy strip club."

"Well," said Key, while looking around for her pants, "it sounds to me like he perfectly fits the profile of an aggrieved narcissist."

In sci-fi and fantasy stories, rebellions are usually the oppressed, impoverished underclasses rising up against their wealthy and powerful oppressors. In the real world, it's often those who are the most comfortable in the system who want to bring it down. As such, lots of mass killers are in the category of the aforementioned incel hero Elliot Rodger, who carried out his rampage in a brand-new BMW his mother had gifted him. The deadliest shooting in American history—the 2017 Las Vegas attack that killed sixty and wounded more than *eight hundred*—was carried out by a millionaire who believed he'd been treated poorly by casino staff. The deadliest school massacre in American history wasn't Sandy Hook, it was a bombing in 1927 that leveled a rural Michigan school, killing thirty-eight children and six adults. The culprit was a local farmer, upset that he lost an election for school board treasurer. What they had in common, in Key's view, was aggrieved narcissism, a total inability to put personal affronts into perspective. Why shouldn't others die for your petty humiliations, when you're the Main Character of the Universe?

"And if so," continued Key, "that would mean there'd be nothing on the record to indicate what's coming—this guy's world-ending grievance could be that local TV blacks out his favorite football team. Don't you remember Marvin Heemeyer?"

"I don't think so."

"It doesn't matter. History is full of guys like this, and we now live in a nation of them, tens of millions of aggrieved narcissists, people willing to raze civilization because they feel personally humiliated. That's the tinderbox, the chain reaction waiting to happen."

"Sure. Now, all we need is some kind of tangible evidence—literally *anything*—that any illegal acts have occurred or are imminent."

"I have to go. I have another call coming in."

She fumbled with her phone's confusing call-juggling interface and, when she answered, heard Hunter Coburn say, "I'm not going to let them railroad my son."

She took a moment to gather herself and radically adjust her tone. Only Patrick got her Patrick Voice.

"Nobody is looking to do that, Mr. Coburn." She hoped he couldn't detect the tone of a woman talking and pulling on her underwear at the same time.

"The shit they're saying about him online is insane. So now it's a supposed parade attack, like that thing that happened in Paris, with the ISIS driver? What happened to the bomb? Or are they saying it's also a bomb?"

"It's all speculation."

"I called my attorney. He said I should contact the police."

"They still haven't reached out to you?"

"He said I should call them about *you*. He looked you up. You're retired. He said what you're doing is illegal, that you have no authority."

She paused. "Do what you feel is right."

"I mean, I can't lose more work over this. We're already behind. So do I just sit here and wait? He's supposedly heading to DC. Do I fly out and try to talk sense into him when he gets there? How would I even know where to find him?"

"I'm not sure there's anything we can do until we get more information."

"But once we have more information, what do we do? I'm not letting them hang a bunch of terrorism charges on Abbott just because he gave a ride to some crazy bitch. Hell, I wouldn't be surprised if she's a fed. I've been reading about how the FBI handles domestic terrorism. They chat with sad losers online, then the fed says, 'Hey, wouldn't it be cool to blow up the Empire State Building,' and the loser says, 'Yeah,' and then they arrest the loser for planning to blow up the Empire State Building."

"That's not exactly how it works, but it's close enough that I won't argue with you."

"All Abbott did was talk shit on the internet. He's never even raised a fist toward anyone, for any reason. He doesn't own guns. If he goes to prison, he won't last five minutes in there. Do you understand? He's a human balloon; he'll pop the moment he encounters a sharp edge. Even if they just give him six months in a plea deal for transporting contraband or some bullshit, that's a death sentence for him. I won't let them do it."

"If he's truly innocent, then I don't want that, either. But there's video from multiple angles of your Navigator driving through a marathon this morning."

"Driving *slowly* and carefully avoiding runners. If I know Abbott, he just took a wrong turn down the wrong street. It's the kind of thing he does. Constantly. Hell, I don't even think that's his first time driving the wrong way through a marathon. He's definitely a menace to society, but not the kind you're thinking of."

"Well, if you come up with a way to intercept him somewhere between here and DC, I am all ears. But if what's in that box is a bomb that can be detonated by remote—and most devices like this are just triggered by cell phone—then we're talking about a very delicate operation. If the rest of a terror cell is waiting in DC for delivery, the moment they hear the police have pulled over the vehicle, they can speed-dial a number and, well, that would be that. If it's rigged to go off when tampered with, the moment somebody tries to open the box, same thing. Remember, the one outcome these people want to avoid is arrest."

"So *what do we do*?"

"It's the same answer for this or life in general: Watch and learn and hope an opportunity presents itself. And pray that this goddamned thing doesn't go boom in the meantime."

13

ABBOTT

While Abbott was driving and stewing in silence, Ether would occasionally try to break the tension with some idle observation ("Did you know that the western border of Texas is closer to California than it is to the eastern border of Texas?"), and Abbott would just grunt in response. This behavior—gruffly shutting down bids for human connection—was something he vividly remembered hating in his father, and he hated seeing it in himself even more, but found himself doing it all the same. Why did *she* get to move on and be happy? The fires of rage must be kept alight at all cost, and there is no justice until everyone has been sufficiently burned.

And so they drove, at one point stopping in the late afternoon at a gas station that was decorated like a mountain lodge. It had a rusty metal statue of a cowboy out front, and the interior featured a stuffed and mounted buffalo head above the tobacco aisle. Then they were off again, and Abbott could feel the exhaustion hitting him and knew that it wasn't just the drive and rough sleep but the anger, that the hours of stewing had drained him. And for what? What had been gained?

So then there was some more silent driving and, when he could stand it no longer, said, "There was an actress who came out recently, talking about how her previous husband had emotionally abused her. He never hit her, but played mind games, undermined her, humiliated her, made her feel worthless. She said it was just as bad as physical abuse. Maybe worse, because there was technically no crime committed and nothing to report. I personally agree with her."

Ether studied him before replying, "Because that's what you've gone through with your parents?"

"I'm saying that we agree that emotional abuse can be worse, right?"

Ether shrugged. "Of course."

"But if so, that means women are actually *more* capable of domestic abuse than men, since women tend to have higher emotional intelligence, more knowledge about how to manipulate. So let's say a woman emotionally abuses a man for years, humiliates him, torments him, destroys his self-worth and peace of mind. Then, finally, he strikes back physically, once. Which one goes to jail? Which one loses their job, their friends? Which one *doesn't* have a shelter waiting for them?"

"And that's something that's happened to you? Someone accused you?"

"No, but it could happen at any time."

"So it's something you heard about in a video. The guy who told you that, did he sell branded merch?"

"I'm saying we're in a world where physical confrontation is off-limits, so everything happens in words and texts, where women have all the power. Then they portray men as violent monsters. 'We women always learn to laugh at a guy's jokes, or else he'll murder us!' It's the same weapon society uses against every marginalized group, painting them as inhuman savages."

"You honestly feel like you've been marginalized?"

"It's not a feeling. Nobody cares about us. If a woman is insulted or humiliated, she gets to call it trauma. Everyone treats it like a crime. But if a man is humiliated, if he's turned down by a woman in front of everyone, he's expected to shake it off. 'It's not like you were beaten up or killed.' Well, make up your minds—is emotional damage a real thing, or isn't it? Because right now, the rule is that it's as real as physical damage—*but only if it happens to a woman.*"

"I promised to listen without rebutting or disagreeing, but from my point of view, you're painting me and all women as sly, evil schemers, when the reality is that we spend every second of our lives tearing ourselves apart with insecurity. And, yeah, even before I'd bought my first bra, I was taught that the wrong encounter with an angry man could get me killed. Not that I had to be told—I think every girl remembers the first time she was wrestling with a boy, just playing, and suddenly realized how *incredibly* strong he was in comparison, that almost every man is stronger than almost every woman—that bell curve barely overlaps. So from then on, yeah, we live our lives in fear of making a man angry, and yes, we develop tools to keep it at bay. You can call it manipulation, but, Abbott, *so much* of it is just self-preservation."

For the second time in two days, Abbott felt rage slipping through his fingers and sensed himself scrambling to hang on, like it was a precious thing. Like he'd be letting the universe get away with something if he allowed himself peace.

"You still don't understand," he said, trying to regain his footing. "If women everywhere, through history, said that there's a certain thing that men do that causes them anxiety, then it would be reasonable for men to adjust. And we do—I don't make creepy comments about women's bodies or what they're wearing."

"Sure. And it's good that you don't do that."

"Okay. Well, when women dress in revealing clothing, it causes men anxiety. It's a form of sexual harassment. But if I dare say that, or ask for any accommodation, I'm an evil oppressor."

She clearly seemed taken aback by this. "Well . . . I'm sure that's true to an extent, but in any kind of a sane world, women should be able to express themselves with—"

"No, see, there you go again with the double standard, saying that women should get to wear whatever they want in the name of self-expression. That's no different than saying men should be able to say whatever *they* want about those women, and their bodies, in the name of self-expression. Either we all have to tiptoe around each other's anxiety, or none of us do."

"But you know that this has happened, almost everywhere, in almost all places, right? What women wear gets heavily policed. Like, by the actual police."

"Yes, and for a reason. A man's sex drive is savage, it's like a drug addiction times ten. But today, in our society, when men say, 'Cover yourselves, it's causing us distress because we have this biological imperative we can't control,' we're called monsters for having this impulse that none of us asked for. There's no cooperation, no attempt to accommodate, no solidarity, like, 'Yeah, we should all work together to help you control this.' Instead it's, 'We should be allowed to expose as much of our bodies as we want!' But, of course, if a man were to expose his penis near a woman, that's a crime—it's not self-expression when *we* do it."

Abbott was once again pleased that Ether seemed to need a moment to gather herself after this. He was causing this woman anxiety, which meant he was winning. Or something.

Finally, she said, "I do hear what you're saying. I do. And I do think it's good that we can talk about it, the two of us. Even if I disagree, it's good that you feel like you can be honest. I acknowledge that this is your lived experience."

"Jesus Christ, what is that, from a psychology textbook?"

"I'm saying, if I listen to you, *honestly listen,* without judgment, can you do the same for me? Because my experience is that fear of assault hangs over every interaction with a man; it's not a scheme that all of us women concocted to screw you over. We're all just stumbling around in the dark, scared."

Abbott scoffed and shook his head. They went under an overpass, and he briefly imagined himself flooring the Navigator into the embankment.

"The clip that got me in trouble," he said, "the one that caused me to get hundreds of death threats from internet feminists, was me saying that I'd rather be raped than be falsely accused of rape. If you get attacked, the world rushes to your aid. If I get accused, even if I'm innocent, I lose my job, my friends, my reputation, everything I have and ever will have, forever. The rape lasts a few minutes, the hell of false accusation lasts forever. Even my obituary would lead with it. I said it then, and I'll say it again: I'd rather be raped fifty times than be falsely accused once. And so would anyone else. So, no, you don't get to throw down your collective rape phobia as a trump card."

That brought silence, and Abbott sensed that Ether was letting it hang in the air. Fine.

"I feel like," she said finally, "you quickly tried to search your brain for an opinion I couldn't possibly agree with or find common ground on. I think instead of communicating, you're trying to shape your words into weapons to deal maximum damage to your 'enemy,' which you have now decided is me. And I would only ask: Is this making you happy? I mean, look at us right now—do you really want to do the next thirteen hundred miles like this, both of us sick with tension?"

"I don't know. Forget it. I'm too tired to keep going back and forth with you."

"Listen: I fully believe that I would think the way you do, if I had lived the life you've lived and consumed the media you've consumed. But I have this theory, that everything that happens on our screens is designed to do exactly what's happening here, to repel us from one another, to create a war of all against all. It's like a filter that only shows you others' bad behavior, blocking the pure and letting through the poison, to make you scared of everyone who isn't exactly identical to you. I think that, long-term, it traps your brain in a prison, that it's designed to keep you inside, alone, with only those screens for comfort. A friend of mine came up with a name for it, for these algorithms, this media mind prison. We call it the *black box of doom*."

I AM FOLLOWING THE NAVIGATOR RIGHT NOW

Posted to r/DCTerrorAttack by CactusDad1999

I've only ever posted on the houseplants sub, but I just happened to stumble across this because a friend told me about it. I am on a drive back to Tulsa from Lubbock and she told me to keep an eye out for the Navigator and showed me this sub. I've been checking at every rest stop and drive-thru, and I JUST FOUND THEM PULLING OUT OF A GAS STATION IN BENJAMIN, TX. We're on 82 and I think they're heading to Little Rock, I'm hanging back as not to be spotted, but I'm trying to stay close enough to see if/when they exit. What should I do?!?

────────────────────────────────────── Comments:

Punisher09: Do you know how to do a Pit Maneuver? You can run them off the road.

JKey: DO NOT DO THAT, that could trigger the device. There's a good chance it's rigged to detonate if the lid is opened, a vehicle impact could doom you and everyone in the vicinity.

ShellyIsWright: There is no device, it's a corpse.

Punisher09: Even if the wreck didn't trigger it, Abbott or GSG could do it. They won't be taken alive. Whatever you're going to do, you can't let them get to a population center. Do you have a gun in the car?

CactusDad1999: No!!!

NotBusey: Punisher how are you not in jail?

ABBOTT

At some point, they passed out of Texas and into Arkansas, passing through the border town Texarkana (at one point seeing a sign for Red Lick, which Abbott decided was the most obscene town name he'd ever heard). Then the sun went down, and Abbott's fatigue turned his mind and body into a lumpy, toxic sludge. Finally, he'd pulled over and begged Ether to take over driving, saying it was either that or wait for him to nod off and kill them both in a head-on collision. So as their headlights led them toward Little Rock, it was Ether behind the wheel, Abbott trying to squirm around and get comfortable in the passenger seat. Then he'd glimpsed the dried blood under him and started to get distressed all over again.

Ether glanced at him with an expression like she was about to try to pick up a rattlesnake by the tail.

"I've never met your dad," she began warily, "so all I have to go on is what you've said about him. But—and you don't have to reply to this, or rebut it, or agree or disagree, I'm just throwing this out there—I think if he knew how that blood got on the seats, that you saw a woman being attacked and intervened, that you stood up to a dangerous man, that the blood was her blood . . . I think he'd be proud of you. I think it'd be the proudest of you he's ever been."

"He'd never believe me. He'd assume I'd cut myself trying to open a foil pudding cup lid. He'll react to these stains like I'd desecrated his mother's grave and killed his dog on the way there. Unless you came with me and told him the whole story, I guess."

"Think about what you're saying, though, that he wouldn't believe you, because *it's too heroic.* You beat your father's expectations! Already, after just a couple of days out of the nest! I mean, I'm not telling you how to feel, but you should feel good about that."

"Hmm."

She glanced into the rearview mirror and said, "Wasn't that car behind us before?"

Abbott checked. It was a little Fiat 500 or some equally tiny car that looked like something the Navigator would shit.

"Maybe. Slow down."

She did, and the vehicle drew closer. Abbott couldn't perfectly see the driver, but the Tattoo Monster made for a distinct silhouette, and this wasn't him. This guy was slim, with cornrows. In the passenger seat was something that looked like leaves, like the guy had a potted plant strapped in with the seat belt.

"It's nobody."

"Okay," said Ether, "but I noticed them a while back, and when we pulled over so I could drive, they passed us. But now here they are, like maybe they intentionally got behind us again."

"Maybe one of your fans? You think they know this vehicle now?"

"I don't know."

"Is there somewhere we can exit, see if they follow? Though I'm not sure what we'd do after that. It's not like we can push a button and make the Navigator drop spikes to blow their tires."

"He's passing us," said Ether, who glanced over as the miniature car drew alongside them. "Just a guy taking his plant for a ride."

Abbott yawned. "Do you know the name of this color, of the outside of this car? You know they can't just say *white.* It has to have some other nonsense word attached to it. It's *Pristine White.* Other people, they would want a color that would hide the flaws. My dad wanted one that would show them off, like if I ever got a scratch on the bumper or a chip from taking it on gravel, he wanted it displayed to the world. One more thing in his life that had been 'pristine' until I came along."

"I feel like that kind of obsession with neatness is just one more way to deal with anxiety. If you feel like you have no control over the world, then you tend to obsessively control the things you—"

There was a jolt and the vehicle lurched sideways.

"HE JUST HIT US!" shouted Ether, just as the Fiat swerved and hit them again. She ran off onto the shoulder and wrestled the Navigator back into the lane. "What is happening?!? Is he doing it on purpose?"

"Get away from him!"

She stepped on the gas and left the little asshole car behind, for a moment. Then they heard its engine whining up alongside them, the Fiat pulling even and then ahead. They were heading toward a bottleneck, a tiny bridge over a creek, two narrow lanes protected by guardrails—there'd be no shoulder to swerve onto.

"WHAT DO I DO? WHAT DO I DO?"

Ether was in an absolute panic, and Abbott was getting there. Was this just how people drove in Arkansas?

Ahead of them, the Fiat reached the narrow bridge and then simultaneously swerved and braked in front of them as if attempting to force them to stop. If so, the driver had badly misunderstood the physics at play: The Navigator was triple the mass of their petite Fiat, and Ether had no time to brake. The Navigator slammed into its passenger door at a forty-five-degree angle, impacting with enough force to send the little car up and over the guardrail, splashing upside down in the creek below.

Ether skidded them to a stop, gasping, her knuckles white on the steering wheel. The dainty little Fiat had vanished from view, but the Navigator had been so unperturbed by the collision that it hadn't even triggered the airbags. Abbott could see the little car's exposed belly just above the surface of the water below, which was definitely deep enough for its driver to drown in. Instantly, he felt an acidic ooze of spiteful glee. It served them right. What was happening to them now, they'd done to themselves.

But then Ether was jumping out and running around the guardrail to the weedy bank of the creek. And that was stupid. This idiot had just tried to crash them; this was their problem and their problem alone. And while Abbott was saying this to himself, he also was jumping out, then sloshing through the surprisingly frigid water. The Fiat's headlights were still on under the surface. A single tire was still spinning. He thought he could see the driver inside, dazed, feeling clumsily around with their hands and trying to figure out why the world had suddenly flipped on its head.

Abbott waded closer, feeling his feet getting stuck in muck and weeds and waterlogged trash. He reached the driver's-side door and found it locked. A panic was rising inside him that had claimed his chest and would soon swamp his brain.

"Hey!" he yelled to the dazed man dangling upside down from his seat belt. "Unlock the door!"

The guy didn't even look that direction. Water was spilling into the interior, and he just hung there like he thought if he just waited out this nightmare, he'd wake up safe in bed. Abbott turned to yell for Ether to get something to break the glass, but she'd already gone to do that and was now on her way back, hurrying down the weedy bank. The tool she'd grabbed was Abbott's father's gun.

She sloshed her way up to the car, gave the upside-down man a warning to protect his face that he neither heard nor obeyed. Then she held the gun underwater, pressing it against the glass at an angle. Abbott didn't even know if you could fire a gun underwater until she did exactly that. The glass exploded, and bubbles flooded out as water rushed in to replace the air.

"Open it!" she yelled. "Reach in!"

Abbott crouched into the water, inches from an actively drowning man, then reached up until he found the interior door handle. He unlatched it, and it took both of them to drag it open. Then Ether ducked in and sliced the seat belt with her Constitution knife.

The man rolled free and crawled out, thrashing his way through the water, sputtering, grunting. He got upright, stumbled over to the muddy bank, and collapsed. He'd apparently cut his head; watery blood was draped down the right half of his face, reddening his white shirt.

He sputtered, "Get the cactus! Please! From the other side!"

Ether said, "Just catch your breath. We'll get something for your head. You're bleeding."

"The cactus! It's over a hundred years old! Please! It's in the passenger seat! It belonged to my grandmother!"

This very much sounded to Abbott like the ravings of a man whose brain had just gotten bounced around his skull.

Then he turned to Abbott, looked him right in the eyes, and said, "Abbott, please. It's all I have of hers."

Abbott was now so thoroughly confused that he complied mainly because he was kind of afraid not to. He trudged over, mud sucking at his feet, and found the potted plant lying across the interior dome light, which stubbornly remained lit under four feet of water. Abbott dragged out the plant, its thick spiky leaves scratching him as if it resented being saved. He brought it over to the man, who clutched the pot to his belly.

"How do you know me? Do you watch my streams?"

The man wasn't making eye contact with him. He was shivering and blinking as if confused about how he got there.

"Stay here," said the cactus man. "Stay here. I called the police earlier. They know about the box. Stay here or—or I'll . . ." He trailed off, examining his plant for injuries. "Stay here or I'll . . . I have to get this water out. It'll rot the roots. She got this as a gift in 1905. Can you believe that? Frickin' planes weren't invented when this plant was born."

"*What are you talking about?*"

"They know about the box. About the bomb. Or the body. Or the alien. Don't try to run. I have friends in Little Rock. I won't let you destroy it. My cousin lives there. No, that's not right. He moved last year, after he got married."

From behind him, Ether said, "Let's go."

Abbott looked back at her. "But what about—shouldn't we wait?"

He heard distant sirens, and Ether ran up to the Navigator. Abbott followed . . . then he saw the damage to the front end and stopped dead in the street.

The entire beautiful chrome grille had been smashed, one headlight was still on but dangling like an eyeball that had been dug out in a street fight. The entire lower bumper was detached, hanging barely an inch off the ground like a mangled jaw. The hood was battered and sitting askew, like a hat on a shell-shocked infantryman. The sight of it hit Abbott like, well, an SUV slamming into an Italian economy car at highway speeds.

Then Ether was yelling for him, and he headed for the passenger's side, soaked from the chest down, his right foot feeling weird, like his shoe had gotten damaged or something. He then saw that he'd lost that shoe entirely, leaving behind a sock caked with creek slime. He stopped because, well, how could he leave without his shoe? He didn't have another pair. You couldn't just drive around with one semi-bare foot. He looked back toward the creek as if he were going to, what, dive in and try to find it?

Ether shouted at him once more, and he climbed in. She peeled away, driving until she could find a side road to turn off onto, getting off the highway, out of view of the oncoming cops.

"I—I lost my shoe. It's back there in the creek. I didn't pack another pair. I didn't think I'd—"

"We'll get you another shoe."

"Where? How?"

She twisted around in the seat for signs of pursuit and, for the moment, found none. Abbott was shivering all over, soaked to the bone. The feel of his wet foot on the floorboard was weirdly unsettling.

"Lots of places sell shoes, Abbott. That's not our chief concern right now."

They drove on narrow roads in various states of disrepair, taking turns seemingly at random. They passed a grocery store called the Mad Butcher. They passed a sign for the Bada-Bing Grille 2 and, immediately after, the Hindu Temple of Central Arkansas Little Rock. There was a flea market, a psychic, and many churches. They eventually turned off onto a random road and parked out of sight at a low, gray building ominously labeled Jack's Motel. Abbott was shivering uncontrollably, for several different overlapping reasons.

Ether asked, "Are you all right?"

"I think so. Are you?"

"I think so. The car seems to run okay. I only see one warning light; it says a parking sensor is offline."

"The whole front end is smashed."

"It's all plastic up there, cosmetic. It'll get us to DC, unless it has wounds it hasn't told us about yet. I don't think the radiator got punctured."

"I don't—I don't understand what just happened. Who was that? Does the Tattoo Monster have associates? Accomplices? Henchmen? Why did he have a cactus?"

"I don't know."

"Will there be more?"

"I don't know."

14

MALORT

Americans, as Malort liked to say, used to be a wild people. It was a whole country descended from hard-barked frontiersmen and those who'd managed to not get slaughtered by them. The USA had sprouted from soil so saturated with blood that the wells tasted of copper, less a "melting pot" than a meat grinder. It was a land of pissed-off underdogs who couldn't be governed, simple folk who were polite and generous but with no desire to ever again feel a boot on their neck. They knew what freedom really meant, that liberty produces risk and pain the way a motor produces exhaust, that the spirit of America means not just accepting that fact but amplifying it so that it can be heard coming from six blocks away. Or that's how things used to be, anyway.

For example, Malort could remember a time when a man could hitchhike all the way across the country, if he so desired. Not because it was safe but because whoever picked you up understood that the world was dangerous and accepted it as such. Maybe they kept a blackjack under the driver's seat in case the passenger revealed ill intentions. These days, a man who looked like Malort would have to be lottery-lucky to get even one ride; it required coming across the exact right driver in the exact right circumstance heading the exact right direction. But after hours of lingering in a truck stop parking lot like an asshole, Malort had miraculously found one: a dude named Chap who was fresh out of the joint himself. He had ink and dreads and was in a beat-up Kia hauling a trailer piled high with what appeared to be all of his worldly possessions. Malort had asked for a ride in exchange for substances that would help the man stay awake for the trip and likely improve his mood in the process. Chap had told him he'd found all his stuff scattered on his mom's front lawn the day he'd come home, and now he was heading east, planning to surprise his brother in OKC and beg him for work in his landscaping business. Malort had thought this plan didn't sound too promising, but hadn't said as much. They'd spent the day listening to a podcast about serial killer Edmund Kemper, who'd murdered eight women, mostly students he'd picked up as hitchhikers, since that was the sort of thing you could still do in the more authentic world of 1973. Now they were reaching the end of the line, and Chap had offered to let Malort off at a busy gas station, so he could try to hit somebody else up for a ride.

"So Kemper, he turned himself in?" asked Chap, seeming almost offended.

Malort grunted. "Called the cops and said he was the serial murderer they'd been chasing. They hung up on him. Thought it was a prank. He had to call 'em back. That's what you learn, listening to these shows; it's never some hotshot detective profiler who catches these guys. The most prolific killer in American history—that we know about—was named Sam Little. You know how they got him? He was living in a homeless shelter, and some beat cop trying to fill his quota pinched him for old drug warrants. It's just morons all the way down."

OKC was coming into view, a factory outlet mall on one side and an RV park on the other.

"I know you're not eager to share details," said Chap, "but whatever property you're trying to recover, it must be worth a lot. And you've got to know they're not gonna let you keep it if getting it back requires you to take actions that get you locked up again."

"It's not the monetary value, if that helps you understand," replied Malort. "It's more about principle. And at this point, I've risked a lot more than another turn in the joint. I came within millimeters of dying this morning, just hours before we met. I didn't disclose that until now, as I didn't want to alarm you."

"What, you wreck your vehicle? That why you were stranded?"

"Nah. Almost got shot by a pod person."

"Is that right?"

He said it like he had just heard some crazy talk and didn't wish to pursue it out of fear of eliciting more.

"Yeah," elaborated Malort. "Twentysomething kid, one of them you see around these days, the ones that can't look you in the eye, so pale that you'd think they've never left their bedroom, on so many prescriptions that all they can do is shuffle and mumble. This thing, this soulless husk of a pod person, pointed a gun at me and pulled the trigger, no hesitation. Barely missed my skull. I turned and looked at him, and what I saw in his eyes was nothin'. Like he thought this was all playing out in one of his video games, like he was used to a world where nothin' was real. It scared the shit out of me because I thought, *That right there is the future.*"

"This is the guy who stole your property?"

"He helped."

They were coming up on a gas station that Malort agreed looked like as good a place as any to part ways. Some people around, not too many. He slipped his right hand into his jacket pocket.

As they rolled to a stop, Chap said, "Well, it was good talking to you. I hope this thing you're doing comes out all right."

"Let me pay you something."

"Nah, you already have. I'd have conked out behind the wheel if I hadn't had you along. I've built up three years of sleep deprivation. Worst part about being inside, there's not a good night's sleep to be had, no matter what you do. Never dark enough, never quiet enough, never cool enough, bed is like sleeping on a bag of doorknobs. And if you're not sleeping right, nothin' else about you is healthy."

Malort's hand remained in his pocket. At the nearest pump was a yellow van that said *Jay's Bouquets* on the side.

Malort nodded toward it and said, "I used to do that, deliver flowers. For a whole summer out of high school, before I got all the ink, when my face didn't scare quite so many people. Best job I ever had. I'd do deliveries at nursing homes on Mother's Day; those old women acted like they'd won the lottery. Their eyes would light up when they saw me coming. Every day, I was seein' people on their happiest day of the year."

"They've got a DRIVERS NEEDED sign taped to the back," said Chap. "Starts at fifteen bucks an hour. You could walk over there right now, button up your collar and roll down your sleeves to cover the ink, tell 'em you've got experience and that you can start Monday. There's nothin' stopping you. That's the only thing I learned on the inside. The world lies to you and says change is hard. It ain't. You can walk out and do it anytime. Just be somebody else."

Malort stared at the flower van. Thinking. "Hmm."

"It's true. And I'll tell you something else, the only thing I learned from therapy: People who had rough childhoods, guys like you and me, you grow up scared of being happy. It don't feel right. You find yourself sabotaging it, because you're so scared that you're gonna lose it that you'd rather just trash it yourself, so at least you can say it was your choice. So, you go hunting for grievances, to give yourself an excuse."

Malort looked toward the store and saw the guy who was probably the flower van driver up at the counter. He closed his fist around the contents of his pocket, then pulled out a wad of twenty-dollar bills. He stuffed them under the visor above the passenger seat, ignoring Chap's polite objections. He had strong suspicions that this guy was gonna need to spring for a place to stay after his brother slammed the door in his face. Malort got out and watched the Kia's taillights shrink into the distance.

KEY

"JESUS TITTY-SLAPPING CHRIST!"

Key had shouted that loud enough that she was pretty sure several neighbors had heard. She was on a floaty in her apartment complex pool, which now featured two printers at the bottom. She was paddling her way toward the edge, adrenaline blasting through her system.

She now knew the intended target of the dirty bomb attack, and the implications were too big for her soggy brain. She was trying to force herself to think through the unthinkable and was fairly certain she was about to jettison the grocery store sushi she'd eaten for dinner.

Key had spent the previous few hours speed-reading through the book she'd confiscated/stolen from the Phil Greene property, Gary Sokolov's self-serving autobiography and business advice book *Life Is Not a Highway*. Sokolov (or, more likely, his ghostwriter) portrayed him as a lifelong misfit and outcast, born in Canada and raised among bikers in Montreal.

He fled to the USA in the '90s after a series of brutal turf wars claimed the lives of everyone he knew. He had since gained nine-figure wealth by—according to him—acquiring from the streets a deep understanding of the rules of human conflict, then applying those rules to financial markets. This prompted him to become an early investor in Bitcoin in 2012 (when it was worth basically nothing), and then, using those same magical biker survival instincts, he'd cashed out after the price skyrocketed but before it crashed back to earth.

As for his politics, he was an extreme Libertarian in the way that both bikers and tech guys tended to be, seeing the rules of polite society as a burden that only prevents the strong from separating themselves from the weak and mediocre. Further digging on Key's part revealed that these days, Sokolov seemed to spend his time starting think tanks with other like-minded weirdos and attending fundraisers with power players at all levels of society. And this was the man who had been sending packages (perhaps full of untraceable cash?) to anti-technology insurrectionist Phil Greene, possibly to assist in the creation of whatever was currently on pace to arrive in Washington by Independence Day. So the one thing Key had needed to know was what was this guy doing on the holiday.

Having hit a dead end, she'd again turned to the pack of friendless obsessives on the subreddit. Twenty minutes ago, she'd posted the following from her pool floaty:

Possible connection to wealthy political donor Gary Sokolov?

Posted to r/DCTerrorAttack by JKey

To be clear: I am NOT suggesting Sokolov is involved in any way and, if anything, he could be a possible target of the attack. It is believed that at least one of the conspirators corresponded with Sokolov, and he is known to live in the DC area. Do we know where he will be on the Fourth? That event could easily be the target of the attack and the destination of the Navigator/device.

Comments:

BOFADeez: Isn't that the biker guy?

Punisher09: Sounds Russian.

MarvinHKing: He's a scumbag who scammed his way into riches. You'll be hearing more about him very soon, I promise.

DarthPenis: This is the glowie, by the way. Anything she says or asks is just letting you know what the feds want you to think.

And that had been it, as far as replies. Interactions on r/DCTerrorAttack were becoming less and less fruitful as its population grew; they were now forty hours into the crisis, and news of it had spread well into the sphere of casual observers, though still with little in the way of mainstream press coverage. The sub was now the home of a core group of posters and a sprawling audience of spectators whose demands for compelling news were growing faster than it could be produced. Attention-seekers were eagerly filling the void, and that, friends, is how you build a bullshit machine.

Out of curiosity, she'd then gone back to the sparsely populated original subreddit, r/AbaddonsNavigator, and posted the exact same question. It had taken roughly eight and a half minutes for the moderator, ZekeArt, to reply, "Is this it?" followed by a link to some DC insider's blog. Key had read the post, read it again, tried to steady her breathing, then read it one more time.

On Monday, Gary Sokolov would be hosting an all-day gathering at his estate in McLean, Virginia. Festivities would kick off at eight in the morning with a concert from a children's choir singing patriotic songs, followed by a brunch, then a "daytime fireworks display." In attendance would be other wealthy donors, CEOs, a few members of Congress, and *three members of the goddamned motherfucking Supreme Court of the United States.*

That is what had sent Key thrashing out of the pool and sprinting up to her apartment. As domestic terror targets go, there were none better, if your goal was to assure and accelerate the decline of the American empire. Members of the Supreme Court are not elected and have no term limits. There is no real mechanism for removing them from office, and their decisions are all but impossible to overturn. They are the closest the USA has to royalty. There is, therefore, no equivalent assassination target in the US government.

If a president is taken out, they are immediately replaced by a vice president of the same ideology to serve out the term—it's barely worth doing. But if these justices were killed, the current president and Senate would replace them with members aligned with the opposing party . . . and those replacements would have lifetime appointments. So this attack would fundamentally change the balance of power in a way *that could only be reversed with another attack on the opposing members of the court.* A line would have been crossed in a way that would all but guarantee it would be crossed again and again. It would be the lighting of a fuse. As such, security at the event would be a small army, but what good would that do if the host of the get-together was himself in on the plot? The Navigator was on pace to have the device at the location several hours in advance. Sokolov, and whoever else was in on it, would have plenty of time to conceal the bomb in an environment Sokolov controlled, at an event he'd planned from scratch.

Key started to dial Patrick, then stopped herself. What would be the outcome of such a call? Was her goal to get them to cancel the event? Arrest Sokolov? For what, the crime of having at some point mailed packages to a SoCal wing nut with no criminal record? Sokolov was a politically connected tycoon, had so far left no direct evidence of his involvement, and at this moment wasn't even in possession of the device. No one on earth was in position to stop this guy.

No one but Joan Key.

She dropped her phone and ran to her toilet, making it just in time.

15

ABBOTT

They found a Walmart somewhere in the wastelands of Arkansas just twenty minutes before closing time. Abbott and Ether split up, she to the pharmaceuticals and Abbott to the footwear. Or at least, that's what he allowed her to believe—instead, he veered off and did what he should have done right after they'd hit the road: He bought a hundred-dollar prepaid smartphone (no subscription or credit card required) and a fifty-dollar usage card.

He then headed out to the Navigator and stuffed it into his bag. He knew Ether wouldn't approve, but as far as he knew, not even the NSA could instantly connect a prepaid phone to a particular user who'd paid cash. He went back in, found some terrible but wearable shoes, and felt the harsh, silent judgment of the cashier at the sight of a visibly one-shoed man buying cheap sneakers minutes before closing time—the ultimate sign of an individual whose life has gone off the rails. Ether had bought bathing supplies as well as first aid for the various damage they'd accrued since waking up in Roswell. She also found a new baseball cap—a white one that said VACAY MODE! in an abrasively enthusiastic font.

An employee locked the doors behind them as they slipped out, and they next headed to a rest area, where they bathed in the sinks with the supplies Ether had acquired. They were both starving by then and soon arrived in some kind of town, passing multiple local restaurants that were already closed (Ether audibly regretting the chance to dine at Mack's Fish House) before finally ordering from a Taco Bell drive-thru.

"Keep going this way," instructed Ether, two bags of dystopian Mexican food on her lap. "There were signs back there that suggested some kind of wilderness; I saw the words *Mossy Bluff Nature Trail* and lots of use of the word *campground*. Those are always good places to stash yourself for a night."

They followed winding roads until Abbott, half asleep and approaching a state of delirium, finally turned down a lane marked "picnic grounds" and eventually parked in a paved spot among some trees, the sound of lapping waves nearby. When they got out, he found the water was directly in front of them—Abbott was surprised he hadn't accidentally drowned them both after having just saved a stranger from the same fate. They ate their lukewarm Taco Bell on the wrinkled hood of the Navigator, Abbott lifting each bite with trembling fingers. He ran his hand along the shattered grille and tried to poke the dangling headlight back up into its socket.

"When I first picked you up," he said, "you told me I wasn't allowed to ask what's in the box. But at this point, considering what I've been through, fuck it. Tell me what's in the box. I'm not asking. I deserve to know. In fact, I'm not taking you any farther until you tell me."

"I don't know."

"What? What do you mean?"

"I mean the man who hired me said it had to stay a secret from everybody, including me. If that seal over the lock gets broken, the deal is off. I don't even have the key. He talked like the world would end if I opened it."

Abbott stared at the Lincoln's battered face. "So you lied to me."

"When did I say I knew what was in the box?"

"You said you definitely knew what *wasn't* in it."

"I said it wasn't drugs, and it isn't. I'm sure of it."

"You're not one hundred percent sure. You can't be."

"It rounds up to a hundred. I mean, if somebody asked you if there was a monkey living in your attic, you'd say no. It's not exactly one hundred percent certain, but there would be some unmissable clues. Screeching, missing bananas, the thud of thrown feces."

"Okay, so what do you *think* is in there?"

"I think it's something very fragile and of great personal value to my employer. Maybe his mother's old jewelry, or antique pottery, or some expensive art. Or maybe just a whole bunch of cash. It's none of my business."

"So it could literally be a corpse and we wouldn't know."

Ether took a bite of her Chipotle Ranch Grilled Chicken Burrito, glanced in the direction of the box, and said, "No. We'd have smelled it by now. Wouldn't we?"

"I'm too exhausted to get mad again," said Abbott, reaching for one of his Cheesy Fiesta Potatoes. "But will you admit that you could have just said that from the beginning? There are things you had to keep secret as part of the deal, but there are others that you kept from me just because you wanted to."

"Cards on the table? I didn't think I'd find one driver who'd take me all the way across the country; I assumed it'd be a chain of, like, five drivers who'd each tolerate maybe a day before foisting me onto someone else. So the policy was going to be total secrecy because I'd otherwise be leaving a trail of strangers who could each go babbling about it online. 'I just gave a ride to the weirdest chick! She said she was doing a job for somebody famous, help me guess who it is, fam!' My original plan was to keep the hat and sunglasses on the whole time, never giving my real name, offering no clues about the sender, recipient, any of it. But at this point, yeah, we should have no secrets from one another. We are very much in this together."

"Okay. So, who are you?"

Ether chewed in silence.

Finally, while still chewing, she said, "If you think about it, there is no miracle of the ancient world equal to this right here. More than eight thousand Taco Bells in thirty-two countries, all of them fully supplied at all times, including perishable lettuce and tomato that has to be shipped with perfect coordination to arrive exactly on schedule. A taco in that Arkansas store will taste the same as one in downtown Tokyo, both cooked on demand and served within minutes. Hundreds of thousands of workers functioning perfectly in sync to feed *two billion* customers a year. The infrastructure to make such a thing possible would have been unthinkable back when this country was founded. Think about all the wars that have been fought just over these spices. Hell, the disposable wrappers and napkins alone would blow the mind of any ancient genius."

"Then they'd spend the rest of the night astonished by one of our modern toilets. Who are you?"

"My name is Karen Wozniak. But I did my videos under the name Butterflaps."

Abbott stopped, almost dropping his Doritos Nacho Cheesy Gordita Crunch.

Failing to hide his disbelief, he said, "*You're* Butterflaps?"

ZEKE

In a last-ditch attempt to squeeze some productivity from the day, Zeke was in bed, using his tablet to alter the commissioned artwork according to changes the client had added at the last minute. The guy now wanted the woodland creatures in the background watching Detective Harry Bosch and cartoon bunny Judy Hopps's lovemaking to be reacting with less fascination and more horror. It was a subtle change, but one that would take time, as there were twelve characters whose expressions needed to be altered, and two of them were visibly pleasuring themselves. Then he received a text from the one friend in the Abaddon chat that had his cell number:

GSG IS BUTTERFLAPS!!!!!

Zeke understood the first five letters of that but not the rest. Was that last word an adjective? One of those Gen Z slang terms that just incepts itself into existence overnight, where suddenly everyone is using it as if it's always been a part of the language? Within a few minutes of browsing the various hubs of discussion, he had the story: The spinoff subreddit had analyzed the GSG selfie posted from the Texas gas station and, based on a tiny sliver of a birthmark visible at the upper edge of the screen, had identified her. She was, it turned out, an internet celebrity.

She was also a well-known psychopath and a manipulator.

Zeke was initially alarmed, knowing what kind of person Abbott was now trapped in the vehicle with, but then felt the sweet relief of vindication. The anti-Abbott shitheads had spent the day calling him an incel and gleefully throwing around accusations of murder, treason, conspiracy, and whatever crime it's called when you steal an alien corpse. This revelation about GSG's identity erased all doubt that she was, in fact, the one at the wheel of this operation, clearly intending to frame Abbott in the aftermath using his old controversial videos as evidence. All she'd need to do is make sure he didn't survive the attack—the dead cannot control their narrative. This, plus what he now knew about the target, meant that Abbott could go down in history as the man who attacked the Supreme Court and sent the country careening off a cliff of reciprocal violence.

No. This woman had to be stopped.

Somehow.

ETHER

Abbott Coburn had been Karen Wozniak's third attempt at a driver.

The first guy who'd pulled up to the Circle K on Thursday morning had looked at her like a piece of meat, flirting even before his tires stopped rolling. The second had presented a little bit of a language barrier and bolted the moment she'd started talking about an off-the-books ride, probably assuming she was bait for some kind of scam that would result in him losing his vehicle or getting deported. By the time Abbott arrived, she'd been in a near-panic about the Tattoo Monster showing up (she had no idea if he'd been tailing her off Phil's property) and had resolved that it was Abbott or nothing. If he hadn't worked out, she'd have had to steal a car. She'd never done anything like that before, but the last thing she'd looked up on Phil's phone before ditching it was a YouTube video on how to hot-wire (if you find the right model and year, it turns out you can do it with a screwdriver).

But then she'd seen Abbott, who looked so pale that he seemed at risk of a vitamin D deficiency and had the vibe of a man embarrassed to be caught in the act of existing. It was like he hadn't socialized outside of the safety of a screen in ten years, so then the question was what type of sheltered indoor kid was he? Guys in that category could be extremely kind or extremely dangerous, depending on their coping mechanisms. Some had white knight daydreams, and some fantasized about mutilating their high school prom queen. Some alternated between the two based on their mood. As such, the first test of their relationship had been her inquiry about whether or not Abbott had packed a weapon. When he'd told her he'd brought along a gun, Karen had tried to calculate the chances of dying at his hands at some point and had quickly notified him that she, too, was armed, playing it off like a casual comparison of travel habits. These were the kind of games you learned to play when living on the streets. Or, well, anywhere else.

Still, she had stuck with him because she knew that to do otherwise would make her a hypocrite. She'd spent months lecturing every willing ear on the modern world's catastrophic loss of interpersonal trust; now here was her chance to prove she actually believed what she was saying. Statistically, most people are not killers, not even when placed in extreme circumstances. Most do want to help, and Abbott clearly wanted to help her, even if he never said it out loud. The question with a guy like him would always be what he would expect in return.

"I had a YouTube channel," she said from her sleeping spot in the passenger seat, already regretting her food decisions. "I started it when I was in college, and for the first five years, nobody cared. Then I had that one video get big, my birthmark cover-up tutorial. This was right around the time all of the makeup influencers started getting famous, and the sponsorship deals were rolling in. I had around two million subscribers at my peak."

She heard Abbott make an impressed noise from the driver's seat, but the number had never seemed real to her. Sometimes she tried to imagine two million people in a crowd, and getting up in front of them to apply makeup to her face while talking about middle school bullying. It never worked; the brain can't accurately picture that amount of anything. And that's not counting her additional million followers on Instagram, a half million more on TikTok.

"I definitely wasn't the biggest, but it was my full-time job, going on camera and gushing about some new palette for twenty minutes. I wasn't as rich as people thought I was, but it was ten times what I'd ever made as a physical therapist—that's what I did out of college. I couldn't afford a mansion in LA or a Lamborghini, a lot of the designer purses and all that came free from sponsors. So I had this one deal going with a makeup brand who'd partnered with Theo Shams. Do you know who that is?"

"Only that they're a really famous YouTuber who talks about fashion while wearing a series of implausible wigs."

"So, this is going to be kind of hard to follow if you weren't part of the scene, but two influencers who were married broke up and went public, each accusing the other of abuse and toxic behavior. Theo sided with one, some other influencers sided with the other, and it became this weird war between the fandoms, everybody sticking up for one partner or the other in this messy relationship drama between internet celebrities none of us had ever actually met. So the opposing fan army came after Theo and started digging up stuff they'd said years ago, some old homophobic jokes, the kind lots of people were doing in the 2000s. I did a video supporting Theo, then those angry fans came swarming into my comments calling us bigots. Then we dug up some old transphobic comments their guy made, so we swarmed their spaces and did the same. This spilled over into every platform, we'd flood each other's Twitter mentions and Instagram comments, and this was my whole day, just refreshing over and over. It went on for like two straight weeks. It was *nuts*."

"So far," said Abbott from the driver's seat, "what you're describing just sounds like the everyday experience of using the internet. Half the people on there are only looking for someplace to off-load their rage."

"So, there was one really nasty girl," said Ether, knowing she wouldn't be able to fully convey the nastiness, "and she kept stalking me across channels, including digging up my personal accounts, my old Facebook, my parents' accounts. Then she photoshopped my face onto some porn and spread it around, including sending it to my family, my family's co-workers, their business inboxes, to people at my church. She was just doing nothing but this, all day, every day, trying to ruin my life, like it had become her full-time job. Her username was, well, it doesn't matter, but her real name was Jolene Brooks. I know, because I did some digging, found her address, phone numbers, everything. I leaked her info to some fans on my Discord, and . . . I don't know what I wanted to happen, but I definitely wanted *something* to happen. And it did."

"Yeah, this is the part of the story I know. It's how I'd heard of you. Or, you know, your persona."

Ether sighed, knowing she was going to tell the story anyway, just to get it out there once and for all. "Jolene lived in Virginia, which is the good Virginia of the two Virginias, but she was in a bad part of the good Virginia. So somebody, not me, decided to do a swatting prank on her. That's where they do a call to the local cops from a fake number, trying to get a SWAT team to show up at the victim's house, to terrorize them. The call claimed Jolene's dad was holding everyone hostage and that he'd sworn to shoot anyone who tried to approach. You probably know what happened next."

It was the SWAT team's body cam footage that went viral. They'd showed up to a dumpy little trailer, the white siding scummed with algae. Jolene's father, drunk off his ass, came to the door and screamed for them to get off his property. Two German shepherds came bounding out from around the man's legs, not aggressive, but running and barking, as dogs do. The cops shot both dogs dead. The man had then flown into a teary rage and charged the police with a hunting knife. They shot him, but didn't kill him. He writhed on his lawn, calling the cops Nazis and crying after his dogs. And there in the doorway behind him stood Jolene, a chubby teenager in a T-shirt and underwear, her hands over her mouth, watching her whole world come apart.

"These people," said Karen, "were poor. Like, *poor* poor. I once did a video about a five-thousand-dollar handbag I got from a sponsor, and I don't think everything in their home would have sold for that much combined. The gunshots to the dad were the kind you see action heroes shrug off all the time—thigh, shoulder, one on his hand. But he's disabled for life now, he has nerve damage in the hand and can't use it, he has a permanent limp, he's in constant pain. He can't work. They tried suing the city, but it didn't go anywhere."

"Do you know who did the actual swatting?"

"Yeah. He was thirteen years old and lives in Belarus. Anyway, the death threats started pouring in after that, coming into my mom's work, my dad's office. Theo did a video denouncing me, all the sponsors left, all the partnerships vanished, all the other influencers joined in the chorus. Meanwhile,

I was sitting there waiting to go to jail, but, you know, nothing I did was a crime. I mean, it used to be that everyone's name and address was published in a phone book; all I did was share it. For weeks after, I just slept all day, trying to stay away from my screens. Once I was disconnected from it and looking back, it was clear that everything we were doing was *insane*. It was the first time I realized there was something truly dangerous about this, the devices, the algorithms. It's like it reduced us to our limbic systems, turned us into mindless zealots in warring tribes. I watch my videos from back then and—I don't know. It's like watching a stranger. And what I couldn't get over is that this technology was supposed to broaden everybody's horizons, you can communicate with people all over the world now, at any time. But for me, the world got smaller. I neglected everything else in my life—my family, my business, my health, everything else just went away in the name of arguing with these total strangers about the lives of other total strangers. I felt like living my life through screens had trapped me in this dark little cell, my own black box of doom."

"I mean, it sounds like she was kind of a nasty kid," said Abbott, clearly thinking he was being helpful.

"We're all nasty at that age—that's what adolescence is for, to be horrible for a few years, to see how it feels. Jolene just wanted to be a part of something bigger than herself, to have a war to fight. It's all anybody wants these days. And she thought she was on the right side of it, you know, her social media is all antiracism slogans, gay rights, trans rights, and she's doing that in rural Virginia, in a trailer where her dad had a Confederate flag hanging over the sofa. Think of the bravery that takes, to be outspoken in that place. And what she was doing to me, what we were all doing to each other, it was just so, I don't know. Phony. We all just wanted to feel something real but to feel it without consequence."

"It's like a game," said Abbott. "You have an enemy on your screen and you click on it, and the enemy's reputation is blown to pieces."

"So after that, I shut down all of my accounts, swore I was going to try to find some kind of life offline. I bought an ambulance. I didn't even fix it up to live in it—I actually bought it from another van-life influencer after they decided to pivot to a gimmick with a softer bed. I took odd jobs when I needed money, borrowed from my parents when that fell through. Then I stumbled into this delivery job that promised to pay enough to do what I really wanted."

"What's that? Go build a cabin in the mountains?"

"To try to make things right, with Jolene and her family. I don't even want her to know the money came from me. I'm not going to do the charity influencer thing, where I have a camera crew follow me as I buy her a new house. No big public apology to try to restore my good name. I just want to quietly route the money to her, change the trajectory of her life. And then . . . I want to try to change the trajectory of the world."

"Oh, is that all?"

"I know how it sounds. But the guy who hired me said he could help with that, if I did the job. And I think he's in a position to actually do it."

HUNTER

He was having the school dream again.

Not that he was back in school but that the roof of a school had collapsed and buried all of the children inside, and it was a roof job his crew had done. It was dream logic, so the school was full of not just children but babies, and now they were all buried under debris, howling over their missing limbs and the ragged red gashes in their delicate skin. Many had been killed, but what was worse was that so many more were still under there, shrieking, whimpering, begging, and there was no way to get them out because the more the rescuers tried to dig, the more the roof fell in, because it had been built wrong, a single step skipped. And the parents were all there, wailing, demanding to know whose greed, incompetence, and laziness had doomed their precious children.

And so Hunter slept, but he was sweating, his system humming with cortisol, his heart pounding. His sleeping brain was racked with shame and guilt and regret and a brutal sense of helplessness that would linger for hours after he woke.

I AM HOME FROM THE HOSPITAL, HERE IS WHAT HAPPENED

Posted to r/DCTerrorAttack by CactusDad1999

Hey guys, just got home, I've got six stitches and a concussion and everything hurts, but otherwise I'm okay. My mom's Fiat is totaled. The police had a million questions and to be honest I wasn't sure what to tell them lol.

As for what happened, I tried to swerve in front of the Navigator to cut it off, but it ran into me and flipped me off a bridge into some shallow water. I was trapped in the car and Abbott and the girl came and got me out. I was delirious with head trauma and I actually asked them to go get my cactus from the car (long story) and they actually did! Abbott brought it over to me and they made sure I was okay but then they left before the police got there.

I haven't been following this story so I don't know the whole situation but it sounds like nobody here does, either? So all I can say is that they had no motivation to help me, I mean if they'd just let me drown, they could have driven off with no worries (aside from me, there were no witnesses to the accident, as far as I know). By fishing me out, they were saving someone who could identify them and pin down their location. If we're trying to gather information and determine how malicious these people are, I think my story definitely has to count as a point in their favor. And I am personally hoping that this whole terrorist rumor turns out to be nothing.

[Post deleted by moderator TruthLover420]

The Butterflaps revelation doesn't disprove Russian involvement, and here's why

Posted to r/DCTerrorAttack by FedThrowaway66974

Some trolls are acting like the Butterflaps revelation somehow disproves the Russian sabotage plan I mapped out earlier. This is why you need to be listening to those of us who actually have inside information, not the kids posting from their basements or those with more nefarious purposes (I'll get to them in a moment).

It's true that GSG aka Butterflaps aka Karen Wozniak isn't from Russia, but she has absolutely been trained by the KGB in infohazard warfare. Our best theory is that at some point, the Russians got to her, maybe with blackmail material or maybe just the promise of a big payoff (I'd definitely look into how easily she got those YouTube sponsorship deals—other influencers were always pointing out how she basically came out of nowhere). The attack on Jolene Brooks was clearly an orchestrated test run of psychological instigation and manipulation techniques. The victims of this attack (which we now know to be the US Supreme Court and dozens of children of DC insiders) have been specifically chosen to generate maximum outrage which will be infinitely multiplied via social media, generating irresistible motivation from the other side to reciprocate.

Now I need to make something absolutely clear:

We have confirmed that the Internet Research Agency a.k.a. the Russian "troll farm" is creating Reddit accounts to spread disinformation on this subreddit. That is the source of these smokescreen posts, those positing a UFO conspiracy, or that the box contains the corpse of a murder victim. I AM CALLING UPON TRUTHLOVER420 TO BAN ANY ACCOUNTS TRYING

TO THROW US OFF THE TRUTH OF A WASHINGTON DC TERROR ATTACK ON JULY 4.

Do I need to re-pot my cactus?

Posted to r/CactusCare by CactusDad1999

Hey guys, it's me again, the one with the heirloom Christmas cactus, I'm panicking right now because this thing got TOTALLY SUBMERGED in water (long story) and it was filthy creek water with all sorts of bacteria and who knows what else. Do I need to re-pot it in dry potting soil? Or can I just let it drain? Do I need to put it out in the sun? I think you're going to say re-potting is the safe option, but I've never done it before and I don't know if doing it wrong can traumatize the plant. Please advise.

Posted to a private horse enthusiast Facebook group by Cindee Teague on Saturday, July 2, at 3:12 A.M.:

First, I want to apologize for the post I made yesterday featuring a photo of myself and YouTuber Karen Wozniak a.k.a. "Butterflaps," whom I met at a gas station in Lubbock. At the time, I was unaware of her bigoted and murderous actions (I did not follow that controversy when it happened, I knew only that Karen had stopped posting to her YouTube channel). There is no excuse for my ignorance and I should have been more careful before posting such harmful content. I have since educated myself and want to say that I absolutely disavow Butterflaps and everything she stands for, what she did was inexcusable and unforgivable. I, like many others, was taken in by an abusive manipulator and I am deeply ashamed for not having seen through her disguise.

I understand that posting that photo was an act of violence and that many of you were harmed. I can only try to make amends and use this as an opportunity to learn and grow. That said, I would beg you to stop messaging death threats to myself and my family. Someone has been sending me graphic photos of stillborn fetuses and saying that they hope I miscarry. I am begging you to stop, again I understand that there is no excuse for what I did, but I feel like that is taking things too far. I have been sick about this all day and I just want to move on. Thank you.

First comment:

LOL look at this abuser trying to play the victim. Zero remorse, no apology, just "Oh, poor me." I'm soooo sorry you actually got criticism for committing literal violence in what had previously been a safe space. The one I really feel sorry for is that fetus, if you have an ounce of humanity you'll abort it so it won't grow up with a psychotic abuser for a mother. You were unmasked today, now we all know what you really are.

DAY 3

The real difficulty is, isn't it, to adapt
one's steady beliefs about tribulation
to this particular tribulation; for the
particular, when it arrives, always
seems so peculiarly intolerable.

—C. S. LEWIS, in a letter to a friend, 1940

16

ABBOTT

From somewhere deep inside a dream, Abbott heard a tapping on the glass next to his head and, in the dream, turned to see a bald, tattooed face behind the twin barrels of a shotgun. But, in the logic of the dream, it was the Tattoo Monster, but it was also his father, or maybe both of them, as if they had merged into a single mockery of the masculinity Abbott had always lacked.

The knocking on the window continued, and now he dreamed it was the police, a SWAT team with guns ready, there not to arrest him but to shred his belly with bullets until the taco shit stewing in his guts spilled onto his organs.

The knocking continued, and now, in his mind's eye, he saw an angry mob, the faces of citizens sneering and laughing in disdain, cameras ready to hold him up to the world for ridicule.

He finally pried his eyes open, turned toward the source of the sound, and found in real life . . .

The police and an angry mob.

The cop was knocking on the glass with a fist, the other hand resting on the butt of his holstered pistol. Around him was a collection of strangers in summer clothes, gathered under the Saturday morning sun, staring, glaring, snickering.

Abbott froze.

The most important thing to understand about spending your whole life in mortal fear of being in Big Trouble is that it's not an irrational phobia—Abbott was constantly getting caught. The rough-edged kids could indulge their darkest desires because they had instincts for getting away with it; they could lie and charm and intimidate. The good kids didn't even have dark desires that needed indulging; they glided through a world that fit them like a glove, wanting for themselves nothing beyond what polite society wanted them to want. It was the ones like Abbott who were stuck in the middle, forever to be the world's punching bag. He was bored by everything normal but lacked the tools to survive excursions into the dangerous and exotic. Now, as always, he would be the one they made an example of.

In the moments he spent staring into the eyes of the cop and the mob, the rest of his life flashed through his mind. Handcuffs. Strip search. Cavity search. Using the toilet in front of a crowded holding cell packed with weaponized mutant versions of all his childhood bullies. Showering with them, sleeping with them, eating with them—zero privacy, ever. His every embarrassing inner thought would be examined by prosecutors at trial, his most intimate chat messages and unguarded emails read aloud in court. A detailed tapestry of his inadequacy, unfurled for the world to savor and deride. And this wouldn't be like past humiliations, a moment of failure that lives on in his sleepless nights. No, this would go on for years, decades. Indignities at the hands of muscular psychopaths and sadistic guards that would continue day in, day out. No escape, his entire body and mind a toy for them to amuse themselves with, his fragility a canvas upon which they would paint their obscene masterpiece. And even if he was eventually released, it wouldn't matter, because those memories would follow him until senility turned all of it into a nonsense stew. He would never crawl into bed with a woman without vivid recall of what had been done to him, the violations, his face pressed into concrete or the metal frame of a bunk bed.

The cop was saying something. In front of Abbott was the water, the pavement sloping down into waves upon which the morning sunlight did a sparkling dance. The lake was crowded with boats and Jet Skis, the revelers celebrating the Fourth of July weekend, basking in the knowledge they, unlike Abbott, were not in Big Trouble.

Abbott set his jaw, started the engine, and floored it, heading directly toward the water. There was a strange object in his path, a raft that seemed to be painted in Spider-Man's red-and-blue color scheme. The Navigator blasted through it, tearing it apart. Someone screamed in outrage. It meant nothing now.

The grille of the Navigator hit the water, and someone else shrieked. The feel of the water thumping against the grille awoke something in Abbott, and he slammed on the brakes. So now the front tires were in the lake, and bystanders were yelling and laughing, and Ether was stirring next to him, mumbling. The cop was running up to them, barking and cursing. In a panic, Abbott shifted into reverse, assuming the Navigator wouldn't obey, that the water had ruined the engine. But after a sluggish start, during which he felt like the water was grabbing onto the front end as if determined to drag them to the depths, they were free. He threw it into drive, the Navigator's absurd turn radius taking them briefly into the water again before heading back the way they'd come, crossing a paved area that was now scattered with families and vehicles that were hauling what looked like homemade rafts. In between Abbott and the road was a black one painted with a yellow Batman logo, being carried by a couple of dudes who yelled and then scattered as Abbott ran it over, the object flattening as if made of paper. He headed for the road with no plan beyond the primal instinct to run and hide.

"Tell me where to go!" he shouted to Ether, who was up and looking out the rear window, trying to piece together what the hell was going on. "The cops are after us. How do I get out of town?"

"You're on the right road. When you find where it splits off onto a smaller one, take it. We'll find somewhere to stop and get out of view." She looked again and said, "I don't think we're being followed. What happened?"

"I don't know. I woke up and a cop was knocking on the window. There were people all around. We got discovered, somehow. Everybody knew where we were. There were hundreds of them."

Ether watched several vehicles pass the other direction, all towing a watercraft of one type or another.

"Abbott, I think they were just there for an event. I think the cop was just asking you to get out of the way so they could get their trailers into the water."

"No. They were—they were all looking at us. They surrounded the vehicle. They knew it was us. The cop knew. Everybody knew."

She continued watching their rear as they flew under a banner that said

WORLD CHAMPIONSHIP CARDBOARD BOAT RACES. They passed signs that indicated they were approaching Fat Possum Hollow, and Ether had him turn off onto a road that seemed to disappear into woods.

And still, no one followed.

Abbott wiped sweat from his face with a trembling hand.

"It's okay," said Ether. "We're all right. Our nerves are fried because of yesterday. But I think it's fine. I mean, it wouldn't make sense for anybody back there to care about us. Who would have pressed charges? The guy who we rescued from the water after *he* intentionally caused an accident? The psychopath who stalked us across multiple states and tried to carjack us at gunpoint? They're the ones who should be in jail!"

"Why didn't you want to stop?"

"What?"

"Last night, when the guy went off into the water. Why did you speed away from the scene before the cops got there?"

"Because," she said, clearly pausing to actually think of why, "while we are not criminals, they would have tons of questions about, well, everything in this vehicle. They would probably take us in, and while I believe we would eventually be released, it'd definitely tie us up long enough to blow our deadline. Oh, and they'd seize all our cash—remember, the cops can do that. They don't even have to charge you with a crime; any large amounts of money are instantly confiscated, and the burden is on you to prove it's legally yours."

"That can't be right."

"It's called *civil forfeiture.* Look it up."

"Well, maybe I'm okay with that. Maybe I want to go back and talk to that policeman. Let him crack open this box and confirm that it's not a dead body or something worse."

"Okay."

"What would you do if I turned around right now and went back there? If I just told the cop everything?"

"I'd go along. What else would I do? It's your choice."

Abbott didn't turn around but felt his anger coming back, wondering why he'd allowed it to dissipate at all. Why do people get mad and then later apologize by saying, "That wasn't the real me"? Why can't the anger be the real you? Maybe the simpering, apologetic version is the fake one.

Abbott said, "I can't continue like this."

"I agree," said Ether, sounding more annoyed than Abbott would have liked.

"What is that supposed to mean?"

She shook her head. "You're not going to like what I have to say, so I'd prefer to just not say it. You do what you want."

"No, say it. We're telling each other everything, right?"

"If I say it, you have to agree to hear it and not just sift through the words for ammo to use in a counterattack."

"Okay."

She took a deep breath and rubbed her eyes. "At some point very, very soon, you, Abbott, have *to grow the fuck up.* You're driving, not me. You've been driving most of the way. I didn't trick you or threaten you; I made you an offer, and you accepted. You're not a victim. Do you want good things in your life? A home, money, a career? It will always look like this, risk and pain and the knowledge that if you screw it up, it's because of *you.* No one else. If you let yourself just blame everybody else every time a gamble goes bust, then that means when you win, it'll only be because the system let you, and you'll never get to fully embrace it. We have two more days of this. So you can stop, or go back, or dump me out, or keep going, but make your choice. I can't handle your whining."

"You didn't tell me a guy would try to kill us."

"The moment you saw me pull out the bundles of cash, you knew there was some danger involved. You decided the risk was worth it. Live with that."

Abbott said nothing, per their agreement.

After a few silent miles, Ether said, "And I'm sick of hearing about your dad. You're an adult. He has every right to be upset about the vehicle getting damaged, but it wasn't your fault, and it's frankly not that big a deal in the grand scheme of things."

"This is probably thirty thousand in damage. And the insurance won't cover it, as there's no police report."

"You know what an adult would say about that? They'd say, 'Ether, I'm demanding another thirty K because of the damage to my vehicle.' It's just money and repairs, a transaction. Stop piling grand emotional significance onto it. That's the other thing about living in the black box— you get trained to turn every little thing in your life into a grand fucking psychodrama."

More silence.

Abbott felt himself deflate and then said, "Okay. No, you're right. You're right."

She spun to face him. "Whoa, really?"

"Yeah. I, uh, needed to hear that. I think."

They fell into silence until they reached another town and stopped at an establishment with the most alarming name for a business Abbott had ever heard: the Bald Knob Truck Stop. They agreed to take turns going inside to get cleaned up so as not to leave the vehicle and foil-wrapped box unattended, Ether taking her turn first.

Once Abbott was alone, he swallowed the final pill in the prescription he'd failed to fill back home. He dug out the prepaid phone, spent several frustrating minutes figuring out how to set it up, then immediately went into his Walgreens account and spent some even more frustrating minutes trying to get his prescription transferred from the Victorville location to one along their route. He checked the map and tried to do the mental math—they would be in Nashville by tonight, unless they were captured or killed along the way. He was not, in fact, able to arrange the transfer through the website and so was forced to get on the phone and go through a lengthy process of claiming that a family emergency had taken him out of town, and so on. He finally was given an address for a Nashville location—Abbott imagined a store decorated with neon guitar signs and cowboy hats—and was told the prescription should be ready for pickup by morning. By the time he was done, he felt like another 20 percent of his metaphorical battery had been drained for the day without even having started the drive. Still, it was a huge relief to know he wasn't going to have to finish the road trip in a state of withdrawal, on top of everything else. Then he logged in to his email, and the whole world tilted under his feet.

Hundreds of messages, mostly from strangers. Bizarre questions, insults, accusations, a crush of notifications from Twitch and Discord and every other app he'd ever used to communicate with the public. He frantically searched his name on various platforms—both his actual name and the Abaddon username. What unspooled was an endless scroll of lies, mockery, and accusations. *Celebrities* were tweeting about him. There were YouTube videos and podcasts. He saw the word *incel* over and over. Strangers were posting links to ancient videos and message board posts, unearthing every politically incorrect thought. But why? *He'd only been gone for two days.* Even if his father had gone public with the claim that his Navigator had been stolen, why would that matter to anyone? Where was the scandal? He had to be missing something.

Another few minutes of browsing sent him into a surreal alternate universe. References to the Russians, and specifically, a female Russian operative. Talk of terrorism and Abbott being a murderous incel collaborator. The word *nuclear* kept coming up along with *radioactive* and *dirty bomb*. There was a video clip of Ether yelling at an old pickup truck and acting like a psychopath, followed by a clip of that same truck surrounded by men in yellow radiation suits.

What the fuck?

Was this an attempt to poison the water supply?

Posted to r/DCTerrorAttack by FatSnape
Having watched the Heber Springs video from multiple angles, it seems clear to me that there was an effort to submerge the Navigator in the lake, an attempt which they then abandoned for unknown reasons. It seems to me that the goal was to contaminate the water supply, infect the tourists gathered there, or both.

The most obvious vector would be some kind of communicable disease that the swimmers and boaters would then spread to friends and family once they returned to their homes around the country. I would research which pathogens spread quickly in water, but without showing symptoms until days later (after the infected have had time to transmit it).

I can't emphasize enough that there HAS to be a reason they did what they did. Remember, there are no accidents.

Have we just witnessed a case of alien mind control?

Posted to r/DCTerrorAttack by AgentSkulli

These posts are getting ridiculous. Every single attempt to explain why Abbott would try to submerge the Navigator is less plausible than the one before. How about you try actually opening your eyes?

If you watch the video closely, you'll see they've wrapped the freezer unit in foil. They clearly sensed they were getting telepathic commands from the EBE trapped inside and attempted to create a barrier to insulate themselves from its influence. It apparently didn't work, as the entity was able to take over Abbott's mind and force him to steer himself into the water (where he and GSG would have drowned, but the EBE would have survived as it does not breathe oxygen).

Also I AM NOT A RUSSIAN TROLL. We need to get this paranoia under control, I've been an active redditor for nine years, I moderate several subs including r/AlienInfiltration and r/ChristopherMeloniAss. If anything, the "terror attack" story is the smokescreen.

[Photo] *I know where Abbott will be tomorrow morning and I can prove it*

Posted to r/DCTerrorAttack by DCThrowaway66

I cannot reveal how I know this, as the information was not come by legally. All I can say is that an employee at the Walgreens store in Victorville, CA, where Abbott Coburn filled his medications just got off the phone with Abbott himself. He called in from a burner and asked to have his antianxiety prescription moved to one of the Nashville locations, to be picked up when the store opens tomorrow (the location is the one pinned in this screengrab from Google Maps).

If the mods want verification, I will privately share proof of everything I am saying.

——————————————————————————— Comments:

TruthLover420: I have examined their evidence and can confirm that this tip is genuine.

ZEKE

The piece Zeke was supposed to be working on—a new commission involving a nonconsensual encounter between Sonic the Hedgehog and a pregnant Jack Reacher—had barely made it past the rough-sketch stage. The bombshells from the Abbott situation were coming in at the exact frequency as to prevent him from ever fully focusing on anything else. He'd gone to sleep on the Butterflaps news and woke to find the Navigator had apparently fled from police after getting spotted at a lake in Arkansas. Before he'd even had a chance to fully digest that, another piece of news came in, maybe the only one that really mattered: There was now a time and location where they knew Abbott would appear next. Not just the city (Nashville, where Zeke had lived his whole life) but the exact spot, which was the pharmacy counter at a specific Walgreens (one that Zeke had absolutely been to before), and a specific time, around eight tomorrow morning.

He had initially dismissed it purely because it seemed too good to be true, an anonymous poster magically stumbling across the one piece of information the hive mind was so desperate for. And yet, it lined up with something that was known among Abbott's Twitch fans but that hadn't previously leaked to the masses: that Abbott was, in fact, running out of his meds. The more Zeke thought about it, the more he thought the tip was real, which meant Abbott and GSG would show up less than two miles from where Zeke was sitting and would presumably find a whole crowd waiting, including a swarm of cops. It meant that all of this would be over by this time tomorrow and that Zeke could, in theory, go watch it happen in front of him. But watch what, exactly? Would GSG allow herself to be taken alive? If it were a bomb, would she trigger it the moment she saw a SWAT team? Or would she pull a gun and get both of them killed by nervous cops?

No. Zeke wasn't going to go watch *that* happen. If he went, he'd be there to make sure it didn't.

Somehow.

ABBOTT

"What are you doing?!?" shouted Ether as she climbed into the passenger seat. "Where did you get that?"

She snatched at the phone, and Abbott yanked it out of reach.

"Did you know?"

"Did I know what?"

"That we're famous? Not because of our stupid internet scandals but for what we're doing now. There's a whole online community based on trying to find us and that box. An entire subreddit. You were wrong, what you said earlier. Everybody knows. The cops know. The feds know. They're all looking for us."

"They are? Why?" She seemed genuinely confused.

"They think that's a dirty bomb in there, explosives wrapped in radioactive shrapnel. They think you're a terrorist or a foreign operative and that you duped me into helping blow up the Supreme Court to trigger a new civil war."

Ether just stared, blinking, as if trying to decide if Abbott were joking or catastrophizing.

"I don't—where are they getting that from?"

"They've pieced it together. They're saying the truck you drove to the Circle K was radioactive; the cops impounded it in space suits."

"*What?* Give me that."

She reached for the phone. Again, Abbott pulled it away.

"Abbott, come on. You get back on the internet, and within five minutes, it's already driven you crazy?"

"I got on here because I moved my prescription to a store in Nashville, so I wouldn't get withdrawal while flying down the highway in the middle of the night. I was actually thinking we could swing by and pick it up tomorrow, like we were still normal people existing in society. Then I go to check my messages and find out I'm the most wanted man in America."

"Abbott, it's not a bomb, nuclear or otherwise. I mean, just listen to yourself!"

"*How do you know?*"

"Because that's stupid. I knew the guy this box belonged to. He wasn't a terrorist, he wasn't violent. And it's not even going to DC. The address is a private home on the other side of the river, in McLean."

"Yeah, and that home is hosting a whole bunch of government officials and judges on Monday morning—the morning when your guy said he *had* to have this box."

"Will you just let me see the phone? I'll give it back, I promise."

He handed it to her, and she read, swiped, tapped, read some more.

"Look, see this? The whole 'dirty bomb' rumor got started because they saw a supposed radiation symbol on the box. This is it, right there." She leaned back and peeled away the foil from one corner. "Look. It's a Megadeth sticker! The metal band from the eighties? They used a radiation symbol because everybody else was already doing pentagrams? There are band stickers all over. They could have looked at the one next to it and decided the box was full of anthrax. Come on, you know how this works. They just run with whatever fiction will stave off their boredom for the next two minutes."

"They're not always wrong! They have access to more information than either of us."

"Using your own judgment, having spent two days with me, do you think I'm a Russian saboteur?"

"You won't talk about what you've been doing these last couple of years. You have big handfuls of cash. You have some kind of untraceable credit card and ID. You know all of these little tricks, like you've had training."

"I learned those tricks because I was literally homeless! And don't say you don't know me. At this point, considering what we've been through over the last two days, you know me as well as anyone on earth. I mean, I'm seeing people on here saying it's an alien corpse! Oh, and here's a guy saying it's the body of some old classmate of yours that you imprisoned and tortured because you're an incel serial killer. If I agree to not believe them about you, will you agree to not believe them about me?"

"That doesn't even make sense."

She gestured toward the truck stop. "*That* makes sense. It's a physical, tangible place. There's a little restaurant inside with breakfast food; they have nice bathrooms. Go in, change your clothes, get cleaned up, get some hot food in you." She held up the phone. "Yes, lots of strangers are saying terrible things about you on here. But look—I just turned it off. Now they're gone. These people walking around this parking lot, in that store, they don't care about any of this. Inside, food still tastes good, water is still wet, you're still alive and in a healthy and strong body. That's real. And when you focus on real things, you'll be shocked at how easy it is to make this"—she held up the phone—"not matter at all."

He wordlessly obeyed, not because he agreed, necessarily, but because he desperately needed to piss. He felt like the pavement was rolling under his feet as he shuffled toward the truck stop, carefully watching the faces of those he passed. None paid him any special attention. A trucker was chatting with the girl at the counter, the huge dude behind him joining in on the conversation—clearly regulars. Everyone else seemed to have swung by on their way to enjoy America's independence in Bald Knob, Arkansas.

Abbott and Ether ate breakfast sandwiches in the Navigator and quickly got moving again, Abbott having no sense of how easily they would be recognized if they remained in the same public location for too long. He knew he should be paranoid, but wasn't certain of just how paranoid to be, which of course is how paranoia works.

"Turn right up here," said the woman he still thought of as Ether, even now that he knew her real name. "We can get back onto the interstate around Memphis and take it into Nashville, maybe find some quiet spot outside the city to sleep tonight. We'll get your pills in the morning, then it'll be onto McLean and then it'll be over. We'll get paid, I'll throw in enough to get the Navigator a facelift, then everything will be fine and normal again."

"Can we even do that, with the pills? For all I know, they've already told Homeland Security that the infamous Abbott Coburn is on the way, hauling a suitcase nuke, an alien corpse, a human corpse, a Soviet You-Tube makeup influencer Manchurian Candidate saboteur, and two bags of illegal guns and cash."

"No. We're getting your medicine."

"What do you care?"

"Because I don't want to hide in the real world because of some bullshit happening on screens. We've done nothing wrong. You need your medication; we're going to go get it. If the cops are waiting for us there, fine. We'll step out with our hands on our heads, obey their commands, and ask for a lawyer. They'll search the vehicle and it'll be scary and traumatic, but then we'll get over it, because despite what the modern world insists, *you can actually get over bad things happening to you.* But I don't even think that's going to happen. I think we are falling into the classic internet mirage that makes it seem like everything that happens there is super incredibly important in the real world when, most of the time, it's nothing."

She hadn't actually given his phone back, and Abbott wondered if she had tossed it.

"Here's the thing," he said, "no matter how this turns out, even if the box is full of lifesaving medicine for orphans, I'm always going to be the incel terrorist. I can live to be a hundred years old, and that's all I'll be. The internet doesn't forget."

"Fuck the internet, then."

"That's easy for you to say."

"Is it?"

"All of my friends are online. It's where I work, it's where I live. If everyone abandons me . . ." He shrugged, unable to even make himself visualize it.

"I'm not going to say that those friendships aren't real," said Ether. "I'm not an asshole. But any friend who abandons you over a baseless internet rumor wasn't your real friend. Whether you knew them in person or on a screen."

"You say so much that sounds like it came off some housewife's inspirational Facebook meme."

"That's another game the cynics play. 'Because this objectively true thing has been said too many times by unoriginal thinkers, we have to reject it and make ourselves miserable just to spite them.'"

Abbott just sighed.

"Also," she continued, "let's say that, hypothetically, you should find yourself walking back some of your views, deciding that maybe the stuff about women and all that doesn't square with reality as it exists outside the black box of doom. If any friends abandon you afterward, if they say you betrayed the movement, they also weren't your real friends. They just saw you as fellow cannon fodder for this war they decided they're fighting."

"Hmm."

She let that sit for a while and, having apparently decided it was safe to do so, ventured one last thought:

"And if you should find yourself in a group of friends who are all united under a cause that makes them miserable, then losing those friends wouldn't necessarily be a bad thing. The wrong friends can make you lonelier than being alone."

From the blog of Phil Greene:

It all started with the Walkman. I was forty years old the first time I saw one, a kid in downtown LA wearing headphones and blasting music from a cassette player on his belt, shutting out the world. This technology had literally invented a new kind of human behavior never previously observed in the species, closing off sense organs to intentionally block out face-to-face social interaction. That was the first time I understood that technology could put the individual in a mental cocoon, replacing the nutrients of tangible socialization with the sweet, processed slurry of passive mass media. When the internet came along a decade later, I knew we were counting down the days until we had the internet version of the Walkman, a portable device that would relieve the individual of the burden to function as a member of society. Only now, instead of the hypnotism of music, it is the parasite of the Forbidden Numbers, rewiring the brain, altering the subject's very ability to perceive the universe itself. All around me are youths under the grip of cluster B personality disorders that used to be rare but now are the norm, minds totally unable to process physical reality. They transmogrify sensory input into a simplistic technicolor melodrama, the only reality they've been trained to understand. I need groceries. I don't know if it's safe for me to drive in my current state of health. The meds are making me sick. I don't want to ask her to take me. She told me they have services now, through your phone, where you can pay a stranger to do your shopping for you. But of course that exists; in a world in which we have all been robbed of the friendships we'd previously have relied upon for such favors, corporations have stepped in with algorithms tuned to the Forbidden Numbers. I feel them calling to me, their promises of eternal frictionless convenience and distraction. A warm, wet, comfortable pod, customized to fit me like a glove. I will not succumb. I will die a free man. I will die fighting.

CONFIRMED: Phil Greene is DEAD and it is believed that GSG killed him

Posted to r/DCTerrorAttack by GoochVortex99

It is now confirmed that Phil Greene, the owner of the property where Karen Wozniak was staying, WAS FOUND DEAD EARLY THURSDAY MORNING, just hours before she was picked up by

Abbott and left town. This is THE THIRD DEATH TO OCCUR AT THIS PROPERTY IN THE LAST THREE YEARS. Phil's daughter, Sundae, passed in February of this year, his wife, Bonnie, died three years ago of an "opioid overdose."

I have attached a map of all missing persons cases from the surrounding area. I'm counting at least eight victims since 2019 who've vanished within five miles of this property. We should cross-reference those victims with Abbott, Phil Greene, and Ms. Wozniak to see if they had prior contact.

All of this fits with the rumors of an underground tunnel network below the Greene property, where bodies (captives?) could easily be stored out of view. A group like this would have made for perfect recruiting material for the Russians, especially if they could have been convinced it was a plan to accelerate the End Times.

17

ETHER

"I hope you don't think I'm being glib," said Ether at a gas station in a town called Earle, "but you know this makes your career, right? As a content-creator? In that industry, it doesn't matter how you get your name out there, as long as it's out there. You'll be telling this story on podcasts and videos for the rest of your life."

The gas station's door was plastered with signs promising that many of their offerings could be purchased with government food assistance credits. There were no other customers in the store, and at the moment, Ether could easily have been convinced that the cashier was the town's only resident.

As they drove away, Abbott glanced at a passing Dollar General store and muttered, "What do people do here? In towns like this, I mean? What do they . . . do?"

Ether watched out her window as they passed a vacant lot, an auto parts store, another vacant lot, a church, and a boarded-up restaurant.

"The same as anywhere. They make friends, they laugh, they fall in love, plant gardens, bake cookies, make art, read books, go camping, have barbecues, drink hot cocoa on winter mornings. And the kids, well, they probably all dream of moving to a city."

"Who would bring kids into this?"

"Some people would rather raise kids here than in an apartment surrounded by noisy traffic. Didn't you just complain that you didn't have countryside where you could go off and have bicycle adventures? Well, here it is. I see woods right over there."

"I don't mean this town, I mean this world. This nightmare. Why would you bring kids into it right at the moment it's all falling apart?"

"Do you really think that? The stuff about how we're living in a dystopia? Or is that just something you say?"

"Are you joking? Oh, wait, I forgot. You haven't been watching the news for the last couple of years."

"Not in the way other people watch it, no. I've been doing plenty of research. About the world, how it's trending. And every time I share it, people get *really* upset."

He shrugged. "People don't like to face reality."

"No, Abbott, they do not. Do you remember the first thing I told you that made you think I was possibly crazy?"

"I'm pretty sure I thought that before you'd even opened your mouth. But at some point, you said you needed to tell me about the worms."

"Yeah. Well, I think now is the time."

"Oh, God. Let me brace myself."

"So, what I'm about to tell you," said Ether, always unsure of quite where to start, "will trigger in you a reflex. First you will deny it, then you will get angry. What I want you to understand is that this reflex has been trained into you, specifically to block out what I'm saying. When we're angry, the listening parts of our brains go dark."

"That sounded like a long way to say, 'Promise you won't get mad,' which I think is scientifically the world's worst way to begin a conversation."

"In our civilization," she began, "stuff has been happening in the background, quietly, out of view. There were these worms. They're born from tiny, invisible eggs. The eggs get into the water, you drink it, the eggs burrow into your intestines. From those eggs hatches a worm that's thin and white and up to three feet long, weaving itself through your muscles as it grows. It tunnels through that tissue until it finds a spot to emerge from your skin, where it creates a blister that feels like it's on fire, twenty-four hours a day. Most people, to seek relief, will dunk the blister in water, which is exactly what the worm wants. It disperses its eggs, and the cycle starts all over again in other victims. To get the worm out of your body, they have to slowly extract it through that burning blister, pulling it through the muscle millimeters at a time, over *months*."

"And this is an . . . alien worm?" asked Abbott. "Is that what's in the box?"

"No, they're from Earth. They've been infecting people for millennia. They're called *Guinea worms*. In the 1980s, more than three million people a year were infested with them. Last year, it was fifteen."

"Fifteen million?"

"No. Fifteen."

"I don't get it."

"What happened is that just in the time you and I have been alive, a whole bunch of heroes coordinated across a whole bunch of countries in Africa and Asia and elsewhere and wiped out the Guinea worm. Countless millions have lived and often died with horrible, three-foot-long worms in their bodies, including lots of children. But no more. While your news feeds were bludgeoning you with stories of school shootings, pathological politicians, and nonstop outrage, this war against the worms was quietly won thanks to relentless, selfless effort by thousands of strangers."

"Okay?" said Abbott, juggling a soda and a bag of Takis chips while he drove. "So that's good news, right?"

"Had you heard anything about it?"

"I don't know. Maybe? Wasn't Jimmy Carter involved somehow? What does this have to do with us?"

"I'm getting to it."

They dumped Haley Swanson's corpse in the water at Greers Ferry Lake

Posted to r/DCTerrorAttack by TrueCrimeTrudy

Everyone here is missing the forest for the trees. Reports are saying the Navigator was parked at Heber Springs overnight before Abbott nearly drove it into the water. Yes, videos seem to show the footlocker was still in the back of the Navigator, but they wouldn't have dumped it along with the corpse for fear it would float back up to the surface. The most plausible version of events is that at some point overnight, somewhere around Greers Ferry Lake or one of the connecting rivers, they dumped Haley out of the box, probably weighing the body down with stones or bricks. They picked that spot on purpose: Heber Springs is exactly 666 miles from Tallahassee, Florida. This completes a satanic ceremony that states if a body is laid to rest 666 miles from its place of birth, its soul will be condemned to hell. The tinfoil around the box is key, as they believe it prevents the soul from escaping before the ceremony can be completed.

This is clearly part of a ritual that Abbott and other members of the cult believe will trigger the apocalypse. These women are OFFERINGS and if we don't stop them THERE WILL BE MORE.

KEY

A plane ticket to Nashville, Tennessee, was purchased approximately three minutes after Key read about the supposed prescription pickup. She told herself that if it turned out to be a dead end, she'd go get some drinks on Broadway, catch some live music, and tell Patrick that she'd taken his advice to do something fun instead of trying to single-handedly stop an apocalyptic terror plot.

So now she was boarding, having snagged the last aisle seat. She found the window seat was occupied by a woman who had already strapped on noise-canceling headphones, the middle seat still blessedly empty. She held out hope that it would somehow, mercifully, remain that way, like maybe whoever had bought that ticket had died horribly on the way to the airport. She settled in and was looking at her phone one final time when an evil shadow was cast over her, surely the looming specter of the passenger who'd come to claim that empty seat. Probably someone annoying, who would demand the armrest and nonstop in-flight conversation.

She looked up to find it was Hunter Coburn.

ETHER

"My grandfather," continued Ether, "who I basically never talk to anymore, one hundred percent believes Christ is going to return to earth at any minute to bring about the apocalypse, due to mankind's sinfulness. He believes everything he watches on the news is a sign: encroaching Communism, the Satanic conspiracy to allow gays to marry, race-mixing, debauchery, pornography, drag queens, the QAnon child sex cult, the climate change 'hoax' he says has fooled the world. He has a TV on every minute he's awake, tuned to these ultra-right-wing news outlets ranting about depravity."

"I know old guys like that," said Abbott. "My dad works with a couple. They're nuts. You can't even talk to them."

"So we can agree that, purely via the carefully filtered media a person consumes, they can come to fully believe in an apocalypse that is not, in fact, occurring?"

"I mean, the world is on fire, just not in the way your grandpa thinks."

"Are you one hundred percent sure, Abbott, that you haven't fallen into the exact same trap, just from the other side?"

"Ah, you're about to tell me climate change isn't real."

"I am not. I've seen the melting ice with my own two eyes. But let me ask you this: When I met you, I asked if you felt like you were cursed to be born when you were, if you felt like you had arrived just in time to see the world end. So I'm guessing that you think the world is collapsing because of the feminization of society, something like that? That we're killing masculinity?"

"I mean, that's definitely part of it. Men are scared to date; no babies are being made."

"Okay, and in my corner of the internet, the harbingers of doom were the opposite: savage patriarchal governments crushing women's rights, taking us back to the dark ages while overpopulation destroys the environment. So that's two groups who both believe the world is ending, *but for totally opposite reasons.* Some say runaway capitalism, some say runaway socialism. Some say it'll be chaotic lawlessness, some say iron-fisted authoritarianism. It's like I have one panicked neighbor saying there's an impending drought and another screaming that we're all about to drown in a flood. Somebody has to be wrong."

"That wouldn't make them both wrong."

Ether groaned and put her head in her hands.

"Okay," she said, trying again. "How about this: What do you think the world will look like in the future, post-collapse?"

Abbott thought for a moment as if picturing it. "Uh, terrified people scrounging for food and running from bandits. Rampant disease, infrastructure breakdown. All the stuff from the movies, I guess."

"No internet?"

"I wouldn't think so."

"No electricity? No running water, no sewage? No hospitals?"

"Probably not."

"Got it. So, what I'm about to say isn't an opinion, it's not a matter of personal philosophy or politics. It is an objective fact that what you're describing is how virtually all humans have lived through all of history. Until, that is, about thirty years ago. Just in the time I've been alive, somewhere between two and a half and three billion people got their first access to clean water and toilets. That's *billion*, with a *B*. About that same number got electricity in their homes for the first time in their lives. Worldwide, infant mortality has been cut in half, illiteracy has dropped almost as much. Suicides are going up here in the US, but worldwide, they've dropped by a third—again, that's all just in my lifetime. Basically, every positive category has skyrocketed: access to communication, paved roads, motorized transportation, international travel, climate control, medicine . . ."

"Okay, it sounds like you're talking about a bunch of good stuff that happened in China and India and—I don't know. A bunch of poor countries I'll never visit."

"I'm talking about how your entire life span has been spent in a *literal reverse apocalypse*. I'm talking about billions of people who lived in what you would consider post-collapse conditions have had those conditions remedied, gaining roofs and lights and safety. A human's chances of dying from famine or natural disasters are as low as they've ever been, ever, in the history of the species. It's been nothing short of a worldwide miracle that makes everything Jesus supposedly did in the Bible look like party tricks. And people like you and me and others in our demographic describe that state of affairs as the world being 'on fire.' I think that's a bizarre mass delusion and that there's a very specific reason for it: we've been trained to cling to a miserable view of the world to the point that we think that *not* seeing the world as miserable makes us bad people. When I spent those months doing hallucinogens, I didn't suddenly see the beauty and harmony of nature; I saw that humans everywhere were working really hard to make life better for other humans and that almost none of us appreciate it. I'm not crediting this miracle to capitalism or socialism or any other kind of ism but to the fact that it's what humans do, because humans are amazing. And it's all invisible to us because the progress occurs behind these dark walls of cynicism, outside the black box of doom."

"That's nice. And again, nothing you said means anything considering the world's scientists have agreed that climate change will wipe out civilization."

"If we don't fix it, yeah. Climate change is a huge deal; it's terrifying. And also, it is objectively true that if we do fix it, the media *will only report it as bad news*. All the headlines will be about the oil and coal workers who lost their jobs, birds dying to windmills—they'll only focus on the negative side effects. And don't tell me we never clean up our messes. There used to be oil slicks on our rivers that would literally catch fire. Sulfur dioxide used to choke the air—when's the last time you've heard about acid rain? Or the hole in the ozone layer? Go read about how previous generations all had lead poisoning or how food contamination used to be a nightmare. I'm not saying everything will be fine; I can't predict the future. I'm saying that it is a one hundred percent certifiable guaranteed fact that it *can* be fine. But people like us have decided that we're never allowed to even acknowledge the possibility."

"Or maybe it's hard for people to care about toilets in India when another maniac is shooting up a school every week."

"You think that happens every week?"

"I bet you have a whole bunch of stats to dump on me about that, too. I'm sure the parents of those dead kids would love to hear them."

"And there's the anger. People hate it when you threaten their nihilism! That's the black box, drawing you back in. Can't you see that it wants you to be afraid to do anything but cower in front of your screens? It only has one trick, one card to play, which is this idea that *bad news is the only news you can trust*. I'm telling you, if you just allow yourself to step outside of it, you'll see it for what it is: a prison where the walls are made of nightmares."

KEY

When Key and Hunter had made eye contact, a terrible, silent understanding passed between them. He'd then wordlessly shuffled into the middle seat, holding a paperback of *Lonesome Dove* that looked like it'd been read fifty times. After settling in, he glanced to his left to confirm that the headphones girl wasn't listening.

He whispered, "I don't understand. Did you arrange this?"

"If I had the power to control who sits around me on flights, I'd travel a lot more," said Key. "What really happened is we both heard the same internet rumor and both booked the first flight out of LAX with open seats, which was this one, which won't get us on the ground until ten P.M. thanks to losing two hours to time zones. There were only four seats left when I booked, so I don't think it took much luck for us to wind up next to each other."

"This was the only one left for me. So the thing about them stopping in Nashville is true. I almost talked myself out of it. I mean, if these two are fugitives, why would they do something as dumb as call in a prescription for pickup? But then I thought, *Oh, right, it's Abbott, that's exactly something he would do*."

"You said he left his devices behind. If they've truly been cut off since Thursday morning, they may not know they're being tracked. Maybe they're just bumbling their way across America, plowing through marathons and cardboard boats, just blithely humming along in a little bubble of obliviousness."

"That last bit should be the title of Abbott's autobiography."

"Anyway, Nashville is our best guess and, if the rumors are true, probably the only plausible chance to get to them before DC." She shrugged. "I figured it was a long shot, but also my only shot."

"*You* figured?" said Hunter, raising his voice a little too much for a conversation they probably shouldn't be having in public at all. "Why are you doing this on your own?"

Key pretended to study the flight emergency manual as if she hadn't heard him.

"Because," continued Hunter, trying hard to restrain his volume, "if this thing is what the internet claims it is, what you seem to agree it is, every field office from here to DC should have every agent working it around the clock. There should be roadblocks, media alerts. The cops should have searched my home, seized everything from Abbott's room, dug through his computer for a manifesto or itinerary. I should have been answering questions in an interrogation room for twelve straight hours about his friends, his behavior, his recent purchases. Instead, it's just you, talking to me at work for two minutes and making no effort to even record my answers. Where is everybody? And how are you any different from the internet weirdos following this out of boredom?"

She was rescued from having to answer that by the flight attendant's seat belt demonstration. They didn't resume talking until they were in the air, engine noise providing at least some minimal cover for a sensitive conversation being held within two feet of seven strangers.

"It's entirely possible," began Key, suddenly desperate to get some airline alcohol into her system, "that there are dozens of agents ready to spring the trap in Nashville. I mean, for all we know, they've got photos from traffic cameras pinpointing the exact route—the Navigator may not even make it to the city. I'm out of the loop."

"Well, that's just great. Is there somebody who can bring *me* into the loop?"

"If you find someone, let me know. Now, I'm thinking you're making this trip for one of two reasons: The first would be that it's just what you said on the phone, that you think the feds are going to railroad your son into a lifelong criminal record over something he just stumbled into. In that case, you're heading out to try to get to him first, to talk him down. The second option is that you're worried that it's the opposite, that the feds aren't on top of this at all. If so, you're heading out to scream to anyone with a badge that they need to do something before your kid gets remembered as the next Timothy McVeigh."

"I don't know which one it is!" replied Hunter, again getting a little too loud. "Everything I read online, it's like they're talking about a stranger. But the more I read, the more that version of Abbott gets overwritten onto my brain. Like maybe I never knew him."

"I would like to say something reassuring right now, but do you know who, thirty years ago, was shocked to find out Timothy McVeigh had blown up a building, including a whole day care full of innocent kids? His dad, Bill McVeigh. He was all, 'My son was always angry and talking shit about Bill Clinton, but he had no violence in him!'"

For the first time, Hunter seemed shaken. He sat back and stared at the seat in front of him, clearly seeing something else.

"Okay," he said, now quietly enough that Key had to lean over a bit to hear, "so who's this rich guy they're talking about, the one who lives outside DC? He doesn't fit the terrorist profile, does he?"

"See, everybody keeps saying that. But I think he may be a Marvin Heemeyer type."

"Who's that?"

ABBOTT

"All of these towns have a Dollar General store," said Abbott as they pulled out of a single-pump gas station in the town of Friendship, Tennessee, population 668. "Dollar General, convenience store, church, school, cemetery, payday loans."

"You know why, right?" said Ether, sucking from a tube of Go-Gurt. "Grocery stores sell processed junk and fresh produce, but they make all of their money off the junk; it's higher margins, less waste. Well, the dollar stores were like, 'Why not just sell the junk and forget the rest of that fresh-food nonsense?' They run the real grocery stores out of the poorest neighborhoods." She studied the map and said, "If we turned that direction, we could go to the town of Frog Jump, Nutbush, or—and this is my favorite—Dancyville. That's kind of fun."

"I'm going to guess it is not, in fact, fun," said Abbott, staring at a road that sliced through two fields that seemed to be growing waist-high weeds. "All that stuff you said about the world getting better, that's great for all of those other countries, for all the poor people in Bangladesh or wherever. But the USA is dying, I mean, that's objectively true. These towns we're passing, you could film a zombie movie in them without dressing the backgrounds. There was a time in this country when you could afford a big house and two cars on one job, with the other parent staying home to raise the kids. Now everybody has to work two jobs to afford one apartment and their student loan payments."

"But who told you that, the thing about everybody affording a big house with one job back in the good old days? I feel like we're getting that from old sitcoms or magazine ads. A quarter of those 1950s houses didn't have indoor plumbing, and almost none had air-conditioning; that wasn't a common thing until decades later. And those houses were *tiny* and packed with three generations of family. I mean, none of this is opinion, you can look it up—the average American now has as much living space as an entire family did back then. And no, they didn't have two cars; they were sharing one, if that. You're right that they didn't have student loan payments, but that's because hardly anybody went to college—hell, in the 1960s, most Americans didn't even finish *high school.* So forget about choosing your dream career; back then, people were still just working in whatever factory kept their town afloat. And if you go back a hundred years, you're in a totally unrecognizable society. In this part of the country, lots of the kids would have goiters from iodine deficiency, illiteracy would be rampant, virtually every adult would be missing multiple teeth. Oh, and it was considered weird if parents *didn't* beat their children. None of what I'm saying requires some deep dive into the research, none of it is disputed. Look it up!

"And then there's the big one, the one nobody ever thinks about: *time.* Everybody longs for those home-cooked meals like in the Norman Rockwell paintings, but those meals only happened if Mom spent *hours* cooking them—most women literally spent most of their time in the kitchen. We make jokes about processed food and drive-thrus, but that stuff is the reason mothers are able to do literally anything other than chop potatoes and knead dough all day. And you can apply that to everything—it used to take much, much longer to shop, to correspond with friends, to travel, to bathe, to wash your clothes, to buy a book. That's the first thing you'd notice if you went back—how your spare time would evaporate because every single little task takes longer, if you can do it at all."

"Okay, I think you're going the other way, now, exaggerating how bad it was."

"No! I've just scratched the surface! Take sex, for example. For most of history, sex education of any kind was forbidden; it wasn't even openly discussed, by anyone, ever. Gay kids, trans kids would've thought they were possessed by demons, and everyone grew up thinking masturbation was this bizarre, grotesque habit only they indulged in—you had actual medical texts that said that boys were at risk of insanity if they touched themselves. They used to sell little spiked rings for boys to wear that would stab them if they got an erection. And did the average man even know how to perform oral sex on a woman until, like, twenty years ago? If you want to get graphic, please remember that you don't have to go back *that* far to find a country that doesn't believe in regular bathing or use toilet paper. Any horny time traveler would be in for a hell of a shock when it came to hygiene. Oh, and until the 1950s, every third bed was infested with bedbugs."

"Why do you know all this?"

"Why *don't* you know all this? This is the fundamental context of your life! I mean, you don't even have to get into the big-picture stuff—life expectancy, infant mortality, literacy, civil rights, way fewer people dying in dangerous jobs—I could spend the next week just listing all of the little everyday improvements we don't even think about. If pleasure was a thing that could be measured, the available pleasure to the average person over all of history would basically be a flat line on a graph that then explodes upward right before you and I were born. In terms of timing, we're fucking lottery winners! Only we know the pleasure of a climate-controlled room, a daily hot shower, of cheap and delicious food and drink, of comfortable shoes and a dazzling ocean of entertainment so vast that we get stressed out trying to keep up. Like music! Music is magic, it heals the soul, and our access to it is *infinitely greater than it ever was before*! And literature—the most beautiful works from the most incredible minds are out there to be read on demand, at almost no cost. And then there's all the little conveniences we instantly took for granted. The ability to read a review of a product you're buying only goes back to Amazon; before that, for all of history, you were just shopping blind. And think about Wikipedia; the guy who invented that deserves a Nobel Prize—it's one of the great inventions in history, and the fact that it's free to use is *insane*. They didn't even have that in *Star Trek*!"

"That's great, when I get back to my phone, I'll go to Wikipedia and read about how fascists are taking over every government in the Western world."

"Yes! Exactly! And that's happening because all of those extremists are selling the same blatant lie: 'The world is falling apart, and we have to get back what *they* took from us.' At that point, it's always just a matter of deciding which vulnerable group to pin the blame on. And it works because their followers are also living in the black box of doom, where screens tell them everything outside their front door is a chaotic hellworld. People become bitter monsters because the box tells them that's the only defense against a world gone mad, so it becomes a self-fulfilling prophecy. It's like I've woken up in a world where everyone not only believes the earth is flat but they're really, *really* angry about it. And they reject any evidence to the contrary because they prefer to be—"

"Oh, goddamn it," grunted Abbott. "It says these Takis expired a month ago. Shit, I knew they tasted off."

HUNTER

"Marvin Heemeyer was a business owner in Colorado," said Key, who Hunter was now pretty sure had started drinking even before she'd left for the airport. "He believed he'd been screwed over in a local zoning dispute.

It had to do with a concrete plant that was going to block the entrance to his muffler shop. In response to all this, he spent a year and a half welding nine tons of armor to a bulldozer."

"Oh, the Killdozer guy! Yeah, I heard about that. I kind of like his style."

"Yes, the Killdozer guy. He dedicated his whole life to turning the vehicle into a tank, including gun ports to fire in every direction. He created a list of targets and welded himself into the cockpit—there was literally no exit; it was a suicide mission from the start. Then, well, he went on a rampage. For two hours, he tore ass around town, flattening the businesses and homes of everyone who'd ever wronged him, destroying thirteen buildings in the process. SWAT teams riddled the vehicle with bullets, Heemeyer just laughed it off—at one point, they supposedly considered calling in the National Guard to take out the Killdozer with an attack helicopter. He eventually got stuck in the basement of one of his targets and had no means to extract himself. There was a gunshot from inside, and that was that—Heemeyer had shot himself in the head after having, in his mind, resolved his zoning dispute. Well, I have this theory that we have been quietly building a society full of Heemeyers, seemingly normal people with middle-class lives and brains full of retribution fantasies. Supposedly mature adults with no sense of scale or proportionality."

Hunter had no problem believing this, as he had, in fact, driven in LA traffic before. Also, his brief time sitting next to this woman had convinced him that she had surely been involved in, or caused, at least three divorces.

"Okay," he said, "let's say that's Sokolov's mindset. Isn't it possible that Abbott has no idea what's going on? I get that every dad says that, but it is extremely hard for me to believe he'd drop everything to go on this suicide mission, and it's extremely easy for me to believe that a girl offered him a cash job and that he let his dick make the call."

"Oh, absolutely," said Key. "It's a common tactic—a coconspirator can't leak details of the mission if they don't have them. A North Korean dissident was assassinated by two girls who thought they were doing a YouTube prank. Strangers offered them cash to rub goop on a stranger's face; the substance turned out to be a nerve agent."

"Well, now, hold on. Doesn't that mean that it's possible this Green Sunglasses Girl *also doesn't know?*"

"Who can say? Maybe she was just offered a pile of cash to transport a sealed container and she recruited the first driver she could find. Maybe this rich psychopath pulling the strings is the only true villain and everybody else is just doing a job. I mean, why else would they feel safe dropping by goddamned Walgreens in the middle of their apocalyptic suicide mission?"

"Then they'd have no reason to resist if they got pulled over, right? Could it be that easy? They get to Nashville, the cops jump out of the bushes, the feds seize the bomb, an investigation clears Abbott because not even his handler knew what was going on. It's not a crime to accept cash to drive someone. It's still a free country, if only in certain specific places, times, and circumstances."

"The problem is that if Sokolov trusted the shipment to a pair of outsiders, it means he'd be even more trigger-happy with a remote detonation. If he gets wind that the Navigator has been stopped, he'd have every motivation to grab whatever burner phone is connected to the trigger and hit Send. Get rid of the evidence and the two key witnesses in one shot."

18

ZEKE

"So your friend is gonna rob the Walgreens?" asked a linebacker of a woman named Rhonda, a.k.a. Beast Infection. "Have you seen those videos from San Francisco, or Portland, or somewhere? Flash mobs just come in and load up carts and walk right out without paying; it's like a crime wave."

"No," said Zeke, "just forget it."

Several large, noisy women had packed themselves into Zeke's apartment, all members of his sister's Roller Derby team. Their Saturday-evening match had just ended, and their postgame ritual was to gather there, have an enormous meal, and then go out and get drunk to celebrate their most recent loss. He was waiting for them to leave because their brassy conversations always made it impossible to concentrate on literally anything—in this case, doing hot-pink touch-up painting around the baseboards of the apartment. At some point, his sister had started talking about the situation with Abbott, and as was her habit, she told the story in such way that made the whole thing sound like juicy gossip.

"No," said Cammy, whose skater name was CamHorror. "They think they're going to be at the Walgreens, but they'll have a bomb with them. Like a big one, bigger than the one from Christmas 2020. Remember that?"

"They're going to blow up the Walgreens?" asked another girl, who went by LaunchLady. "Why? Does it have to do with that thing with Butterflaps swatting that little girl a while back?"

"No," said Zeke, from his prone painting position. "They're going to try to blow up Washington, DC. But they're stopping at Walgreens. Or at least, they were planning to. Tomorrow morning, apparently."

"And there'll be a SWAT team waiting for them," promised Cammy. "And *the two probably won't be taken alive*!"

"Oh my god," said another of the girls, Terror Kata Pot. "Why haven't I heard about this? Was Butterflaps the one with the birthmark on her head?"

"It's all over the internet," replied Cammy, who was tracking a pizza delivery on her phone.

"And how does Zeke know the guy?" asked Beast.

"They're internet friends. He's actually a streamer, he goes by—what is it?"

"Abaddon," said Zeke. "A-B-A-D-D-O-N. It's from the Bible, I think."

Yet another woman, Fountains of Pain, said, "Is this him?" She held up her phone. "He made a video praising Harvey Weinstein?"

"What? No. Ignore that. He got into an argument with some YouTube feminists. It was stupid."

"It's the first thing that comes up when you search that name. It says he's an incel and likes Hitler."

"He's not! And no, I don't even know what they're talking about. Hitler? Ignore all that. That's all—it's all taken out of context."

"This is *crazy*," gasped LaunchLady. "They're saying here that Butterflaps is an undercover Russian? They found an old picture of her with Putin when she was little. And she's an alien? And they're in a cult?"

"Nobody knows what her deal is. I just know that she abducted Abbott and he's probably going to die when they get here, and nobody cares."

"But he's, like, an incel terrorist or something?"

"He helped us out last year," said Cammy. "Remember when the van broke down? The engine blew up and it was going to be like five thousand dollars to fix it? Abaddon and his fans did a fundraiser, and they paid for the whole thing. They've never even met us; they just stepped in because they knew we were having a rough time. It saved our asses."

"That's cool," said Beast. "Oh, this girl who made the video criticizing Abbott is a real bitch; it came out a while back that she was bullying her staff. Or I think that was her. Have you told the police about all this?"

"The police are the ones who are going to shoot him," said Zeke. "You know how the cops are; they don't care. Their goal is to make sure neither of them can set off the bomb. They probably won't even give a warning— they'll just jump out and pump five hundred bullets into the car."

"Zeke wants to get Abbott away from her before that happens," added

Cammy, before looking out the door and saying, "Ugh, the pizza driver missed our turn. Every time!"

"Could you get a warning to him somehow," asked Terror, "that the cops are waiting to ambush him?"

"Even if I could," replied Zeke, wiping a pink drip from the baseboard, "if it causes them to bypass the city and continue on their terrorism mission, it's not like that's better. I'd go to jail for aiding and abetting the attack. I want to get Abbott out of the car so the cops will only shoot the girl."

"So we have to somehow get to him in advance, but not *too* in advance. How would that work?"

"Well," said Beast, "you'd have to do it in a way that the girl doesn't get spooked and set off the bomb." She took a hit off a vape that stank like bubble gum.

"That's right," added Terror. "You'd need to stop the vehicle somehow on the approach, like block the street or something, in a way that makes them both get out. Then we pull up alongside, grab your friend, and drive away. Then maybe the cops could come in while the vehicle is stopped. Done, disaster averted."

"But," said Beast, "we'd have to know the exact route they'd take."

Zeke was absolutely baffled as to the direction the conversation had taken. "Who's 'we' in this scenario?"

Ignoring him, Terror said, "Somebody pull up a map."

Abbott and GSG are NOT in Nashville to pick up a prescription

Posted to r/DCTerrorAttack by FedThrowaway66974

As others have pointed out, it obviously makes no sense for Abbott to resurface and fill his anxiety meds in the middle of a worldwide manhunt. The FBI believes the "prescription" he is picking up is actually code for five kilos of fentanyl.

The drug will be added to the radioactive material that is lining the armored case so that, upon detonation, it will also contaminate the shrapnel ejected from the device. Fentanyl in this pure form can trigger an overdose through skin contact alone, so the goal would be to get granules into the victims' open wounds and to generally contaminate every surface in the vicinity. This would poison first responders and emergency room personnel, creating a wave of additional patients and incapacitating medics just when they are most desperately needed, which of course will only compound the chaos already caused by the radioactive material.

This type of dirty bomb is known as a "Pandora's Box," a device containing as many different contaminants as possible to create mass disruption of rescue and recovery efforts. There is talk internally that the terror cell may have also acquired some quantity of the nerve agent sarin as well as a weaponized form of the group A streptococcus bacteria, which, if introduced under the skin via a puncture wound becomes necrotizing fasciitis, a.k.a., the flesh-eating bacteria. This is so far unconfirmed.

Also, this is NOT a suicide attack. Karen Wozniak and Abbott Coburn both have substantial streaming audiences, their intention is to operate the vehicle via remote and stream every step of the attack from some safe location. The goal is to create such a sheer volume of traumatic video across so many social media accounts that it will be unavoidable, a shock that ripples through the population in waves, totally dominating all social traffic and headlines. In addition to a government left in chaos due to decimation of the Court, imagine dozens of children suffering fentanyl overdoses and having their flesh eaten by bacteria and radiation, the body horror streamed for audiences in real time. Imagine every viewer terrified that their town is next, that any one of their neighbors could be recruited for a similar attack.

I've also received some shocking intel that I've not yet been able to confirm, so I am going to hold off on sharing it for now.

Needless to say, if it is true, it is a bombshell that could change how we think about all of this. Be sure to follow this account for updates.

KEY

"Now that you're here," said Key as they waited in BNA's baggage claim for the machine to shit their luggage, "what's your plan?"

"Well," said Hunter, "considering there is zero chance of me getting even one minute of sleep tonight, I intend to rent a car and pass by every single hotel in the Nashville area to see if one of them has a big white Navigator parked there. If so, I'll find his room and brace myself for the dumbest conversation of my lifetime."

"Do you have any idea how many hotels are in Nashville?"

"Nope."

"Around three hundred and fifty. And some have valet parking with the lots scattered miles away. You'd be lucky to hit ten of them before morning."

"Then I'll try to get into his head and guess which one he'd pick. Unless you have a better idea. I mean, what was *your* plan?"

Key sighed, having dreaded this very question. "I have friends who feed me inside information," she began, "sometimes, when they feel like it. If JTTF is setting up to collar Abbott and the girl, I'll sit back, watch it go down, and feel some closure when the bomb squad examines the box and finds that it's full of, well, whatever they find. But if it turns out they have no such plan, then I will see if I can do something myself."

Hunter let that sit for a moment, then asked, "Like what?"

"I have no arrest powers. But, as a citizen, there is nothing stopping me from engaging the couple in a conversation, should I happen to run into them. And if, in the middle of that conversation, the girl should reach for a gun, well . . . I'll do what any armed citizen would do in that circumstance." She saw the question on Hunter's face and said, "I don't travel without the Glock."

After a chilly pause, Hunter said, "And if it's my son that reaches for a weapon?"

"It sounds like he's not the type."

"He's the type to panic. Whether it's you or some FBI agent in a blue windbreaker, he's not going to take the confrontation well. And if that agent—be it you or someone else—thinks there's a bomb in the back that could irradiate several city blocks, they may start shooting the second Abbott makes a move toward anything that looks like a detonator, or toward any pocket that could hold such a device. He could get shot reaching for his asthma inhaler."

"So you're saying that you'd prefer it be you who confronts him, before that happens."

"Yes, I'd like it to be us," he said, casually cementing a partnership with two little letters. "Me because I'm his dad, you because you want credit for the bust, not the FBI or the Joint Terrorism whatever."

"I don't care about that."

"Several hundred dollars spent on a plane ticket tells me otherwise. And I'm guessing your friend inside the bureau knows that, which is why they're not telling you anything. And why I bet you didn't tell them you were making this trip."

She sighed. "I booked a rental car in advance. Did you?"

"No."

"Well, there's no need for us to both pay for one. We'll just use mine."

"Yeah," he said casually. "That makes sense."

ETHER

"Do we risk a hotel?" she asked, through a yawn. "We're on the cusp of Nashville; they've probably got some good ones."

Abbott shook his head. "I'd just spend all night worrying that cops or fans or vigilantes would be blocking the door come morning."

"So you're saying that regardless of the quality of the bed, your worries would ruin the experience."

"Are you going to try to stretch that into a metaphor for my whole life? That I'm physically comfortable but my brain won't let me enjoy it?"

"Well, it's not a metaphor, it's literally what's happening, right?"

He scoffed and gave an ugly smirk that made Ether think she'd maybe crossed a line. She found herself holding her breath.

"You think you have it all figured out," he said, sounding more exhausted than anything, "but the way humans work, the current world is the baseline, that's what we know. Then our mood is based on whether we think that's going to get better or worse. So, as a white woman, yeah, you've been on this winning streak that promises to continue. But all I hear is how *my* life needs to get worse. Everything is about how we straight white men have had it too good for too long, that we need to step back from the good jobs to make room, that we should consume less for the good of the planet—but *only us*. And before you tell me this is some media narrative, here's my individual, actual reality: I don't own a home or a car. I have no trust fund. I don't have a degree or any skills society deems useful. I'm not strong enough for construction—you can ask my dad. I tried to learn to code and couldn't wrap my mind around it. Everything else is either bottom-of-the-barrel stuff—janitors and plumbers, or women's work—customer service, nursing. That's my reality, and even your four wads of cash won't save me from that."

"Okay, but are you honestly worried you'll wind up on the streets? You're a smart guy, able-bodied. The odds are overwhelming that you'll spend the rest of your life sleeping in warm beds and eating good meals, with access to a doctor if you break your leg. So what are you really worried about? I don't think it's fear of poverty; it's fear of humiliation, that other people will think you're a loser. Because objectively, you'd still be living better than any royalty from the past."

"Well, that's just a ridiculous thing to say."

"Is it? Those palaces got so cold in the winter that their drinks froze in mid-meal. If an ancient king got an infection, some quack would stick a leech on it, and then they'd hack off the limb without anesthetic. But what he would have, that you don't, is respect."

They hit a pothole, and the box jostled behind them. Abbott shot a nervous look back at it, and Ether had caught herself doing the same.

She clicked on the dome light and studied the map. "Take this next turn. I think there's a state park we can stay in. Unless you want to get a hotel in the city. Last chance."

"No. I mean, if this thing is a homemade nuke, it's probably wise to keep it away from people as much as possible. You know, just in case the cynics of the world happen to be right about this one thing."

They parked in a pitch-dark wooded area, Abbott retrieving a sleep mask from his bag after forcing Ether to promise not to laugh. This turned out to be quite a challenge—the mask was in a camouflage pattern—but soon she had closed her eyes and begun her "sleep anywhere" technique, which involved slowly relaxing all the muscles in her body, beginning with her face. This was supposed to be accompanied by a mantra of "Don't think, don't think, don't think," but she instead found herself repeating another phrase, over and over:

"The box cannot be a bomb, the box cannot be a bomb, the box cannot be a bomb," again and again, until the sounds became nonsense.

She ransacked her memories for evidence to the contrary. Phil Greene had definitely known how to design and build; he'd cobbled together his own solar hot water heater, his own geothermal HVAC system. He knew where to get parts, prided himself on circumventing regulations at every step. "My water gets hot enough to boil your fingers like hot dogs," he'd boast, "and the shower's got enough pressure to scour off your tattoos."

But, also, she'd once seen him stand stone-calm in the face of a meth head screaming racial slurs, Phil grinning and saying, "Sonny, you didn't come out of the womb knowing those ugly words, and cursed be the man who taught them to you, for he was doing the devil's work, and it's that same serpent that wants you and I to fight right now."

There was rage in him, justified rage—Phil had not seen one minute of societal or karmic justice in his time on earth. But she never saw him take it out on a living thing. Never. And still, she could feel the box behind her, wrapped in foil that did nothing to block the dark energy that seemed to radiate from it, the box itself now planting doubts in her mind—

"I want to ask you something," said Abbott, nearly causing her to jump.

His tone implied it was an opening for an argument, and she was so, so tired. What she'd learned about Abbott was that he was the most comfortable in conflict, mainly because that was the only time he knew what to say. Maybe arguing was the sound of his childhood, and it soothed him.

"Okay," she muttered.

"When we first met, you asked me how you smelled, and I gave you an honest answer. And you said that's what you value about people like us."

"Sure, I remember."

"So be honest with me now: Is there seriously *anything* I could do to make myself attractive to women, aside from suddenly winning the lottery? And yes, I know that me just asking that question makes me unattractive. That little paradox of 'If you have to ask, you don't deserve to know' is what makes us blow our brains out."

Ether took a moment to carefully arrange the words before they left her mouth.

"Scientifically," she began, "humans tend to match at their own attractiveness level. So usually when guys ask this question, it turns out they actually have encountered willing girls, but thought they were repulsive. If you're not out there seeing what kind of women you actually match with, your view of attractiveness is shaped by movies where they cast an actor in the top one percent of attractiveness as the loser's girl-next-door love interest. So you think, *Well, I'm a loser, so I should get one of those,* but she's a Hollywood four and a real-life nine. Then when you see someone who is actually at your attractiveness level in real life, you're disgusted by your own reflection. If you're just looking to hook up, start by lowering your standards."

"See, you accuse me of having this confrontational mindset, but any time guys ask questions like this, it always gets framed in the most cynical way possible. I'm not just looking to hook up."

"Okay. Remember, you asked for honesty."

"I know."

"Are you *sure*?"

A pause. "Yeah. I guess."

"Girls know your type. If a guy's last girlfriend was a screen, it means he's used to all of the pleasure flowing one direction. If we were in a relationship, I just picture you staring at screens all day until you're in the mood to have sex, at which point, you'd expect me to be right there to provide it, then you'd go back to your screens. Girls call this *porn brain,* the guy expecting us to always be on standby, groomed and waxed while he barely remembers to brush his teeth. I think you'd love doing the occasional nice, showy favor for me but only on your terms, when you felt like it. I think you would whine like a little boy if I told you I wanted to go hiking, or boating, or to visit my mother in San Bernardino. I think you'd zone out any time I told you about my day and feel insulted if I asked you to take a shower. No real woman can give you the frictionless relationship of a media-augmented jerk-off fantasy."

"It sounds like you're saying I have to become a totally different person. Somebody who likes to go out and do things, somebody who's extroverted and fun to be around."

"Why not? You're miserable as who you are! I swear if the black box of doom had a slogan etched across its door, it would be, 'We hate ourselves and will kill anyone who asks us to change.' Who told you that no partner who demands compromise is worth it? Can't you see the conclusion they're leading you to? 'Unless I somehow get this perfect, effortless relationship, I'm better off alone, with my screens.' The box doesn't train you to do anything but remain in the box."

She closed her eyes and decided she'd sleep through any further questions. *One more day,* was her final thought. *One more day, and it's done.*

ZEKE

"The cops are gonna come by if we just keep sitting here," said Zeke to the three very drunk women around his van. "They're going to think we're running a prostitution ring out of the Walgreens parking lot."

"They should thank us!" barked Cammy, before taking a pull from a can of wine. "We're doing their jobs for them!"

Some wine flew out of her mouth when she said that. Zeke checked the time on his phone. It was two in the morning, maybe six hours until showtime.

"This van does kind of look like we're peddling weird sex stuff," said Beast Infection, who was drinking from a cardboard box of wine she'd set atop said van. "It'll make it easy for the cops to track us if we have to make a getaway afterward."

Zeke was talking to them from behind the wheel, acting as the designated driver, as he generally had to avoid alcohol due to his various medications. "Why would we need to make a getaway? We're not going to be committing a crime—we'll be saving somebody from a kidnapping."

"What if this lady gets violent and we have to beat her down?" asked Terror, the only other member of the Roller Derby team who hadn't abandoned them for a bar or a bed. "It could happen, you know."

Zeke didn't know exactly what strain she'd been smoking, but she smelled like a skunk that had been set on fire.

"No!" he shouted. "Whatever we do, it can't be violent, it can't be criminal."

"What are *you* worried about? You're in a wheelchair. They don't put disabled people in jail; it's against the law. There was a Bond villain like that. They had to just keep letting him go."

"He's right," said Cammy, "we need to wrap this up. Look, if they're coming in off the interstate, we know exactly how they'll get onto this street. The off-ramp is about two miles in that direction, by the school. It's one lane. You block that, you stop them. And we have to do it at the last second, after they've exited, before they merge."

"Again," said Zeke, exasperated, "the problem is we'd somehow have to know the exact moment they're coming down the ramp. How do we do that? If we knew how to track the vehicle, we'd just go find them now."

"Somebody will spot them," said Beast. "The whole internet is watching, and *the internet sees all.*"

KEY

"You seriously don't remember the Nashville truck bombing?" said Key, in disbelief. "In 2020? Christmas Day?"

"I don't know—I think I remember hearing something about it."

She and Hunter were watching the Walgreens parking lot from inside a Waffle House across the street, the only eating establishment they could find still open at that hour. At the moment, there was a single vehicle parked in the pharmacy's lot, a colorful van surrounded by a few highly animated women.

The Walgreens had turned out to be nestled among several hotels, and Hunter had gotten his hopes up that Abbott had decided to just stay at one of those, maybe planning to wake up and hit the pharmacy before jumping on the interstate to Armageddon. But a check of their lots had revealed a dozen white SUVs, none the one they were looking for. They were both starving by that point and so had decided to grab some night breakfast and down as much coffee as the restaurant would allow before the staff ejected them from the establishment.

"The scene was something out of a movie," said Key. "This RV pulls up to a spot downtown and starts playing a computerized voice warning everyone to evacuate the area. Then it announces a bomb is about to go off and starts a countdown, while playing 'Downtown' by Petula Clark. The cops evacuated everybody according to the bomber's instructions, and at six thirty in the morning, *boom*. It collapsed one building, wrecked sixty others, and took down an AT&T switching station that knocked out communications across several states. A lot of people lost 911 service; one airport lost air traffic control. But there was only the one fatality, the bomber. And I think there's a really specific reason why you haven't heard more about it."

"What's that?"

"There was nothing to argue about. The bomber had no politics; it was just an old guy who believed aliens had secretly invaded Earth in 2011. If he'd been an Islamic extremist, you'd have had the president yelling about a new Muslim travel ban. If he'd been a Nazi, you'd have had the other side yelling about new hate speech laws and a domestic terror crackdown. All of the yelling would have created online engagement and TV ratings and ad revenue. But because the bomber didn't trigger any particular raw nerve, there was no media money to be made, so we all just shrugged and moved on."

"I'm starting to sense you're something of a cynic," said Hunter as Key watched the Walgreens lot, imagining morning light reflecting off fresh blood and shell casings.

She had drunk too much before the flight and during the flight and after the flight, and now she could feel herself getting dull and sleepy, which was triggering her anxiety because she knew she had to stay sharp for what could be the biggest day of her life, and possibly the last. So now she was scorching her digestive tract with coffee and rehearsing the scenario in her head, struggling mightily to focus. Her stomach was simultaneously telling her she needed to eat and vomit, and also, she was 99.7 percent sure that the incel terrorist kid's dad would fuck her if she offered.

"What do you think those people are doing over there?"

Hunter directed his attention over to the Walgreens lot. Key counted three women and one guy who stayed behind the wheel of the van they'd arrived in. The van had a custom paint job on the side depicting a cartoon woman with large breasts and rabbit ears.

"Based on my previous visits to Nashville," he said, "I'd guess it's a bachelorette party. Maybe the van is a party bus. So, is this what you did at the FBI? Domestic terrorism?"

She paused to dump sugar in her coffee, knowing it was no longer hot enough to dissolve it. Sometimes she liked to have a little puddle of granules at the end; it was like the coffee's dessert.

"Let's put it this way. There was an apartment building in the old Soviet Union, now Ukraine. In the 1980s, everyone who lived in a particular apartment got sick and died. Leukemia. Nobody could figure out why. Even weirder, the first to die usually slept in a specific room, against a particular wall. Well, after almost a decade of this, somebody finally investigated. It turned out that, years earlier, a guy working in a quarry had lost his radiation level gauge—that's a rock-measuring gadget with a tiny little capsule of cesium-137 inside. The tool got ground up with the gravel, which got turned into concrete, which got turned into that apartment building. That little capsule of radioactive material embedded in the wall of that apartment killed at least four people and delivered heaping doses of radiation to seventeen more. Silent and invisible."

"So is that what you did, track radioactive material?"

"Yeah, but I like that story as a metaphor. I track radioactive ideas, virulent narratives that develop in insular little subcultures until they burst out onto the scene. One random guy posts a hoax to 4chan in 2017 under the pseudonym 'Q,' three years later, weirdos wearing Q T-shirts are storming the Capitol Building. Did you hear about Facebook's role in the genocide in Ethiopia? And Myanmar?"

"I don't think I heard about those genocides at all."

"Well, the company had teams devoted to it, as in, 'They are clearly trying to organize an ethnic cleansing on our website. What do we do?' They have war rooms set up to discuss which countries are at risk of the same. The USA is on that list."

"So, did you retire to pursue another career? Write books?"

Good god, she thought. *The man is definitely flirting with me.*

"No," she said into her coffee. "My only plan was to get away. If I had to go punch in at that office one more time, with those people, I think I'd have started looking into how to make a truck bomb myself."

Jesus, did she just say that out loud?

"Come on," said Hunter. "You have to have a purpose. You're still young. People live forever these days. I've got a grandpa who's still alive—he's a hundred."

Key imagined living to a hundred and almost passed out. "Is it possible those people and their anime sex van are some of the internet weirdos who've been following this case, scoping out the scene?"

"They wouldn't be that stupid, would they? To get in proximity of a toxic car bomb, just for fun? I mean, I guess they could say we're doing the same."

"At least I have training."

There was a suspicious pause, and Hunter said, "Hey, I want to make something clear. Whatever happens a few hours from now, I want you to know, I fully intend to survive it."

"Okay? I'm, uh, glad to hear that."

"Because I've continually asked what exactly you want out of this—a rejuvenated career, a medal, just to have done a good deed—and it really kind of seems like you have no thoughts that extend into the future. That, whether or not you're conscious of it, that you . . ." He trailed off, like he had previewed the rest of that sentence in his head and decided to cancel it.

"I what?"

"That you wouldn't mind it if you didn't survive this. That if the act of stopping this ended up with you dead on the pavement in a shoot-out or explosion, your name living on in all the news stories and true-crime podcasts to come, with all your old colleagues finally realizing how awesome you were, that you'd be pretty okay with that."

Key sipped the lukewarm sugary remnants of her coffee and said, "If so, that's nobody's business but my own."

DAY 4

I have pleasures, and passions, but the joy of life is gone. I am going under: the morgue yawns for me.

—OSCAR WILDE, in a letter to a friend, 1897

From the blog of Phil Greene:

I used to try to befriend like-minded folks, those who were prepared, self-sufficient, ready for the collapse. I watched as one-by-one they disappeared into their own black boxes. They were certain there was a war to be won against this group or that, some puppeteers who could be taken out, the people finally set free. I ran into many who cut me off the minute they saw the color of my skin, as if I'd have nothing to offer in the aftermath. I've forgotten more skills than these fools ever bothered to learn, but thus is their mindset: all they want is to fight. Can't they see that that is the Forbidden Numbers at work, that they long for conflict because they've been trained to believe that conflict is entertainment? As long as they demand the universe be entertaining, then the real world will always lose out to the box. The real world, where authentic beings live, *is boring.* Or at least, it is boring to the infected mind under command of the parasite that relentlessly demands the next hit of novelty. This is the true strength of the box, that anything can be subsumed into its walls, even rebellion against the box itself. The only hope for rebirth is to create a world that is, mostly, a quiet place. Knowing the kind of actions that would be required to restore this silent state to the world weighs heavy on my heart. Karen took me to the grocery store today. I didn't ask her, she just came around and offered. I suppose she'd done the math and knew I had to be running out of some essentials. I refused her three times, but she wouldn't take no for an answer. We didn't talk much on the way there and wound up arguing on the way back. I accused her of having an angle, of wanting my money, or my land, after I was gone. I could tell she was hurt by that and she started crying, and honestly, I don't know why I said what

I said. I think I've always had a meanness in me, and I worry I've become too sick to keep it reined in. Maybe the Lord knew that to be suited to this task, I would need to be amenable to solitude, and placed this coarseness in me to facilitate it.

19

ETHER

"Have you ever pan-fried string cheese?" asked Ether while chewing a vending machine danish in the parking lot of the Johnny Cash Rest Area in Dickson, Tennessee.

The sun had barely risen, but the day was already a sauna, clouds hanging overhead like steam off a pot of chili. Thunder rumbled somewhere in the distance.

"Like, that rubbery white tube cheese?" asked Abbott, who Ether had now firmly decided was not a morning person. "It doesn't taste like anything."

"It doesn't when it's raw! But what you do is, you put a pan on your hot plate or fire, put the string cheese in the pan, let it melt until it's crispy on the edges, eat. It's a nice little treat for something you can make quickly in the back of a van. Can you believe how many humans have lived and died without ever tasting melted cheese?"

Abbott made some kind of a response noise, and she knew she wasn't capable of untangling his ball of nerves. The pharmacy would open in half an hour, and they both felt like shit. At the outset, she had gently mocked Abbott for suggesting a cross-country car ride would be physically taxing, but miles always take their toll, no matter how you traverse them.

"It's funny," she said, scanning the long paragraph of ingredients on her danish, "when I went off-grid, I had it in my head that I would subsist off natural foods. I was imagining myself eating nuts and berries. It turns out that's not possible; the only reason we can have a produce section in the grocery store is because of all the highways and trucks that bring it in from wherever it's in season. When old people talk about how much better fruit tasted in their youth, they're not mentioning that you could only buy that stuff in certain places, at certain times of the year. There are parts of this country that never *saw* an avocado until the 2000s, when they started bringing them in from Mexico and shipping them all over. I wound up eating tons of processed junk from gas stations. Stuff that came in individual wrappers, to keep the bugs off it. I gained a lot of weight."

"Are we going to die today?" asked Abbott, who was eating a sleeve of little waxy chocolate doughnuts. "I mean, even if this thing at the pharmacy comes off without a hitch, we'll be in DC in, what, seven hundred miles? So, late tonight. That's the last chance for anybody who wants to stop us, and they'll just get more desperate as we get closer. So I guess, before we head into the city, I just wanted to know: Is this my last day on earth?"

"No more catastrophizing after this, okay? I mean, even if we were going to die, I wouldn't want to spend all day dwelling on it. Come on, let's go."

He started the engine but didn't shift into gear. "If you want me to calm down," he said, "you can explain exactly why you're so sure the previous owner of this box wasn't a terrorist and/or an amateur bomb builder. I know this is getting into personal stuff you hadn't wanted to share, but I think we're past that now."

"I agree," she said as Abbott pulled into traffic. "From here on out, no secrets."

[Photo] *I AM TAILING THE NAVIGATOR ON MY MOTORCYCLE AND I AM FREAKING OUT*

Posted to r/DCTerrorAttack by ExpertLaneSplitter
Took this pic while stopped at a red light. Was camping in Natchez Trace state park and came across their vehicle, pulling out. We're now heading into the city. Streaming live from my helmet cam here: *[link]*

ETHER

"So, the thing about living in an ambulance," Ether began, "is that they have lots of storage and such, but they get horrific gas mileage. And when they break down, they are very expensive to fix, and mine had an especially hard life those first few months. I had joked to my family that I was going to escape to the Arctic Circle, and, well, I actually did that. I took a monthlong road trip up the Dempster Highway, through Yukon. You think the USA is empty, it's nothing compared to Canada as you head north—just vast, open stretches of hills and wilderness. You eventually hit a point where the houses are elevated on concrete pylons because otherwise their foundations would melt the permafrost and sink in the mud. It also turns out there are tons of used RVs for sale up there because they died on the way up—that road is *brutal*. It wound up popping two of my tires, and I almost froze to death, due to poor planning."

She could have talked for an hour about this part, how she'd shivered under her blankets and pondered how all that lay between her and eternity was whether or not someone happened to pass by. The kindness of a single stranger was the reason she still drew breath.

"And this is when you were doing shrooms the whole time?" asked Abbott. "Discovering the hidden truth about modern society and all that?"

"Yeah. And what I discovered was that so much of the self-help and wellness advice I was getting was entirely about solitude. 'Meditate, alone! Do yoga, alone! Work in your garden, alone! Walk through the woods, alone!' Like 'alone time' is the one thing we're all missing. Anyway, I scurried back to SoCal and started looking for a place to stay that wouldn't cost anything and also wouldn't require me to be some weird dude's sex slave. I heard about an old guy and his daughter who had a little shack on their property, and the offer was I could stay for free but had to take care of it. Keep the vandals out."

"These are the people who had the box, right? If not, I want to skip ahead to that part."

"Yeah. You'll want to get into the far-right lane. It's going to become your exit up here." They were not yet in view of the city, but traffic was definitely becoming more dense and aggressive, exuding the grumpy morning energy of a population center. "So, the guy was in his seventies and the daughter was in her fifties, but she could have passed for much younger. I mean, she was a knockout. Come to find out, there was a tunnel connecting their house to the shack, like an escape route, should they have to go on the run."

"So they were criminals."

"No. Paranoid. Or at least, the old guy was. Phil Greene was his name; the daughter was Sundae. And Phil was a literal genius. An eccentric, somebody who'd worked the same boring job for decades but who had a million weird hobbies. He'd set up his house so it was totally off-grid. But his wife, Bonnie, had passed a few years ago. They said it was an overdose from painkillers she'd gotten hooked on after a surgery, but I always got the sense that maybe it was on purpose. After that, Phil had started getting a little weird, like you could ask him about the weather and he'd start talking about how human evolution had been hijacked by software algorithms, our brains rewired to turn us into zombies."

"So, he was a skilled builder, and paranoid, with secret chambers under his house. This is off to a great start."

Ether knew how it sounded. How could she convey the warm humanity of the man and his daughter? It would sound like platitudes if boiled down to mere words. A flood of gentle memories washed in: Phil and Sundae laughing on the porch and watching the sunset while they ate peach cobbler. The old man rotating through his vast collection of profane trucker caps, at least one for every day of the year. The three of them having a playfully fierce competition over fantasy football.

"In an effort to try to understand Phil, I really did try to listen to him, and the thing is, *a lot of what he was saying was right.* You know, all conspiracy theories start from there, a core of truth. But then you make it your religion, and at some point, I don't know, you forget how to be a person. He used to clip out reading material for me, pin it up in the shack so I couldn't miss it. Anyway, I had assumed the daughter had moved in to help take care of him in his final years, but it turned out it was the opposite. She had breast cancer that had spread. She was in decent shape when I first moved into the shack, but she went downhill really fast. They started inviting me into the main house more and more so I could help out, and toward the end, I kind of became part of the family."

"Even with this guy ranting about his conspiracy nonsense all day?"

Again, what was there to say? The headlines would probably reduce Phil's entire being to labels: "conspiracy theorist," "anarchist," "prepper." This man with a thousand stories from a lifetime of traveling the country, a vibrant mind with a yawning loneliness at its core. The world would never understand all his flailing attempts to reclaim some meaning in his life after everything he'd cared about had been placed in a box and lowered into the ground, or the tenderness he felt toward his daughter after decades of estrangement, Sundae having come back home with her own long list of unbelievable tales. This frail old man who waited on his dying little girl hand and foot, convinced until the last that she would recover, certain that fathers did not bury their own daughters next to their own wives. One human soul could surely not be asked to swallow that much sorrow.

"All I can say," said Ether, "is that I never saw him mistreat anyone face-to-face, never saw him pass up an opportunity to help a neighbor. They all borrowed his tools, they all had some *MacGyver* repair job that Phil had done for them, getting their AC working again when they couldn't afford to replace it. But then Sundae finally passed—that was earlier this year—and the old man and I did kind of fall out after that. He got more and more paranoid, especially about anything having to do with signals—5G, Wi-Fi. I mostly kept to the shack, assuming that one day he'd demand I leave there, too. In the end, I think he only talked to the cats—he had all these strays that would come by, he'd leave the gate open for them in the evenings. By that point, that's all he wanted, an audience that wouldn't push back. The only time I saw him was when he'd come out to the shack and use my laptop to upload his latest rant to his blog. I never pointed out the hypocrisy there."

"I'm sorry, but it really, really sounds like he could have been building a bomb that whole time."

She rubbed her eyes. *If Abbott could have just met him . . .*

"So," continued Ether, "one thing I knew about Sundae is she used to run with these biker guys. One day, Phil comes up to the shack with this box, says he needs it out of the house, that if anybody tries to touch it, I should kill them. Especially if they're big, inked-up biker dudes."

Abbott let out a theatrical sigh. "See, now it sounds like it's full of drugs again. Or a body."

"No, Phil hated drugs, so did Sundae—remember how Bonnie died. A few weeks later, I get a call in the middle of the night from somebody I've never talked to before. He says he's a friend of the family. He says Phil is dead, insists it's due to natural causes. He says Sundae always spoke highly of me, said I was trustworthy. He offers me one million dollars to bring this box to his place outside Washington, DC. He says there's at least a quarter million in cash stuffed in a mattress, money he'd sent to Sundae but that she'd never spent. With Phil gone, he says the cash is mine, and if I bring him the box, he'll give me another seven-fifty. But he needs me to go immediately, no waiting around and seeing to Phil's arrangements. I have to pack a bag and go, traveling totally off-grid. We kept the Ranger pickup parked by the shack. I wrestled the box into the back, took the tunnel to the house. I got the cash from the mattress and found Phil's phone, as I didn't have my own. Then somebody starts yelling, and I realize I'm not alone. The Tattoo Monster was there; he'd been searching the house, and he starts chasing me, demanding the box. I get back into the bedroom, lock the door, go through the closet, and back down the tunnel. We had a little space heater in the shack—a gadget Phil had made; it screwed to the top of a propane tank. I turned it on and threw a blanket over it, starting a fire over the hatch, so the Monster couldn't follow me. I sped away from the scene with no plan whatsoever for how I was going to get to DC. Then I met you, and that's that."

She'd decided on the fly to leave out the detail of ordering multiple rides until she'd found the right driver. She wasn't sure how Abbott would feel about that.

"And the guy who called you, he's a celebrity of some kind? You said he was, back when we first met."

"He told me his name when we spoke, and I looked him up while I was waiting for you. He's a tech millionaire, a big political-donor type. He was an old boyfriend of Sundae's. I'd heard his name come up a couple of times. Gary Sokolov."

"Okay, can you vouch for *this* guy at all?"

"No. This is your exit."

He took a deep breath and adjusted his grip on the wheel.

She said, "Hey: we're not going to die today."

Abbott didn't reply. A barrage of fat raindrops detonated across the windshield.

KEY

"Now hold on," said Hunter from the passenger seat of the rental car. "Are they here for Abbott or the crowd?"

"They're almost definitely here for the crowd," replied Key, unable to believe what she was seeing.

They were referring to two squad cars containing exactly four cops that had pulled up to the Walgreens at around seven thirty A.M., just as the rain started. She and Hunter were parked at a CVS pharmacy down the block, Key imagining the two stores in a bitter turf war. It's impossible to know exactly how many residents of the Nashville area had previously been following the Navigator situation, but it was clear that number had grown as news got out that the infamous SUV was set to arrive on their doorstep.

And now the Walgreens parking lot was *packed.*

She saw lots of young males, and some rednecks who'd come armed. They had started arriving in the predawn hours, like they were lining up to be the first to get the store's hot new model of toe fungus medication. Key imagined all of them capturing a police shoot-out and subsequent bomb detonation live on stream before perishing with their phones in their hands, their surviving loved ones seeing the engagement stats and weeping a single tear of pride. What Key did *not* see was police setting up a staging area nearby, preparing to swoop in and surround the Navigator. Only these two squad cars had appeared, and she was guessing they were here in response to store employees complaining about a weird internet flash mob clogging up their lot. But, hell, what else had she expected?

After the OKC bombing, Timothy McVeigh only got caught because the highway patrol happened to pull him over for driving without plates, the doofus greeting the cop in a SIC SEMPER TYRANNIS T-shirt with a Glock in a shoulder holster.

"If Abbott and the girl are clueless about all this," said Key, "they're definitely not going to pull in if they're greeted by this scene. These idiots will start screaming the moment they see the Navigator. Abbott will freak out and speed past."

"I don't understand," said Hunter. "Are they here to stop him? Cheer him on? Warn him away from the cops?"

"I think each of them thought they'd be the only ones here. They imagined themselves inconspicuously filming as it played out. It didn't occur to them that they would be part of a crowd."

"The same as us, in other words."

"Have you checked the internet chatter in a while?"

"No," said Hunter. "Resisting the urge to create a Reddit account and call them all imbeciles always gives me a migraine."

Key pulled out her phone, browsed to the subreddit, saw the top post, and said, "Oh, shit, we need to move."

"What?"

She started the car, wishing she had a magnetic siren to slap onto the roof, like in those old cop shows. "Somebody is following the Navigator into town. They have live video."

ABBOTT

He hated driving in the rain, and he hated driving in a strange city. Though Abbott also hated driving on sunny days in familiar cities. It was a relentless barrage of overstimulation and tense standoffs, automobiles having a magical ability to make humans abandon all concepts of empathy and self-preservation. For example, some asshole on a purple crotch rocket motorcycle had been tailgating them for miles, the rider probably pissed that he'd gotten caught in a thunderstorm in a vehicle with no roof or windshield. He'd been weaving around back there and acting like he wanted to pass, but never did, despite plenty of chances. Abbott would have assumed it was another member of the Tattoo Monster's biker gang, but he seemed more like a Harley guy—if you showed up on one of these, they'd probably beat your ass. Yet when Abbott took the exit into the city, so did the motorcycle.

Almost immediately, they'd been forced to stop on the off-ramp, greeted by a row of stationary brake lights behind a veil of windshield rain splatters. They remained stopped for too long, much longer than they'd have needed to wait for, say, a cautious driver to merge. Embers of panic glowed behind Abbott's sternum. Someone honked. Someone yelled. Someone else honked.

Abbott, fighting his urge to catastrophize with all his might, muttered, "I don't like this."

Ether, who was already scanning the surroundings as if looking for escape routes, said, "Neither do I."

To Abbott's right was a patch of trees; to his left was a grassy hill leading up to the four lanes of interstate they'd just left, which led to an overpass. He noticed Ether looking in that direction, and the fact that they were clearly both asking themselves the same question—could he crank the wheel, climb that hill, and get back onto 40—instantly made the panic embers in his chest flare to life.

He edged over to the left, trying to create an angle to see ahead. What he saw made no sense: A colorful van—baby blue with what looked like an anime-style airbrush job—was parked horizontally across the lane. It was as if they'd blocked the lane on purpose and done it exactly when Abbott had taken the exit.

There was no fucking way this was coincidence.

"Uh, Ether, I think we have to—"

"WHO IS THAT?!?"

Abbott barely had time to look. Someone was shouting out there, and he thought he could hear his own name among the shouts, then suddenly Ether's side of the windshield was pink. The wipers swooped across, smearing it to the point that only the left quarter of the glass was still transparent. And through that clean bit of glass, he saw a second figure run toward him, a large woman in a backward baseball cap, brandishing a small bucket. She yelled and slung its contents toward the Navigator, and now the entire windshield and most of Abbott's side window were coated in paint the color of Pepto Bismol.

Ether was yelling at him to drive, to back up, to get away, but behind him was the man on the purple motorcycle, who would be flattened if they went in reverse. In front of him was nothing, he was blind, the wipers sweeping solid pink arcs across his field of vision. Even if he could get out of the stalled traffic, the Navigator was undrivable until the view was cleared.

Now the woman on Abbott's side was slapping the splattered glass of the side window and screaming, "ABBOTT! COME ON! WE'RE WITH—" and a word that sounded like *Z* or *See* or *Seek.* Then the other voice was shouting the same thing, and Abbott looked to Ether for guidance, but now she was crawling into the back, digging around in Abbott's bag. When she came back around, she was holding his father's gun.

"What are you doing?!?"

Before she could answer, everyone outside started screaming and scattering.

HUNTER

Abbott's father was on foot now, hustling through the driving rain, Joan having swung her rental car onto the shoulder once she saw all the cars backed up on the off-ramp. The colorful van they'd observed in the Walgreens lot hours ago had intentionally blocked the lane, and there, about five vehicles back, was Hunter's Lincoln Navigator. The top half was now painted pink, for some reason, including the windshield. The front end was badly damaged, one end of the bumper dangling just inches off the ground. So now he and the former FBI agent were running across traffic, Joan motioning to the oncoming cars as if she had some kind of traffic control authority. Up on the ramp, idiots were shouting and, now, running.

He heard Joan say, "Oh, shit!" and then Hunter felt time slow almost to a stop, the raindrops hanging in the air, all noises fading to silence.

He had never, for even a moment, truly believed his son and this mystery girl were transporting a bomb. Life simply wasn't that exciting. The world was full of sad sacks thinking they're going to die in the Revolution, or Armageddon, or in the throes of civilizational collapse at the hands of sentient AI. Statistically, almost all of them were destined to pass quietly in hospitals with tubes sticking out of every hole, or on the sofa while sleepily watching a baseball game, or in a head-on collision after deciding they were fine to drive home on sixteen beers. The world is boring, you do your job, and eventually, you die from the same mundane misfires that escort everybody else into the dirt. So, yeah, the box probably contained drugs, or illicit cash, or maybe some documents chronicling felony tax evasion. Everything else was, in Hunter's view, wishful thinking. Minds desperate for something, *anything* to happen, good or bad, as long as it was interesting.

But in that stretched-out moment, he saw that the Navigator was boxed in: vehicles all around, the windshield covered, morons slapping on the doors. So if this vehicle did contain a bomb, its inhabitants would know that it was now or never—either set it off or be resigned to a failed mission and a lifetime in prison. This was likely the pivotal point of the affair, of his life, of his son's life, maybe in the history of the nation.

And then he saw what had caused Joan Key's outburst: barreling onto the scene was a yellow van with a festive bouquet of flowers on the side. It had jumped off the interstate and was plowing down the grassy hill. Hunter sensed time snap back to full speed as the van T-boned the Navigator, the impact pushing the top-heavy vehicle over, sending it and his boy tumbling into the trees.

20

ABBOTT

There was glass in his eyes, and Abbott thought he could smell smoke. People were yelling, screaming to get back, that a nuclear bomb was about to go off. Rain was pelting his ear.

He brushed away jewels of safety glass and cautiously opened his eyes. The view out of the windshield was still nothing but pink. To his left was the sky and tree branches. He didn't know what had happened, only that the window next to his head had exploded, and then he was being whipsawed this way and that. Now gravity was pulling him in the wrong direction, and it was raining on his face. He was dangling by a seat belt that was cutting into his pelvis, and his shoulder was resting against something soft.

Yeah, he could definitely smell smoke.

Some part of him knew he should be taking action, that the vehicle was on fire, that death was looming nearby, gazing upon him with its unfathomable indifference. He should be escaping, fighting, climbing out. But . . . why? To what end?

It was over. The trip was done, the Navigator was wrecked. He would never see any of the money—even if he grabbed his bag and climbed out, he'd instantly be arrested, the cash impounded and eventually distributed back to someone who wasn't him. Even if the box's contents were innocuous and he avoided prison time, he wouldn't be going back to his old life but to some much worse version of it. His father would kick him out, he'd have to beg his mother to let him stay with her in Houston and, if she refused, live on the street. He felt himself getting drowsy. He thought he could now feel heat from an unseen fire. That was okay. This seemed like as good a place as any to end his story. It wasn't extremely comfortable dangling from the seat belt and resting his shoulder against whatever softness lay beneath him, but he'd definitely slept in worse positions.

He closed his eyes.

In the end, Abbott Coburn had simply not been made for this world. He was one of those extra screws you find in the box after assembling a piece of furniture. He had nothing to offer and was going to get flicked into the garbage at some point, either today or tomorrow or next week or ten years from now. Why draw it out? Why be that curious object that lives in a drawer, always in the way?

He felt the softness under him shift and turned to find Ether lying under him, grass and twigs pressing themselves up through the shattered passenger-side glass. She opened her eyes, blinked, and Abbott jolted himself into action.

He said, "Are you okay?" but it was a dumb question. She wouldn't know if she was or wasn't; it was just what people said in situations like this. Her chin and cheek were covered in blood.

He unbuckled himself and climbed up, immediately gashing his palms on the shards around the edges of the window, trying to find a place to put his feet that wasn't Ether's face. He raised his head out of the Navigator. Up on the off-ramp was a yellow flower delivery van, its front end crumpled from the impact.

Smoke stung his eyes, raindrops pelted his scalp. The exposed underbelly of the Navigator was on fire, and he could absolutely feel the heat now. Abbott didn't know a lot about the anatomy of cars, but he knew the gas tank was in that vicinity. He climbed up and out, stepping on Ether in the process, then lay on the side of the vehicle and extended a hand down. Black smoke was now rolling off the bottom of the Navigator, and flames were licking up next to him. He heard a tire pop. He imagined twenty gallons of gasoline boiling inside the tank, explosive vapor building and building . . .

"COME ON!" he yelled to the woman who was already unclasping her seat belt and trying to get her legs out from under the dash.

There was a noise from behind him, and Abbott looked back to find someone was stomping around at the rear, yanking the back doors open.

He thought it might be a Good Samaritan there to aid the rescue, then saw the bald head and realized what had happened: the Tattoo Monster, having wrecked the Navigator, was now rescuing "his" black box from the imminent gasoline explosion.

Abbott turned away to focus on helping Ether out of the vehicle, and now both of them were coughing and the door panel he was lying on was hot enough to sear exposed skin. When she got far enough out to see what was happening at the rear, she tried to yell something at the Tattoo Monster, but he gave only a cursory glance their direction, hauling the heavy trunk up through the brush.

By the time Abbott hauled Ether the rest of the way out of the Navigator and jumped down, he couldn't open his eyes against smoke that was like something deployed against World War I trenches. They ran away from the wreck, farther into the trees. When Abbott looked back, the interior was engulfed, along with all its contents. His money, his belongings, the gun—he was literally left with nothing but the clothes on his back. Next to him, Ether was bent over at the waist, coughing and spitting up blood.

And now someone was running toward them through the trees, having come from the direction of the street below the off-ramp. They ran directly to the engulfed Navigator and frantically kicked in the windshield, unleashing a frenzy of rage against which the glass stood no chance. For a crazy moment, Abbott thought they were trying to deliver a final round of punishment to the Navigator before it was consumed by the flames, but then the man yelled into the windshield, calling for Abbott, whom the man apparently believed was currently roasting alive inside.

Abbott shouted, "We're over here! We got out!" and the man turned, and it was his father.

Abbott was, in that moment, more terrified than he had been at any single point of the trip, including when he'd just been inside that burning vehicle. The backstory of his father's appearance and the implications instantly played out in his mind: he'd been dragged away from his work, his home, from all the things that actually mattered to him, to come two thousand miles to retrieve his pride and joy, which had been stolen and then forever ruined by his idiot son. His father's fists were clenched.

He had salt-and-pepper stubble on his jaw, like he'd been up all night and hadn't bathed. And now he was coming toward Abbott, stomping through the trees and the pouring rain, backlit by the roiling hellfire of the dying Navigator. He closed the distance and was saying something, over and over, inaudible under the ringing in Abbott's ears.

When he got close enough, Abbott could hear him say, "I thought you were dead. I thought you were dead. I thought you were dead," in a low monotonous tone, like he didn't know he was making those sounds, and Abbott saw that the man was crying.

Almost too stunned for words, Abbott muttered, "We're okay. I think." He turned to Ether to ask if she was, in fact, okay, but she was already scrambling up toward the off-ramp.

Going after the box.

KEY

Hunter had gone after the vehicle in hopes of retrieving his son, but Key's job wasn't over there. Her concern was a black box that may or may not contain an improvised weapon of mass destruction that may or may not be seconds away from detonation. And at the moment, that box was being dragged toward the rear of a flower delivery van by Malort, whom Key had last seen at a Victorville gas station. Somehow, she'd always known they'd meet again and that one of them would leave that meeting very unhappy, if they left it at all.

If this dirtbag had some kind of altruistic reason for crashing the Navigator—like if, say, he'd wanted to stop a potential terror attack—here is where he'd be looking for an authority figure to take the device off his hands and award him the Key to the City. Instead, he was opening the rear of his flower van to load up the box.

Because he wanted it for himself.

Because he had his own agenda in mind.

Key pulled the Glock. All moments had converged to this.

Trees were catching fire around the crashed Navigator below, and smoke was rolling up across the street, blowing up toward the interstate. Just as she was approaching Malort from behind the three glowing dots of the Glock's sights, there was a *whoomp,* and a ball of fire rolled into the sky, the gas tank rupturing. The bystanders gasped and recoiled.

"STOP AND GET ON YOUR KNEES!"

Malort glanced back at her while in the act of lifting the black box. It was half-covered in ragged strips of aluminum foil like a takeout burrito in the hands of a drunken college student. Malort didn't seem to recognize Key, but he did recognize the gun. He showed no fear—she sensed it was not his first time having one pointed at him, or the tenth—and also did not comply with any part of her order beyond the first word. He gently set the box back on the pavement and turned to stare her down. The combination of the rain and acrid black smoke was reducing visibility by the minute. Cars were slowing up on the interstate, drivers either being cautious or turning into spectators.

"You a cop?" grunted Malort. "Or did Sock send ya?"

Key pulled her shirt up over her mouth and nose. The air was turning lethal.

"GET ON YOUR KNEES. PUT YOUR HANDS ON YOUR HEAD. Just stay calm and we'll sort this out."

He didn't do any of that.

As he stared her down, she heard the first drone of police sirens.

Malort seemed to be working through his own thought process, and it wasn't hard for Key to guess what was going on in his ugly, bald head. There were no other officers on the scene, but there would be soon. There was a general state of chaos all around, and visibility was poor. He outweighed Key by probably 150 pounds. She could see the predatory gears turning in there, the guy calculating if he could close the distance before she could react, if he could overpower her and escape in the ensuing chaos. Or maybe he was the type of scumbag whose brain didn't work that way. Maybe he just didn't like being told what to do. Maybe he'd rather get shot with an entire magazine of .40-caliber hollow points than kneel before a shouting woman. And if he came at her, she decided, it *would* be the entire magazine.

Key opened her mouth to shout that this was his final warning, when a horrific noise came howling down from the interstate. Malort turned that direction, and so did she. From her vantage point below, she could only see the tops of the vehicles moving from left to right along I-40, all of them having slowed to a crawl as cars passed cautiously through the plume of smoke. The vehicle nearest to her was a concrete truck, the drum in back rotating its cargo. Behind it was the densest part of the smoke, and dread hit Key as it became clear what was about to happen:

The awful noise was the sound of an eighteen-wheeler that had come up on the traffic stoppage too fast, the driver realizing too late that the smoke and the rain was concealing multiple stopped vehicles, one of them hauling twenty tons of wet concrete. Key heard gasps and shouts as the semi screeched and swerved. The cab missed the concrete truck, but the trailer was raked across it, its side wall ripping open on contact. An avalanche of cargo flew out the side, pallets of small white containers that rained down and burst and splattered, turning everything white. She had a brief moment to wonder what in the hell they'd been hauling when she looked back toward Malort to find he was lunging for her.

He had apparently calculated that this had been enough of a distraction to allow him to make his move.

And, it turned out, he was right.

ABBOTT

The black box was sitting unattended by the flower van on the off-ramp, strips of torn foil flapping in the wind. Above, total chaos had unfolded on the interstate; thousands of white plastic tubs had rolled and burst and spilled down the hill, splattering chunky white liquid. A short distance away, the Tattoo Monster was fighting a woman, looking like he was trying to wrestle a gun away from her.

Ether, whose shirt was smeared red with blood she'd wiped from her face, shouted at the man and ran in that direction, unarmed and seemingly with zero plan. As she did, the Tattoo Monster stood up, the woman lying at his feet, her gun now in his hand. He pointed it right at Ether, and she skidded to a stop. The man was soaked from the rain, his eyes were red from the smoke, and he was bleeding from his nose. He looked like he badly wanted to shoot someone, whether it served his goals or not.

Abbott yelled, "NO!" and found himself in between Ether and the gun, his body somehow having thrown itself into that position without Abbott's knowledge or consent.

"Heeeey!" said the Tattoo Monster, with an odd note of amusement in his voice. "I remember you!"

"It's over!" said Abbott, or at least that's what he tried to say before his words sputtered into a wet coughing fit. "The cops are coming. There's no place to go," he wheezed.

The Monster snarled and aimed the gun.

Out from the smoke behind the Tattoo Monster came an arm that wrapped around his thick, inked-up neck. Abbott's father yanked the Monster backward with surprising ease, the latter grunting in pain and rage. He aimed the gun behind him as if attempting to shoot his attacker off him.

Abbott watched as his father caught the gun hand, then worked his fingers around and depressed a button that caused the magazine to slide out of the grip and tumble onto the grass. Then, the gun still in the Tattoo Monster's fist, his father yanked back the slide and ejected the one remaining bullet from the chamber. Abbott's father never saw combat in the Marines but, as he liked to mention now and then, he had learned a few things.

The two men tumbled into the grass. Abbott looked to the woman the Tattoo Monster had been fighting earlier to see if she was dead. She was already getting to her feet, though, blood running down her forehead, looking more enraged than Abbott had ever seen a woman. His father and the Monster were locked in a stalemate, the former with his arm still tight around the other man's neck, the Tattoo Monster trying to pry himself loose and failing.

The woman turned to Abbott and yelled, "Go flag down a cop!"

She was pointing back in the direction she'd come. Abbott could see red and blue lights through the smoke and assumed that somewhere in that area were several cops stuck in traffic, trying to figure out what in the possible fuck was going on.

He took off in that direction, and Ether followed, but then she stopped and screamed, "Where did it go?!?" in a tone like a woman discovering her baby stroller was now sitting empty on a busy sidewalk.

Abbott turned and almost asked what she was referring to, but of course that would have been the world's dumbest question. What else would it be? Where the box had been sitting near the back of the flower van—which, Abbott noted was, in fact, full of shattered vases and scattered bouquets—there was now only empty pavement.

Then Ether, now in a full-blown panic, yelled, "Who are *they*?!?"

She was pointing to two men in black suits and wraparound sunglasses who were quickly hauling the box up the hill toward the interstate, stepping through spilled white tubs and grass smeared with pale, chunky lumps. A third man was guiding them up, a fourth was coming down the hill toward Abbott, his hand inside his jacket as if resting on the butt of a gun. Ether shouted at the men with the box to stop, but these guys looked like Secret Service or someone equally serious and official. Did Nashville have cops that looked like this? Were they feds of some type?

Ether went running up after the box, slipping on the wet and creamy grass, avoiding the man with the hand in his jacket who'd tried to snatch her arm as she passed. Abbott followed, cautiously. Scattered all the way up the hill were hundreds of ruptured tubs of what he could now see was cottage cheese. The torn-open semi loomed above them next to the cement truck, nestled among a whole bunch of stationary cars and several confused, soaked drivers who'd gotten out to see if they needed to flee the scene before something else exploded.

The two men with the box either had better shoes than Abbott or they somehow had much more experience scaling a wet, cheese-slicked hill. They were already up on the interstate and rolling the box in between stopped vehicles, their shoes kicking aside cottage cheese as they went. Abbott saw a stray cat in the middle of the street, happily licking the pavement.

The man with the gun in his jacket caught up to Ether from below and snatched her by the bicep, yanking her back.

"Let go of me!" shrieked Ether. "That belongs to me!"

"It is the property of Mr. Sokolov," said the man. "You failed to make the delivery, so he came himself. Your services are no longer needed."

"What? No, you still owe me! Tell him he still owes me! Hey!"

"You may keep the cash you have already been paid. Mr. Sokolov appreciates the work you have done. We've got it from here."

"That money burned up in the car! I don't have anything! Hey!" she was shouting past him, trying to get the attention of the men with the box who'd vanished behind the stopped vehicles.

Abbott made as if to follow them, no clue what he'd do if he caught up, then everyone started screaming again. He turned to the left and was greeted with the hellish shriek of eighteen more tires scraping across pavement.

Another semi had arrived at the pileup, again going too fast. This one jackknifed, and the trailer skidded around and toppled over, the roof of the trailer buckling and flying open under the weight of its shifting cargo. Thousands of red plastic squeeze bottles burst through and tumbled onto the street, spilling and popping and pinwheeling down the hill. Bystanders shrieked as they were splattered with burning droplets of sriracha hot sauce.

And now Ether was free, having used the distraction to yank herself from the suited thug's grip. She ran, disappearing between the stopped vehicles on the interstate, following the path of the men with the box. The black suit took off after her, and so did Abbott, weaving through the rain and the cars and the toxic air. They all arrived just in time to see a black SUV parked in the median, a man closing the rear door just before it pulled away, doing a U-turn to head southwest, away from the pileup. The man who had closed the door entered a second, identical vehicle, which immediately followed. A third black SUV remained, and from that vehicle emerged two more men in dark suits. They did not draw weapons, but their demeanor implied it was only because they didn't think they'd need them to deal with the two soaked, bleeding wretches before them.

The first man said, "We're done here," and the pair, along with the third man who'd tried to restrain Ether, headed for the final vehicle.

Abbott turned to her. "WHAT DO WE DO?!?"

Before Ether could answer, there were violent footsteps from behind them. The Tattoo Monster came charging into view, dodging around the stalled cars, his clothes streaked with white and red like he'd just fought his way out of a lasagna. He barreled past Abbott and Ether, paying them no mind, running after the final black SUV as it did its U-turn and headed off into the rain. He didn't catch it, of course, and eventually stumbled to a stop, shouting curses into the sky.

The fact that Malort was out here running free immediately made Abbott wonder if his father was now lying somewhere down in the smoky chaos with a broken neck. He turned and ran back the way he'd come, across the pavement, trying to gracefully trod down the spicy, creamy, wet hill and wound up sliding all the way down on his ass. He found his father standing down there with that woman he'd arrived with, who was currently inserting the magazine back into her pistol. His father's shirt was ripped and his hair was a mess, and he seemed to have a bloody bite mark on his forearm.

From behind Abbott, Ether shouted, "Sokolov's entourage took the box!"

Abbott's father seemed confused as to how that string of sounds could be a sentence, but the woman with him only said, "Where did they go?"

"They're heading that way," replied Ether, having apparently decided this woman was on her team, "but they're just getting away from the traffic jam! It's three black Porsche SUVs! Do you have a car?"

"This way!" Then she felt her pockets and turned to Abbott's father. "Wait, do you have the keys?"

"You had them!"

"Shit, they must have fallen out while I was fighting the gorilla."

At that moment, said gorilla ran into their view, sprinting down the street.

A realization seemed to hit the woman and she said, "NO! He's taking the car!"

Sure enough, the Tattoo Monster ran all the way down the off-ramp, toward a sedan parked on the shoulder of the connecting street. He pulled keys from his pocket and jumped in. The woman pulled her gun and sprinted toward him, only to see the man reverse down the shoulder until he found a gap in traffic, at which point, he swung across both lanes and got going the other direction. The woman stopped and bent over, staring at the ground, her hands on her knees.

Eventually, she walked back toward them and said, "Hi. I'm Joan Key, retired FBI. Everybody calls me Key, because there was another Joan in my class at Quantico who everybody liked more. I came here with Abbott's father. Not in any, uh, official capacity."

Ether said, "I'm Karen. Everybody calls me Ether. Or, at least, I started making people call me that once Karen became a slur." She turned and spat out blood. "I bit all the way through my cheek."

Key nodded. "You and I need to talk."

"She doesn't know what's in the box," said Abbott. "They had a tamper seal thing on the lock, they told her if she opened it, she wouldn't get paid."

"If so, he did you a favor. I'm pretty sure that if you'd opened it, you'd both have been dead one millisecond later."

"I'd ask how you and my dad got partnered up on this, but I'm sure it's a whole thing."

Many police cars and at least two ambulances had now made their way to the scene of the chaos, but the focus of all personnel was getting bystanders away from the area. The Navigator was now at the center of a blaze that was crawling through the trees and toward some houses. Abbott sensed the vegetation here hadn't had rain in a month, and what was coming down now was too late to stop the blaze; the dry branches were just too eager to burn. Meanwhile, it appeared that the spectators who'd gathered at the Walgreens had slowly made their way down to the scene, and now they were yelling at first responders that there was a nuclear bomb inside the burning SUV, spreading panic among the very confused bystanders and Sunday-morning drivers.

Abbott looked to his father and said, "Uh, sorry about the Navigator. When I took the trip, I didn't know it was gonna be"—he gestured to the surrounding hellscape—"this."

His father winced as he touched the bleeding bite on his forearm and said, "It fulfilled its one purpose: It kept you safe. Side impact, rollover, you both walked away with just cuts and bruises. That's all you can ask from a vehicle."

"Though it should be mentioned," said Ether, "a normal car with a lower center of gravity probably wouldn't have tipped over at all. Good to meet you, by the way."

"Got to have a tall vehicle these days, or else you can't see around all the other tall vehicles."

"I'm sorry," said Key, "just to clarify, who here among us believes there is a weapon of mass destruction on its way to the nation's capital at this very moment? And that the man hauling it is wealthy and powerful enough that this nation's law enforcement apparatus is helpless to stop him?"

She raised her hand.

Abbott's father raised his and said, "She convinced me it's at least plausible."

Abbott said, "I honestly don't know."

Everyone looked to Ether, who said, "I'm going to try to get the box back regardless. If he's not gonna pay, he's not gonna get his box. Otherwise, this was all for nothing."

"If he's a terrorist mastermind, you're definitely not getting paid," noted Key.

"I'm saying that none of us here want this box to make it to its destination, or even out of the city, if we can stop it. And I for one am perfectly willing to flee the scene of another accident to try. If the police get to him, fine, but if not . . ."

"Are we willing to steal a car?" asked Abbott. "Because we're stuck otherwise."

At that moment, the powder-blue van pulled up on the shoulder, on the side of which was painted an anime girl with large breasts and bunny ears who was winking and making a V with her fingers.

"Abaddon!" shouted the guy behind the wheel. "Get in! It's Zeke! Zeke Ngata!"

Abbott was afraid to admit he didn't know who this person was, but as usual, his expression apparently gave it away.

The guy said, "ZekeArt, from your chat?"

"Oh! Yeah. Is this the van?"

"This is the van! Runs like a dream. I painted it myself. Get in!"

Nobody moved.

"Are you the one who blocked the street and then threw paint on our windshield?"

"Yes!" proclaimed Zeke proudly. "The cops and an angry mob were waiting at Walgreens. You were walking into a trap! We wanted to stop you before you got there but didn't want to risk injuring anybody. The paint was Cammy's idea."

He pointed to the passenger seat, where a broad-shouldered woman with teal hair smiled and waved. "A couple of my friends helped, but they went home; they don't like cops. Get in!"

Zeke asked, "Did the Green Sunglasses Girl burn up in the car?"

"Uh, no," said Abbott, "she's right here."

Ether waved. "I'm Karen. Everybody calls me Ether."

Zeke stared. "Oh."

Abbott said, "She's not in on it. This is my dad, uh, Hunter, and this is—I'm so sorry, I forgot your name. She's an off-duty FBI agent, but she's gone rogue or something."

"Joan Key, K-E-Y. Zeke, you and I have spoken multiple times, on the subreddit. I'm the glowie." She turned to Ether and said, "This guy broke the case, interpreted a note you discarded, and figured out your route, then pinpointed the exact destination. He did it so fast that it kind of scared me a little."

"Oh," said an increasingly confused Zeke. "Okay. Right. Yeah. Nice to meet you."

"And we've lost control of the device. It's currently in a convoy of black movie-villain SUVs heading southwest on I-40, and I don't think the police are stopping them."

"Oh, shit. That's Sokolov's people?"

"Yep."

"Well, get in! Let's go!"

Abbott's father said, "You guys are free to do what you want. Abbott and I need to stay here and get things straight with the cops. That's my vehicle they're trying to extinguish over there. And as far as I'm concerned, I've done my part."

Abbott saw the indisputable logic in what his father was saying and knew he had no rebuttal that would hold up in the face of it. Winning an argument with his father would be like a dropped egg winning an argument with gravity.

Ether looked at him and, as usual, his feelings were transparent to her. "Do you agree with that, Abbott? You're just going to go back home, make some popcorn, and watch how this plays out on a screen? Become just another member of the audience?"

He stared at his shoes, which were creating ripples in a puddle of rainwater. His clothes could not physically absorb any more liquid than they currently held.

"I mean . . . what else can I even do?"

"You can *finish the job you were hired to do.*"

"I did! The job was to deliver the box to this guy, this Sokolov. Now he has it. This thing about it being a bomb, either it's a paranoid fantasy, in which case there's no point in doing anything, or it's an actual bomb, in which case it needs to be handled by somebody more qualified."

"And what becomes of me? Huh? This guy"—she pointed to Zeke behind the wheel of the van—"he came for you, he's your friend, he has no reason to let me in that vehicle, because as far as he's concerned, I'm probably a terrorist or a Russian spy or whatever the internet is saying. So what do I do? What do I have? I'm just a homeless woman stuck in fucking Nashville with nothing, not even a vehicle to sleep in. And what becomes of you? What are you going back with? A cool story to tell a bunch of strangers on your stream?"

"As opposed to what?"

"As opposed to *seeing it through.* This thing we started, this thing we have almost died several times trying to do."

Key said, "One of those cops down there is looking right at us. If we're leaving, we need to do it now. Otherwise, we hear about the detonation tomorrow from our fellow inmates in a holding cell."

Abbott was relieved by the interruption. He knew exactly how this next part would go: His father would put his foot down and everyone else would back off, relieving him of the burden to decide. If he fully cooperated with the police, his dad's lawyer by his side, he could be sleeping in his own bed by tomorrow night at the latest. What was he guilty of, aside from giving a ride to a stranger and almost getting killed by an outlaw biker who probably had a rap sheet a mile long? The cops would care about Abbott's testimony, not Abbott himself. He could still get out clean.

If he got out now.

He looked to his father. "I mean, we have to go talk to the police, right? For the insurance? And just, you know, so we don't get in trouble?"

His father gave him a look that Abbott couldn't quite identify, because he had never seen it before.

"I think you have to make that decision, Abbott. You're an adult."

And now his father was staring at him from one direction and Ether from the other, and this guy Zeke and his sister and this FBI lady—everyone was watching him, this decision all on his shoulders, somehow. He felt the weight of it and hated it, hated that he was being saddled with the consequences of whatever happened next. He hadn't asked for this.

And yet, all eyes were on him just the same.

He heard himself say, "Okay, let's go," and slid open the boob-painted side door.

"Well, if you're going, I'm going," said his father. He paused to study the painting on the side of the van and asked, "Do you have another vehicle, by chance?"

"Nope!" said Zeke. "Get in!"

Key said, "To be clear, you're just getting us somewhere safe where we can regroup and I can find a car. You're not pursuing the bomb convoy."

"I can explain why you're wrong about that later! Let's go!"

"Hold on," said Ether. "I have to check something. I'll be right back."

Key glared at her. "Where are you going?"

"You see that school down the street? Park around the rear and wait for me. If I'm not back in five minutes, just go."

Then she ran off toward the crowd and the smoke and the chaos.

The Navigator has been destroyed, the whereabouts of Abbott, GSG, and the bomb are unknown

Posted to r/DCTerrorAttack by TruthLover420

There have been sixty-five submissions on this. To keep discussion in one place, this will be treated as the official post going forward, all others will be deleted. Abbott and GSG are likely less than ten hours from the capital and we are likely less than one day from an event that could trigger the end of the United States as we know it. All we can do is keep trying to get the word out. If we stop this, we'll be remembered in the history books.

How can anyone deny EBE mind control at this point?

Posted to r/DCTerrorAttack by AgentSkulli

I'm seeing people claim the two semitruck drivers were in on the scheme, to create a distraction for Abbott and GSG to escape. But we have already established that the EBE in the freezer case is capable of mind control and it simply orchestrated sufficient chaos for its own purposes. What matters now is that Abbott and GSG are NO LONGER IN CONTROL OF THE EXTRATERRESTRIAL BIOLOGICAL ENTITY—there are witnesses at the scene who saw Men in Black take the case on board government vehicles and transport it out of the city. This means that right now, there are exactly two possibilities:

1. The EBE is on its way back to a military facility where it can be secured and studied;
2. The EBE has mind-controlled the MIBs transporting it and it is now on its way to Washington, DC, where it will be brought into proximity of certain people in positions of power so that they, too, can be manipulated.

At this point, I would have to say anyone here who denies alien mind control has to themselves be under the influence of the EBE.

[Video] *Worst Pizza Ever: Hundreds of Gallons of Cottage Cheese and Sriracha Spilled on I-40 in Nashville, TN*

Posted to r/WackyCatastrophes by CrashBoy6942069
They have shut down I-40 in both directions while hazmat cleans up the hot sauce. Fifty people had to go to the hospital, but nobody has died. That white you see all over the streets in the news footage is the cottage cheese, the red is the hot sauce. I can't imagine the smell.

——————————————————————————————— Comments:

DrFartMcFart: Why is this making me horny.

21

KEY

The bomb was on the move, but the van was not, and it was driving Key nuts.

"I've got to say," said Zeke from up in the driver's seat, "I'm voting 'bomb' on this. The symbolic date, the target, the evil millionaire mastermind, the ties to a criminal organization in the form of these bikers. I listened to a podcast about Hells Angels. They would use C-4 to blow up rival biker gangs; guys like that would know how to get the goods. And Sokolov would be creating the perfect alibi for himself, attacking his own event. Anybody who accused him would sound like a nutjob, especially if he's set it up so that he doesn't survive the attack."

After Ether had returned to the van, they'd sped away, and Key had instructed Zeke to quickly get them to a safe spot away from the chaos. They'd then engaged in an excruciating debate about the best way to hide the absurdly conspicuous vehicle from public view, finally landing in the middle of the packed parking lot of a buffet restaurant outside of town. Zeke had noted that if there was a group of people least likely to recognize two internet celebrities, it would be the elderly Sunday morning breakfast buffet crowd.

"As long as we're all in agreement that we need to intercept the box," said Ether, "then I kind of don't care what you think is inside it. Bomb, human corpse, alien corpse."

It turned out the reason she'd run off was to see if, by some miracle, Malort had left Phil Greene's old phone behind in the stolen flower van. Key and the rest of the misfits waited longer than the five minutes Ether had requested, and Key had seriously considered asking them to either take off or let her out to find another ride. Then Ether had come sprinting back, phone in hand, diving into the side door and yelling, "GO, GO, GO!" Then she'd shown Key the tracker app, the dot marking the location of the box curling down around the city on 440, making its way back east. Key had taken one look and thought that this young woman might have just saved the world. The problem, she had quickly realized, was that while knowledge of its location was necessary for action, it wasn't at all clear if any action was possible. So much of a modern life was just sitting back helplessly and watching disaster unfold, in real time and in high definition.

Hunter said, "Whether or not it's a bomb is going to matter quite a bit when this whole thing comes to a head. Sokolov's reaction will be very different if the box contains a suicide bomb versus a bunch of Krugerrands."

"All I know," said Ether, "is that I spent my whole life assuming the worst about people, and I'm not doing it anymore."

"Well, in my job, if I don't assume the worst at every stage, the roof falls in. Maybe not that day, but somewhere down the line. One employee's mistake leaves a gap that lets water through, and well, that's all it takes to erode a Grand Canyon. A little water."

"But you do have a crew. Now imagine if you assumed the worst about people to the point that you were scared to hire anyone, doing every job solo. Not many roofs would get done that way, right? Okay, now imagine if a whole society started operating like that. If there's no trust, there's no roofs. No civilization."

"I don't see what that has to do with whether or not this box contains a bomb."

"I think you guys believe it's a bomb because, deep down, you *want* it to be a bomb. That would justify all the time and energy you've put into chasing it down. If it's anything less—I mean literally anything, even a million dollars' worth of heroin or stolen diamonds—you're going to feel cheated. So if it comes down to—"

She was cut off by the sound of Key's phone ringing.

It was Patrick.

Key shushed everyone and answered the call with, "You got my text?"

"It's over. Are you alright?"

Key sat upright. "What do you mean it's over?"

"Highway patrol pulled over the convoy south of town. They spoke to Sokolov. There was no device."

Every pair of eyes in the van was staring at her: Zeke and his sister from up front, Hunter next to her, Abbott and the girl from behind. Key didn't know what her own face was doing in that moment, but it was apparently very confusing and/or alarming to these strangers.

"What do you mean?" she asked. "Did he open the box for them? What was in there?"

"They didn't specify over the phone, but they confirmed it was not an explosive device."

"And there was no hit from the dogs?" Key thought there was no way they'd actually had time to get bomb-sniffing dogs onto the scene, but she wanted to make Patrick say so.

"I don't know that a dog was brought in."

"You mean they took his word for it. Who has the box now? Nashville PD? For the love of God, tell them to hold it until they can analyze the contents. And not to try to open the lid, unless they want their building to become the site of a radioactive crater and future memorial."

"They had no grounds to confiscate it."

"*What?*"

"Joan. I understand you've just been through a traumatic situation, and I understand why you are so invested in this. But take a step back and think: We have no direct witness testimony of anyone involved being in possession of explosives—or any other illegal materials, for that matter. We have no testimony or documentation from anyone who sold them such material. We have no witness claiming they saw a bomb being built or that Phil Greene ever even expressed intent. We have no records of purchases or any other terror-related transactions. You have a lot of lore and rumors and shady characters, but at the center of it, there's just a box, and now multiple veteran police officers saying that box contains nothing of interest."

"The box that was riding with an ultra-wealthy political donor whose social media is probably full of Blue Lives Matter memes."

"Come home, Joan."

"So to be clear," she said, "they're now driving this box to Washington, DC."

"They're driving to the airport, to take Sokolov's private jet back."

She groaned. "And there's nothing I can say right now that will get them stopped by the TSA."

"On what grounds?"

"Okay."

"It's over."

"Okay."

"Are you coming home?"

"Yes."

"Good."

"As soon as *I'm* sure it's over."

"Joan—"

She hung up and said, "We're on our own. Just like I thought." She looked at Zeke. "Can you get me someplace to rent a car?"

Abbott asked, "What's the plan?"

"Well, they're flying to DC, so unless you know where I can find a fighter jet or a surface-to-air missile, the capital is my next chance to intercept that thing. So I'm driving to DC. Or that DC suburb, whatever."

The girl, Ether, said, "McLean, Virginia. It's across the river, where all the DC big shots live."

Zeke said, "I don't understand why we're taking separate vehicles."

Key threw up her hands. "*Why would you be going?*"

"Why would *you* be going? Neither one of us is getting paid to do this!"

"Here's how I see it," said Zeke's sister, Cammy. "If we spend all day driving out there, and it turns out to be nothing, we'll feel pretty stupid, right? But if we stay here, then watch on our phones while a terrorist bomb blows up a bunch of children and politicians, I personally am going to feel even worse. Can you guys pitch in for gas? We'll have to fill up six times for the round trip."

Exasperated, Key asked, "What exactly do you think we're all going to do once we get out there?"

"How long is the drive to Virginia?" asked Zeke.

Ether said, "Ten hours, if we go the fastest way nonstop. Longer if we take some side roads and stop repeatedly to piss."

"Okay," said Zeke, nodding and fastening his seat belt. "Then we've got that long to figure it out."

The man who rammed the Navigator in Nashville is a biker named Richard "Malort" Little, a hero who risked his life to try to save millions

Posted to r/DCTerrorAttack by QueefMachine91
Little's whereabouts are currently unknown but it's clear this guy must be a redditor who has been following these events via this sub. He knew where Abbott and GSG would be and managed to disable their vehicle, which is more than any of us accomplished.

Malort, if you're out there and if there is anything we can do to help, let us know. If anyone knows of a fundraiser to provide him assistance, please post the link so we can donate.

ABBOTT

Everyone stank of smoke and cheese and hot sauce, and it was turning Abbott's stomach.

It was decided that, once they were some safe distance from Nashville, they needed to stop somewhere for gas, supplies, and some clothes that weren't covered in pepper sauce and cheese curds. Cammy said she knew just the place but didn't clarify. So now Abbott was in the very back of the van with Ether, who had stuffed her mouth with tissues to stem the bleeding. They were both slumped back, exhausted. He was oddly soothed by the sensation of having others in charge of the driving and navigation, even if they were heading toward some kind of doom.

Ether looked at him and, quietly, said, "Thank you, by the way."

She'd taken the crimson wad of tissues from her mouth and seemed to be inspecting the damage with her tongue.

"For what?"

"Coming along. Helping me see this through. The upside of being responsible for your own choices is you get to celebrate when you do the right thing. Don't forget to do that part."

"Maybe we should see how this turns out first."

"Are you going to be okay without your meds? It's funny, there was so much chaos back there that I'm now wondering if we couldn't have just swung by Walgreens on the way out without anybody noticing."

Apparently, Abbott's father had been eavesdropping. He looked back from the second row. "Which prescription was it?"

Abbott said the name of the antianxiety medication, and Cammy, who had apparently joined in the eavesdropping, said, "Oh, I have that. I can definitely spare one."

"Hey," said Key, "I've got some of those."

Zeke said, "Me, too! I have the higher dosage, but you could split a pill if you had to."

Then, after a suspicious pause, his father said, "I do, too. Zeke's dosage. But they were in my bag, in the rental car."

"Maybe Malort will take a couple," said Key. "Calm himself down."

A pill was handed back to Abbott. He wasn't even sure whose he'd wound up with.

Zeke glanced back at Key and said, "All right, glowie, what do we know about our enemy, here? This Sokolov?"

"Are you telling me you haven't read up on him online?" Abbott noted an odd smile when she said this.

"I have, but I guess I was assuming you had, you know, insider information or something. Is he really a prison genius who got rich off tech investments? That story feels a little too Hollywood for me."

Key said, "Yeah, the reality isn't quite that neat."

MALORT

The only thing Malort really used the internet for was watching a particular genre of video: vehicles running into low bridges and getting their tops scraped off. He could watch that shit for hours.

There was one infamous bridge in Durham, North Carolina, that only had a clearance of eleven feet, eight inches, and locals called it the "can opener" on account of how it would peel the tops off tall trucks that ignored all the low clearance signs. This occurred with sufficient frequency that a live feed of those incidents had gained quite a following over the years. The Bankhead Tunnel in Mobile, Alabama, was almost as good, only twelve feet high and plenty of signs warding off semis that routinely run thirteen or higher. Its live camera captured truck after truck getting violently wedged into the tunnel after their electronic navigation systems led them right into roof-scalping doom. But by far the best clip he'd ever seen was of a train that somehow got routed under a bridge six inches too short for its cars. Unlike the trucks getting decapitated by the low clearances, the train couldn't just screech to a halt; it just kept going and going, the bridge peeling back the corrugated roofs of car after car after car, destroying the cargo in the process (several million dollars' worth of brand-new Ford Explorers). Malort had watched that video at least a hundred times. This situation reminded him of that.

He was in the rental car he'd borrowed from that cranky lady with the gun, but he knew rental cars had trackers installed, so now he was looking for something to steal. This situation wasn't gonna pan out the way he'd wanted, that much was clear, but he was a freight train and these were his tracks. Bridge or no bridge, there was nothing to do but keep grinding forward, until the sheer violence of the wreckage finally stopped him for good. Malort had spent most of his adult life understanding that, at some point, he would mess things up so bad that they couldn't be put right. He'd cross the wrong line and wind up in prison so long that he'd just die there, or cross the wrong dude and get stabbed in the throat. Malort was now fairly certain he would never see LA again, or another Christmas, or even Tuesday. But these were the tracks that had been laid for him and, one way or the other, he intended to look Sock in the face one last time before this ride finally came screeching to a loud, painful end.

Malort had met Gary "Sock" Sokolov back in the '90s when they had both migrated to California's Central Valley to start running crank, what they called meth back then. The pair hauled ephedrine up from the border and lived free in ways that men don't anymore. Malort had been born in

Montana and had grown up unaware that there were parts of California poorer than Mississippi, a haven for biker clubs and 1 percenters that, it turned out, suited him just fine. After a few years, they'd put back enough cash to open a titty bar outside Fresno and dreamed of spending the rest of their lives getting paid to shoot pool and get shit-faced. One of the girls they hired went by the name Sundae, and Malort and Sock both fell in love with her before all of her had even passed over the threshold. But she took to Sock, as he was the smooth talker between the two, and Malort always got told that he was like a brother to her. It was always sweet to hear and, at the same time, cut him like a knife.

The three of them stuck together after the bar went belly-up and after the next dozen ventures met the same fate. When Sundae decided she'd wanted to move to LA with what Sock and Malort both knew were secret dreams of fame, Sock agreed, because he always agreed with whatever she said, and Malort followed them down, because that's what he did. Always waiting in the wings, ready to break the bones of anybody who wronged the one person he truly loved. Then, in the fall of 2012, a ticking time bomb was planted in their lives.

That's when the three of them went off to do a cross-country bike ride, Sundae in Sock's sidecar. They'd planned it for months, a tour they'd drawn up to be a preview of the apocalypse, passing through all of the best ghost towns in America. They hit Picher, Oklahoma, population 20 (evacuated by the government after the whole place got contaminated by a lead mine), Putnam, Texas (population 94, dried up on its own due to Circumstances), Centralia, Pennsylvania (population 5, due to an underground coal fire that'd been burning since 1962), and a dozen others. On the way to the Quabbin Reservoir in Massachusetts (the site of several small towns that had been intentionally flooded to create the reservoir) they stopped in Springfield, where Sock had insisted several appropriately unruly dive bars could still be found.

They hit up what seemed like a decently grimy joint and wound up playing pool with the most repulsive category of humans on earth: smug college boys. These were the guys who knew their lives were gonna be one long, freshly paved road, that none of their vices or perversions would get them into hot water, as they were simply too valuable to the system. There were several of them, led by this tall drink of mayonnaise with movie star hair and carefully mowed beard stubble. He'd been openly hitting on Sundae, telling her she looked like Beyoncé, which already was enough to get him pulverized, but then he'd doubled down by trying to hustle Sock at eight ball. They played for drinks, the kid doing that shit he probably saw in a movie, intentionally throwing close games to lure the mark into going all in, at which point, he planned to then turn around and unleash his true skills. Sock had gone along with it, always keeping it close until the kid put five hundred bucks on a final best-of-three match. At which point, Sock, who Malort sincerely believed was one of the hundred best pool players on the planet, chalked up his cue and calmly ran the table twice, the kid never even getting a turn.

Nobody had put cash on the rail, because gambling was forbidden at the establishment, and both Sock and Malort had known from his manner that the kid didn't really have the five hundred—that was, of course, the whole point. They took him out to the parking lot and punched him in the gut hard enough to make him puke and probably shit blood for a week, all his coward friends hanging back and insisting they were gonna call the cops. The kid then took them to his car—a beat-up old Ford Taurus—and offered them his laptop computer as payment. It was an old model covered in scratches and stickers, and Malort had figured a pawnshop wouldn't fork over more than fifty bucks for it. Leave it to the two of them to shake down the one rich kid who happened to be poor. Then, in an act of desperate bullshitting that Sock would be telling as a funny story for years after, the kid had insisted there was five thousand of some kind of new computer money on the laptop. They had laughed in his face, beat his ass, smashed his windshield, and rode off with the laptop in Sock's saddlebag. Once they were back home, Malort had asked a nerd friend if the computerized money was somehow real. The guy had taken a look and said that on the laptop was a "key" to a "wallet" with computer coins worth about twenty bucks, and only if you could find some other nerd willing to trade for them. Sock had tossed the laptop onto a shelf in a closet and forgotten all about it.

Several years went by, and Sock tried to go more and more legitimate, as he'd done some time by that point, and Sundae had said she'd leave him if he ever went away again. His life became a cycle of taking jobs that lasted right up until a superior busted his balls a little too hard, at which point, he'd lash out and get fired again. After getting canned from the best-paying legal work he'd had in his life—a welding job on an oil rig—Sock had started scrounging around his place for parts to sell. He remembered the old laptop computer and showed it to Sundae, who did some research and told him the computer money on that hard drive was called "Bitcoin" and that a Bitcoin was, as of that moment, worth $43,000. Sock had almost broken down in tears at the news—43K was enough money to get him out from under the old bar loans, enough to go see the doctor about why his piss sometimes turned blue. Then Sundae had to clarify: $43,000 wasn't the value of what was on that computer, that was the price of a single Bitcoin.

That laptop gave him access to five thousand of them.

That hunk of metal and plastic that had been gathering dust next to Sock's old Kaiser helmet and *Easy Rider* magazines was worth over two hundred million motherloving dollars.

KEY

"The funny part," said Key, "is the price of Bitcoin actually went up another fifty percent or so after he cashed his in; he could have sold at sixty if he'd sat on it a little longer. But the point is, this guy's business acumen consisted entirely of trying to hustle a poor college kid and then failing to ever clean his closets. So, yeah, somewhat different from the story he tells in his biography."

Abbott said, "I wonder why the kid never tried to track down the laptop after the price of Bitcoin went to the moon."

"He probably did, but you're talking about a couple of bikers he saw almost a decade earlier, probably while drunk off his ass, who lived on the opposite side of the country. And why would he assume they still had the laptop, as opposed to pawning it or tossing it at some random strip club in Kentucky?"

"But wouldn't he have recognized Sokolov after he became a public figure? Put two and two together?"

"Maybe, but so what? He has no legal claim to the coins. It's no different from selling a painting at a garage sale and then having it shoot up in value because the artist got famous or died. Anyway, to his credit, Sokolov immediately decided that he had accidentally benefited from some kind of weird alien technology that he in no way understood and, instead of trying to understand it, immediately converted the coins into cash in chunks and used that cash to buy land."

"Actually," said Hunter, "I have to give him credit. Knowing how you're dumb is one of the most valuable kinds of smart there is."

"I suppose. I mean, he didn't know real estate, either, but he'd ridden across America and saw how all the small towns were bleeding their population into the cities, and he understood the basic concept of supply and demand. So, he googled the fastest-growing cities in America and bought entire neighborhoods' worth of distressed properties and vacant lots—anything that kind of looked like it would someday hold an apartment building or a new development of McMansions. Then he bought an estate outside DC and started figuring out how to get himself invited to the right parties. The guy probably just missed his window to visit Epstein Island."

"All I'm hearing," said Hunter, "is that these are amoral dirtbags who suddenly came into unfathomable money and power. That sounds exactly like a recipe for the civilization-ruining nightmare scenario."

Key said, "I agree on the second part. But it wasn't all the dirtbags who came into money. It was just Sokolov."

MALORT

It seemed fitting that Malort had been in prison when he heard that Sock had struck it rich. Sock had always been the one with the luck, born with looks and brains and the ability to always sidestep the blowback from his endless fuckups. Malort, on the other hand, had gotten stuck with a five-year sentence for aggravated assault and trafficking stolen auto parts, when all he'd done was rent some garage space to a friend who was doing the actual work of stripping precious metals from catalytic converters, then stab that friend when a disagreement arose over payment. Still, Malort had taken Sock's good fortune as the best news of his life, thinking "they" had struck it rich, the three of them. He imagined the day of his release, Sock and Sundae picking him up at the gates in a Rolls-Royce with a hot tub instead of a back seat.

That's what you get for assuming the best about people.

Instead, Sock had disappeared in a puff of smoke like the goddamned Road Runner. Sundae told Malort that he'd started acting weird as soon as he realized the old laptop was a gold mine, telling her he needed to get away, to protect himself from the hundreds of former associates who'd murder him for that laptop the second they found out about it. After vanishing for a month, he came back and told her they were moving to Virginia. Sundae hadn't been a fan of abandoning everything and everyone she knew and found Sock's vision of their highfalutin future to be frankly terrifying. The discussion had descended into a screaming match, and Sock had stormed out. This, Malort wasn't ashamed to admit, had also come as good news. Maybe once he got out, it would just be him and Sundae. That would be better than the money, by a mile.

Within a year, Sock was wearing suits and doing press appearances talking about his rough criminal past, like Malort and Sundae existed only as colorful reminders of the misguided miscreant he used to be. Everybody said the money changed Sock, but that wasn't it. If he'd just wanted to be rich, if he'd fucked off to Honolulu and spent the rest of his life on the beach, who'd have blamed him? But no, Gary Sokolov thought he deserved to decide what kind of world it was going to be for everybody else. When they'd been doing their apocalypse bike ride, Sock had made the comment that after things fell apart, the hardest part would be figuring out what to do with all the soft cubicle dwellers, the herd animals who wouldn't know how to behave without somebody telling them the rules, how to dress, which words they were allowed to use this week. Sock had spent his whole life saying the system was bullshit, but what the money made apparent was that the only thing he hated about the system was that he wasn't the one running it.

A year before Malort got out of prison, Sundae had sent him a picture Sock had taken with the president of the United States. Malort had thought it was a joke, like maybe they'd had a cardboard cutout at a party or something. And it *was* a joke, to be sure. It's just that the universe happened to be in on it.

22

HUNTER

"There it is," said Cammy, a lilt of wonder in her voice. She swept her hand across the vista in the windshield. "Take it iiiiiinnnn."

Hunter heard Ether say, "What the hell? I thought it was a gas station, but it just. Keeps. Going."

Cammy cackled. "You've never seen a Buc-ee's before?"

It was pronounced like "Bucky's," and it surely was an imposing sight for those who had not previously witnessed its majesty. It was an ostentatious mockery of a normal convenience store: A hundred and twenty gas pumps next to a sprawling facility stocked to feed and equip an army, every inch plastered with its bucktoothed beaver mascot.

Zeke said, "When the first one of these opened in Tennessee, the governor and both senators came to the grand opening."

Abbott shook his head. "When humanity dies, a picture of this place should be on the tombstone."

Key said, "In and out, guys. Food, clothes, bandages, gas. Don't be dazzled into a stupor by the spectacle. The man we're chasing is boarding a jet as we speak."

Hunter volunteered to hang back to pump and pay for the gas, as he suspected he was the only one in the party who was not currently in some state of financial desperation. Everyone hurried into the store . . . everyone except Ether, who approached Hunter with a look like she was about to beg her boss for a raise.

The trip had been rough on her: She wore an unflattering tank top that was pink with blood diluted by rainwater, her ear had been mauled, her hand was bandaged up. One knee of her jeans was covered in smeared cheese curds, and the other was red with hot sauce that had to have been blistering her skin by now.

She said, "Hey, uh, I want you to know—if I thought even a little bit that this thing was a bomb, if I thought there was that kind of danger here, I wouldn't have asked your son to come along."

"If it's *not* a bomb," replied Hunter as he slid his credit card into the pump, "we're all going to have a lot of explaining to do. And some stiff legal fees in our future."

"But if I'm wrong and your friend is right, if it turns out that I've accidentally facilitated a terror attack on the government—get yourself and Abbott to safety. Leave me to try to do, well, whatever can be done. Don't put yourselves at risk."

"I have to ask: How in the world did you even get Abbott to go along with this?"

"If we're both being frank, I kind of bullied him into it; I was a little desperate at that moment. But as for why he stayed with it after things started to turn ugly, ah . . ."

"What?"

"Honestly? He didn't feel like he had anything to go home to."

Hunter sighed. "Of course he would say that. If he can't sit in his room and play video games full-time, then life isn't worth living."

"I've only known Abbott for a few days, so I don't pretend to understand your whole father-son dynamic, but you should ask yourself what you would say to Abbott if you knew it was the last conversation you'd ever have with him, and make sure that you make time to say it between here and McLean. Because, well. You never know."

KEY

Inside, Key stared at a case of what she estimated to be eight hundred flavors of beef jerky and tried to think. The store was packed with tourists who'd apparently come to Buc-ee's as their destination, not a stop. Everything smelled like smoked meat and warm sugar. Nearby was a giant sign that said, RESTROOMS: WORLD FAMOUS! which sparked many questions in her mind.

She absolutely still intended to ditch the rest of the van misfits as soon as she could find another vehicle. Otherwise, even if everything went perfectly and they made the heroic save, it would be difficult to explain why she had turned up at the scene with an incel streamer, his dad, a disgraced makeup influencer, and a Roller Derby girl in a blue hentai van being driven by a disabled furry porn artist.

"Hey," said Ether, who had crept up behind her at some point. "Jesus, this is an alarming amount of jerky. If this place flooded, it would rehydrate into a stampede."

Key glanced back at her. She didn't particularly need Ether/Karen/whatever, but she definitely needed Phil Greene's old phone and its tracking app. When Key separated from the group, ideally it would be with that phone in her pocket.

"Is the package in the air?" asked Key, hoping it would prompt Ether to pull out the phone to check.

"As of about five minutes ago," she answered, without doing that. "It was stuck on the runway at the Nashville airport for a while and I imagined police surrounding the plane, but I guess that was too much to wish for."

Key sighed. "Almost everything is."

Ether paused in that way that people do when they're loading up the thing they'd actually come to say. "So . . . if I can be super honest right now, I feel like you're planning to ditch us as soon as you can find a car."

"Well, now that you've suggested it, yeah, that's probably the most reasonable course of action. I'm trained in this, you guys aren't. And unlike you, I agreed to take these kinds of risks the moment I decided to pursue this as a career."

"Just understand that I'm making the trip one way or the other. If you leave me behind, you'll just be complicating things, because we'll be working separately instead of together, getting in each other's way. And no, you won't talk me out of it."

"This paycheck means that much to you? Or do you secretly believe it might be a bomb after all?"

"I can't believe that. I can't allow myself to. I'm sorry, I knew these people. I lived with them."

"Dennis Rader—the BTK killer—was married the whole time he was active; the wife never had any idea while he was butchering at least ten victims. So who would you say knew Rader better: his wife or the people he killed?"

"And what percentage of the population is truly capable of doing something like that? Like what are the odds?"

"Unfortunately, a tragedy here wouldn't require a majority of people to be terrorists. Just a few."

"Okay, then how do you know I'm not one of them? Everybody online seems to think I'm a conspirator. What convinced you otherwise? Honest answer."

"You won't like the honest answer."

"Try me."

"You don't fit the profile." She glanced around. "I need new clothes. This cottage cheese is starting to ferment."

ZEKE

"I have my Mace in my purse," said Cammy over a sloppy barbecue brisket sandwich that Zeke was pretty sure she wasn't supposed to be eating inside the store. "Do they sell guns here?"

She scanned her surroundings, presumably for the Buc-ee's assault rifle aisle.

"Probably at the Texas locations," replied Zeke. "But you've got the right idea. This device probably isn't on a timer; that's mostly a Hollywood thing. That means it's set to be manually activated by remote. Incapacitate the man with the switch and your problems are over."

"And then what?"

"The police finally figure out what's going on, they rush in, say, 'Thank you for doing our jobs for us.'"

They were circling an island of counters in the middle of the store, inside of which was a man chopping a huge pile of beef brisket on a cutting board. Behind him, a vat was stirring warm pecans into a coating of sugar and cinnamon. Nearby, a woman was slicing a board of freshly made fudge. Along one wall were dozens of fountain drink stations boasting every flavor modern chemistry can convey to the human tongue.

"Will we win an award or something afterward?" asked Cammy, some brisket flying out as she spoke.

"They'll probably send us a bill for the damage."

Cammy watched the brisket guy chop charred flesh and said, "We're not gonna die, are we?"

"I don't know, Cam. Are you having second thoughts?"

"I mean, do we trust this girl? Ether? I thought we had decided she was behind all this."

"I don't trust anybody, just by default. But if Abbott trusts her, that's good enough for me. If he's wrong, well, I'd rather have her in the vehicle with us than out there pursuing her own agenda. If she's going to DC because she wants to be the one to trigger the bomb, then we'll be there to stop her. It'll be five against one."

A voice from behind them asked, "Are you finding what you need?"

Zeke assumed it was a store employee, but he looked back to find it was Abbott's terrible father, Hunter. Jesus, what a stupid name.

Cammy said, "We're trying to figure out if they have weapons here."

Hunter examined the Malort bite wound on his arm and said, "I think if this situation descends into a pitched battle with the security team of a wealthy and politically connected ex-con, we'll probably be on the losing end even if we arrive with every dangerous object Buc-ee's has to offer."

Zeke said, "Hmm," and thought he had a fairly solid grasp on why Abbott couldn't tolerate this guy.

"Hey, I wanted to ask something. You watched Abbott's streams, right? You're a fan?"

"Yeah."

"Why? I don't mean that in a bad way, I mean—what are people getting out of it? Legitimately asking."

"We weren't jerking off to it," replied Zeke, "if that's what you're wondering. He plays games and chats with us. And, you know, he's funny. I put him on in the background while I work. It's just like hanging out with a friend."

"Okay, but sometimes he's eating?"

"Yeah, once a week he does fast-food reviews. You know, like if there's a new menu item, he reviews it. But it's just a joke, like he's making fun of the channels that do that stuff. He acts like he doesn't actually know how to eat, there will be this big windup where he's introducing the food and going into extreme detail about how it's made, then when it comes time to try it, he smashes it into the side of his face, like he missed his mouth. Then he goes, '*Mmmm!*' It's always the same joke, but I laugh my ass off every time. I guess knowing it's coming makes it funnier. But there's not much to it other than that; we just hang out. A bunch of us, together. It's a community."

"And they fixed our van," said Cammy. "When it broke down, Abbott got everybody together to chip in. It saved our asses."

"I didn't know that," said Hunter, and Zeke had a whole lot of things he wanted to say in response but figured there was no point.

"To the tune of five thousand dollars," added Cammy, "so if Abbott needs help seeing this thing through, I figure this is the least we can do."

ABBOTT

While moving through a maze of Buc-ee's–branded merchandise, Abbott started to wonder if this place wasn't a dying hallucination he was having while his body was cooking in the crashed Navigator. There was a pickup truck parked inside the store, its bed full of stuffed Buc-ee beavers. They had beaver-branded bikinis and pool floaties. Abbott needed pants and a shirt—his back and butt were caked with what fellow shoppers must have assumed was vomit—but the only pants he saw at the moment were yellow pajama bottoms covered with that deranged cartoon beaver's face.

His father strolled up and, in the matter-of-fact manner of speaking he used to convey every motion except rage, said, "Hey, I feel like this might be the last chance at a private conversation we'll ever have, for a variety of reasons. So there's, uh, some things I guess we should say."

It hardly passed for a private conversation considering Abbott was having to shuffle aside once a minute to allow another shopper to pass, but he supposed nobody eavesdrops on the words of vomit-covered men.

"Why did you come out here?" asked Abbott, rather than wait for his father to deliver whatever speech he'd prepared. "Was it the internet rumors, or did you just want the Navigator back?"

"Come on, now. When have I not been there for you? What crisis was I absent for? I may not have been all smiles and sunshine, but I was always there. Always."

"Do you know the names of any of my friends? Before the ones you met today, I mean. Have you ever watched a single one of my streams?"

"I feel like that goes both ways. Do you know any of the guys I work with or what's going on with the business, day to day? When I come home in a pissy mood, do you ask *why* I'm in that mood? Do you know if I've tried dating after your mom went away? It seems like we both have that personality; we keep to ourselves. It's kind of unfair that parents are expected to be a certain type of person."

"I learned how to shave from the internet. Not from you. That's where I learned how to tie a tie, how to get rid of pimples, how to fill out my taxes—a bunch of strangers taught me, other people's dads. I never learned how to talk to girls or anything else having to do with how to be a man. And, you know, there's a lot of guys out there like that, but they were raised by single moms. I had you in the same house, but your only method for teaching me anything was to shame me for not already knowing, then storm off to the garage. And, hey, maybe you're right, maybe I'll be the same kind of dad to my own kid, if I ever have one. Whatever. It is what it is."

"Abbott . . . do you know how much pain I'm in, every day? This work has destroyed me. When I'm old, I won't be able to walk, I won't be able to sleep through the night, the pain is going to follow me around like a curse until I die. And I did that for you, to provide. I could have kicked you out when you turned eighteen, but I didn't. I kept providing. Even when you refused to grow up and move on, I still fed you and housed you and kept you safe."

"I'd have rather been poor and had a dad who didn't hate me."

That stopped him. Abbott was glad it did. He made a show of examining a rack of T-shirts. One featured an American flag behind the words, SORRY, CAN'T HEAR YOU OVER THE SOUND OF FREEDOM RINGING.

Another proclaimed, FREEDOM IS NEVER MORE THAN ONE GENERATION AWAY FROM EXTINCTION.

"I never hated you," said Abbott's father, looking everywhere but at him. "I just . . . I would give anything, *anything* to be that guy, the one who radiates warmth. I don't have it in me. I never have. I don't feel what other people feel. I look at a puppy, I look at a baby, I look at my own mother and I don't get this fuzzy gush of emotion. I lack those brain chemicals. But I *do* feel the urge to give them good lives, to protect them. I would die for my family, my people. And I walk around every day knowing that no matter what I do for the world, no matter what I build or how much money I make, people can sense what's missing in me, and they stay away. I'm going to die alone, I know I will. I know you won't come visit me, wherever I end up. And I'll understand. But, Abbott, the way I am. I didn't choose to be this way."

"Well, neither did I."

Abbott found a pair of black pants on which the beaver was slightly less conspicuous. Nearby was a blue T-shirt that featured a cartoon dog wearing American flag sunglasses. It seemed to be the least gawdy shirt in the store.

His father, seeming to examine a woman's shirt that read, AIN'T NO HOOD LIKE MOTHERHOOD, said, "I know. *But* what you can choose is whether or not to take action. And I watched you choose to do this, to see this thing through. To do something, rather than be a spectator."

"That's nice that you have a good feeling about me for the first time. But I shouldn't have had to earn it."

"I'm saying that if my job was to get you ready for the world, then it looks to me like I've done it."

"So that's what you wanted for our maybe-final private conversation? To try to justify yourself for the ten thousandth time? I guess as final conversation subjects go, that's as appropriate as any."

Abbott could sense his father getting angry and, for the very first time, could sense himself not giving a shit.

"Maybe you won't hear this," said his father, "because I know I definitely didn't listen to my dad at your age, but I have to at least try to say it: you don't know yourself, Abbott. Nobody knows who they are until they go out and adversity strips away the phony parts, makes a mockery of all the lies you tell yourself. Inside your little cocoon, you can convince yourself that you can do anything, that you could succeed if you were given the right chances. But that's all just an illusion until it's tested. You're still new. Nobody's taken you out of the package yet."

"Until now?"

"Maybe."

"*Maybe?*"

"Let's put it this way. Let's say we go out there and it all goes to shit and a bunch of people die because of it. But let's say you survive and have to spend the rest of your life with that knowledge that you tried with all you had and failed anyway. *Then* you'll know what it's like to be a man."

"That sounds awful."

"It is, sometimes. But just think of what it'll be like if you succeed."

"Here's what I think," Abbott said, after a terrible pause to browse beaver merch. "I think that you're probably right. My bedroom, my screens, that's my comfort zone. But I think those rooftops are your comfort zone and where you get scared is in situations like this, talking to me, or thinking about why you are the way you are. I think that because the roof stuff is physically harder, you think you're being tough, but you would rather be up there for twenty straight hours in a hurricane than, say, sit down and actually try to work things out with Mom, to understand where she's coming from, to see why she did what she did. I think you and I are both scared to come out of our shells, but you don't see a problem with yours because your shell happens to make you a lot of money."

"And yet, Abbott, I'm here." His father paused while he picked up a shirt, then said, "We both are."

The secondary attack will involve the mass assault of abducted prominent children

Posted to r/DCTerrorAttack by FedThrowaway66974

I know you guys have been fiending for an update, and I've got a juicy one for you. Be sure to follow me to be notified as soon as these come in.

The FBI has confirmed that, in the aftermath of the upcoming attack, there are plans for fake ambulances and crews to carry away the wounded children. In the midst of the chaos at the various hospitals around the DC area, those children will be routed by Coburn and Wozniak to a secret location, where they will be imprisoned and, over the coming weeks and months, repeatedly sexually assaulted and tortured live on camera.

The young victims with radiation wounds and flesh-eating disease will be left to rot live on stream, their tissue literally melting off their bones as they scream, day and night. These acts will be blamed on a specific activist group that the Russians have calculated will incite maximum outrage, I'll leave it to you to discuss which one that is (if you want more info on that, you can subscribe to my newsletter—it's $4.99 a month, but it's worth it as certain facts aren't safe to share on Reddit).

The broadcasts of the children's defilement will be pay-per-view, and it is believed that the millions brought in from eager audiences around the world will be used to fund the next operation. This was the reasoning behind the spilling of the red sauce and white cheese at the scene of the Nashville distraction. It was intended to taunt the public, an artistic representation of the blood and semen that will be spilled in the coming months. We have tried to warn the parents of the children who will be attending the Sokolov event tomorrow morning, but it is believed that they are in on the operation, that they were paid a fee to sacrifice their own children for torture as part of the false flag to incite the coming revolution.

If you think these people aren't capable of that, you need to open your eyes.

23

ETHER

"It's official," said Ether. "They've overtaken us. I guess that was inevitable."

They were all back on the road, half of them in Buc-ee's garb. The blue dot marking the location of the black box was currently soaring smoothly over Kentucky. Ether was trying to gauge Agent Key's demeanor, sensing that Key felt like she'd been made to sit with the losers in the cafeteria and that it wasn't her first time. The former fed was wearing a new T-shirt featuring a bald eagle on a motorcycle.

"Hold on," asked Abbott, "you can just load a nuclear bomb onto a private flight? Nobody searches the bags or anything?"

"Nope," said Key. "The TSA *can* search private planes, but they almost never do. The aircraft and passengers are considered low-risk on account of being fabulously wealthy."

"Jesus Christ."

"And now you see the genius of Sokolov's plan. Not a single mechanism of this country's counterterrorism apparatus would stop a wealthy, well-connected conspirator. Hell, even after the bomb goes off, he'll probably have politicians and pundits defending him on TV."

"Now, as for Sokolov's estate," said Zeke, using his non-driving hand to scroll through what looked like a listing from a real estate website, "he's got a seventy-million-dollar mansion overlooking the Potomac, the grounds surrounded by a wall and a gate. There are five other buildings on the property for servants and guests, then a gatehouse right at the main road. From there, a driveway leads to a motor court in front, then around to a luxury glassed-in garage in back. That's next to the lawn and swimming pool, so guests can admire his many exotic cars while listening to the live music he books to play in his backyard. It looks like U2 made an appearance last Christmas, for an audience of CEOs from around the world. So that's the kind of parties *he* has."

Hunter said, "The way you're describing this place kind of makes me want to blow it up myself."

"I'm not seeing a fence along the riverbank. I bet they don't have one, as it would obstruct their view. So, there you go: all we need are six tuxedos and six wet suits to wear over them. We crawl out of the water, strip off the scuba gear, and blend into the party like James Bond."

"If I'm right," said Ether, "and if I just walk up to the gate and demand payment, I say there's a fifty-fifty chance Sokolov lets me in. He wouldn't want me making a scene in front of his guests. I at least have to try. It could resolve the whole situation in five minutes."

"And if you're wrong," said Hunter, "you've tipped him off that we're coming."

Cammy said, "Ooh, I think I just had an idea of how to get inside." She turned to Zeke. "Look up which town on our route has a Party City and find out what time they close. And a craft store or hardware store. Someplace with paint and stencils." This was met with silence until she said, "Unless somebody has a better idea?"

Key said, "How about you give us the details, and then we'll have between now and the nearest Party City to come up with something better."

I am an officer in the US Marine Corps and we have been mobilized to seize control of the capital

Posted to r/DCTerrorAttack by SemperFiAnonymous

Two entire divisions of the US Marines have been mobilized to Washington under the guise of a training exercise. It is my understanding that we secretly will be there to impose marshal law in response to tomorrow's attack on the Supreme Court. The president has already prepared a statement blaming the attack on the Russians (not that this will stop him from flipping the court with openly Communist replacements). I told my commanding officer that I would not go along with any effort to suspend the US Constitution, as that would violate my oath. He strongly implied that any of us who did not go along would be executed for treason.

We will all have to pick a side soon. I know which one I'll be on.

This is Haley Swanson, I am not dead

Posted to r/DCTerrorAttack by Haley_Swanson99
A friend pointed me to this subreddit, I have no idea what's going on but I barely remember Abbott Coburn, he did not murder me and I am very much alive. I left home for Clearwater a few years ago to become a Scientologist, my family freaked out and filled out a missing person's report and it made the news. A few months later, my mother found me but didn't tell the press because she wanted to keep the Scientology thing quiet. I got out of the church last year but changed my name for reasons having to do with personal safety. Please stop badgering my parents telling them you know where my corpse is, they just saw me at Easter. Also, there is no way I would have fit in that box.

Thank you. Stop being weird.

—Haley (no longer my name)

ETHER

After hours of discussion, it had ultimately been decided that Cammy's plan was laughably unrealistic, and also the best of their available options. They'd found a Party City in Roanoke, Virginia, and filled a cart minutes before the store was set to close. Now they were back on the road, Ether sorting through bags of balloons and painting supplies. She figured they were a little more than two hundred miles from the destination—she'd come more than 90 percent of the way.

"If you think about it," she said, "Party City is kind of the apex of human civilization. An entire chain of almost a thousand stores that sells nothing but cheap plastic party supplies. Think how many parties it takes to support that."

"Six months from now," said Key, who was opening a package of balloons with her teeth, "maybe it'll be a festive little POW camp."

"Do you guys really think the country will descend into civil war if this thing plays out like the bad guys want?" asked Cammy while examining a set of paintbrushes. "I mean, how would that even work? I'm thinking about my trans friend in Austin being asked to fight for, what? The new Confederacy? The Independent Nation of Texas?"

"It would definitely be messy," said Key. "But the way I see it, America was never really united. In Alabama, the line where the seashore used to be about eighty-five million years ago now marks which counties vote Democrat. That old shoreline created rich soil that was perfect for cotton. That meant slaves; their descendants still live there. That's America, full of these fault lines, open wounds that never healed. If you head a few miles that direction and cross into West Virginia, the average life expectancy drops five years. The average person born over there dies six years sooner than if they'd been born back in California. Same nation, different worlds."

Ether said, "And nationwide, the average life span has gone up ten years since 1960. We've gained *an entire extra decade of life* just in that time, and nobody cares, because apparently progress doesn't count. The plane has landed, by the way. It's at something called Leesburg."

"It's a small, fancy airport for rich people. Now, what was supposed to hold all this together was religion, that we'd put aside our differences because we're all children of God and so on. But half of us don't go to church anymore, so now that's your biggest fault line. Abortion, gay marriage, trans rights, the War on Christmas—it all boils down to old-school religion versus new-school secularism, and both sides secretly believe that, eventually, the other will have to go. Now add to that the fact that we're all just *bored.* Our whole society is idle and overeducated, and nothing spices things up like conflict. There's an old saying that a child not embraced by the village will burn it down to feel its warmth. I'd update it to say the child not sufficiently entertained by the village will burn it down for the spectacle."

"You keep talking about Phil like he was crazy," said Ether, "but the two of you could have chatted for hours without ever disagreeing."

"I've been inside his tinfoil house. He may have had a point in the way that the Unabomber sort of had a point, at one time, before isolation drove him off the deep end. Phil Greene appears to have spent his final days ranting to empty rooms about Satan and 'the Forbidden Numbers,' whatever that is."

"I can tell you what that is, if you want to know."

Abbott paused while inflating a red balloon and said, "I'm almost afraid to find out."

"It sounds creepy," said Cammy.

"You have no idea." Ether tied off her first finished balloon and tried to think of where to start. "So, who here remembers the old website AmIHotOrNot.com?"

"I do," said Abbott. "It was in the early 2000s. People uploaded their pics for strangers to rate their attractiveness on a scale of one to ten. The rating was public. It destroyed the self-esteem of millions of average-looking people who grew up in ugly neighborhoods."

"Yeah. Well, that's an example of the Forbidden Numbers."

Key muttered, "Oh my god."

"No, seriously. It was just a silly idea somebody had. It took them a week to code it, but it was objectively the most important and influential website ever created. Mark Zuckerberg started Facebook to be a HotOrNot ripoff, YouTube was launched to be a video version of it—that's a trillion dollars' worth of market cap right there. That's because they'd stumbled across a world-changing concept: applying a numerical value to human behavior that had never before been quantifiable. Up until then, for all human history, any individual could lie to themselves, could secretly believe they were more attractive than they are, or smarter, or more creative, or nicer, or richer. Or, and this is the big one, that their beliefs were popular. The Forbidden Numbers strip all that away; your true spot on the social hierarchy is revealed for all to see, in the form of likes and followers. It doesn't matter how comfortable or well-fed somebody is; if you humiliate them in front of their peers, they'll want to burn the system to the ground. Well, social media algorithms are a twenty-four-seven humiliation machine. That, Phil believed, is how a population is primed for authoritarian rule. And that's just one example; we're essentially teaching machines how to hack human insecurity."

Key said, "Okay, I admit that so far this is like ninety percent the same as what I wrote when I was at the FBI."

Ether nodded. "If you relentlessly attack people's self-image, they'll scramble for something, anything to preserve it. Every cultural faction has their own scapegoats—the government, their childhood trauma, their mental illness, the evil billionaires, immigrants—and it doesn't matter the degree to which any of them are valid, because all the system cares about is that *you surrender your own agency.* 'I cannot be blamed for the state of my life, because I am at the mercy of this other, more powerful thing.' Phil's theory is that people *want* that powerful thing to exist, to take over their lives. At that point, we will have finally surrendered the entire concept of free will, the one thing that makes us human."

"So that will make them vote for a dictator?" asked Cammy. "I think they're already doing that now."

"It will, and they are. But Phil didn't think even that would be enough. What the people want is a cruel, all-powerful being that they can simultaneously obey and also endlessly complain about. He thought it would take the form of an artificial intelligence, one that would spontaneously create itself."

"Ah," said Key, "I wondered when we'd veer off into Crazytown."

"Look around you. How many people out there are addicted to internet gambling, or games, or porn, or outrage headlines they compulsively click and share? See, the Forbidden Numbers work on the back end, too, dialing in on exactly what pixels on a screen will subdue the human animal. And we go along willingly because *we want to be subdued.* The whole appeal of being in a media-induced flow state is that you block everything else out. We want to be zombies. Puppets. So, we're growing our own puppeteer."

Hunter said, "Yeah, I think he's convinced me that we should find this thing and destroy it."

"No! There's nothing to destroy! That's just another lie the system tells us, that the only solutions worth considering are the ones that are exciting to think about. Spectacle, like Key just said."

"I can't help but notice," said Key, "that this guy who kept warning the world that we were all going to die alone, did exactly that. So it kind of sounds like this trap he thinks the system has laid for us got him, too, one way or the other. So maybe, *just maybe,* he decided he wanted to go out with a big bang after all. Maybe just to wake us all up."

Ether thought about Phil, whose body was presumably now lying naked and cold in some city morgue, and found she'd lost the desire to speak further. They continued down the highway, accompanied only by the huffing and squeaking of the balloons.

MALORT

Many words had been used to describe Malort over the years, but *woodsman* had probably never come up even once. He'd almost gotten lost stumbling through the trees along the Potomac, but fortunately, his navigation challenge was fairly straightforward: he just had to keep the river in sight and keep moving until he saw Sock's ridiculous mansion on the other side of the water. This was a stretch where the river got narrow enough that a strong man could chuck a cat across it, should the need arise.

The trip to DC had taken him fourteen hours and involved eight different stops to find a single decent vehicle to steal. His plan required a pickup, and he'd eventually found one in the parking lot of a home improvement store in Roanoke, where he'd stopped to buy the props he'd need to pull off this operation. The plan also required Malort to be in disguise, which wasn't exactly easy considering his frame and overall physical appearance. He'd wound up swinging by a Party City to buy the least ridiculous wig he could find, figuring he could wear it under a do-rag that would hide most of it. He didn't know if his face was now known to the public thanks to the fiasco in Nashville, so he'd simply stuffed the wig down his pants and quickly slipped out, the staff up front mostly distracted by some gang of idiots buying every balloon in the store.

He'd been an hour down the road before he'd even noticed that his stolen pickup had a hunting rifle mounted to a rack in the rear window. This saved him another stop, which represented one of maybe three lucky things that had ever happened to Malort in his entire life. Still, by the time he made it to his destination, it was technically already the Fourth of July.

He stumbled over a root and fell to his knees for the third time. The rifle slipped off his back, bouncing into the leaves. Malort imagined it falling just the wrong way and shooting his balls off. The fatigue was getting to him. He knew he needed to get an hour or two of sleep at some point if he was to have any hope of seeing this thing through. He needed to do this first bit, though, before he could relax—

There it was.

Sock's estate overlooking the river turned out to be comically easy to spot, as it was sporting obnoxiously bright security lights, blasting across the water to ward off any thieves or protestors who would attempt amphibious access to the property. Hell, the asshole had probably packed the hundred feet or so of river with those spiky submarine mines.

Malort found a decent log he could prop the rifle on and got down into the dirt like a sniper. The gun wasn't a cannon, just something the owner had probably used to pick off varmints from his backyard. It did have a scope, though, and that gave him a clear enough view. Hell, Oswald was twice as far from Kennedy when he'd made his shots, and that was a moving target . . .

He listened. Malort had no idea how well-patrolled this area was or whose land he was even on. He waited for the sounds of angry shouts or an approaching engine or the snapping of twigs. Nothing. Satisfied that he was operating with some privacy, he viewed the Sokolov property through the scope. Crews were working overnight, building some kind of a stage with an elaborate arch decoration overhead. Getting ready for Sock's Fourth of July blowout. Just off the lawn to one side was a glassed-in garage, showing off a row of trophy vehicles.

Malort scanned around with the crosshairs until he found the right window, absently wondering who would have jurisdiction over a shot fired from the District of Columbia into Virginia.

He aimed, waited, held his breath, then pulled the trigger.

DAY 5

I am not well, and I am afraid to come
to see you now for fear something
melodramatic might happen.

—ROBERT OPPENHEIMER,
in a letter to a friend, 1926

24

ZEKE

The universe had been trying to murder Zeke Ngata from the moment he was born, and he took that personally. His parents were told he wouldn't survive infancy, then childhood. On his eighteenth birthday, Cammy had baked him a cake shaped like a middle finger, which became the annual tradition thereafter: "Fuck you," it said, "I'm still here."

Each time he surpassed some doomer milestone, the doctors acknowledged that the diagnosis had probably been incorrect and the most recent one could be boiled down to, "We don't have a name for this yet; please stop bothering us." Zeke personally believed his current symptoms—a creeping loss of limb control that started with his feet and rose as if he were being steadily lowered into the void—were the result of a botched surgery, one performed at an early age due to the first misdiagnosis. He also secretly believed that no one wanted to admit this, because doctors don't like to rat on each other. Well, he "secretly" believed this in the sense that he told it to everyone he saw, at every opportunity. He'd survived long enough to make it through art school, then struggled to find work-from-home jobs in graphic design that didn't pay peanuts. He'd wound up making far more by taking commissions for cartoon erotica, which might seem to an outsider to be a "last resort" type option, but it had actually been the second thing Zeke had tried. A month ago, he noticed a periodic tremor in his drawing hand, making precision work difficult. So what. He'd figure it out.

And so now Zeke was driving through McLean, Virginia, at six in the morning, daring the universe to try to kill him again. Cammy was in the passenger seat, and the only thing visible in the van behind them was red, white, and blue balloons.

"Okay, we've got a name!" said Cammy. "Holy crap, they actually did it."

She was on her phone, scrolling the chat from Abbott's Twitch channel. They'd recruited the fans there for an overnight task, and it appeared that this group of astonishingly bored weirdos had come through. Zeke had never doubted them.

"Is it the name of the party planner?" asked Zeke. "Sokolov's assistant? Somebody like that?"

"No, I think we've got something better. It's—OH, SHIT."

She was reacting to what was now visible through the windshield: they'd rounded a curve and could now see the gates to the Sokolov estate on their left.

"What?" asked Key from within the balloons behind them.

"There's a crowd at the gates," said Zeke.

"How many?" That was Hunter's balloon-muffled voice.

"Maybe . . . fifty people?" said Cammy, though Zeke thought it was probably more.

It had the feel of a protest, in the sense that some of the members of the crowd had brought signs. One said, JUSTICE FOR HALEY, another said, SEEK THE TRUTH, followed by a URL in an unreadably small font that seemed to have the letters *UFO* in it. But most were waving hand-painted yellow-and-black-striped signs that simply said, STAY AWAY. Everyone was packed tightly in front of the gates as if determined to prevent any vehicles from entering.

"Oh!" said Cammy. "Look! It's the police!"

"How many?" asked Abbott from somewhere back in the Balloon Zone.

"Two patrol cars. They don't have their lights on."

"They're coming to clear the crowd," said Key. "Just keep driving. Get us out of sight."

Zeke did, noting that a rough-looking pickup was pulling up to the gate, looking so out of place that he figured the guy had to have gotten the wrong address.

MALORT

The battered Chevy S-10 pickup Malort was driving rolled up to the gates of Sock's compound, where a handful of cops were trying to subdue a crowd of shouting kids protesting something or other, as if any of the billionaires and big shots at this shindig would even notice. Malort hadn't dug into the details of the event; he knew only that on the morning of the Fourth, Sock was holding a big blowout on his lawn for some strutting flock of assholes. The main thing from Malort's point of view was that it meant Sock was going to be home.

He pulled up, the Chevy's bed showing off its contents to the world: the biggest pane of glass he'd been able to find at the home supply store in Roanoke, a plastic tub of random accessories he'd bought with it, and a pair of toolboxes that had belonged to the truck's previous owner. Malort thought it looked like the vehicle of a salt-of-the-earth independent con- tractor who'd agreed to do an emergency window job. He'd tied a ban- danna around his neck to conceal his identifiable tattoo and wore a beanie that covered most of his bad Party City wig. He also had neglected to shave over the course of his cross-country journey, and the facial hair changed his look to a shocking degree (he'd never had a beard, and this one came in completely white—something Malort had absolutely *not* been prepared to see). He put on a pair of prescription reading glasses he found in the glove box. They gave him a headache, but he felt like they, along with the rest of the disguise, made him unrecognizable to any stranger working off, say, a grainy security cam photo.

Outside the gate was a little box on a pole with a screen and a single button. Malort punched said button while idiots shouted around him, some trying to get in front of the gate, the cops shoving them away. Malort put on his grumpiest expression, the look of a man who has been told by his boss he has an early-morning rush job on what he'd thought was going to be a drinking holiday.

As soon as a security guard's big, stupid face appeared on the screen, Malort grunted, "Hey, I can do the glass today, but they'll have to come back to do the tint."

This was a technique he'd learned over the years; you could ambush people by throwing them into the middle of what sounded like somebody else's argument. It makes them afraid to ask too many questions, lest they get sucked in. The guard looked confused and annoyed, like he'd already been about 90 percent of the way to just walking off the job before Malort had even shown up.

"This is about the window?" asked the guard.

"Now, this is Soft Coat Low-E," said Malort, making a show of shouting to be heard above the ruckus, "you don't have to worry about UV damage to the cars. It's not gonna match what you already have installed, not until we can have Mike or Rob come by and do the tint. I don't do the tint. I'm not trained in that. They had me do it once, but apparently, I did it wrong, and Rob had to come in and redo it—"

"Just a moment."

The screen went dark while the guard presumably called somebody on the house staff. As daytime break-ins go, if smash-and-grab wasn't an option, your best bet was to convince them to just let you in. The only way a man who looked like Malort would be allowed into a place like this was if there was dirty work that needed done in a hurry. If he'd had the ability to somehow clog Sock's toilets and show up as a plumber, he'd have done that. Instead, he'd shattered a window, one in a spot where it'd have been easily visible to the partygoers. He figured it would have to qualify as an emergency, as a man like Sock couldn't let it appear he didn't have his property squared away.

A moment later, the monitor blinked on, and the guard asked, "Who put in the order?"

Malort had been anticipating this, figuring they would ask the head of the house staff, who either had not, in fact, called anyone about the shot-out window yet or had called and been told nobody would be around until business hours, because it was goddamn six in the morning on a holiday.

"They identified themselves as a member of the staff," he said, in a tone like it was his hundredth time answering this question rather than the first. "Or maybe it was an assistant. Tony took the call. They said they needed this done and me gone before the guests got here. Now, I'm not sure that's enough time even if you let me in right now, but I'll do my best.

And like I said, it's gonna be clear glass, not smoked like the rest; that's just until Mike or Rob can come by. If that's gonna be a problem, I need to know now. But I was told there was an event today and that the home-owner didn't want the broken window with all the guests around. I've got the glass in the back if you wanna look it over prior to install."

The monitor blinked off again without a response from the guard. This plan had depended on Sock getting his beauty rest at this hour and no one on the house staff being brave enough to wake him. Sock did not like to be roused prior to his designated waking time and, in Malort's ex-perience, sometimes would respond with violence. Maybe it was a blood sugar thing.

Minutes passed, unruly dickheads yelling around him. If this didn't work, his backup plan had been to just ram the gates, but looking at them now, he was pretty sure he wouldn't get through even if he reversed and got a running start. So that idea was out the window unless he came back with a tank.

He prepared himself for Sock's stupid face to appear in the monitor and mock his feeble attempt at a disguise, but instead, the gates swung slowly open without another word from the guard. Malort rolled in, watching the cops fighting to keep the crowd from following him through.

ABBOTT

There were no sidewalks in this wealthy suburb, because of course there weren't. In places like this, a lack of sidewalks was a status symbol. The land actually sloped up on each side of the road like a riverbank as if to twist the ankles of any foolish pedestrians. Abbott and Ether stood out-side the van, which was stopped in the road maybe half a mile from the gates.

From the passenger seat, Cammy said, "Okay, we got a ping on the box. It's still in the garage."

"It makes sense that he'd leave it in the vehicle," said Key, whose head had emerged from the balloons to look over Cammy's shoulder. "That garage overlooks the lawn from the side; he could drive it out among the guests and set it off, or just do it from inside the garage. If there's twenty-five kilos of Semtex in there, that's powerful enough that the glass wall would only add some sparkle to the blast wave."

The sun had risen fully, and Abbott estimated that the humidity was approximately 300 percent. What awful weather to die in. Or live in.

"You ready?" asked Ether. She took off her VACAY MODE! cap and tossed it into the van, revealing her birthmark.

Abbott sighed. "Nope. Let's go."

They walked along the shoulder, morning commuters whooshing by. They'd ultimately agreed that Ether would be given her chance to simply ask to be let in, and they'd come up with a way to maybe even use that to their advantage. So now they had split up the party, and Abbott wondered if he'd ever see anyone in that van again.

He let out a long breath and said, "I'm not sure I can do this. I feel sick."

"Yes, you can. You can do anything. You came all this way!"

"I feel like the drive was the easy part and stealing this incredibly dangerous box from a billionaire's fortified compound is the hard part."

"It's impressive how in one sentence you managed to exaggerate the danger of the box, the wealth of the man, *and* his home's fortifications."

Soon, they were in view of the gate crowd, which had doubled in size just since they'd driven past. Squad cars were now parked along the opposite side of the street. A few faces turned toward them as they approached and showed no signs of recognition.

At first.

As they drew closer, Ether put on her green sunglasses. Then someone registered what they were seeing, and maybe they thought it was a random woman playing a prank or doing true-crime cosplay, right down to the infamous Butterflaps birthmark on her forehead. But then they saw Abbott, and the news permeated the crowd right before his eyes. Abbott and GSG were here, in the flesh, coming their way. Immediately, several people performed what Abbott now recognized as a modern dehumanization ritual: they pulled up their phones and started recording, breaking eye contact to focus on their screen instead. This gesture had a clear meaning: "You are now no longer a person but a vector for engagement. Whatever happens to you from here on out matters only in terms of the quality of content generated."

"Can we put the phones down?" said Ether once she was close enough to be heard. "There's been a huge misunderstanding here. But to work through it, we need to talk. If you've got your cameras out, then we're not talking, we're performing for an audience. And that audience doesn't want resolution, it wants conflict, purely because that's more fun."

That, of course, did nothing to affect anyone's actions—the most entertaining subjects were those desperate not to be filmed; half of the thrill was in the violation. Now some were shouting questions and accusations, and Abbott felt a larval panic twitching in his gut. He wondered if this could turn physical if there wasn't at least one person here who not only believed the rumors but believed them hard enough to take action. It would only take one. He was picturing somebody pulling a utility knife and spilling his intestines onto the grass, leaving him to writhe in this terrible heat.

Frustrated at the lack of productive responses from the crowd, Ether pushed through to the box outside the gate and hit the button.

A guard appeared on the screen, and Ether said, "This is Karen Wozniak and Abbott Coburn. We need to speak to Mr. Sokolov about an unpaid invoice and reimbursement for a totaled vehicle."

The man's face did not change in response to this, mainly because it seemed like he'd already been at maximum exasperation from the moment he'd answered. "One moment."

The screen went black, and they were once again left with the rabble outside the gates.

"Everybody be calm," said Ether to the rabble. "There's no bomb, there's no anything. We're not part of a domestic terror plot."

A big dude with wild hair, sunglasses, and a beard said, "Why did you flee the scene of the accident?" He asked this through his phone, his eyes on the screen to make sure both Abbott and Ether were in frame.

"Which one?" asked Abbott, before he could stop himself.

Ether said, "Listen to me. For most of this trip, we have been harassed and stalked, scared out of our minds. In Nashville, a maniac tried to kill us, we literally had to crawl out of a burning vehicle. And all of this has been over a dumb misunderstanding, just rumors that got out of hand."

The wild-haired man pointed the phone at Abbott. "So you deny being a member of any hate group."

"Well," said Abbott, "that's a weird question because I don't think any groups, even hate groups, consider themselves hate groups, so if I was a member of one, I wouldn't say I was. So when I say I'm not a member of a hate group, I can only say it with confidence because I'm not a member of any group, of any type."

Ether glared at him. "*Why can't you just say no?*"

From behind the hairy interlocutor, another kid with spiky frosted tips said, "So you deny being a Nazi child groomer?"

Abbott needed a moment to process that last part into a legible accusation.

"I don't groom children to be Nazis, if that's what I'm being accused of. I don't do any other combination of those words, if you were trying to accuse me of something else."

"Then why did you defend Hitler and pedophiles on your stream?"

"I . . . didn't? I mean, I've streamed for hundreds of hours, but I don't think I've—"

"Get the video!" yelled someone. "We've got the receipts!"

Ether gave him a worried look, and Abbott found himself longing for someone to jump out at him with a blade.

MALORT

Sock's property was absolutely infested with serious security types in black suits and sunglasses. As soon as the gate closed behind Malort, they checked his stolen pickup with bomb-sniffing dogs and made him explain five different ways that he was there to fix the broken window. They examined the glass; they checked his toolboxes. *Who in the hell was coming to this party?* Did they know it was hosted by a man who once celebrated the Fourth by firing a roman candle that was clenched in his asshole? Indoors?

Malort knew Sock had big-shot friends, but the setup made it look like the goddamned president was coming. Wait, *was* the president coming? Wasn't that a thing that could plausibly be happening? Malort imagined trying to sneak a large item off the property with this level of security, then wondered if it was possible that he would fuck this up so hard that he would wind up killing the president and going down in the history books. It would definitely show all of those elementary school teachers who'd insisted he'd never amount to anything, including the woodshop teacher he'd stabbed with an awl.

Still, Malort had been in situations like this before, having crossed borders and infiltrated places he was absolutely not supposed to be. He handed over one of his fake driver's licenses and made a big show of feeling inconvenienced and impatient, explaining about the tight schedule, and the tint. Eventually, it was decided that yes, the broken glass that some thoughtless hunter or hooligan had shot out the night before needed repair, and nobody else had shown up to do it, so the esteemed Mr. Sokolov must have ordered some lackey to make the call. After what felt like half an hour of standing around, Malort was finally turned loose on the job.

He pulled the truck up to a glassed-in garage that was like a blown-up version of a display case for a kid's model cars. Inside was a cherry-red 1968 Mustang Shelby GT, a white 1986 Lamborghini Countach—two cars a young Sock had been obsessed with—and a series of other gleaming vehicles driven exclusively by assholes who didn't deserve or appreciate them. There was a European supercar that looked like it came from an alien planet, a luxury sedan that looked like something a dictator would ride in, and some kind of electric bullshit. Not a scooter in sight, not even some kind of ostentatious custom chopper to connect to his roots. Malort wondered if the last time Sock had sat on one was for his pretentious book cover . . .

There. On the end.

It was one of the black SUVs he'd seen in Nashville, styled like a European sports car to try to hide the fact that these things were all just disguised minivans for soccer hags. Malort glanced around to make sure he wasn't being watched—the one security goon nearby had his back to him at the moment. The lawn was buzzing with worker bees setting up the ridiculous stage and chairs, including caterers in tuxedos fussing over an outdoor banquet table with silver-domed platters. *Don't mind me,* thought Malort, *just one more drone buzzing around the hive, making honey for the assholes . . .*

He made his way over to the shattered window that ran from floor-to-ceiling, then pulled out his hammer and knocked out the rest of the glass. Then he stepped through, pausing to examine the frame with his tape measure as if to confirm the dimensions. Then he casually walked past the SUV, glancing inside.

And there, at last, was the box.

Holy shit, he wasn't even going to have to break into the main house. Sock had just left it in the back of his grocery-getter like some shopping he hadn't felt like hauling inside. Malort gripped the hammer so tight that he thought it was going to turn into splinters in his palm.

ABBOTT

"That's not what I said!" shouted Abbott into twenty simultaneous live streams. "Look, what happened was, this feminist YouTuber made a video saying that Adolf Hitler was a pedophile, because Eva Braun was only seventeen when they met. All I said was that seventeen was legal in Germany at the time!"

"Why were you defending Hitler?" asked someone from the back.

"I wasn't! He's a monster! But he's not a pedophile! You can't just pass a law today and then project it backward in time and declare that everyone who was in violation is retroactively a deviant! If in the future, they decide the age of consent is twenty-six, they can't then retcon all of us into predators! You can't just say stuff that's incorrect, even if it's about somebody everyone is supposed to hate."

"What do you mean *supposed* to hate?!?"

"I hate Hitler! He was history's greatest monster! But that doesn't mean we should just make shit up about him! We should never be making shit up—that should be a blanket rule!"

Someone shouted a rebuttal, but Ether cut it off, saying, "Guys, this is a perfect example of what I'm talking about. Can't you see that *nobody involved with this actually disagrees*? Abbott, how would you feel if tomorrow your dad brought home a seventeen-year-old girlfriend?"

"Bad! It would be one of the worst things to have ever happened!"

"And yet, you found yourself sucked into an internet debate where *you were on the side of Hitler,* knowing that the only possible winner was the platform profiting from the engagement. You are all having arguments that are specifically designed to go in circles, forever! Don't you see the system doesn't care what you believe, that it only cares that you keep yelling into your screens, getting enraged at strangers you barely disagree with?"

Someone shouted back that *they* didn't agree that Hitler and pedophilia were good, but the crowd's attention was diverted to three vehicles that stopped across the street, unloading another pack of protestors. More were approaching from the other direction, on foot.

"Listen!" said Ether. "What I'm saying is that *I don't disagree with you on what needs to happen.* I don't know what is in that box, and I don't have it. I was hired by Mr. Sokolov to transport it across the country. In Nashville, his security team seized it and brought it here. I personally don't believe it's a bomb, but just in case it is, *Abbott and I agree that we need to prevent any more people from getting in.*"

Abbott thought her timing was a little on-the-nose, as, at that moment, down the street came the baby-blue van, the side decorated with a cartoon girl whose enormous breasts had been freshly repainted into a pair of balloons. On those balloons were the words ALL-AMERICAN PARTY SUPPLY. Below the woman, it now said, ARLINGTON, VIRGINIA, followed by Zeke's actual cell number. Below that was a URL for the business, and anyone who checked it would find a fully functioning webpage that a sleep-deprived Abbott had designed just hours ago, complete with stock photos of impressive balloon displays arranged around happy partygoers. Through the windshield were the faces of Zeke and his sister; around and behind them was nothing but balloons in the colors of the flag.

"Don't let them in!" shouted Ether—as if the crowd needed her encouragement.

ZEKE

The tiny monitor on the call box instantly blinked on without any action from Zeke, revealing the face of a security guard who seemed to long for the sweet release of death.

As a greeting, the guard said, "What is it now?"

"First load of balloons," said Zeke. "We've got five hundred in here. Should be able to get all two thousand in three loads once the crew is out and they're not displacing so much space."

"One moment."

The screen went dark. Zeke glanced over at Cammy. The police were pushing the protestors back, but there weren't enough of them now, and the crowd was yelling, getting bolder. Abbott and Ether had joined them, shouting that the van wasn't to be let in, hopefully creating the impression for the guards that they were in no way on the same side.

The pivotal moment was coming, the part Zeke had rehearsed in his head approximately five hundred times in the last few hours. After what seemed like a very long time, the monitor finally blinked on again.

"Who put in the order?"

Zeke didn't want to reply too quickly—if this were real, he'd have to search his memory for the name, and he definitely wouldn't say it like he was throwing down his trump card, which he absolutely was.

Instead, Zeke glanced at his phone as if scrolling for a work order. "Uh, it says it came from Tay-Tay."

That was the name that had been unearthed by the sleuths in Abbott's chat. It was the nickname of Gary Sokolov's twenty-two-year-old girlfriend, Tanya Taylor, whom Sokolov did *not* want the public knowing about. Zeke had guessed that the house staff also weren't supposed to know about her but that they almost certainly did. She was not set to be at today's event—no rumors of their relationship could be allowed to waft through this particular gathering. If Zeke and the gang had gauged the situation correctly, it would be plausible enough that this woman had gone rogue and ordered some extra balloons, but the delicate nature of her relationship to Sokolov would prevent anyone from making a call to double-check.

The man in the tiny monitor muted the sound on his feed and turned to say something to another guard nearby. The shouting from the protest was loud enough that it was getting hard to hear, and Zeke made no effort to hide his fear that any delay would be putting him and his crew in danger.

Zeke said, "Hey, can you hear me? I have the work order right here. Six hundred and sixty-six red, six hundred and sixty-seven white, six hundred and sixty-seven blu—"

Zeke was cut off by the thunk of a heavy object having been hurled at the driver's-side door.

"You—" He paused to allow someone to scream that he was going to die. "You can check the contents—it's wall-to-wall balloons and three members of my crew, two of whom may have suffocated by now, I don't know. Who are these people out here? What's happening?"

"Just a moment," said the man, and the monitor went dark.

"Hey!" shouted Zeke, not sure if the channel was even still open on his end. "These people are throwing things! Hey!"

KEY

This was a type of claustrophobia that Key had never felt before, probably because she had never spent time at the bottom of a Chuck-E.-Cheese ball pit. They'd wanted her and Hunter to be invisible from outside the van during the approach and had inflated additional balloons to fill the space the two departed passengers had created. From the other side of the van's walls, she felt the occasional bump as protestors smacked the vehicle, and she could hear muffled yelling about how passing through the gates meant death. And, well, they probably weren't wrong. She imagined the device going off and the cleanup crews in hazmat suits being baffled to find her balloon-encrusted, Buc-ee's–branded corpse in the aftermath. She felt her phone vibrate; probably another voicemail from Patrick, who had been trying to contact her ever since the fiasco in Nashville. She had nothing to say to him at this point. If the FBI wasn't at Nashville, they weren't going to be here, either.

She sensed movement. Holy hell, had the kid actually gotten them through the gates? They drove for a bit and stopped again. She heard more talking, then there was a surprising amount of additional driving, and Key wondered if she'd misunderstood the direction of movement and if they were now, in fact, heading away from the estate. But eventually, the side door was pulled open, and she and Hunter stepped out into the lawn of a fabulously wealthy shithead. Balloons cascaded out with them, and this was the key moment when she'd find out if the security staff had been told to keep a lookout for her. The gambit with the balloons was to ensure that they didn't see her face until she was on this side of the gate so that, if discovered, she could make a desperate final run for the box.

A guard gave her a long look but then just did a scan with the metal-detector wand and gave her a pass—her Glock was, at the moment, hidden in the spare-tire compartment of the van, under hundreds of balloons. Another uniformed guard was leading a dog as it sniffed around the van. The balls on Sokolov, letting bomb-detecting canines nuzzle every visitor while an entire armload of Semtex was probably just a stone's throw away . . .

Cammy was helping Zeke into his chair, and the latter was giving orders about balloon placement as if working off detailed instructions. The mission was straightforward only in the sense that it didn't take long to explain it: they needed to somehow get the box into the van, get the van out of the gates under the guise of leaving for the next load of balloons, then take the van to a remote location—one they'd found the previous night—where hopefully no bystanders would be harmed by a potential detonation. The part of the plan that Key had not shared with the team was that she intended to drive the van out to that remote location alone. Then she would pry open the box, and one of four things would happen:

1. She would find it was full of some totally innocuous but valuable bullshit, like Sokolov's rare sneaker collection—in which case, Key would be ruthlessly mocked and shunned from public life forever.

2. She would find the box was full of some nonexplosive contraband, some drugs or cash that Key could proudly claim had been her target all along.

3. She would find inside an improvised explosive device, at which point, she would call Patrick and then wait for her apology and lucrative book deal, possibly with film rights.

4. It would turn out the box was, in fact, rigged to detonate if the lid were opened, and Key's brain wouldn't even have time to receive any pain signals before she was vaporized. Her theory would be proven right, the feds would go about rounding up the conspirators, and the EPA would spend months scraping radioactive fragments out of the surrounding soil. They wouldn't necessarily put up a memorial statue of her in the aftermath, but she'd definitely get a plaque on the Wall of Honor and probably a movie made about her, if not a miniseries. This one seemed like the least amount of hassle and stress on Key's end. She wasn't necessarily *rooting* for it, but she wasn't rooting against it, either.

She examined the layout of the property, imagining future documentaries and podcasts doing the same. There was the Potomac, then the sprawling lawn, then the sprawling swimming pool, then the sprawling white mansion. On the lawn, staff were busy setting up a temporary stage; arcing over it was a massive eagle with its wings spread, clutching an American flag in its talons. Just behind the stage were rows of canisters and wiring that Key assumed were the "daytime fireworks." Some research had revealed it was a display of airburst powders that would paint the sky in red, white, and blue, forming detailed shapes thanks to computerized precision timing. Though it just now occurred to her that the "daytime fireworks" promised in the invitation was probably a dark joke inserted by Sokolov himself. "Oh, there'll be fireworks, all right."

To Key's left was a glassed-in display of a wealthy aging man's Emotional Support Cars. According to the tracker, the box was behind that glass, in one of those vehicles, no more than fifty feet away from where she was standing. It was entirely possible that all of world history would pivot on Key's ability to move that box from one spot to another. At least it had wheels. Parked in front of the car aquarium on a circular driveway of intricately interlocked stones were a number of vehicles from the caterers, decorators, and other professionals. Zeke had parked the van awkwardly, away from all of them, one tire off on the precious, perfect turf.

Zeke said, "Okay, they want these scattered by color, red over here, white in the middle, blue over there."

For the most part, the rest of the party staff were ignoring them, though one woman who was attaching labels to the folding chairs in front of the stage was now watching them, confused. Key assumed those labels were marking where the various donors, politicians, and judges would be seated and imagined months of behind-the-scenes jockeying to determine who would be given the places of honor, not knowing they were really being positioned according to who would be guaranteed to catch the most lethal part of the blast.

She turned to Hunter and, loudly enough that any eavesdropping staff would hear, said, "Hey. Get this vehicle out of their way. Get it over there by the garage. We'll carry the balloons over from there."

Hunter was no dummy, Key had learned that a while ago, so he played the part and acted mildly annoyed that a coworker had loudly made demands of him in front of everyone. He jumped in and moved the van toward the garage, backing up to a particular spot where she now saw a black Porsche SUV on the other side of the glass. He was parked alongside another vehicle that had done the same, a rusty pickup that didn't seem to belong, some kind of contractor. A guy was crouched in the bed, packing up, screwing around with some cardboard. Maybe he'd built the eagle.

Key followed the van on foot as if eager to get started hauling balloons. Her heart was hammering. She glanced back—the staff member who'd been eyeballing them was now talking to Zeke and Cammy. Key retrieved her Glock from the van and stuck it down the back of her pants.

The next challenge was finding a door into the garage that could somehow be opened without triggering an alarm—she assumed that wouldn't be easy even on a normal day, as it appeared there were several million dollars' worth of cars in there. She rounded the corner and found not just a door but one that was currently being propped open by a toolbox.

Well. That was convenient.

She looked back. No one was watching her at the moment, though now two more staff were talking to Zeke and Cammy, seemingly confused about how their current party setup would accommodate two thousand untethered balloons. She couldn't really hear them at this distance, but one of them seemed to be complaining that they'd get into big trouble if the wind blew the balloons into the river.

Key stepped into the garage and braced herself for some kind of alarm or an intercom voice to shout at her from the other side of a security camera. Was Sokolov so arrogant that he wouldn't even consider the possibility of someone infiltrating and sabotaging his plan? Maybe Cammy's idea had, in fact, been too crazy to anticipate.

She circled to the back of the black SUV and decided that if anyone approached, she would jump into the vehicle and lock herself inside. She would open the trunk—blowing the lock with her Glock if she had to—and if the device went off, well, that would be tragic for the caterers and party planners, but it'd be either that or let it take out the intended targets later. She wasn't quite sure how history would judge her, but at that point, it would be someone else's problem.

She held her breath and, quietly, pulled open the rear doors of the SUV.

It was empty.

She frantically looked around, then quickly grabbed Phil Greene's phone and brought up the tracker. It showed the box—or at least the AirTag—was nearby. Not inside the garage, but . . .

She heard an engine start. She looked up to find the rusty Chevy pickup on the other side of the glass and saw that in its bed was a steamer trunk–size item that had quickly and clumsily been covered in cardboard. It was currently pulling away, heading down the driveway, out toward the gates.

"NO!"

Key flew toward the door and, for the first time, noticed that one of the glass panels was missing, and she could have just stepped through it instead. She drew her sidearm—

And now rough hands were grabbing her, twisting the Glock out of her grip. She thought it was Hunter for a moment, but Hunter was face down on the fancy driveway stones. She twisted around to find Zeke and Cammy arguing with men in black suits, Cammy with her hands behind her back like she'd been cuffed. As soon as she saw that, Key felt thick zip-ties cinch her own wrists.

She heard Zeke say, "Stop that truck!" The kid was smart; he'd pieced together that the pickup was being driven by the Tattoo Monster. But he wasn't *that* smart because if he were, he'd have realized that they should now be rooting for him to escape. That truck was hauling the bomb away from where the judges and children would be gathering within the hour, presumably to take it back across America. Key imagined herself getting free and chasing it to California, then having to do it again, and again, and that would just be her life from now on, chasing this weapon of mass destruction as it bounced back and forth from LA to DC like a tennis ball.

And then black suits went jogging up the driveway, and Key wondered if Malort had the ability to detonate the device and if they'd get to him before he was able to do it. Did he have a burner phone with a particular number in its contacts, where three taps could send the lethal signal?

From the ground, she watched as the truck and its pursuers disappeared around the house, and she held her breath, waiting.

25

ABBOTT

"I never said I wanted to have sex with her!" shouted Abbott to a crowd that now extended along the road in both directions as far as he could see. "I said that you can't simultaneously say that a sixteen-year-old girl is too young to consent because she has the simple brain of a baby and then in the next breath insist that all of the world's governments take her advice on climate change! If a sixteen-year-old boy makes a racist joke, you want to ruin his life forever. Well, make up your minds: Are sixteen-year-olds fully formed adults or not? You can't just switch back and forth based on what wins your current argument!"

"But do you understand," said Ether, who had seemingly joined the prosecution, "*how you picked the most off-putting possible version of that argument?* How you just said whatever would antagonize your opponents the most? What positive outcome did you think would result?"

"Why are you taking their side?!?"

"I'm not! I'm just saying—"

There was a stir in the crowd, people yelling, pointing. The gates were opening, and the police formed an arc to keep the mob from rushing inside. Four men in dark suits emerged, scanning the crowd. Abbott turned to Ether and saw the hope in her eyes, knew that in this moment she believed she'd been vindicated, that here were Sokolov's men to negotiate payment, to maybe even reveal the contents of the box and put the rumors to rest. And in that moment, Abbott wasn't sure what he wanted to happen. Christ, did he really dread an anticlimax more than death?

One of the men in black said, "Mr. Coburn, Ms. Wozniak, your friends have requested you come inside to join them. Please come with us."

Abbott intuited that, despite this phrasing, the situation had in fact gone badly wrong and that he should take off running down the street.

But . . . then what? He struggled to imagine how, at that point, he'd be able to affect the outcome one way or the other. So, Abbott allowed himself to be escorted inside the gates, and Ether followed.

KEY

The four of them were seated in a spacious sunroom—Key, Hunter, Zeke, and Cammy. A glass wall overlooked the pool and, beyond it, the party setup on the lawn. The good news, as Key saw it, was that none of them were restrained. The bad news was they'd confiscated her Glock.

She'd demanded the security guard look in her wallet and, upon discovery of the former FBI ID, they'd cut the restraints off her and Hunter both. Zeke had not been cuffed because they presumably knew the optics of that would not be great. Cammy had been restrained because she had attacked a member of the security team who had put their hands on Zeke's wheelchair to roll him away, and Cammy considered that a form of assault. They had cut her loose, too, on her promise that she would be good as long as nobody else tried to drive Zeke's chair without his consent. "You don't do that," she'd said. "Ever."

The sunroom was a space of white marble and uncomfortable loungers that probably looked great in publicity photos. Behind where the four of them were seated was an expansive bar with bowls of fruit—Key imagined some servant coming every three days to throw all of it away to be replaced with new, like flowers. There were metal rails on the ceiling, and it appeared that the entire glass wall could be raised to open one continuous space with the pool, room for a few dozen power players to ogle bikini girls while enjoying cocktails and bumps of silky-smooth cocaine. The ceiling and two of the walls seemed to be made of concrete, which implied some parts of the house might be well protected from the blast. But this sunroom was definitely not.

Two men lifted the black box from the bed of Malort's presumably stolen pickup, one of them directing another staff member to get the ugly vehicle out of sight. They'd already moved Zeke's hentai van, and event staff were now hurriedly gathering up and popping the balloons Key's squad of misfits had brought in. She found herself oddly offended by that.

Hunter, Zeke, and Cammy all seemed to be waiting for Key to do something, ready to follow her cue, as if she had a plan. At the moment, she was waiting to see where Sokolov's people would stash the box, wondering if running out there and shoving it into the swimming pool would blunt its effects. It would still be a mess—twenty-five kilos of Semtex was a hell of a lot—but surely the water would catch most of the toxic shrapnel . . .

The door flew open, and Malort was escorted in, scratched and bruised, both hands behind his back in multiple zip ties. He was directed to a chair at gunpoint, where he sat, sparing only a moment to glance at Key and the rest of her crew, shaking his head in disgust/disappointment. Key worried for a moment that Sokolov's people were going to leave them alone with this inked-up shaved bear, but more security guys in black suits immediately filed in. Key wondered how much those guys made and if any of them were retired feds. It seemed like a pretty sweet job. It turned out they were escorting Abbott and Ether into the room, both allowing themselves to be directed to stools at the fruit bar.

"Mr. Sokolov will be here in a moment," said one of the security goons.

Key saw what she thought might be the man himself striding around the pool outside, pointing toward the staff who were handling the black box and directing them toward the sunroom. Meanwhile, a group of older men in suits arrived at the party and were escorted toward their seats.

The VIPs had started to arrive.

Sokolov made the sunroom hostages wait as more guests filed in and found their seats, staff hustling to and fro to fill drink orders. Old men in suits shook hands with other old men in suits, Key imagining them exchanging pleasantries about their grandchildren and golf games. It was clear that Sokolov had intentionally given her a front-row seat to her failure. It felt as carefully orchestrated as the rest of the event, and now she wondered if this hadn't been his plan all along, if the same diagrams he'd drawn up to place specific guests in the blast zone didn't also have this sunroom designated as the viewing area for certain attendees who weren't on the guest list. As for why, well, that was obvious: Key and the van misfits would be framed as the perpetrators in the aftermath. Would she even have Patrick to vouch for her? She imagined all of the stories about her coming out over the following weeks, her erratic behavior in her final months on the job, the enemies she'd made, the drunken conversations she'd had with colleagues about how she intended her retirement to be short, and not because she planned to reenter the workforce. Sokolov, with all his wealth and powerful friends, could push whatever narrative he wanted, the one crafted to most viciously stoke the embers of resentment glowing in the bowels of the culture. Everything, it appeared, had worked out exactly how he'd wanted.

And then the man himself strode into the sunroom. Handsome, with a powerful build and a face that had spent a lot of time in the sun and a lot of time smiling. He looked like a TV preacher or an aging Hollywood heartthrob. He surveyed the collection of detainees and rubbed his forehead as if he'd just come home to find his dog had dragged garbage all over the house.

Finally, he looked down at Malort and said, "I have you on night-vision cameras shooting out my window last night. My people have been tracking you this whole time. You probably think I'm gonna start busting your balls about this half-assed attempt to get onto my property, but instead, I'm going to point out a much better method you could have used, a little technique I call, 'Pick up the phone and tell my best friend that I want to talk to him in person.' We could've worked this all out over a classy sunrise breakfast in this very room. Instead, you do all this, violating your parole every which way, because your first resort is and always has been to act like a psycho."

Malort shook his head and scoffed. "'Best friend'? Motherfucker, you better tell your boys to kill me; otherwise, I'm gonna find a hog and drag you by your ankles all the way back to LA, until all that's left is your feet in those fancy fucking shoes, which I'll toss into the ocean for the sharks."

Ether raised her hand like a kid in a classroom and said, "I'm sorry, but I still think this is all a hilarious misunderstanding."

As she spoke, Key saw a group of probably fifty children in choir robes were now ambling toward the stage. Her mouth went dry.

"If you're about to ask me for your paycheck," replied Sokolov, "I cannot even begin to quantify all the ways you screwed this up. I ask you to drive this box out here as discreetly as you can, and within twenty-four hours of your departure, I'm on a conference call with three of my lawyers and the heads of the FBI's domestic terrorism task force asking me if it's a nuclear bomb. Then I wake up this morning to a call from my people saying you're all at my gate, hiding in a pile of balloons. Jesus, and I thought Mal's plan was stupid. How is your generation going to run the world when we're gone?"

The door opened once again, and two members of the household staff entered, rolling in the black box, band stickers and all.

Key noted only two exits from the sunroom: the door to the lawn that those staff members had just used, which was to her right as she faced the glass wall, and one behind her, which led to the rest of the house. Both were guarded. She estimated that between the box and the gathering outside was fifteen feet of swimming pool and twenty feet of lawn. It looked like a decent distance, but explosions don't work like they do in movies, where a fireball and shock wave will propel the hero to a safe landing. In real life, the blast and all its accompanying toxic shrapnel would be traveling at *eighteen thousand miles an hour,* ten times faster than a bullet. No one in that crowd or on that stage would see or hear the explosion before their brain matter was bouncing off rooftops in DC. And that was no exaggeration. One handful of Semtex would blow a car apart; twenty-five kilos would mean they would likely find human teeth embedded in the trunks of those trees across the river.

To Sokolov, Ether said, "I gave up my old life to do this job, because you promised enough cash to make it worth it. I need that money, I have a debt to pay, and I'm not leaving here until I get it. And I know you have it. A million bucks won't force you to skip a single cocktail on your next vacation."

"Why am I not surprised," said Sokolov, "that someone of your generation wants a participation trophy?"

"Why am I not surprised someone of your generation wants me to work for free?"

Outside, the guests were seated, and the children on stage had assumed formation and were now singing "America the Beautiful," which

Key considered to be the worst song she'd ever heard, always pulled out of storage for singers who didn't have the vocal range for "The Star-Spangled Banner," which she considered the second worst. She realized that the climax of this song would be the perfect time to detonate the device, if the villain wanted to be cinematic about it. It really came down to whether or not Sokolov was determined to die in the explosion—the man was, at the moment, standing just six feet from the box. She saw no device in his hands that could act as a trigger. She watched and tensed herself and waited for the moment he moved to put a hand into a pocket. When this occurred, she would have only seconds to try to close the distance and alter the course of events before her organs were perforated by the goons' pistol slugs.

Hunter said, "I'm sorry, are we being detained? And if so, on whose authority? If you're accusing us of attending your Fourth of July party without an invitation, you need to either escort us off the property or call the police. But it looks to me like you have some stuff to work through with your gorilla friend. If you and your people insist on holding me and my son in your capacity as private citizens, there's a point where that becomes kidnapping."

Outside, Key heard the children sing of alabaster cities, undimmed by human tears. As if any city was ever built without tears, and sweat, and blood. The guard closest to her had taken off his jacket. His arms were crossed, the butt of his sidearm in a shoulder holster. It looked like a Heckler & Koch P30L. The guy looked lazy and bored, and Key wondered if she could get to that gun before he could. Shoot Sokolov, then the glass, shove the box into the water—

Sokolov said, "Oh, the police will be here soon enough," in a tone Key couldn't quite pin down.

Ether said, "Open the box."

Sokolov looked at her. "Why?"

"Just for me. I need to know."

He shrugged and dug into his pocket for his keys. He took a step toward the box and Key made her move.

She launched herself at the nearest security goon, reaching for his holstered automatic. There was the briefest moment when her fingers brushed its plastic grip, but then the goon expertly repositioned his body, hundreds of hours of training doing their work in an instant. Because of course these were top-of-the-line luxury goons, the type who escort oil tycoons through war zones. So as Key thrashed and fought to seize the man's sidearm, a second goon got on her back and put her on the floor while a third stepped in to assist, pressing her face to the tile. Sokolov gave Key only a brief look of mildly amused pity, then went about his task. Of course he'd known she'd try that. Of course.

She could only watch from the floor as Sokolov stood over the box, glancing out at the children's choir bathed in the light of a blistering July morning. He ripped off the yellow-and-black tape protecting the lock and inserted the key.

The children sang, "From sea to shining sea—AAAHHH!!!!"

There was screaming and the horrific noise of structures rent asunder.

MILES

By the time Miles O'Toole was nineteen, he pretty much had the world figured out.

He was born in 1992, his own consciousness forming in parallel with the World Wide Web. He had mastered his father's PC by the time he was six; by age eight, he'd successfully sneaked into his elementary school's network via a password a secretary had stuck to her monitor with a Post-it note. He wrote his first virus at ten.

Miles had quickly decided that he'd been born into a society that was very much a solvable puzzle. The powerful wanted to hold down everyone else, but they were not clever and could be defied if the clever were willing to break their arbitrary rules. In high school, Miles read about a new technology called *blockchain* and instantly believed that he had glimpsed how civilization could one day be saved from the brutes. Here was a system of recording transactions that was anonymous, decentralized, and free, a method by which goods and information would be traded in a manner that literally could not be regulated or suppressed by any outside authority.

It was the birth of a system that would break the grip of all states, corporations, and churches, of anyone who would look to get between individuals who wished to transact. The gold in this new system would be cryptocurrency, and the first currency to matter was Bitcoin.

By 2011, Miles owned a dedicated Bitcoin-mining rig (he was one of the early adopters of GPU versus CPU mining), and by the fall of the following year, he'd mined a hundred blocks, which at the time counted for fifty coins each. He'd begun his third semester at MIT and had already come to the conclusion that the institution had no more to teach him. He ran with a group of guys who called themselves the Chain Gang, and they spent their weekends charting out a path to create a start-up, one that would make them millionaires by age twenty-two and that would reformat the entire economy before they hit thirty. And then, in October of that year, Miles died.

He didn't know he'd died—most people don't realize death can be a delayed release thing. It was Columbus Day weekend, and he and his buddies had driven to Miles's hometown of Syracuse. On the way back, they had stopped at a bar in Springfield after having already spent much of the day drinking. Miles found himself talking to the hottest girl he'd seen in his entire life, and then he started showing off at pool, first beating his friends and then a couple of strangers, the losers buying the next round. Then a biker dude spoke up, drunk off his ass, and asked to join in. Here was a chance for Miles to do his move, which was to hustle a stranger at pool in full view of whoever he wanted to impress, then refuse to take the stranger's money, insisting it was all for fun. It wasn't about the cash, after all—it was about savoring the look on the losers' faces when they realized that they, like everyone else, had underestimated him. He imagined his life would be an endless chain of similar rubes left reeling in his wake.

And so they played a couple of friendly games, Miles losing each time, playfully bantering to let them know this was all in fun. Then he asked for a final, big-money match, a race-to-two, Miles ready to turn it on. The biker dude then got the luckiest pair of breaks he'd ever seen and cleaned the felt while Miles could only stare, the gorgeous girl next to him gasping, "Oh my god," as the big dude called shot after shot, suddenly stone sober. The eight ball went in for the last time, and the guy had demanded Miles pay up, at which point, he'd had to admit he didn't have the cash—he had fifty, but not the promised five hundred. The biker and his even bigger bald friend had then escorted him outside, and when Miles had suggested he could get the cash from an ATM, the bald one punched Miles in the gut so hard that acid rushed up his throat and sprayed from his mouth. He was then on the pavement, gasping, feeling like the blow had shattered his organs. Miles's worthless friends were all by the door muttering mild protests, saying this wasn't cool, dude. But no one was coming to save him, and in those few seconds, Miles O'Toole received more of an education than he'd ever gotten at MIT.

He'd wound up begging the bikers, offering them anything, everything, to get out of this situation with his life. He ended up giving them his laptop, which wasn't his school laptop or his gaming rig—it was his Bitcoin cold storage. He told the biker as much, that the price on those coins was going to the moon within a year or two, that it'd be worth ten times what he owed. They took the laptop and all of his cash and, before leaving, slapped Miles on the ear so hard that he was briefly knocked out, draped across the hood of his own car. Then they'd smashed his windshield, laughing the whole time, sauntering away with the hot girl Miles had been hitting on.

And as he lay there, feeling sudden wetness down his leg and realizing he had pissed himself, everything Miles thought he knew about the world turned to dust and blew away. None of his techno-Utopia bullshit mattered as long as bullies could punch you in the gut and take what was yours. The only way for him to get his laptop back was to go to the cops, but that would mean that even the possession of Bitcoin was determined by men with guns operating on behalf of the state, which defeated the entire point.

Miles never spoke to the Chain Gang after that. He dutifully finished his degree and went to work for a mobile medical billing start-up that accumulated a respectable pile of VC money before getting bought out by the largest player in the space. Miles married his best friend, a woman with frizzy hair and glasses and crooked teeth whose smile could outshine the sun and whose cutting sense of humor could disarm a firing squad. She was an acclaimed artist who worked in metal, always out in the garage grinding and welding, traveling to shows all over the world. They bought a lovely waterfront house in Lake Placid, both working from home with their three dogs. Miles's modest investments kept going up, his wife sold her angular rusty sculptures for sometimes five figures. Then the other shoe dropped and Miles remembered that, oh yeah, he was dead.

With the economy flooded with pandemic stimulus money, Bitcoin finally mooned—it shot up to ten thousand, then fifteen, then twenty. Miles refreshed the price on his phone every hour, calculating in his head what he had lost all those years ago. He watched as those five thousand stolen coins became worth ten million, then fifty million, then a hundred. He didn't eat, didn't sleep, didn't laugh at his wife's jokes, didn't make love. That was generational wealth he'd lost, enough to set up his future kids and grandkids, a dynasty. It was private planes, Hollywood red carpets, parties at dance clubs with rappers, literal supermodel girlfriends. It would have made him the envy of billions, literally billions, of lessers. Instead, he was running out the clock in obscurity with his smelly dogs and ugly, cackling wife.

Where was that old laptop now? Surely in a landfill—even if the thugs had pawned it, the tech was badly out of date by now. No one who'd bought it at the time would have recognized the wallet keys for what they were. Then, one day, Miles got word that some mysterious person was dumping vast quantities of coins, cashing them in at a rate that was actually moving the price, and Miles *knew*. Somehow, he knew. By the time Gary Sokolov turned up on TV talking about his amazing business acumen and outlaw biker background, Miles's wife had moved out, taking the dogs with her, begging him to get help, to please see someone about his depression, to get medication. As if somebody makes a pill that un-fucks reality.

Once she was gone, Miles was free to devote himself to a new project full-time, utilizing the welding and metalworking skills his wife had taught him across dozens of lazy Sundays. It would take months to complete, but he knew how to do it because it had been done before; there were plans and a template to follow.

Only he would do it better.

26

ABBOTT

Abbott Coburn had spent much of his twenty-six years in a state of uncontrolled, frantic paralysis. So it was appropriate that in the moments before chaos was unleashed on the Sokolov estate, he was furiously imagining a dozen possible courses of action while his body remained perfectly still.

Somewhere from outside came a hellish chorus of destruction and terror. Captors and captives alike rushed to the glass wall of the sunroom but could see nothing—the source of the chaos seemed to be behind them, back at the gates. There was a mechanical roar and the shrieks of metal twisted and torn, then shouts and cries. And then gunshots, in rapid succession. There was no mistaking that last noise for firecrackers or anything else—this was the sound of humans trying to kill other humans, and it was growing nearer. Abbott imagined the gaggle of protestors out front somehow having broken through the gates, and now some of them were almost certainly dead, unless they were the ones doing the shooting.

But then came the roar of an engine, rising with proximity. A wave of screams washed toward Abbott, the lamentations of all who saw what had just pierced their bubble of tranquility. The VIPs up by the stage were now standing, looking back at where the fancy driveway wrapped around the house, unable to yet see the visage of their oncoming doom. An older woman was trying to usher the terrified children's choir off the stage, but she, too, seemed uncertain as to what exactly was the protocol. Abbott imagined her having worried herself sick about this performance, having visualized a hundred possible outcomes, none of them within a thousand light-years of *this*.

And then, into view rolled a rumbling hunk of metal that Abbott's mind couldn't fully comprehend.

"Holy shit!" shouted Key, her face pressed to the glass. "Somebody built a fucking Killdozer!"

The monstrosity was on tank treads, shielded from all directions by steel plates that had been crudely welded into place. It rumbled up the driveway, cracking the intricate stonework as it went. Across the blade in front was painted one word: BITCOIN.

The pilot—who must have been viewing the scene from cameras, as there certainly was no windshield—apparently saw the fancy cars on display in the glass garage and veered off in that direction. It smashed through and began crushing one vehicle after another under its treads, then jets of flame emerged from both sides of the Killdozer, setting the structure ablaze. Of course they'd equipped the machine with flamethrowers. Of course.

The lawn outside was now utter bedlam. In the sunroom, everyone had frozen in place until they saw Zeke's wheelchair roll into view and realized he'd already gone out to try to deal with the situation. Then Cammy rushed out after him, and everyone followed. Zeke was yelling for the guests to head up the driveway, toward the gates, telling them that nowhere here was safe from the Killdozer unless they knew how to swim. An old guy with his wife and a couple of assistants actually heeded his instruction, and Abbott wondered if Zeke was now out there issuing commands to a Supreme Court justice. But then in from the driveway came the protestors, who'd poured through the obliterated front gates, blocking the only escape route. On both sides of the property were walls and then woods; behind was the Potomac. This only left the house as a possible refuge, which at the moment was home to what may or may not have been an improvised weapon of mass destruction.

Abbott rushed out onto the lawn just as the Killdozer erupted from the other end of the garage, leaving a row of flattened and burning cars in its wake. Two guards were shooting at the cab and having no effect, while at least two others were screaming at them to stop firing, that there were kids around. Then the Killdozer headed right to the stage, where fifty children had stood moments earlier, all of whom were now shrieking and running with the rest of the crowd. Abbott saw the woman who was presumably in charge of the choir trying to corral the children and usher them to safety, but she was herding them toward the house, and the box. And there was

Sokolov in the middle of the chaos, directing everyone toward the sun-room Abbott had just vacated. Was this all planned, the Killdozer there to cluster the victims around the bomb? If so, it seemed like a somewhat overcomplicated way to achieve that goal.

The Killdozer barreled into the stage, bashing into the first column holding aloft the overhead eagle, causing the whole structure to come tumbling down around it. Abbott spotted Key nearby waving around her FBI badge, yelling to everyone to go toward the gates, to push through the protestors, to avoid the house. But some of the protestors were yelling and demanding to be taken to the alien corpse, while others had started grabbing choir children and pulling them toward the driveway, telling them they were about to be abducted into a torture cabal, the intricacies of which they were struggling to explain over all the noise. So now guests and security were pulling the kids away from a crowd of strangers who were, in fact, escorting them away from danger, but for the wrong reasons.

Abbott couldn't find his father or Ether, the two people he realized he was depending on for instructions. He felt a wave of debilitating panic ripple up from his chest. Would anyone notice if he just left, got breakfast somewhere, and waited for all this to blow over?

Then he saw it: the bulldozer rolling toward a collapsed bit of the stage structure, a hunk of the eagle's wing leaning at an angle on broken wooden supports. An older man and a child were cowering under it, and Abbott didn't have to ask why, because he knew why: they were waiting for someone to come and tell them what to do, somebody who knew what the fuck was going on. But no one was coming, no one else even saw what was about to happen, there was only Abbott, and now Abbott was running and yelling at them, grabbing the little boy by the wrist and snatching at the lapel of the old man.

"HE'S COMING! MOVE! MOVE!"

He dragged them away from the leaning structure approximately two seconds before it was flattened by the treads of the Killdozer. The old man was shouting questions at him, but Abbott couldn't hear over the roar of the Killdozer's engines and the sound of boards cracking and popping as it did doughnuts over the flattened remnants of the stage.

"GO TOWARD THE GATES!" yelled Abbott, wildly gesturing that

direction in case the man and the child didn't have superhuman hearing. "SEE THE GUY IN THE WHEELCHAIR? LISTEN TO HIM! THAT'S THE ONLY SAFE PLACE! RUN!"

The guy and the kid—Abbott had no idea if they even knew each other—kind of hobbled off in that direction, clearly wishing they had a better option than traversing the gauntlet of crazies. Then Cammy appeared and grabbed both of them, hustling them through the crowd to safety and, Abbott thought, probably etching her name into future history books in the process.

KEY

As the Killdozer rolled the stage remnants into a pancake of splinters, Key's mind was flailing, trying to make sense of the scenario. Had one of the internet weirdos built this contraption specifically to try to thwart the terrorist attack? If so, what was their plan? Maybe this was to be the second phase intended to run roughshod over first responders, and they accidentally started early? A word had been painted on the front of the Killdozer, but she couldn't see it clearly. It looked like it may have been BITCH.

At the moment, the armored monstrosity was rolling toward the catering tables off to the side, the tuxedoed staff having long departed. As it crushed silver platters of croissants and muffins, Hunter passed into her view, urging Ether along with him, climbing across the stage debris to the complicated setup behind it that Key believed was the "fireworks" display, rows of black tubes designed to launch the airbursts of colorful powders over the Potomac.

She turned away from them. She needed to prioritize, and the box was still a greater potential threat than the Killdozer. She looked back toward the house and was hit with the nauseating sight of dozens of idiots packing the sunroom to get away from the rampaging mechanical beast, many of them crowded around the bomb box. At least two children were now sitting on it.

She ran in that direction, rounding the pool. She waved her ID as she burst in the door and shouted, "Retired FBI!"—the second word said much louder than the first. "It's not safe in here!"

An array of faces turned toward her, including two she recognized as senators and one as her least favorite Supreme Court justice.

She said, "LISTEN! This is a planned attack, and the house is a target! Follow me or you are going to fucking die!"

She led them toward the door back into the house, only to find it had already been kicked open.

ABBOTT

The Killdozer had finished flattening the catering and was now rolling toward the fireworks apparatus behind the stage. There among the tubes and cables, Abbott saw his father, his jaw set with determination, screwing around with wires and switches back there as if he knew what he was doing. And there was Ether next to him, along with some party attendees in suits who may or may not have been some of the most powerful humans on the planet. Ether was exhorting Abbott's dad to work faster as she lifted the apparatus to aim the tubes horizontally. Then there was a noise like a blast of cannons from a pirate ship, and the air in front of Abbott turned red, white, and blue, the bursts erupting in neat rows that he suspected were in the shape of a flag, if viewed from a distance. He had thought this seemed like an extraordinarily ill-conceived plan on his father's part, as not even actual fireworks would have done much to damage the homemade tank. But when the air cleared and Abbott wiped chalky red powder from his eyes, he found the Killdozer had rumbled to a stop, now coated from front-to-back in the colors of the flag. The goal had not been to destroy it but to blind it, the pilot presumably steering via cameras whose lenses were now obscured.

The Killdozer rolled forward a few feet, then back, then attempted to turn as if the driver was trying to get his bearings. Victims seized this opportunity to flee, including those behind the stage who'd just been saved from getting flattened and/or flamethrowered to death. The Killdozer continued to edge itself around, cautiously, like the driver was trying to mentally estimate the location of the final standing structure: the enormous mansion.

Zeke was still herding fleeing victims toward the front gates. Cammy was now carrying two children in that direction, both slung over her shoulders like bags of animal feed. Then the Killdozer was on the move again and heading roughly in the direction of the house. Abbott turned and watched dozens of faces in the sunroom shout and point, but none of them were moving, as if they'd rather die than miss the spectacle. Inside, Key was screaming at them, waving around her badge.

The powder-coated Killdozer rolled forward, and the blind driver did the one thing they had almost certainly hoped to avoid: They ran right into the pool. The driver must have felt the machine tilting down because at the last moment, they'd tried to brake, then reverse. It was too late; the Killdozer tipped into the water, blade-first, rolling forward until its whole body fell in, sending a tsunami of pool water splashing over the side. Then the mostly submerged Killdozer came to a halt, and Abbott allowed himself to believe it was over.

His father and Ether ran up, and the latter said, "The fireworks were his idea!"

His father's gaze, however, was fixed on the submerged Killdozer. "It's still running."

Abbott saw that there was, in fact, a vertical exhaust pipe extending out of the pool, still belching smoke.

"What should we—"

Before Abbott could finish the question, the blade of the Killdozer rose up out of the water. Then the machine rolled forward a few feet so that the blade was positioned over the lip of the pool. The blade was lowered, which had the effect of pulling up the Killdozer's front end.

"Shit!" said Ether. "I think he practiced this!"

The treads got traction on the edge, and the machine lurched forward with shocking speed, water cascading down its sides, erupting from the surface like a sperm whale.

MALORT

Watching the growling and clinking monstrosity rampage around Sock's fancy lawn party had convinced Malort that not only was God real but that he cared only about making the absolute funniest possible thing happen at any given moment.

He had been watching it all play out and trying to figure out how to take advantage of it by getting the box off the property amid the madness. The problem was that his stolen pickup had been moved to some other building on this sprawling, obnoxious campus of bullshit, and he had no idea where. That meant he needed to steal another vehicle and to somehow do it among what was soon to be the greatest concentration of cops in one place since 9/11.

As soon as the chaos had begun, Malort had snapped his zip ties—he'd learned the technique years ago—and retreated farther into the house (that part had required bashing open two sturdy locked doors with a total of five solid kicks). He'd passed from the sunroom into a giant white kitchen for assholes and then through to a giant white dining room for assholes. Several rooms later, he eventually landed on a huge decorative motor court for visiting assholes, where he found a series of luxury town cars and SUVs and wondered if the god of making hilarious things happen might allow him to get away in the attorney general's Mercedes.

He went back through the house to the sunroom to get the box, only to find the room was now packed with confused old men in tailored suits and panicked children in patriotic choir robes. The woman who kept claiming to be an FBI agent was yelling at them and started pushing them past Malort into the house. He saw the box in the middle of the room— some choir kids had been using it as a sofa—and moved toward it just as shrieks erupted from all around him.

Through the glass wall, he saw the armored bulldozer contraption was rising from the pool like Godzilla, climbing up the side. Its blade smashed into the sunroom, and all fucking hell broke loose, important assholes running in every direction. Malort tried to grab the box, but scrambling bodies were bumping into him and falling down, stampeding into choke points at both exits.

The machine rolled farther into the room, but its canopy—a solid metal box that its nutcase driver had apparently welded himself into—was six inches too tall for the room. Years of watching bridge crash videos primed Malort for what was to happen next: The bulldozer lurched forward, the concrete ceiling grabbing the armored canopy and peeling it off in one piece. The plates were fused together but were apparently attached to the body with just brackets and gravity.

As the bulldozer entered the room, Malort saw the driver in the now-open cockpit: a pale, chubby man, slick with sweat, wearing only a red Speedo. His eyes were wild, and there was a moment when he saw Malort and a look of recognition hit his face, even though Malort had no memory of ever meeting the guy. The bulldozer was immediately angled in Malort's direction, and he went to yank the box out of its path. All of this, from pool emergence to this moment, played out over a total of four seconds, and Malort's brain barely had time to form the thought that he wasn't going to be fast enough.

ABBOTT

After racing around the pool to the door of the sunroom he'd just exited several minutes earlier, Abbott found the doorway packed with panicked and stumbling party refugees, everyone trying to squeeze out at once. His father and Ether were behind him, and both went to help pull fleeing guests through the exits.

Then Abbott saw that the Killdozer was bearing down on the Tattoo Monster, who was dragging the box away, pulling it by its handle, his hand just inches from the radiation sticker. There was a brief moment when it seemed like the bald man was intent on dying with the box; he stopped dragging it and hugged it as if he thought the crazed, mostly nude man at the Killdozer's controls would swerve to avoid flattening him, even though it seemed clear that flattening people was his whole deal. Then, at the last possible moment, the Tattoo Monster dove out of the way, and the BITCOIN-branded blade of the Killdozer rose and passed over the box, leaving it for the treads.

Abbott stared as the treads first knocked over the box, then tipped it, then bulged the wooden sides.

And then the lid popped open, and Abbott thought, *This is the last thing I will ever see.*

27

ETHER

She was in the process of helping a security guy who'd dropped his gun in the stampede—she didn't want some choir kid to pick it up—when Ether heard Malort the Tattoo Monster yell, "NOOOOO!"

She assumed he was in the process of being crushed by the Killdozer, but it wasn't Malort under the treads, it was the box. And she felt his reaction in her gut, because the destruction of the box also meant the end of her mission, of her hopes for seeing this through. But lingering behind all that was doubt, the fear that maybe she was wrong and everyone else was right, that the box she'd transported twenty-six hundred miles into a pack of potential victims was, in fact, designed to detonate if its container was disturbed. And so, she held her breath as the box opened and split, the plywood panels popping loose.

First, she saw a black canister the size of a coffee can tossed around in the guts of the box's contents, then the canister was crushed and a puff of gray powder burst out, coating nearby victims. Then the treads rolled across the rest of the box, and its entire contents were sprayed in every direction.

It was mostly paper, bundles of it, full of colorful photos in tones of flesh.

Magazines. One landed by her feet, and on the cover was a fully naked woman draped across a chopped motorcycle. It was a magazine called *Hog Momma* and appeared to be at least twenty-five years old. The Killdozer rolled to a stop, and the man at the controls seemed to be working some switches, the floor around him now carpeted in vintage pornography.

A small flame appeared from a nozzle on the side of the machine, and Ether knew what was coming next. She screamed for the remaining sunroom victims to escape through the shattered glass wall. They dove into the pool as hellfire erupted from the Killdozer.

Everyone got out, she thought.

All but one.

Malort had been on the floor, snatching up magazines and growling and whimpering as the Killdozer's flamethrowers were unleashed. He recoiled from the fire, howled like a wild animal, then jumped up onto the Killdozer, his pants and shirt ablaze. He grappled with the driver, trying to choke him or tear his head off his body entirely. The driver stepped on the accelerator and crashed through the rear wall of the sunroom, and then the wall behind it, leaving a roiling inferno in his wake.

ABBOTT

The three of them—Abbott, his father, and Ether—stood just outside the burning sunroom, surrounded by the cacophony of fleeing VIPs and choir children, some of whom were now splashing their way out of the pool. The remnants of the box and its contents had vanished behind the flames, already reduced to blackened debris.

All this, thought Abbott, over that.

He met Ether's eyes and saw relief and triumph and exhaustion, and he knew in that moment that she'd harbored her doubts and could now set them free. Then he looked to his father, who was visibly shaken and had, presumably, spent the last several seconds believing his entire body was about to be dispersed into another state.

"Hold on," said Abbott. "Was the attack sponsored by Bitcoin?"

His father ran a hand through his hair, wincing at the heat radiating from the inferno and said, "Man, Joan is gonna be pissed." Then he looked around. "Wait, where is she?"

MALORT

He was burning alive.

He was so mad that he didn't even care.

Malort had the bulldozer idiot in a choke hold, and together, they crashed through a wall and then another one and then another, turning the mansion into a blast furnace as they went. Then they reached the vast marble entryway and bashed through a bay window, shards of glass raking Malort's scorched arms and gashing his head.

And then they were bearing down on another loose crowd, a confused flock of suits and choir robes with the FBI lady who'd led them to what she'd thought was safety. The crowd parted like the Red Sea, and the bulldozer smashed into the parked VIP rides, pushing three of them along until they ran into a tree. That, finally, was enough to halt the Killdozer's progress. A moment later, its flamethrowers ran out of fuel and sputtered out. Malort still had the driver in a choke hold but realized he was no longer resisting or doing anything. He let him go, and the man slumped over.

Malort jumped off, leaving behind what he believed was the first person he'd ever killed all the way, tossing aside his burning jacket, slapping flames off his jeans. He sprinted back toward the mansion, which was now fully engulfed, filling the sky with smoke. He rushed toward the bulldozer-shaped hole that was now the maw of hell itself and was met by a solid wall of heat, the furniture and curtains inside going up like they were coated in magnesium. He persisted through the pain, felt it air-frying his face long before he got to the house. He didn't give a shit. He intended to run into the fire, through it, to get her out of there, or what was left of her.

But just before he reached the hole in the wall, he was tackled from the side and thrown to the turf. It was Sock, holding him down, and Malort growled and punched the man in the head, tried to claw out his eyes and pull off his ears. And the whole time, Sock was breathlessly grunting, "She's not in there, man. She's not in there. She's not in there."

Malort knew that on any given day he could take Sock apart, either now or in the past, that Sock had always been soft, hadn't been in an evenly matched fight maybe ever. But Malort was burned and bleeding and exhausted and choking on smoke. And now he had his hands around Sock's neck, and it was like one of those bad dreams where your limbs don't do anything, because he had no strength in his fingers, could not make them squeeze.

"She's not in there, Mal," said Sock as if he'd lost the ability to say anything else. "She's not in there."

And finally, Malort just let him go and closed his eyes, listening to the house burn.

ABBOTT

The burning mansion was impassable and, God willing, vacant, so Abbott, his father, and Ether had to circle around, and that turned out to be a shockingly long distance to travel on foot. By the time they reached the front motor court, they found the Killdozer had come to a rest against a million dollars' worth of guest vehicles and a stout tree. A flock of party survivors were standing around in a state of shock and/or confusion.

Joan Key ran up to them and said, "The box. Is it—"

"It was full of vintage pornography," said Abbott's father and, in response to Key's facial expression, added, "I'm not joking. It's all burning up on the other side of the house."

Key looked in that direction and said, "I don't—I mean, what happened? What have we been doing? Who was that guy?" She gestured toward the Killdozer, where a mostly nude corpse was slumped over in the seat.

Abbott finally noticed the Tattoo Monster being led away from the heat of the burning mansion by Gary Sokolov before both collapsed into the grass. The bald man, now covered in blood, scratches, and some wicked-looking burns, rolled over and stared up at the sky as if waiting to ascend.

As Abbott approached, he heard the man say, "I've wasted my whole fuckin' life, Sock. I've wasted my whole fuckin' life."

Sokolov glanced over at him and said, "Mal, I think you're about to have your name in *The New York Times* for saving the lives of multiple members of at least two branches of the federal government."

"Fuck, that's even worse. Who did you piss off bad enough that they came after you with a tank?"

"That there is the college kid we roughed up years ago because he tried to pay a lost bar bet with Bitcoin. Seems like he decided he wasn't happy with the transaction. He'd been posting threats online. My people assured me it was all talk. But you know. It's always talk till it's not."

"I'm sorry," said Key, "but *what exactly was in that fucking box?*"

28

MALORT

Sundae Greene got kinda famous after they moved to LA, and she stayed famous for a while, longer than most. It was an odd type of fame, the kind where they'd be out at a bar or rally and there'd be a double take from a dude thinking he recognized her, then he'd process *how* he recognized her, and quickly look away before his old lady noticed.

Sundae had regularly appeared in over a dozen skin magazines and in many more adult videos, back in the apex of the DVD porn era, when guys in grimy adult bookstores would plunk down twenty bucks or more for a single flick. And Malort kept at least one copy of every single magazine, calendar, poster, and video Sundae ever appeared in, neatly bundled in one of the road cases Sock had kept from his brief time as the lead singer in a Canadian death metal band called Twat Chuggler. When she got older and sort of found Jesus, Sundae had wanted to throw it all out, but Sock and Malort had begged her not to, told her that she'd regret it if she did, that when she looked at those old magazines, she wouldn't see the depravity but would remember the old life they'd had, all the adventures on the road, the wild youth she'd miss when she was old and gray. But of course, she wouldn't ever get to be old and gray, she wouldn't even make it to sixty, and could have passed for forty in her coffin. Or that's what Malort had heard, anyway.

One thing he'd learned in prison was that the other old-timers all shared the same fear, not of dying while incarcerated but of losing people, of getting that call that mothers or brothers had passed and that their own fuckups had kept them away at the end. Well, not more than two months after getting the ridiculous news about Sock winning his convoluted lottery, Sundae came to visit and told Malort the other news, that she had cancer and that she'd apparently had it awhile. She insisted there was still hope, smiling while Malort fell apart on the other side of the glass. It was like the universe had taken the infinite good fortune that was owed to Sundae and handed it to Sock instead.

She'd held on longer than expected, gave the cancer the fight of its life, but had passed just months before Malort was set to be released. But of course she had; this was all a cosmic joke from start to finish. When Malort had gotten the news over the phone, he'd started bawling, and the huge Mexican dude on the next phone over came and put an arm around him, and there was silence all around. Everybody in there knew that the single thing that scared them most had happened right in front of them, that a man had lost the one most precious to him and that he hadn't been by her side at the end, hadn't said goodbye.

Sundae was cremated according to her instructions and her ashes went into the box, along with her photo albums and all the letters Malort had sent her from inside. That box was what remained of Sundae Greene, the only tangible remains of her face, her smile. As soon as he got out, Malort went to Phil's apocalypse compound to claim the box, but the crazy old bastard wouldn't hand it over, saying that Sundae had sworn off her relationship with all of her scummy old biker friends, which was bullshit— she'd answered his letters, she visited him once a month. But Phil was off his rocker by that point, and Malort couldn't exactly blame him. He, like Malort, had woken up one day to find the sun had left the sky and taken all the stars with it.

Malort, with nothing much going on in his life, had made a habit of occasionally driving past the Greene property and its solid rust fence topped with razor wire. Then, on the night of Wednesday, June 29, he'd passed to find the fence's sliding gate standing wide open. He entered the house to realize it was like that because Phil had died to a tag-team finishing move delivered by paranoia and gravity. He took this as a sign and went all through the house looking for Sundae's box and was consumed with rage when he realized what must have happened: that fucking Sock had taken it, thinking he had some kind of a claim to Sundae's memory even after he'd abandoned her for his money. Malort had called Sock— getting only his voicemail, as always—and demanded it back, unspooling curses and lamentations until the time limit ran out on the recording.

What Malort didn't know but had since figured out was that this phone call had served to notify Sock that the old man was dead, and *that* had been his cue to dispatch a flunky to collect the box and deliver it to him—the flunky being this random homeless girl Phil had living in his escape shack. If Malort had just been 1 percent more patient with his search, if he'd just taken a few deep breaths and realized the box could be stored somewhere other than the main house, he'd have probably found it within an hour. But that had never been Malort's way, and God had clearly decided that more comedy could be squeezed from the situation. And now here he was, thousands of miles away, feeling burns turning into blisters all over him as a chorus of sirens approached from every direction, knowing that he'd just lost Sundae for the second time.

The Sokolov mansion was burned to conceal the contents of the case

Posted to r/DCTerrorAttack by TruthLover420

For every single doubter and naysayer in here, I hope you've learned your lesson and hopefully some humility in the process. Whatever was in that box, what we now know for sure is A) they wanted it covered up badly enough to burn down a $100 million mansion to hide its contents B) they killed the one man who got close enough to see what was inside, and C) they engaged the entire apparatus of the government and news media to disseminate the same cover story.

Also note that they made that cover story as ridiculous as possible (stating that the box contained innocuous personal mementos of a family friend, which is laughable in the face of the evidence, such as the residual radiation). This is specifically intended to rub it in our faces, to crush our morale. They want us to know that we are powerless, that they can do whatever they want in plain sight, and there's nothing we can do but lay down and take it.

Here's my question: Will you?

Miles O'Toole is a hero who thwarted a terror attack and nobody gives a shit

Posted to r/DCTerrorAttack by RubberAssFactory

This is a man who, like us, knew what was coming but who, unlike us, actually took effective action. He built a machine with radiation shielding and broke into the location and destroyed the device, sacrificing his life in the process.

The fact that these early reports are painting him as some kind of a crazy loner with a personal beef is more proof that they just want to sweep this whole thing under the rug. What we know is that some kind of attack was planned on the government, elements within the government were in on it, and all evidence for it is being buried.

Miles has a surviving wife and the community has launched a fundraiser (link below) to help cover the funeral and living expenses. In a just world, they would clear away the debris of that mansion and replace it with a statue of Miles O'Toole and his Lifedozer.

Abbott Coburn and Karen Wozniak have made a deal with the FBI to turn over info on their Russian handlers in exchange for immunity

Posted to r/DCTerrorAttack by FedThrowaway66974

I know there is a lot of shock and disappointment that neither of the perpetrators were taken into custody, but you have to understand that they are not the big fish. There is an underground organization in place to recruit and arm domestic terrorists and the first goal has to be to dismantle it. It is my understanding that six Russian nationals have been apprehended and transported to a black site for questioning. None of this will be publicized, for a very simple reason:

As soon as it is made public that there is an apparatus in place to pay and arm domestic terrorists with the goal of destabilizing the country, literally tens of millions of Americans *will seek it out and volunteer.* Our analysis found that approximately 45–50% of Americans would assist in an attack on civilians if promised sufficient payment, often as low as $500. This is why I believe that efforts to stop this are futile. Understand: the USA is uniquely positioned in the world to be almost totally immune from invasion by a foreign power. When the attack comes, it will be from your neighbors and coworkers. And, yes, your family. No matter what happens with Abbott Coburn and Karen Wozniak, the fuse has already been lit.

YOU CAN TRUST NO ONE. You should be focusing on your physical fitness and stockpiling nonperishable foods and uncontaminated water. You should have a go bag ready to move away from the city centers at any moment. The government is going to use the coming violence as a pretense for a crackdown and it is my estimate that within six months, anyone you pass on the street will be ready to turn you in, to have you and your loved ones transported to the camps. And you'll be shocked to find out how many of your "friends" will stand and applaud as you go.

Stop waiting for the collapse. It's here. I've turned in my resignation so that I can prepare for what is to come. If you want news on these events before anyone else, subscribe to my newsletter at the link below. It's $7.99 a month, which I'm thinking is a pretty small price to pay for survival.

Dark times are ahead.

29

KEY

It was late afternoon before Key finally took Patrick's call, not because she was avoiding him but because her Fourth of July Monday had been an interminable chain of meetings and conference calls with representatives from seemingly every domestic law enforcement and counterterrorism entity in existence, as well as her attorney and the head of the private security firm that protected Gary Sokolov and his property. As she answered her phone, she stared out at the Potomac, where a guy was paddling by in a kayak.

Patrick began his call with, "I've got a flight out there at seven P.M. your time, into Dulles."

"There's no need, I'm fine."

"Fine? It sounds like you personally escorted seventeen high-profile assassination targets to safety just moments before the room they were in was destroyed and set ablaze."

"I think it's how I got onto the scene that'll give me trouble."

"What are you telling them?"

"The truth," said Key, through a sigh. "It would all have come out, anyway."

"How many media requests have you gotten?"

"I don't know. Every time I check my messages, I start to get a panic attack. It looks like I've been offered a Buc-ee's sponsorship deal, too. I was head-to-toe in their merch at the time."

"I can't tell if you're joking."

"At this point, my brain is so fried that I can't even tell myself."

"Are you sure you don't want me to come out there?"

"No, I'll head back out as soon as I'm allowed. We'll have lunch. Bring your wife and kids. I never get to see them."

"Sure thing. I'm glad you're okay."

"I know you are. I have a feeling I'm going to regret asking this question, but nobody here can or will tell me why Phil Greene's possessions were radioactive."

"Oh, that. He spent thousands of dollars on 'negative ion' pendants. They sell them online as anti-5G devices—those are the weird amulets you saw hanging all over his walls. It turns out they're made of thorium dioxide, basically radioactive mining waste. We think he crushed some of them up in his shop and mixed them with paint and coated his truck with it, I guess to protect him from 5G signals while he was driving. His leukemia was unrelated. Your stolen Semtex was, who knows, probably burned or buried by the thief years ago, before he got arrested."

She sighed and rubbed her eyes. "If this idiot in the bulldozer hadn't shown up, I'd have never lived this down."

"Well, remember when we met over breakfast a few days ago, you mentioned anonymous internet posts warning of a world-changing event on the Fourth. We believe those were from Mr. Killdozer himself. So I say your instincts were spot-on, even if you didn't get the details exactly right."

There was a time in the past—long passed—when Patrick and Key could have wound up together, and for the millionth time, she wondered what their life would have looked like. Mostly she came to the conclusion that he'd dodged a lethal bullet. He'd married a perfect woman, and they'd had perfect children while Key couldn't even keep her plants alive.

"Also," he said, "if you need a laugh, when it first came across the wire that a bulldozer was tearing ass around the Sokolov property, I, uh . . ."

"You what?"

"I, for just a moment, assumed it was you driving the bulldozer."

ETHER

Gary Sokolov's guesthouse was nicer than any home Ether had ever lived in. Its patio featured a grill that looked like it could feed a professional hockey team.

The entirety of the hentai van squad had been detained on the property ever since the morning's attack. The endless stream of concerned and confused officials in dark suits seemed very worried about any of them flying back to SoCal without explaining their role in the incident approximately one thousand times. Ether had expected at least some of them to get taken into custody, but Sokolov had summoned a phalanx of lawyers before the firefighters had even gotten the house fire under control, and in the end, not even the Tattoo Monster had wound up in cuffs. The one man the feds most wanted to question and arrest was also the lone death in the incident, the thirtysomething software engineer who'd apparently abandoned his life and family to pursue a career in mechanized vengeance.

In the middle of the afternoon, Sokolov had demanded everyone—including the former FBI agent and the biker who'd repeatedly tried to murder them—to meet at the guesthouse about a quarter mile up the riverbank. She'd assumed he wanted some kind of private meeting to discuss a coherent legal and media strategy, but when she'd arrived with Abbott and his father, she found Sokolov manning the grill while household staff unwrapped cuts of meat from seemingly every edible species. Malort, who was 40 percent covered in bandages, was standing over jars and pitchers arranged on a banquet table, brewing some kind of concoction. Off to one side was a hot plate bringing the bright orange contents of a stewpot to a boil.

Sokolov said, "We've got a whole spread in the works, including non-meat for you non–meat eaters. A lot of my younger friends are vegan. I've mastered grilling tofu, jackfruit, you name it. It's the Fourth. If nothing else, we should at least get to kick back and chew on some charred fat. Otherwise, what's the point?"

Without looking up from his chemistry, Malort said, "I'm so hungry I could eat the front tire off a menstrual cycle."

Hunter said, "So you think we're all friends now?"

Sokolov shrugged. "I can't make anybody be friends or enemies with me. I learned that a long time ago. But you've got to understand that where Mal and I are from, when you've got beef, you clear the air, with fists if you have to, but at that point, it's over, done. That's probably the only useful thing I ever learned in my wild years. The clubs that survive are the ones that don't let problems fester, members whispering behind each other's backs, letting bitterness stew in their guts. If there's conflict, you hash it out and *then you bury it*. Even if your house gets burned down in the process. Mal was upset with how I handled the money situation, but I've cut him in, and I'm lending him my lawyers to get him out from under any charges coming his way. We'll get him off with community service, filming some internet PSAs about the dangers of drugs and riding a motorcycle without a proper helmet."

"One question," asked Ether. "Why were you so insistent that the box had to be here by today? You know that was half the reason everybody thought it was part of a plot."

"I was set to leave town tomorrow!" said Sokolov as he flipped strips of marbled meat on the grill. "I'm spending a month in Dubai with a friend. I wanted to see that the box was secured before taking off. Sit, sit. Relax. When's the last time you've been able to relax?"

"We haven't been able to relax," said Zeke, who'd apparently arrived while Sokolov was talking, "*because of you*."

"That's why we need to sit, break bread, hash it out! I'm saying we need to make peace, you're saying, 'How can I make peace with an enemy?' and I'm saying that's the *only* time you can make peace! Why hold on to anger? Sit! I'm grilling sliced pineapple on the side. You ever had that?"

Ether sat at the table, and that seemed to break the seal for everyone else.

She looked at Malort's brewing operation. "What the hell is that?"

"Creamsicle moonshine," grumbled the man who'd tried to smash her skull on the pavement a few days ago. "In the pot is a gallon of orange juice and a pound of sugar. Bring it to a boil, add a bottle of vanilla coffee creamer, a splash of vanilla extract, and a bottle of vodka. We had a version of this we used to make in prison with juice and creamer packets. It was a special-occasion thing."

Zeke said, "I think one cup of that would kill me dead. Like medically dead."

"None of the young people I know drink these days. I don't get it. It's unhealthy. Science agrees that it takes two drinks just to make you a normal person."

From the grill, Sokolov said, "Wherever this man and I have gone, chaos has followed. I'd thought that maybe unfathomable riches would change that, but here we are again. None of you want to hear my life story, but part of me thinks getting rich is the worst thing to ever happen to me."

Cammy said, "We'll be happy to take the money off your hands if it's a burden."

"Ha, be careful what you wish for. But I should ask: What all have you guys lost in this situation? If I'm putting an itemized bill together, what are we looking at?"

Hunter said, "A 2022 Lincoln Navigator, full luxury package, less than forty thousand miles. A round-trip plane ticket, car rental. Any legal fees that arise."

"Zeke needs a better wheelchair," said Cammy. "It didn't get damaged in the attack, but that's what we want, anyway."

Sokolov raised an eyebrow. "You understand this man is on video organizing the evacuation before anybody else even knew what was going on? I'm guessing every manufacturer of wheelchairs on earth will be thrilled to gift him their most tricked-out model as long as he agrees to say the brand name in a video. What you should be asking for is access to a world-class physician to see if his condition can be treated. Or, at least, kept from getting any worse."

"Oh yeah," replied Cammy. "We want that."

"Speaking of," said Ether, "I just want the money you owe me, but I have special instructions for it. There's a girl, she doesn't live too far from here. Her dad is disabled because he got shot by the cops. I want most of my payment routed to her, I want them taken care of. There's a whole story behind it, if you feel like you need the context."

Sokolov said, "I know who it is. I've got the internet."

Key said, "You don't owe me anything. I chose this. I don't want your money."

"Just to be clear," said Abbott, "if you'd settled up with the Killdozer kid after you cashed in his coins, none of this would have happened. I don't think it's chaos that follows you around; I think your supposedly amazing conflict resolution skills could just use some work."

Ether added, "Generally, when you find yourself constantly in the middle of drama, it's because deep down, you want it that way."

Sock brushed some sauce onto charred meat and said, "Well, in my defense, I am a huge dumbass."

There was a silence as the meat sizzled, and Malort said, "We had a good fuckin' thing going, you know. All those years. I don't understand why the money had to end it."

Sokolov let the meat sizzle some more, then said, "We talked one time about what you'd do if I ever won the lottery. Remember that?"

"Yeah. We'd open a titty bar again. Hang out and shoot pool and never care if we turned a profit."

"No. You said that's what you'd do if *you* won the lottery. You said if *I* won the lottery that you'd slit my throat and steal the ticket to cash it in for yourself."

"Come on, man. You knew that was a joke. You laughed."

"When I found out what was on that computer, I got scared, like I've never been scared before. I thought I was having a heart attack, but it was just a panic attack, the first of many. By that point, you had years left on your stretch, and I wanted out of that life, to try being respectable. Well, you weren't gonna come out here and be respectable; that wasn't your way. So what was the alternative? Leave you a chunk of the money? I figured you'd have partied yourself to death within six weeks of your release. You've got to understand, I felt like I'd inherited some kind of cursed artifact or an atomic bomb. I love you, Mal. You and Sundae were the only family I've ever had. But the thought of you with tens of millions of dollars to spend and no job to go to, it'd have been like throwing a dog into Willy Wonka's chocolate river."

"But how could you leave Sundae behind?"

Sokolov shook his head, continuing to study the meat before him. "We did nothin' but argue from the first day the money arrived. She had it in her head that the cash meant I could pay off all our various debts and then retire. Get a place by the ocean, eat fancy food, and throw parties for all our new, boring friends. You know, take it easy. And, yeah, maybe that's what you do with *one* million dollars. But two hundred million?

Man, that's a seat at the table. You can move the needle with that kind of scratch. We used to sit around and bitch about the government, the taxes, and the cops and the speed limits. This was a chance to reshape the world. Not all the way, but a little bit. Sundae wanted no part of that. She didn't want to move, didn't want to be at my side for photo ops, thought her past would come out, all the magazines and the movies she'd made. I told her we'd have the kind of cash that'd make sure nobody cared about that. But she just imagined herself around high society and getting judged wherever she went, her old pics turning up in political attack ads. Never mind that my track record was ten times worse than hers. And, you know, I figured she'd come around, that I'd fly her out for a visit, and when she got a taste of the life, she wouldn't want to go back. But then she got sick and—" He shook his head. "We never got the chance."

"You should've stayed," said Malort, who was ladling his orange concoction into a series of Mason jars. "You should've told her, 'This money, this power, it's not worth losing you.' You should have tracked down this kid we got the coins from and just gave him the computer back. Those last couple years you'd have had with Sundae, it'd have been worth the money ten times over."

Sokolov stared at his steaks, smoke wafting up into his eyes, and said, "Goddamn it, Mal, don't you think I know that?"

Twitch chat logs from the stream posted at 5:04 P.M., Monday, July 4, by user Abaddon6969:

DeathNugget: Abs we were 100% certain you were dead.

Tremors3: I can't believe this is real.

CathyCathyCathy: I can, only reality can be this stupid.

ZekeArt: There's way more to the story than what he just told but I'm sure he'll fill you in later. But I have a request: There was a porn star from back in the late 90s and early 2000s named Sundae Greene, she did her work offline in magazines and home video, did a lot of biker-themed stuff (including some calendars and posters). She only did solo and girl-on-girl, most of it pre or early internet. I need you to see if any of it made it online. Stills, video, anything.

DeathNugget: I'm desperate to find out what this can possibly have to do with the Killdozer attack.

Tremors3: I wouldn't know how to search for pornography on the internet and in fact have never heard of it before today but . . . yes, I am now watching a video of Sundae Greene.

CathyCathyCathy: Me too. And maybe this is a weird thing to say but this porn star has the kindest eyes I've ever seen.

ZekeArt: Thank you. Yeah it's really hard to explain but it's important.

SkipTutorial: So back to what I was saying, I don't think the judgment of the public after you're rescued from the desert island plays into it. There's no way you can claim that the morality of society extends to an island separate from that society.

LumpShaker: What if we trick the old man into eating the baby, then his punishment for the crime of cannibalism is everyone else gets to kill and eat him. Boom, two birds with one stone.

SteveReborn: Why can't you just eat the two birds?

30

ABBOTT

"This is," said Abbott, "the drunkest I have ever been."

It wasn't helping that the way the seating in the limo worked, he was going down the road sideways.

"The candy-flavored liquor sneaks up on ya," said Malort, who as a precaution had moved on to guzzling straight vodka from the bottle.

"Oh my god," said Cammy, who was sitting next to Malort and sharing the bottle with him. "One of the girls on the Roller Derby team mixes Miller Light and Mountain Dew. It's incredible. I got so sick off it. Zeke got so mad at me."

"Mountain Dew was invented as a whiskey mixer," said Sokolov, who was pounding through bottles of Michelob Ultra at a stunning rate. "Couple of brothers from Knoxville came up with it in the forties, for that specific reason. Now it's the nemesis of every dentist in Appalachia."

Ether was next to Abbott, nervously bouncing a knee. "I don't want her to see me," she said for the fifth time on the drive. "I'm only coming to make sure it gets done."

It was getting close to eight o'clock, and they were just entering a town that, like so many they'd passed through, was barely there. It wasn't yet fully dark, but the sound of amateur fireworks could be heard popping in the distance. Backyard celebrations. The spontaneous barbecue at Sokolov's guesthouse had devolved into Ether tearfully explaining exactly how she wanted her payment delivered to swatting victim Jolene Brooks, at which point, Sokolov had stood at the table and said, "Hell, let's just go do it now." And so, a few hours later, they were heading into Jolene's tiny hometown, at the moment passing a lit-up sign by the side of the road that simply said, REPENT.

The cover story would be that a wealthy, somewhat anti-police Libertarian had heard the tale of Jolene's family's hardship. In response, he was offering to provide in-home care to her father and a full-ride scholarship to the university of her choice, hopefully one far away from that father. This news would be delivered directly to Jolene's door by one of Sokolov's attorneys and a bodyguard, who were currently trailing the limo in a black SUV. The reasoning for this, according to a mostly drunk Sokolov, was that any such offer delivered via phone, mail, or email would simply be disregarded as a scam. A presidential limousine and a gleaming SUV pulling up would be a little harder to ignore. A search of Jolene's social media had confirmed she'd be home, as she didn't attend fireworks displays because she needed to comfort her new puppy through the cacophony.

They pulled up to a trailer that Abbott vaguely remembered from the infamous body cam video, though it seemed to be in a state of even more disrepair these days, the green scum having completely overtaken the siding. He watched through the tinted side window as the two men knocked on the door. Next to him, Ether was staring straight down at her lap. She'd said she didn't want to see Jolene or her reaction and seemed to Abbott like she wanted to curl in on herself, terrified of a real-life encounter with a specter previously glimpsed only in a nightmare.

Abbott said, "She's answering the door."

Jolene Brooks had gotten taller and had let her hair grow long, dyeing it bright red. But yeah, it was her. Ether reached over and grabbed Abbott's hand, not with affection but like she'd snatched it while dangling off a ledge, squeezing so hard that he felt his knuckles grind. Over the next few minutes, Jolene listened to the men, her face transitioning from apprehension, to confusion, to, well, not happiness but a cautious optimism. The prospect of everything being okay, so okay that you don't quite trust it.

"She's asked for her dad to come to the door," narrated Abbott. "So now they're explaining it all over again to him. He's clearly suspicious, but they're showing him the documents. He keeps looking over at the limo, and yeah, I think the cars are making it real to him."

"How does he look?" asked Ether, still staring at her lap, still destroying the bones in his hand.

"He looks okay. About how you'd expect."

In fact, he looked thirty years older than he was, gaunt and unkempt, a man with nothing to do with his day but drink and be mad at the world. Abbott would be shocked if he had another year of life in him.

"How is Jolene taking it?"

"You know how sometimes you have a nightmare that's so bad and so vivid that for a few minutes after you wake up, you're still not sure you're really awake? She looks like that."

Zeke said, "Once you got Gary here drunk, you should have convinced him to just give her millions of dollars so she wouldn't have to work at all."

Abbott's father, who had taken a couple of drinks to calm his nerves but who was now nursing a bottle of water, said, "I totally disagree. When did that become the dream, to just be a parasite who sucks up food and electricity that other people make? Don't you want to be great at something, to make stuff, to contribute? All I hear is, 'Your job shouldn't be your life!' but why not? I mean, if you get rich, maybe you don't charge for the work, but don't you want to wake up every morning knowing that you've helped somebody? That you fixed their leaky pipes or cooked them a meal? I don't care if you're doing it for a corporation or the government or just for the hell of it—there's nothing better than doing work that helps somebody. Nothing."

At the door, the two representatives were shaking hands with Jolene and her father, leaving them with manila envelopes full of documents.

"Why don't my videos count?" asked Abbott.

"Count for what?"

"Why don't they count for work, for doing good for somebody?"

"I guess it does," he replied, "but I'd ask you this: Do your customers *need* you? Are you making yourself essential? I just know fans can be fickle, that's all. I've seen how they turn on you if they suddenly decide they can get more entertainment from your downfall. It feels tenuous."

"I can vouch for that," muttered Ether. "Are we done?"

Sokolov glanced back at Jolene as she closed the screen door of her trailer and said, "Looks like it. Do you think they do a fireworks display in this town? It'd be tragic if we don't get to see a show tonight."

MALORT

They drove toward Richmond, figuring that would be a big enough place to have a decent fireworks display, and wound up parking outside a stadium that boasted it was the home of the Flying Squirrels. The parking lot was full, but a block away, a bunch of overflow spectators had set up camp on the sidewalk, and there was a guy doling out barbecue from a smoker towed behind a truck with a cartoon pig painted on the side. Malort had gotten a basketful of baby back ribs that he decided after the second bite were the best fucking thing he'd ever eaten.

"She was teaching me to play guitar," said Ether, who was sitting on the hood and eating an ice cream cone they'd gotten from a drive-thru on the way into town. "Phil would sit on the porch and watch the sunset and drink his coffee, and Sundae would teach me chords and tell stories about her wild youth, all the places she'd been, all the trouble she got into. She didn't mention you guys by name, and, you know, I think she didn't want to invite a bunch of questions about prison or sudden riches. It was always, 'One time, on a ride with some friends . . .' and it was like listening to an old veteran talk about their former comrades in the trenches."

She'd been telling Sundae stories since they'd left that girl's trailer, and Malort had noticed that the whole time, Sock hadn't said a word, just stared out the window.

"It was weird," she continued, "but you know Phil needed care as much as she did; he was sick himself and never really came back from his wife passing away. But I think that actually extended Sundae's life. Like it gave her energy, being with someone who needed her. Not just because of feeling like she had to stay strong for Phil but that she needed to be needed. I think that's what I learned from her, that you have this modern thing where the goal is to be totally disconnected from any burdens or obligations. But I think we all need to be needed."

"Did they recover anything from the fire," asked Malort, "from the box, I mean? I know sometimes stuff doesn't burn up all the way."

"I don't think so," mumbled Sock. "Fragments."

"Well, I was going to wait to tell you this," said Zeke, who was making a mess of a banana split, "but I asked our chat friends to see if any of the, uh, professional pics Sundae had taken wound up on the internet. I don't know what percentage of them did, but they've come up with over a hundred and fifty images and an additional twenty-seven video clips. And you know they can crop those, if you want just her face, without the, uh, context."

Malort tried to say something in response to that, but the words caught in his throat.

Abbott, who looked like he was going to puke if someone poked him in the right spot, turned to Sokolov and said, "So, you know all sorts of powerful people. Do they think this country is on the verge of tearing itself apart? I heard rich guys all have apocalypse shelters. When I get to be your age, is the USA still going to exist?"

"Who knows," said Sock in the tone of a man who'd asked himself that question many times and never arrived at an answer. "Maybe one day, you'll sit down with your own grandkids in some burned-out building and tell them what the country used to be like, that you could get drunk and eat ice cream and watch fireworks, and nobody would bother you. And they'll say, 'Damn, that sounds real nice. What happened?' and you'll have to try to explain how everywhere, all at once, everybody lost their fucking minds."

"I wrote whole reports on this," said Joan the FBI lady, who'd vomited twice in the last two hours but was now taking bites from an entire ice cream cake she'd bought, eating it right out of the box. "Nobody liked my conclusion. The only thing that will save us is a new cold war. Or, you know, a new actual war, against a real enemy, not some impoverished country where we send billion-dollar cruise missiles to bounce around the rubble of some buildings that got blown up three wars ago. A single enemy is the only thing strong enough to unite us."

"I refuse to believe that's the only way," said Ether.

Joan nodded toward the fireworks. "The original colonies all hated each other. The only reason the USA exists is that they finally united in their even worse hatred of the British."

Hunter shook his head, gnawing on his own rack of ribs from the barbecue trailer. "People just need to get a taste of it. When they figure out that instability isn't about cool gun battles on the street but empty store shelves and power outages, that all your credit cards stop working and the hospitals go dark, they'll come to their senses."

Malort turned to Sock and asked, "Do you have an apocalypse shelter? Some island you've bought that you can escape to if everything goes kaboom?"

"No," said Sock, a little too quickly.

"Well, if you're lying, I want a spot in it. I want that to be part of my deal, a room in your island fortress if society descends into chaos."

"I thought you wanted me to buy you a titty bar. You need to pick one or the other. Apocalypse shelter or titty bar, not both."

"Okay, I'm sticking with the titty bar."

"Ooh," said Cammy, pointing to the sky. "I think this is the finale."

31

ABBOTT

In the aftermath of chaos, the early narrative is the one that tends to stick, as everyone has usually moved on by the time it gets corrected. At least, that's what Sokolov had told them. He had an entire floor of professionals operating out of a tower in New York dedicated to image management (they were the ones who'd gotten a slapdash, ghostwritten autobiography to the top of the bestseller lists a mere five months after Sokolov had the idea), and they'd pushed the narrative that Abbott and his friends were heroes who'd rushed to McLean in order to thwart a rumored attack. The world seemed intent on rewarding Abbott by stress-testing his social anxiety to the breaking point, as he was already scheduled to fly back to Washington, DC, for a series of ceremonies and meetings, which he'd accepted only because he'd been advised it was a good idea by Sokolov's team. They'd said it would ensure that future search results for his name would be entirely about this, rather than any controversial opinions expressed in the past. The more events he attended, the more coverage was generated, the more positive content would drown out everything else.

Then, he'd received an invitation from some political organization to join their lecture circuit for a shocking sum of money (the Killdozer driver was a member of the opposing party, and they were trying to turn that into a thing), and Abbott decided he'd rather drive for Lyft the rest of his life than live out his days as a political outrage sponge. He hadn't even known the identity of the old man he'd saved from getting squished by the Killdozer and certainly hadn't known his politics.

"This is your turn," said Ether, pointing toward a dusty road, well-hidden by the surrounding brush.

They rounded a hill, and into view came a rusty corrugated steel fence, the gates secured by a heavy padlock for which Ether was holding the key in her left hand. The copy of Phil Greene's will that left the property to Ether was dated shortly after Sundae's death, but before he and Ether had their falling-out. If he'd created an updated version of the document to cut her out of it, he'd not left it where it could easily be found.

When Abbott entered the house, he was expecting the place to be an oven, but the interior was cool and dark, like a cave.

"The AC runs off his solar panels," said Ether. "It's funny, he was obsessed with being off-grid because he couldn't trust anyone, but those panels were manufactured in Germany with Chinese parts, sold by a corporation with employees and stockholders all over the world. Just try to count how many humans operating in perfect sync it took to build and ship all the stuff he needed to live 'off-the-grid.'"

She ripped down the wire and foil from the living room bay window, and sunlight spilled into the space. The light revealed the walls were coated in crazy scrawls of nearly unreadable text.

Abbott said, "Jesus."

"Yeah, toward the end, he started doing his journals on the walls. He was afraid of forgetting or getting brainwashed and figured he'd always be able to look at this and remember. We need tools. This chicken wire is screwed into the studs."

Abbott wandered into the hall and found where the writing seemed to end. "I think this is where it leaves off. He may have written this right before he died."

"Who knows," said Ether. "I'm trying not to read any of it. I want to remember him how he was before, you know. Before he got like this."

"It looks like this part mentions you."

"I'll paint over it. Zeke says he'll put a mural on one of the walls for free."

"He's going to fly out from Nashville?"

"Not fly. Cammy wants to do a road trip out here in the fall. She insisted. Zeke says flying can be a nightmare if you're in a wheelchair—it's a whole thing. That should give me enough time to get the place fixed up. Did you know they're going to see him at the Mayo Clinic? He said they've scheduled scans he's never even heard of."

Abbott checked his phone and said, "Oh, wow. I missed a call from my mom. I don't think I heard from her this much when we lived under the same roof."

"Tell her you have a new mom now."

"That isn't funny."

"Ha! Maybe not, but your reaction always is."

Joan Key had started writing a book about social atomization in the smartphone era, funded by an advance from Mr. Sokolov's new think tank on the subject. She'd immediately said she could use the assistance of Abbott's father, a roofer who did not use social media and who only read books about the Old West. So now Abbott's father was at Key's apartment for days at a time, and for some reason, nobody involved could just come out and admit they were fucking.

"I think the mural would go there," said Ether, "so it's the first thing you see when you walk in."

"I hope you like that anime style. I'm pretty sure that's all Zeke can do."

"We should brainstorm what to have him paint. Something inspirational, to keep the nudity tasteful."

"Well, it's up to you, it's your house."

"Yeah, but you're going to have to look at it every time you come over. All right, let's go through and uncover all the windows first. Let the light in."

The final journal entry of Phil Greene, scrawled on the northern wall of his hallway:

Some Mormons or Jehovah's Witnesses or some other religious types came to the door today, that's what I get for leaving the gate open. I've often thought that what we need to counter what's coming is a new religion, where the like-minded form bonds through touch and kindness and soft conversations over home-cooked food, practicing human connection as it has been done for tens of thousands of years. I don't know exactly what rules this new faith would impose on its congregants, but I think that going door-to-door and interrupting folks while they're trying to have dinner should be considered a mortal sin.

I intend to finish the ceiling of the workshop tonight, I can still feel the signal coming in through there, I think it leaks in around the light fixture, way up in the rafters. It should be a two-man job, but it's not like I can bring somebody in. They would see how I live, and they wouldn't understand. I would go over and ask Karen, but these days, she doesn't understand, either. Yesterday, or maybe it was two days ago, I can't stay on top of the movement of time, she came by with tacos from El Pollo Loco, saying she'd accidentally been delivered a double order, but I knew she'd ordered extra for me. I told her no, and I know I was rude about it. I don't even know why. I was hungry, too. If Sundae were here, she'd tell me I was wrong to do that. If Bonnie were here, she'd read me the riot act, maybe slap me on the back of the head just for emphasis, and march me over there to accept the young lady's kindness and apologize for acting how I did. I'm sorry, girls. I don't know what is happening to me. Maybe tomorrow I'll go over and try to smooth things over with her. But I'll finish my work in the shop first. I want it known that I just wish to be friendly and that I'm not just looking for somebody to hold my ladder.

AFTERWORD

At the front of every novel is a block of legalese explaining that it is a work
of fiction and that no people or places are intended to represent reality.
Almost no one ever reads that part, and even those who do apparently
don't believe it. These days, most discussion around fiction involves trying
to figure out which opinions expressed in the text are those of the author
and which people were copied from the real world to populate its cast of
characters. So let me say this in my own words:

This is a work of fiction. In every circumstance in which I had to
choose between the reality revealed in my research and a bit of fantasy
that would make the story more entertaining, I chose the latter. There is,
in the real world, a domestic intelligence and security service called the
FBI, but nothing about its procedures or the disposition of its employees is
accurately represented here unless by coincidence. The method of procur-
ing the elements for the hypothetical bomb described in this book would
not work in the real world, and even if it did, the resulting device would
not be terribly effective. Contrary to what multiple characters in this story
believe, the drug fentanyl cannot cause overdose via casual skin contact.

Likewise, there are corporate chains in the real world called Walgreens,
Circle K, and so on, but their representations in this story are not necessarily accurate in terms of their procedures, policies, or even in which
items they stock. This is a work of fiction, designed to be authentic only
in terms of the characters' humanity. I do not know, for example, whether
or not consuming a brisket sandwich inside Buc-ee's will get you ejected
from the store, and what was depicted in this novel should not govern
your future behavior in that specific scenario or any other.

Furthermore, the opinions expressed by the characters in this story are true and valid only in the sense that they are truly the opinions held by these fictional characters who, and I cannot make this clear enough, do not exist outside of this tale. Likewise, no character in this book is intended to represent any category of real person; they are individuals whose beliefs and worldview may not be replicated by any single real living human, let alone any entire demographic or ideology. They speak only for themselves. Obviously, the ideas expressed in this book (and, hopefully, every book) are intended to be thought-provoking, but that phrasing should imply it's the start of a conversation, not the conclusion. If you are looking for the final answer on how to solve any societal problem, from chronic loneliness to domestic terrorism, you have a tremendous amount of research ahead of you, and none of it will involve reading novels. This book was not the work of an expert, unless two decades as a professional storyteller has made me an expert in that particular field. Even then, it's not like you have to take a test and get a license. I'm only here because, in the late '90s, I realized they'll basically let anybody do it.

Finally, the fates of these characters do not represent what the author believes they deserve, or what any equivalent real person would deserve. If you feel like certain bad people in this story got off too easy or that certain innocents had it too hard, that is only because, in this particular fictional universe, karma doesn't exist.

If you wish to follow up with me personally, at the time of this writing, my username is JasonKPargin on TikTok, X (formerly Twitter), Instagram, YouTube, and several other platforms that probably won't even exist by the time you read this. Feel free to drop by one of them and ask any questions you might have. I likely won't answer them, but asking will be good for my engagement metrics.

That's it, book's over. See you next time.

—*Jason Pargin*
January 2024

ABOUT THE AUTHOR

Jason Pargin is the *New York Times* bestselling author of the John Dies at the End series as well as the award-winning Zoey Ashe novels. He previously published under the pseudonym David Wong. His essays at Cracked.com and other outlets have been enjoyed by tens of millions of readers around the world.